The Regency

LORDS & LADIES
COLLECTION

*Two Glittering Regency
Love Affairs*

Carnival of Love
by Helen Dickson

&

The Viscount's Bride
by Ann Elizabeth Cree

The Regency

LORDS & LADIES
COLLECTION

The Regency

LORDS & LADIES
COLLECTION

Helen Dickson &
Ann Elizabeth Cree

*M&B™ and M&B™ with the Rose Device
are trademarks of the publisher.
Harlequin Mills & Boon Limited, Eton House,
18-24 Paradise Road, Richmond, Surrey TW9 1SR*

First published in Great Britain in 2001 & 2003

THE REGENCY LORDS & LADIES COLLECTION
© Harlequin Books S.A. 2008

The publisher acknowledges the copyright holders of the
individual works as follows:

Carnival of Love © Helen Dickson 2001
The Viscount's Bride © Annemarie Hasnain 2003

ISBN: 978 0 263 86653 7

052-0608

*Printed and bound in Spain
by Litografía Rosés S.A., Barcelona*

Carnival of Love
by
Helen Dickson

Helen Dickson was born and still lives in South Yorkshire with her husband on a busy arable farm where she combines writing with keeping a chaotic farmhouse. An incurable romantic, she writes for pleasure, owing much of her inspiration to the beauty of the surrounding countryside. She enjoys reading and music. History has always captivated her, and she likes travel and visiting ancient buildings.

Chapter One

1789

The Italian May was surprisingly warm, and through half-closed eyes Lavinia looked up into the Saracen blue sky, which was a canopy of ever-changing hues. The sun's warmth had an invisible, embalming quality and she sighed languidly, apathy and inertia calling the tune, the lull and gentle rocking of the boat cradling her nerves as she listened to the gentle splash of the oars and the lap of the water against the hull.

She was content to forget the passage of time as Giuseppe, clad in the scarlet and black livery of the Scalini household, guided the black-gilded boat slowly among a host of other vessels passing hither and thither on the San Marco Canal, some of them sailing too close and approaching too fast for comfort at times.

Basking in the heat, the city of Venice rose out of the calm waters of the lagoon like an exquisite, elaborately adorned crown, seeming to float in the iridescent haze which skimmed the surface of the canal. Virginia creepers unfurled their leaves as they climbed the peeling and

stained stuccoed façades of convents and palaces like huge
fishing nets hanging out to dry. It was a city full of candle-
lit palaces and churches built on water, shuttered and secretive, magnificent and ancient, its towers and crenellated
buildings soaring at random.

'Isn't this just perfect,' Lavinia murmured to her companion Daisy Lambert, where they lounged side by side on
silken cushions under a gold-fringed scarlet canopy.
Daisy's mother, after consuming a little too much wine
earlier and finding the heat of the day too much, had fallen
into a light doze across from them.

They were returning from a visit to the Lido, which extended along the mouth of the lagoon. There they had
strolled along the spit of sand, gathering seashells and pic-
nicking at noon, before heading back to the house of Signor
Leonardo Scalini and his wife Valentina in the Castello area
of Venice.

The Scalinis were an old family of merchant stock. They
had become close friends over the years with Mrs Lambert's husband, who had been a merchant. Venice, being a
key trading centre where spices, silks and other Eastern
luxuries were exchanged for necessities of the West, was
where he had spent much of his time, before being struck
down by some kind of undulant fever—which Mrs Lambert
was certain he had contracted from the noxious vapours
rising from the canals—eighteen months ago.

The Scalinis, wishing to relieve Mrs Lambert's sorrow,
had invited her and her daughter Daisy to stay at their home
for a while. The invitation had been extended to included
Mrs Lambert's niece, Julia, who was the widowed daughter
of her late brother. Julia's half-sister Lavinia, and Lavinia's
betrothed, Robert Feltham, had also been invited.

Before coming to Venice they had visited Rome and
Florence, but Lavinia loved Venice most of all. She was

overawed by its decaying elegance; despite being weathered with age, it retained a certain patina of charm. The moment she had set foot on one of its hundreds of small islands—like writers, poets and artists throughout the ages who had been drawn into its mesmeric aura—she had embraced it at once, feeling it close around her like a warm blanket.

Daisy, two years older than Lavinia, sighed languidly, stirring on the cushions to feel the warm sea breeze on her cheeks, and to gaze at the hundreds of small boats and the uniformity of the gondolas in funereal black spread across the water. It was a rich kaleidoscope of colour, an amazing spectacle of life and gaiety, against the backdrop of the city.

'I only hope Giuseppe is in no hurry to reach the house,' Daisy murmured. 'I feel rather like Cleopatra must have felt on being rowed down the Nile on her royal barge. I could stay on the canal all afternoon. We've been in Venice two weeks now, and I can't for the life of me think why we haven't been to the Lido before today. We must go again before we leave.'

'The reason we haven't been before is because there's been so much else to occupy our time,' breathed Lavinia, watching in fascination as bare-chested men swooped up and down the rigging and busied themselves on the decks of the large sea-going vessels, ranged along the Giudecca quayside to the left of their boat.

They had both taken to the sightseeing and social whirl that Leonardo and Valentina had plunged them into with enthusiasm. Their hosts, eager to make their stay in Venice as pleasurable as possible, had seen to it that they visited the opera houses and the theatres, and had taken them to the grand houses of their many friends where they dined in style.

'I only wish we had been here for the end of the Car-

nival—instead of spending so long in Florence,' said Lavinia with regret. She would have loved to take part in the
Carnival celebrations, which spanned the winter months to
the eve of Lent. 'Valentina says it's such an exciting time
to come to Venice, the Carnival being a riotous affair, when
Venetians don their masks to hide their identities as they
indulge in revelry. The merriment goes on night and day,
with pageants and parades and masked balls.'

'I can well imagine. But Valentina also says that the
anonymity of the mask gives free reign to fantasies, roguery
and all manner of licentious behaviour. Little wonder Robert chose to spend so much time in Rome and Florence
before coming to Venice,' Daisy said drily, referring to
Lavinia's betrothed—a man she had little liking for. Robert
was confined to his bed after eating something which had
disagreed with him, and had been unable to accompany
them to the Lido. 'His disapproval of such wild and deca-
dent behaviour—when all social distinctions are thrown to
the wind and men and women become truly incognito, from
the Doge down to the meanest beggar—would have sent
him into a fit from which he would never have recovered.
Had we arrived during Carnival time he would have chaperoned you every step of the way.'

Lavinia smiled. What Daisy said was true. Robert, who
was certainly not lacking in moral restraint and regarded
any kind of frivolous entertainment with severe disdain,
would not have allowed her to partake in the festivities.
Not being one to indulge in flamboyant display, a sightseeing tour of the city and its many beautiful churches and
treasured works of art were more to his taste.

'Perhaps you're right, Daisy. Poor Robert. If only he
would let himself go from time to time. Still, we do have
the costume ball to look forward to.'

Valentina and Leonardo had arranged to take them to the

ball, which was to be held at one of the palaces along the Grand Canal. It was an important social event to celebrate the twenty-first birthday of an Italian nobleman's son, and promised to be an exciting occasion. However, because it did not coincide with Carnival time—much to the young man's regret—he had decided that it would be a costumed ball with all the extravagance of the Carnival.

'It will give us the chance to dress up and wear Carnival masks,' Lavinia continued, 'and there's to be champagne and music and dancing till dawn. Even Robert would not be so ungracious as to turn down such an invitation as that. I think Sir John and Lady Evesham and their daughter Sophia have been invited, too. You remember, Daisy...we were introduced to them by Valentina at the theatre the other night.'

Daisy wrinkled her nose with obvious distaste. 'Yes. I remember. Sir John and his wife seemed quite nice, as I recall, but I can't say I liked Sophia much. She has a mean, peevish look about her, and she is so plain it's hardly surprising no suitors were forthcoming when she made her debut a year ago. Her parents thought she might stand a better chance if they exhibited her around Europe. Valentina has invited them to call on us but I can't remember when. No doubt we'll see them at the ball.'

Both girls were looking forward to what promised to be an exciting and glittering occasion, and Lavinia had already chosen her costume, having found it in a chest holding a wide variety of Carnival clothes which Valentina kept for such occasions.

'What will you wear, Daisy? Have you made up your mind yet?' Lavinia asked, idly watching a colourful, boisterous group of travelling players, singing and clowning, float by on a barge to perform on the Lido, one young man entertaining them on his guitar, the melodic notes of a love song and their laughter trailing behind like ribbons.

'No, I haven't decided. It's between the lilac and the red velvet.' She turned her head and looked admiringly at her companion. 'But no matter what I wear, I will not look as splendid as you, Lavinia,' she murmured. Being small and with a tendency to put on weight, Daisy envied Lavinia her slender shape and delicate features. With hair like spun gold and eyes turquoise blue and as vivid and deep as the Venetian lagoon, her friend really was quite lovely. Everywhere Lavinia went heads would turn and admiring eyes would follow her.

'Nonsense, Daisy,' countered Lavinia, looking warmly at her friend, having become extremely fond of Daisy during the months she had known her. This trip to Europe had thrown them together, and they had both been relieved to discover that they got on well. Daisy threw herself into whatever it was they were doing with such enthusiasm, which was one of the characteristics which made her such a stimulating companion. 'You will look very nice in either—but if you want my opinion, with your colouring and dark hair, I think the red suits you best.'

'I think you're right,' Daisy replied, knowing she would bow to Lavinia's eye for colour and sense of good taste in the end. 'I wonder what Mr Feltham will say when he sees you in your costume, Lavinia. Considering how brusque and high-handed he always is towards you—and how he is always telling you not to lend yourself to gossip—I'm surprised he allowed you to choose it without his prior approval.'

'I know,' Lavinia replied, remembering the moment when Robert had told her he would trust her this once to choose something suitable to wear for the occasion, as if he had been bestowing a vast favour on her. 'But there's nothing provocative about it. It's not revealing in any way, so Robert cannot disapprove.'

Having seen Lavinia's costume on her in all its simple, triumphal glory, Daisy wasn't so sure about this and gave her friend an arched look. What Lavinia didn't know was that the fluidity of the white silk outlined every curve of her body when she moved. It shimmered and made her look as though she were floating on air, and was far more revealing and alluring than if she were going to the ball stark naked. Robert Feltham might cut a fine figure, but he was a man who shunned frivolity and excesses, and Daisy would take mischievous delight on seeing the horror he would be unable to conceal when he saw what his betrothed was wearing.

Content to bask in the pleasant warmth, a lengthy silence fell between them, but Lavinia suddenly became alert, her eyes widening in alarm when she saw that a barge being rowed at speed was coming perilously close to their own. On a gasp, she scrambled to her feet, shouting to Giuseppe, who was facing away from the oncoming barge. Turning quickly, he saw to his horror the barge bearing down on them and tried to steer the boat out of its path, but it was an impossible task.

Waving an arm, he ordered Lavinia to sit down, but it was too late. The barge collided with their own, which then rammed into another. When the bow of their boat rose, to her horror Lavinia found herself unable to maintain her balance, and was cast into the water.

Gasping for breath, she flailed and floundered about wildly, but she was unable to swim. Her heavy skirts pulled her down and she felt the cool water close over her head. Gripped with terror and panic, she was certain she was about to drown. After bobbing up to the surface she was immediately dragged down once more, having hit her head on the hull of a boat—whether the Scalini boat or someone else's, she had no way of knowing—but the sharp stab of pain exploded inside her head.

From somewhere a long way off she could hear her name being called above the roaring in her ears. With her mouth full of water she was unable to breath and felt as though her lungs were bursting. Looking up, she could see the underneath of a mêlée of boats and a brightness which seemed to dim by the second as she sank further and further. A red haze was beginning to cloud her vision. Gradually a sense of peace and calm began to descend on her as the world as she knew it and her consciousness both began to recede; at that moment death seemed almost certain.

Just when she thought all was lost she was conscious of someone beside her, coming between her and death, condemning her to live. Grasping her arms, he pulled her towards his naked chest and held her in a paralysing grip. As he swam with her to the surface she saw the bright light coming closer, larger, until she burst through its centre and felt the warm sun on her face once more, finding it strange that she was unable to move, that her body didn't seem to belong to her any more.

'Hold on to me,' said a man's voice in English, which seemed to come from far away. 'We'll soon have you back on board the boat.'

Instinctively Lavinia obeyed, unable to do anything else. The stranger held her close, with arms wrapped round her like a vice. Hands reached out of the boat and took hold of her, pulling her up, her rescuer lifting her with what seemed to be superhuman strength. Half-drowned, she was hauled over the edge and into the boat where she collapsed, motionless, face down on to the bottom. The air was rent with voices, Italian and English, all talking at once.

'You're safe now,' she heard Daisy say, but she couldn't move. Everything seemed so far away and her body felt like lead.

Lavinia became conscious of someone's hands moving urgently over her, tearing her dress down the back in an attempt to loosen the lacings of her tight bodice, before kneeling at her head, raising her arms and placing his hands on her shoulder blades, his fingers spread out over her bare flesh as, with a rhythmic movement, he began to pump the water out of her lungs in an attempt to revive her. Pink-faced, all Mrs Lambert, who had been woken by the commotion, and Daisy could do was watch as the man paused and lifted one of Lavinia's eyelids, which flickered at his touch.

Eventually she began to cough and splutter as she tried to rid herself of the water which had almost consumed her, labouring to drag breath into her tortured lungs. The pain in her head, which had momentarily disappeared, returned to torment her with a savage vengeance.

Seeing that she had regained consciousness, the man ceased his pumping and gently turned her over on to her back, wiping back the veil of wet hair and looking down for a moment in silent contemplation at the pale, heart-shaped face which was fragile and fine-boned, her lips shell pink and perfect.

'You'll be all right now,' he murmured. 'You're out of danger.'

With one arm flung above her head, Lavinia's eyes fluttered open to see a darkly handsome face, bronzed by the sun, bending over her, out of which looked a pair of questioning, clear blue eyes, which shone as bright as jewels. Black brows were puckered together in frowning concern.

'My—my head,' she managed to whisper.

Lavinia's rescuer, who seemed to have taken charge of

the incident whilst the others looked on in anxious shock, took her face gently between his lean fingers and turned it to one side, brushing back tangles of her hair to reveal a small gash just above her ear, from which a thin trickle of blood oozed.

'You must have hit your head on the boat when you came up beneath it. The wound is superficial and I don't think any permanent damage has been done—but no doubt your head will ache for a while.' He smiled down at her, his teeth dazzling white between his slightly parted lips, making an instant appraisal of the lovely young woman sheathed in wet clothes whom he had just fished out of the canal. She was a golden girl, slender as a wand, and had been as light as thistledown when he had lifted her up into the boat. 'You were lucky not to drown.'

'Which is thanks to you.'

His eyes went to her bodice which only just covered the soft curve of her breasts. 'Your dress is ruined,' he apologised. 'I had to act immediately, and because it restricted your breathing I had no alternative but to tear it.'

Lavinia managed to summon up a smile and answered him in a weak voice. 'It is nothing. I owe you a great debt, sir. I am truly sorry for any trouble I have caused you.'

'It wasn't your fault. It was lucky I was standing by the rail of the ship and saw the boat career into your own, casting you into the water.'

'And you immediately jumped in to rescue me,' she whispered, trying not to let her eyes dwell on his athletic physique, on the wet, powerful muscles of his tanned chest, which tapered to a narrow waist and gleamed beneath the hot sun.

'Something like that.' He grinned. 'You had a close shave, it's true, but you're safe enough now.'

Meeting his gaze, Lavinia saw that his eyes were lively,

with a hint of humour in their depths, and shining like a light out of an otherwise dark countenance. His hair was short, jet black and gleaming. It curled vigorously, and droplets of water dripped off the ends and ran slowly down his lean face. Stark black brows were slashed across his forehead and his mouth was wide, his chin indented in a firm, thrusting, arrogant jaw.

The stranger's masculinity was obvious and complete and, despite his bare chest and feet, there was a certain refinement in his well-defined handsome features. She wondered at the character behind them, sensing strength, impatience and steely determination.

Lavinia was curious to know the identity of this man whose prompt action had saved her life.

'Thank you for saving me. But for you I would be lying on the bottom of the lagoon.'

By this time Daisy had recovered sufficiently from the shock of Lavinia's tumble into the water and had gathered her shattered wits about her.

'You gave me such a scare, Lavinia,' said Daisy softly, kneeling beside her and placing a cushion beneath her head in an attempt to make her more comfortable, disturbed by this handsome stranger who had jumped into the water from a nearby sea-going vessel to rescue her friend, his only article of clothing being a pair of tight black breeches, which clung to his masculine body in such a manner that she had to avert her maidenly eyes.

The stranger got to his feet, continuing to gaze down at Lavinia. 'I shall leave you now that I can see you are sufficiently recovered and in capable hands.'

'Thank you, sir,' said Mrs Lambert. 'We cannot thank you enough. We'll get her straight home where she will be put to bed and the physician sent for.'

'I would advise that. Do you have far to go?'

'No. But who do we have to thank?'

He smiled crookedly. 'Maxim Purnell at your service, madam. And you are…?'

'Mrs Esme Lambert. This is my daughter, Daisy—and the young lady you so gallantly rescued is Miss Lavinia Renshaw.'

Maxim inclined his head slightly, his eyes settling on Lavinia propped up on the cushions, gazing up at him intently. 'I am happy to make your acquaintance—although I wish we had met in less traumatic circumstances.'

The offending boat that had collided with their own went on its way after much irate shouting and gesticulating between the oarsmen, and others, which had been alerted to the crisis and stopped to watch, also carried on about their business.

Lavinia struggled to sit up when her mysterious rescuer disappeared over the side of the boat, watching in fascination as he ploughed his way through the water back to his ship with powerful strokes, his black head bobbing up and down and his strong shoulders gleaming as they broke the rippling surface of the water.

On reaching a rope ladder hanging down the ship's side, Maxim effortlessly hoisted himself up before vaulting on to the deck, where he turned and looked in Lavinia's direction, calmly watching her boat continue on its way. The incident had brought a moment of relief from his own troubles, and he would welcome many more such incidents if it gave him the opportunity of making the acquaintance of women as lovely as the one he had just plucked from the lagoon.

It was the tense situation in France that had brought Maxim to Europe, his anxieties compounded by the deepening political crisis in that country. The growing unrest had produced panic and was badly affecting markets throughout Europe. Public order had also collapsed in many regions and, like everyone else, he was very much afraid that open insurrection could be transformed into revolution.

Owning warehouses in ports in France and Italy, warehouses which were filled with commodities he shipped to various countries in the world in his own vessels, he had come to see the heightening crisis at first hand, and to order the emptying of those warehouses should his worst fears be realised and revolution did break out in France. Its possible implications could prove disastrous.

A jovial, middle-aged man by the name of Tom Player and in the same state of undress as Maxim, came to stand beside him. Knowing that Tom was in Venice at this time unloading a cargo from the Levant, Maxim had arranged his journey so that he could spend a few days in the ancient city and see this old friend. Having witnessed the incident and been faintly amused by it, Tom clapped his companion good-humouredly on the back.

'You haven't been in Venice forty-eight hours, Maxim, and already you are plucking damsels out of the lagoon. Who is she, did you ask?'

'Of course. She is English and her name is Lavinia Renshaw.'

'Will she be all right?'

'Yes—although I only just reached her in time.'

His friend glanced at him sideways, a wicked gleam glinting in his eyes. 'And was she worth getting wet for?'

Maxim grinned, his blue eyes gleaming wickedly. 'Well worth it.'

'And is there a chance that she might show her gratitude?' Tom asked meaningfully, his weatherbeaten face wrinkling with lines of humour and a wicked twinkle dancing in his eyes.

'No, Tom, you old rogue. I could tell at a glance that

the young lady is much too refined and chaste for what I know you are implying.'

His friend chuckled. 'Same old Maxim—giving nothing away. How many ladies have you left dangling for your favours back home, eh?'

Maxim frowned, his expression suddenly serious. A muscle moved spasmodically at the side of his mouth and his voice was rough with emotion. 'Just the one, Tom. Just the one.'

Tom looked at his friend in taut silence, knowing precisely the woman he was referring to. All at once Maxim seemed like a man being stretched beyond the limits of endurance. 'So, it's still Alice, is it?' he scowled, nodding slowly with understanding. 'So—the wench is still chewing away at your gut, is she?'

'She is, and her teeth get sharper the more she chews.'

Alice Winstanley was the daughter of a small shipping merchant—and mother of Maxim's three-year-old daughter. Alice was charming and pleasing to the eye, but she was as greedy and as ambitious as her father had been before his demise over three years ago—and in Tom's opinion she was as immoral as sin.

Tom sighed deeply. 'I remember the time when you took up with her and I tried to warn you about her, knowing through my long acquaintance with her father—and her mother being my cousin an' all—what she was like. I recall how you would swear and curse at me for speaking out against the girl who roused such intense feelings in you. So she still won't marry you.'

'Not without a grand title. Whatever there was between us was over and done with a long time ago, Tom, when I became aware of the unsavoury depths to her character that I couldn't possibly know about on first meeting her. Her hold on me is stronger than it ever was because of Lucy, and she damned well knows it. Nothing and no one has claimed my heart like that child has done. I would give her anything she wanted—even the moon if I could reach it. I curse the day I made Alice aware of the title—for she has given me no peace since.'

'And is it not within your power to acquire the title? After all, it is yours by right. You are the next Earl of Brinkcliff. All you have to do is go and see your uncle and reconcile your differences. He's been hankering after a meeting with you since your grandfather died—to affirm you as his heir.'

Maxim tensed and looked straight ahead, his fists clenched by his sides and his mind locked in murderous combat against the idea of going to his uncle. When his grandfather had been alive, the old man had turned his back on the elder of his two sons, Maxim's father, disinheriting him and banishing him from his home because he had dared to defy him to marry the woman he loved, a woman his grandfather had deemed unsuitable to be the Countess of Brinkcliff, chatelaine of Brinkcliff Hall.

On his death the inheritance had passed to Maxim's uncle, Alistair Purnell who, hounded by illness throughout his life, had never married. Feeling a belated sense of regret for the long estrangement and wanting to make Maxim his heir, he had written him frequent letters in an attempt to mend the breach. But Maxim could not forgive what his grandfather had done and, because Alistair had done nothing to right the wrong done to his father when he had been alive, he considered his uncle's conduct over the whole affair no better.

'It's not as easy as that. It's too damned complicated and you know it,' he growled between clenched teeth. 'Out of sheer spite Alice is determined to stand against me on this—regardless of the shame she not only brings on Lucy but also on herself.'

'Since when did Alice Winstanley possess the capacity to feel what would cripple any other mortal?' retorted Tom with biting scorn.

'I have no illusions where she is concerned, Tom. Had it been any other decently bred young woman she would have hidden her condition and married me instantly. But not Alice. Maybe if her father had not died around that time, he would have succeeded in persuading her to marry me. But one way or another, while ever I have breath in my body, I'll fight to gain custody of my daughter—to have her live with me permanently.'

Tom gave him a questioning stare. 'Why, has something changed? I thought Alice and little Lucy were living with you at your London house.'

'They were—have been for the past twelve months or more—until this mess with France blew up. When Alice knew I was coming to Europe, in a fit of anger and resentment at my refusal to allow her to accompany me—for she was convinced my trip to Europe was one of pleasure and not of business—she went to live with her stepmother, taking Lucy with her. I have to do something, Tom. I have watched my daughter grow from a babe in arms to a sturdy three-year-old. I am the centre of her everyday world, and she attaches herself to me like a shadow. I will not lose sight of her because her mother is too stubborn and too ambitious to bow to reason. Nor will I be held to ransom by Alice.'

'I can't begin to conceive what kind of life you'll have married to a woman of Alice's ilk—and I certainly don't envy you—but if you intend making an honest woman of her and keeping Lucy, then you'll have to swallow your own pride and let bygones be bygones. What is past is past.

It's the future you have to consider. Go and see the old man. He's been trying to make amends for what your grandfather did to your father for years.'

'It's too late for that, Tom.'

'Better late than never. And how do you know it wouldn't be what your father wanted? You know I have no liking for Alice, Maxim, but I think you'll have to give her what she wants in the end. It's the only way you'll get to keep your daughter.'

'Maybe you're right. But much as I want Lucy with me, I have no great desire to saddle myself with Alice for the rest of my life. If there is any other way I can obtain custody of Lucy, then I will find it. For some time before I knew Alice was to bear my child, our relationship was cooling and I had decided to end our affair, but when Lucy was born I knew I could not banish the perfidious bitch to obscurity or cast her memory aside. She doesn't love Lucy as a mother should love her own child. She sees her as nothing more than a means to an end. Aye, she is callous and ambitious—and treacherous into the bargain.'

'You loved her once, Maxim.'

'Maybe I did but, whatever it was, it wasn't meant to last.'

Shaking his head Tom moved away, leaving Maxim to do battle with his conscience and to mull over what he had said, hoping that in the end common sense would prevail. Tom, who had captained Maxim's father's one and only ship plying coal from Newcastle to London—an old barque Maxim's father had purchased with a few gold coins after his split from his father—now captained a much finer vessel, one of a fleet of ships owned by Maxim, which flew his flag and carried cargoes from all over the world.

From an early age it had become clear to Maxim's parents that he was a highly intelligent child with an insatiable thirst for knowledge. With the help of his mother's family, he had been sent to a school in Westminster and afterwards to Cambridge to finish his education. But in the meantime he'd had to suffer the loss of both his parents, whose entire fortune was wrapped up in the three-masted sailing ship.

Possessing a shrewd and clever brain, on finishing his education Maxim had attacked life with a single-minded determination. Immediately putting his meagre inheritance to use, he had sold the vessel and gambled on a series of investments which had paid off. Learning fast, he survived and prospered—in fact, it was as if he could do no wrong. He had embarked on new ventures, buying land in England and America, land which yielded its riches of gold and tin and coal. Tom had laughed with admiration, telling him that his father would have been immensely proud of his son who had turned out to be a brilliant businessman of the first order, a man who had obviously been born with the Midas touch.

Maxim thrived on taking risks and was forever driven by the thrill of the wager, always winning and becoming richer by the day, his wealth bringing him untold luxuries, but no apparent happiness. At best, he was a fiercely proud and private man, guarded and solitary, a man accountable to no one. At worst, he was a man with a wide streak of ruthlessness and an iron control that was almost chilling. He could be cold, calculating and unemotional, which was how his business adversaries thought of him.

Where his grandfather and his uncle, the Earl of Brinkcliff, were concerned, Maxim was as hard and unforgiving as his father had been before him, but Tom knew that Alice had found the chink in his armour by providing him with a daughter outside wedlock—although a son would have given her more leverage in persuading Maxim to become reconciled with his uncle. How long would it be, he asked himself, before Maxim lost the battle to stand firm against his uncle and went to see him?

Deep in thought, Maxim continued to watch as the boat carrying Lavinia Renshaw went on its way. The incident which had just occurred had left its effect on him, and he had a strong desire to see her again. Her pale features and those incredible turquoise-coloured eyes amidst the mass of corn gold hair had drawn him like a magnet.

Unbidden, he remembered the last time he had seen Alice, when she had flounced out of his house in anger. Things had been thoroughly unpleasant between them for so long that not for one moment had he considered going after her. Alice was a gifted, ambitious schemer with a highly refined sense of survival, and he didn't give a damn where she went or who with, providing Lucy was not harmed. He was determined not to let Alice and her unreasonable demands cut his heart to shreds. Because of his daughter he had allowed her into his home and his life, but he was damned if he would let her become the centre of it. No woman would ever have that much power over him.

Chapter Two

Despite her unfortunate ordeal, when they reached the Scalini residence Lavinia managed to get to her room where she was bathed and put to bed to await the doctor. The elderly physician praised the gentleman who had bravely jumped into the canal to rescue her, for he had no doubt that his prompt action and knowledge on how to treat people who had almost drowned had saved his patient's life. As a result of the knock to her head, no doubt it would ache for a while but, apart from that, the doctor was sure she would suffer no ill effects.

There was a good deal of fussing and concern from everyone in the Scalini household. Lavinia lay in bed as people came and went, her head so crowded with impressions and suppressed emotions that she was quite bewildered. Julia swept into her room with her usual exuberance.

Over the years Lavinia had learned to cope with her half-sister in her own way, which was largely to avoid her whenever possible. This had been quite simple when Julia had married, but on the death of her husband—who had left her with nothing but a pile of debts—she had returned to live at Welbourne House in Gloucestershire.

On his death two years ago, Alec Renshaw, Lavinia's

father, had left his considerable estate to his son, Edgar, who was seventeen and still pursuing his education at Oxford. Alec had granted his stepdaughter a generous allowance—although not as much as she would have liked, which was the cause of much of her complaining and discontent—and that she could continue living at Welbourne House until such a time as she decided to leave. To Lavinia he had left a legacy of thirty thousand pounds, which was to be held in trust until she was twenty-five, or to be made available on her marriage.

Julia, who was eight years older than Lavinia, was outspoken and callous and always undermining Lavinia and taking her to task over something or other. In fact, she constantly made life downright unpleasant for her. With dark hair, flashing brown eyes and full red lips, Julia was a handsome woman. As usual she was dressed in the height of fashion—a gown of the finest silk clung to her figure, showing to anyone who was interested that it was full and shapely. She was such an overpowering person that most people felt subdued in her presence, and she put Lavinia's quietness down to her ordeal rather than her own domineering manner.

'Well, Lavinia? How do you feel? It must have been a terrifying ordeal for you,' she said imperiously, unmoved by what had happened to her half-sister, making it abundantly clear that she had come to enquire about her health out of duty rather than any concern she might feel for her well being. 'It is clear that your rescuer saved your life.'

'Oh, yes, Julia. I owe him a great deal,' Lavinia murmured.

'I hope you have everything you require.' Her eyes did a quick sweep of Lavinia's pale face and slender shape beneath the covers. 'You look well enough, to be sure.'

'I am. Thank you.'

Lavinia looked at Julia, sensing there was something different about her. Her expression was as cool as ever, but there was an excitement behind it and she appeared to be suppressing some inner emotion. Coming to stand close beside the bed, Julia's eyes were inscrutable. Lavinia recalled how Daisy had commented just the other day on the amount of time Julia and Robert spent together, and her friend had laughed when she had told Lavinia to watch for the way Julia fluttered her lashes and how the tone of her voice would change when she spoke to him. Daisy was convinced that Robert was aware of it, despite trying to conceal his feelings behind that marble façade of his. *Why*, Daisy had said, *he puffs up like a mating bird every time she goes near him.* The words had been innocently spoken and soon shrugged off by Daisy, but they had left Lavinia with a feeling of unease, and she found it strange that she should think of it now.

'Your escape was a wonderful piece of luck,' Julia told her, 'but it is over now and you must put it behind you.'

'I intend to. Have you been shopping, Julia?'

'No—not yet. I'm just on my way. Leonardo and Valentina had to go out and so I decided to delay my shopping trip until later—in case Robert should need anything, you understand. Someone had to stay and look after him.'

If it was Julia's intention to make Lavinia feel guilty for leaving her betrothed alone when he was unwell, she did not succeed. Robert was not the type to have anyone fussing around him. Schooling her features into a polite mask, she gave Julia a cool look. 'I expect he was grateful for your concern, but he was not so ill when I left him to go to the Lido, Julia.'

'He may have appeared to be a little better but he was far from it. You really should have put off going to the

Lido until he was well enough to accompany you,' she chided.

'We can always go again,' Lavinia told her lightly, determined not to be intimidated by her sister. 'Where is he, by the way? I thought he would have been in to see me.'

'He has been told what has happened and will be in to see you directly—as soon as he has dressed.'

Julia was looking at Lavinia steadily. Did Lavinia imagine it, or was there a malicious gleam in her eyes and a secret, rather smug smile on her sultry lips? A horrible possibility that there might be some truth after all in what Daisy had said dawned on her, and for the first time she eyed her sister with mistrust. It had never occurred to her that Julia might resent her forthcoming marriage to Robert—that she might want him for herself.

With a thin smile on her lips, in a cloud of heavy perfume and a rustle of silk skirts, Julia swept out of the room. Lavinia was left staring at the closed door, glad that she had gone, turning over in her mind the suspicions which had been implanted there by Daisy. But then she shook herself, telling herself not to be ridiculous, and that her tumble into the lagoon must have addled her wits. Robert was an honourable man whom she trusted implicitly.

News of what had befallen Lavinia forced Robert from his sick bed. Of slender build and with thin, greying hair and sharp features, he was not handsome but striking, in a distinguished kind of way. He was also twenty years Lavinia's senior. Everything he did was meticulously thought out and controlled. From poor beginnings, he had inherited neither title nor wealth, yet by hard work and frugal living he had managed to amass a considerable fortune and had purchased a fine property close to Welbourne House.

Lavinia was under no illusion that her legacy of thirty thousand pounds had drawn Robert to her but, feeling there would be no Thomas Dorsy in the future to capture her heart—the young man she had loved with all the passionate ardour of her youth, the man she would have married had he not been killed serving King and country in India—she had accepted Robert's suit. However, she had grown very fond of Robert, and always looked forward to his visits to her home. She saw no reason why they shouldn't be happy together.

Robert entered her room, adjusting his cravat, giving the impression that he had dressed in a hurry. His face was pale and pinched, which was his natural state and had nothing to do with his sickness. He came directly to the bed where he stood looking down at her.

'I trust you're suffering no ill effects from your ordeal, Lavinia?'

He was angry about what had occurred. Lavinia sensed it and braced herself for a ticking off. 'Apart from a headache caused by hitting my head on the bottom of the boat, I am fine, Robert.'

'Good. I am glad to hear it. The doctor says you are to remain in bed for the rest of the day. But perhaps the accident might have been avoided. According to the boatman, if you had not been standing up in the boat at the time, you would not have been thrown into the canal.'

'I know,' she admitted, giving him a wan smile. 'But when I saw the other boat about to ram us, I didn't stop to think.'

'No—which is proving to be a failing in you, Lavinia,' he reproached her harshly.

With growing anger, Lavinia glared at her betrothed from beneath half-lowered lids. Only Robert would make it sound like it was all her fault, she thought crossly. No doubt he blamed her for drawing attention and making a spectacle of herself, as though she had fallen into the canal deliberately. Heated words rose to her lips, which at any other time she would have stemmed, but, fuelled by her thumping head and tired of always trying to keep on the right side of his temper, a rebelliousness stirred inside her that she could not repress.

'Contrary to what you may think, Robert, I did not fall into the canal on purpose. However, it is over now and no serious harm was done. However, with all my faults, I cannot for the life of me think why you want to marry me at all. There is certainly nothing romantic about our relationship, is there?' she said scathingly, astounding herself that she dared voice her thoughts. Warnings of danger that she had gone too far flashed into her mind, but ever since she had regained her senses and looked into the clear blue eyes of Maxim Purnell, nothing was the same as it had been before her tumble into the lagoon.

Robert was looking at her with disapproval, but was also a little nonplussed and surprised by her sudden outburst. 'We are not discussing romance but reality, Lavinia,' he said sharply.

'No doubt Julia has been looking after you in my absence,' she said, making a sudden play of adjusting the pillow behind her head. Catching his sudden frown and the sharp glance of unease he threw her way, her suspicions that hidden forces were at work about which she knew nothing increased.

'She has been both thoughtful and attentive in your absence. But you defied me, Lavinia,' Robert accused coldly, leaving Lavinia with the impression that he wanted to veer the conversation away from her sister.

Again she bristled at the harsh tone of his voice and raised her chin with a touch of defiance. 'I did no such thing.'

'I said I would take you to the Lido when I felt up to it,

but you were determined, you and Daisy—who in my opinion is far too high-spirited and frivolous—and if this insolent outburst is anything to go by, her influence where you are concerned is proving to be far too disruptive. No doubt she found it exciting taking you on some hair-raising adventure.'

'That's ridiculous, Robert. It was merely a trip to the Lido—and I certainly cannot call my tumble into the lagoon an adventure. I was almost drowned. I certainly didn't want it to happen.'

'Nevertheless, after this unfortunate occurrence I must ask you not to leave the house again unless you are accompanied by me. Is that understood? No doubt by tomorrow I shall be feeling a good deal better.'

Despite her annoyance at Robert's unreasonable manner, Lavinia felt obliged to ask after his health. 'How are you, Robert? Has the sickness left you?'

'I believe I am somewhat restored.' His expression guarded, he lifted his brows in bland enquiry. 'And to whom do we have to be grateful for your deliverance from the lagoon?'

'Someone by the name of Maxim Purnell.'

Robert frowned, becoming thoughtful, as if the name was familiar. Lavinia looked at him curiously.

'Do you know anyone of that name, Robert? Have you heard it before.'

'I believe so—only in passing, mind. If they are one and the same man, that is.'

'It's hardly a common name. The man I saw was tall, very dark—and undoubtedly handsome,' Lavinia told him boldly, probing to learn more about her rescuer, knowing Robert would find her description of him annoying and distasteful. 'Tell me about the Maxim Purnell you know.'

'I believe I might have seen the man once or twice in

London, but I can't say that I know him or recall what he looks like. Despite the time I spend in London, I move in very different circles to Mr Purnell. I only know that he's said to be the nephew of the Earl of Brinkcliff, who resides, I believe, at Stannington in Oxfordshire.'

'Said? What do you mean?'

'That nobody knows for sure. What is known is that the Earl is an old man without an heir.'

'But if Maxim Purnell is his nephew, then surely—'

'I have told you that nothing is known for sure, Lavinia,' Robert answered irritably. 'It is rumoured that when the Earl of Brinkcliff's older brother wanted to marry a woman not of their class, their father threatened to disinherit him, believing it would have the desired effect. But the old man underestimated his son because he went off and married her anyway. I believe Maxim Purnell to be their offspring. True to his word, the old Earl disinherited his eldest son— an action which, by all accounts, the present Earl has come to regret.'

Lavinia listened with immense fascination. 'So the man who saved my life could be the nephew of the Earl of Brinkcliff.'

'It's possible. But much good it will do him if he isn't reconciled with the old man.'

'How does he live? What is his profession?'

Robert looked at her coldly, disapproving of the interest the man had aroused in her. 'Handsome he may be, but his social standing is far from impeccable. I do not approve of his lifestyle. I believe the man is an adventurer and a gambler, Lavinia. A professional gambler—successful, too, by all accounts.'

Lavinia's eyes opened wide. 'But if he's as successful as all that, then he must be very good at it.'

Robert gave her a withering look. 'Gambling is not an honourable profession, Lavinia,' he admonished.

'No—of course it isn't, Robert,' she said quietly, feeling well and truly reproached whilst forcing herself to repress a smile.

'But if the man who pulled you out of the lagoon is the same Maxim Purnell, then he appears to be one of nature's survivors to me.'

Lavinia and Daisy had arranged to purchase their masks for the ball the following day, but because of Lavinia's mishap they put it off until the day after. True to his word Robert accompanied them, but when they reached the Mercerie, the main street in Venice which linked St Mark's Square with the Rialto, he and Julia left them, preferring instead to while away an hour or so beneath the tall tower of the Campanile in St Mark's Square drinking coffee at Florian's, giving Lavinia the freedom to shop with Daisy and her mother.

Protected from the hot Venetian sun under pretty parasols, the three of them wandered at leisure, meandering through an enchanting maze of alleyways, squares and bridges. All around them was an amazing spectacle of life and gaiety, full of noise and colour and teaming with people, but it also had a seedier side, for the alleyways leading off were where courtesans offered their services to all comers.

The many shops were filled with curios and sumptuous goods from the East, and caged nightingales sang sweet melodies above the heads of the crowds. They found the mask shop Valentina had recommended almost immediately, and Lavinia became so absorbed in her task of selecting one to go with her gown for the ball that she failed

to notice the tall man standing a little to one side, who was watching her with studied interest.

The whole window of the mask shop was festooned with beautifully created masks on display. Lavinia gazed at them in wonder, undecided which one to choose. There were all colours—silver, white and bronze—some sequined and decorated with ribbons and pearls. Some were elaborately adorned with soft feathers, others with delicate tissue and gold leaf.

'Come along inside, Lavinia,' said Daisy breathlessly, her eyes as wide as the empty eye-hole sockets of the masks looking back at her through the window. 'We must try some on.'

'Yes, yes, Daisy—but look,' gasped Lavinia, dragging her back as she was about to move away. 'See that one in the centre—the gold silk with sequins and beads.'

'Yes, I see it. Oh, Lavinia, it's adorable,' she enthused. 'But Robert would never approve. It's far too costly and elaborate for his taste. You know he never spends a guinea when a shilling will suffice.'

Lavinia looked a little downcast on being reminded of Robert's miserly ways. It was as if a cloud had suddenly descended on her. 'Well, what of it?' she replied with a hint of rebelliousness in her tone. 'It would certainly go with my dress.'

'That's true. But you would have to dig deep into your pocket to pay for it—or perhaps I should say Robert's, considering he's paying for it. Which is strange, don't you think, when he clearly thinks that any item of luxury to be some kind of sinful indulgence?'

There was just a hint of scorn in Daisy's voice when she spoke of Robert which Lavinia noted and decided to ignore. The man she had chosen to marry would never meet with her friend's approval, so there was no point arguing. 'I suppose you're right,' she admitted with a wistful sigh, gazing at the forbidden mask with longing. 'Although it is perfect, isn't it? Still—it's going to be hard enough for Robert to accept the dress without adding to his vexation by appearing in something he would consider too expensive and frivolous by far. Let's go inside and look for something else.'

An assistant welcomed them into the shop which was full of people and crammed with masks of every description. There was a strong aroma of paint and glue emanating from the workshop at the rear, where masks were made from clay moulds for the nobility and general public alike.

Watched over by Mrs Lambert, both girls excitedly tried on one mask after another. The majority was made from papier mâché, but there were others made from leather and canvas, all skilfully made and exotically trimmed. They delighted in the anonymity to be achieved by the wearing of something so small, the masks creating an atmosphere of secrets and mysteries, the empty eye holes giving them a sinister air.

Inside that small shop the many faces of the Carnival came alive to them. Some were grotesque, some comical and others tragic. Some were linked with characters of the underworld, while many of them represented characters from plays performed by bands of actors who travelled through Italy. The most familiar of these Commedia dell'Arte characters were Harlequin, Columbine and Brighella, and the long-beaked clown Pucinella.

'I had no idea there were so many different kinds,' gasped Daisy excitedly. 'There are so many to choose from I shall never be able to decide.'

Eventually Lavinia chose a plain white oval mask, thinking it suited her and would go well with her dress. Mrs Lambert was trying to help Daisy make up her mind between a red silk mask or a black sequined half-mask, and it was proving to be extremely disconcerting for Daisy, who always found it difficult to decide on anything when presented with a choice.

While she was waiting Lavinia couldn't resist the temptation to try on the mask that had caught her eye in the window. The assistant was only too willing to oblige and handed it to her before turning away to serve a gentleman.

Lavinia gazed at the mask, fingering it with sheer delight. It was a half-mask, a work of superb craftsmanship, of gold silk and intricately sewn with winking gold sequins and tiny gold beads. Holding it up to her face she looked into the mirror, aware of someone coming to stand close behind her and taking the delicate ribbons in his fingers

'Allow me,' said a voice, low and soft like velvet.

Lavinia's breath caught in her throat when her eyes met those of her rescuer from the lagoon in the mirror, and she was unable to do anything other than watch in astonishment as he deftly fastened the ribbons at the back of her head before leaning forward so that his face was beside hers, his eyes watching her in the mirror in speculative silence before saying quietly, his breath warm on her cheek, 'I think this becomes you extremely well.'

Lavinia expelled the breath she hadn't realised she was still holding, and she turned and stared up at him through the eye holes of the mask. The dazzling charm of his lazy white smile was doing strange things to her pulse rate. 'You!' she breathed. He was so incredibly handsome, with eyes that seemed to look deep into her heart. Until then she had thought she remembered exactly what he looked like— the image she had of him in her mind's eye was that of a man who had just emerged from the lagoon, with black unruly hair and flashing white teeth, wet and gleaming with health and vitality, everything about him exuding brute strength.

This arrogantly handsome man was in such contrast that it was difficult to believe they were one and the same. He was dressed immaculately, his thick black hair well groomed. The dark green cloth of his superbly cut frock coat stretched across his broad shoulders, and the pristine whiteness of his silk neckcloth emphasised his bronzed features. There was a leashed sensuality about his face, and his finely sculpted lips were slightly parted in a lazy white smile as he regarded her.

It was the clear blue of his eyes that told Lavinia it was indeed the same man who had come so quickly to her aid and her heart soared. As a result of the tender care and her day of rest after her tumble into the lagoon, she presented a fresh and blooming countenance to the man she had every reason to be grateful to.

'I—I did not expect to see you here—or again, for that matter. Forgive me,' she faltered. 'I—I hardly recognised you.'

Maxim arched a sleek black brow. 'Why? Because I appear before you fully clothed? Or can it be that you have forgotten me already?' he asked on a note of mock regret.

'Oh, no—no.'

'I am happy to see you suffered no ill effects from your accident,' he said, smiling a slow, dazzling smile that swept across his tanned features; its effect on his face was as startling as the effect it had on Lavinia's senses.

Maxim felt his heart slam against his ribs when he looked at her, unprepared for the shock of purely physical desire that swept through him. Dressed in a delicate shade of pastel pink, with her golden hair arranged in delicate curls about her heart-shaped face, Miss Lavinia Renshaw was eternally female, elegant and slender, with an air of serene composure. It was as much a part of her as her magnificent eyes—large, translucent and deep turquoise, with a darker rim around the iris, which gave them a glowing intensity.

And her mouth—never had he seen or wanted to place his own lips on a mouth like that. Maxim was certain it must have been shaped by one of the famous sculptors whose statues graced the many beautiful churches of Venice. It was chiselled to exquisite perfection, wearing a smile as tantalising and mysterious as the silks and brocades that floated behind the gondolas on the canals at Carnival time.

'I am so grateful for what you did the other day. Your prompt action saved my life. As you see I have made a full recovery, but thank goodness you are such a good swimmer.'

Maxim's cool blue eyes warmed with amusement. 'I've had plenty of practice. However, I don't make a habit of jumping into the lagoon to rescue people. You are the first.'

'And the last, I hope,' Lavinia laughed, looking up at him.

'My advice to you is to learn to swim.'

'I would love to—but unfortunately there are no facilities where I live.' She moved to one side to make room for another customer at the counter. 'I had no idea so many people would be buying masks outside Carnival time.'

'That is because so many tourists—especially the young gentlemen on the Grand Tour—find them ideal gifts to take back to female relatives and friends.' Maxim eyed her quizzically. 'And you? What is your reason for purchasing a mask?'

'We are to attend a costume ball tomorrow night. It's being held at one of the palaces along the Grand Canal.'

'I do know of it. And have you decided which mask you are going to buy?'

Lavinia sighed, removing the gold one and fingering the plain white on the counter. 'Yes. This is the one.'

Maxim frowned, looking at her closely, seeing the unmistakable regret mirrored in her lovely eyes, having heard it in her voice. 'It is not nearly as becoming as this,' he told her, indicating the gold one. 'It is evident to me which one you prefer.'

Lavinia caught her bottom lip with her teeth, an unconscious habit she had acquired as a little girl when she was about to do something she would regret. 'I know. But—'

'But?' Maxim queried.

'If I appear wearing anything as extravagant as this, my—my betrothed will be quite put out,' she explained, wondering why she should suddenly feel so reluctant to mention Robert.

If Maxim was disappointed to learn she was betrothed, he gave no sign of it. 'So—you have an escort to the ball.'

'Yes. Why do you ask?'

He grinned. 'Because I would have asked to take you myself.'

Lavinia's eyes lit up. 'Oh! Are you invited?'

'I am.'

Lavinia was thrilled to know this, and she tried to ignore the dull ache of disappointment in her chest, shocked to realise how much she wished he was to be her escort instead of Robert. A slow, lazy smile swept across Maxim's face.

'Perhaps it's sensible of you to choose a plain mask.'

'Do you think so? Do you mind telling me why?'

'Because it will help stave off the many contenders for your hand that a mask with so much seduction sewn into it with those sequins and beads would be sure to attract.'

Flushing softly, Lavinia handed the mask to the assistant, who shook her head with dismay as she was about to place it in a box, telling her in broken English that the ribbons had worked loose and would have to be fixed. But it was no problem. She would have it done and delivered to her address before the shop closed. After giving the assistant the Scalinis' address—an address the assistant was well familiar with—Lavinia turned back to Maxim. The crush inside the shop made it virtually impossible to move.

'Come outside,' he urged, taking her elbow.

Lavinia turned to Daisy, who was completely unaware of Maxim's presence as she frowned in desperation, her eyes going from one mask to the other, racked with indecision.

'If you would like my opinion, Daisy,' Lavinia laughed, coming to her rescue, 'I think the black will complement your red dress perfectly. The red mask might not be of the same shade and might clash.'

'Do you think so, Lavinia?'

'Yes. I'll wait for you outside the shop. It's so crowded in here.'

After extricating themselves from the crush, Maxim and Lavinia found themselves out in the street, where the crush was almost as great as inside the shop. Holding Lavinia's arm firmly, Maxim cut his way through the crowd like an irresistible force, coming to a halt across the street where it thinned out, but still able to keep an eye on the shop so that Lavinia would see when Daisy and her mother emerged.

'So,' said Maxim, his bold gaze sweeping over her shining hair, a smile of frank admiration gleaming in his eyes when they settled on her upturned face, 'you are staying with Leonardo Scalini and his wife.'

'Yes. Are you acquainted with them?' she asked, managing to keep her expression calm at finding herself in such close proximity with him, but her treacherous pulse was racing twice as fast and her mind was in absolute confusion. No other man had ever had this affect on her before.

'Only slightly. The Scalinis are an old, established family in Venice—and much respected. There are few who have not heard of them.'

'When you jumped into the lagoon to save me you were on board a ship. Are you a sailor?' Lavinia asked, curious to know if he was the same Maxim Purnell Robert had told her about.

He laughed. 'Heaven forbid. No. I was merely visiting a friend of mine, who just so happens to be the captain of that ship.'

'So you are not staying on the ship?'

'No. I am staying at an apartment of a friend of mine in the San Marco area—not far from here. In fact,' he said, taking her arm and drawing her into the street a little way and indicating a rather grand-looking creamy yellow mansion with green shutters down one of the narrow streets, 'that's the building down there.'

'Yes, I see. And are you in Venice long, Mr Purnell?'

'No. A few days at the most, then I have to leave for England.'

'And where do you live when you are in England? Where is home?'

'Kent.'

Lavinia could see Daisy and her mother coming out of the shop and she smiled up at Maxim. 'Here are my friends. I—I must be going. Goodbye, Mr Purnell. I can never repay you for what you did.'

Reluctant to let her go, Maxim moved closer, seeming to tower over her. 'Yes, you can.'

'How?' A nervous quaking jarred through her when she saw how intently he was looking at her.

'By saving a dance for me at the ball tomorrow night.'

Lavinia caught her breath, teetering on the edge of an abyss, trying not to blush at the wicked thoughts that sprang to mind. Maxim Purnell was making her feel things she had never felt before. It was like she was completely helpless, finding herself being pulled to this man by some invisible force she couldn't resist, no matter how hard she tried. 'I—I don't think that would be wise,' she whispered. 'Robert, my betrothed, would not approve.'

'Surely he would not object to one dance,' Maxim pressed, not the kind of man to be put off. 'And Robert will have to give way at some time during the evening. The night will be one of intense revelry when everyone throws off their inhibitions. Robert will find that I will not be the only man wanting to dance with you.'

Lavinia found it impossible to resist his request—and secretly she didn't want to. She smiled. 'Then what can I say? Yes, Mr Purnell, I will by happy to dance with you—with Robert's permission, of course.'

'Of course. Until tomorrow night,' he said, turning to Daisy and her mother and indulging in a few polite greetings before excusing himself and moving off into the crowd.

Lavinia watched him go with unconcealed interest in her wide eyes, and a whole bewildering array of emotions sweeping over her. She had an uneasy feeling that there was something dangerous about Maxim Purnell, that the fine clothes and indolent manner were to lull the unwary into believing he was refined and civilised, when beneath the disguise he was primitive and barbarous, the sort of man who had done and experienced things both dangerous and terrible, things that had hardened him. Yet he was wickedly handsome, she thought. He reminded her of a black panther—sleek, beautiful and dangerous.

Reluctantly she tore her eyes away from his retreating

figure and began walking in the direction of St Mark's Square to find Robert and Julia, her steps as light as her fluttering heart.

Later in the day when the gold velvet box containing Lavinia's mask was delivered to the house, she took it to her room to try it on, accompanied by Daisy. Upon lifting the lid of the box she let out a gasp of surprise, for, instead of finding the one she had ordered, it was the other—the exquisite gold silk which had so caught her eye.

'Oh, Daisy, look,' she whispered, taking it gently out of the box and staring down at it, seeing it had been studded with shining jewel-like objects which winked and shone when they caught the light. Lavinia was sure they hadn't been there before. 'There must be some mistake. I certainly didn't order this.'

Daisy came to stand beside her, her eyes wide with amazement when she saw the mask. 'Good Lord, Lavinia. If you didn't order this, then which one did you order?'

'It was white—plain white—and I couldn't bring it with me because the ribbons had become loose. The assistant promised to have them repaired and delivered to the house. I cannot keep this—Robert will have a fit. It must be returned to the shop immediately.'

'No, wait. What's this?' said Daisy, reaching into the box and picking up a small card from the bed of velvet. 'It just says—This becomes you better. M.' She looked at Lavinia's stunned face in question. 'M?'

'Mr Purnell,' whispered Lavinia, experiencing a shock of quivering excitement mingled with alarm when she realised what he had done. 'Oh, Daisy! He was there when I tried it on in the shop. He told me this mask suited me better than the white. He must have returned and told the assistant to deliver this one instead of the one I ordered, paying the difference himself. But what can it mean?'

'It means, Lavinia, that you have made quite an impression on Mr Purnell. Why else would he send you something so exquisite?'

'But it is quite wrong of him to place me in such an embarrassing position. He should not have done it.'

'You cannot blame him, Lavinia. How was he to know you are betrothed to Robert?'

'Because I told him. You must see that I cannot possibly accept a gift from any man without Robert's approval—especially not such an expensive gift as this. It would be too rash. And see—those sparkling stones were not in the mask we admired. It is either a different mask or they have been added on Mr Purnell's instructions. They cannot possibly be real.'

Daisy studied them closely. 'Well, I'm no expert on such matters, but they certainly look real to me. And besides, I wouldn't say Mr Purnell is the type to buy fake anything—that it has to be the real thing or nothing at all.'

Real or not, the mask had certainly thrown Lavinia into a quandary. 'Oh, what can I do?'

'Accept it. I would,' Daisy said firmly in answer to Lavinia's questioning glance. She shrugged. 'Why not? You're never going to receive anything as expensive or as exotic as this from Robert. Besides, he'll never know if you don't tell him. It's not as though he's going to be asked to pay the difference, is it?'

Daisy spoke with so much force that Lavinia was almost persuaded. She looked at her, feeling herself weakening, aware how dire the consequences would be if she were to accept it and Robert found out. On seeing the unconcealed encouragement and mischief lurking in Daisy's eyes, she knew she would succumb to temptation, unable to believe that a chance meeting with Maxim Purnell could have created such a rebellious change in her. The unconventional event of their meeting would be indelibly and importantly marked for all time if she accepted his gift.

'But—I can't do that. It would be deceitful—wouldn't it?' Her lips trembled into a smile.

Daisy giggled softly. 'Madness, I'd call it, but it isn't as though you intend becoming involved with him, is it? Besides, Robert has his head so high in the clouds most of the time that he will never know. Enjoy yourself while you can, Lavinia. Life will be no bed of roses when you're back in England and married to Robert. At least you will have this wonderful time you have spent in Venice to look back on—to know that for a while you were admired—albeit from afar—by the extremely handsome and exciting Maxim Purnell.'

Chapter Three

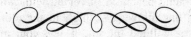

Dressed in all their finery, the large party from the Scalini House went by water to the ball. Just as Daisy expected, Robert almost threw a fit when Lavinia presented herself in her white silk dress. If Valentina and Leonardo hadn't come to her rescue and enthused about how lovely she looked, Daisy was certain he would have ordered her back to her room to change into something else.

Robert was so incensed that he failed to notice the expensive, exquisite beauty of the mask his betrothed was wearing, which twinkled with expensive jewels. Valentina raised her eyebrows in surprise as her sharp eyes inspected it closely, but she made no comment other than to smile secretively and say how beautiful it was. But she was curious to know how Lavinia got away with wearing something which her expert eye told her was far too expensive for Robert to have purchased, and she would dearly like to know who had.

The Grand Canal was alive with gondolas and barges ferrying people to the palace where the ball was being held. Light streamed from the arched windows of the many grand houses on either side, the moon reflecting its silver sheen on hundreds of rooftops. Arriving at their destination, the boatman secured the craft to a wooden post and they alighted and climbed the steps. The palace, with its intricate, lace-like façade, was of fifteenth-century architectural elegance, very grand and awe-inspiring, although not as large as Lavinia had expected it to be.

They moved into the ballroom which had frescoed walls and a magnificent carved and gilded wooden ceiling, panelled with beautiful scenes of Venice painted by leading artists of the time. Flowers were bursting out of baskets and vases and music filled the air. It was like a magnificent theatre and no expense had been spared.

Lavinia could not have imagined such a spectacle. It was lavish, with so many people in a variety of dazzling, exotic and sumptuous costumes and bedecked with jewels. Many of the families attending the ball were part of the hierarchy of powerful families which ruled Venice. There was such gaiety and so much colour. It was like make believe, like stepping back to a medieval age, and Lavinia felt absurdly happy as she mingled with the throng on Robert's arm, who had surprised them all by wearing a Harlequin costume. But it was plain that he was feeling ridiculous and finding it impossible to relax.

Lavinia was light-headed, which had nothing to do with the wine she drank as the evening progressed. There was no discretion, only a sense of boldness, of daring and recklessness as the Carnival atmosphere of the ball invaded each and every one of them and took them over. A sense of fantasy and unreality prevailed over the whole night.

She was conspicuous because of the simplicity of her attire among so much flamboyance. She had chosen to wear a dress that was like a shining column of white silk, with long flowing sleeves and a high stiffened collar which framed her face, her only piece of jewellery being a gold brooch at her throat. Her dress was extremely flattering and alluring, showing the curvaceous outline of her body when she moved, and hinting at her small waist and hidden delights.

A white wig, short and softly curled, covered her hair, and the golden mask sent to her by her admirer covered the upper part of her face. The colour, set against the startling white of her attire, emphasised the brilliance of her turquoise eyes.

Lavinia immediately became the focal point of several masked revellers, and she was surprised when Robert raised no objection to her being whirled on to the dance floor by one of them. As the ball gathered momentum her feet didn't touch the ground as she danced with one partner after another, each one totally unrecognisable, but all the time she was waiting in excited anticipation for one man in particular to come and claim her for the dance she had promised him. But as the evening wore on she felt her spirits begin to wane when he didn't appear.

'By the way, Lavinia,' Robert said, having come to stand by her side after conversing with Sir John and Lady Evesham, who were accompanied by their daughter Sophia. 'It may interest you to know that I have heard something concerning the man who pulled you out of the lagoon—Maxim Purnell.'

Lavinia was all attention. 'What have you heard?'

'It would seem he is the same Maxim Purnell I have met on occasion in London.'

'Oh? How do you know that?'

'I have made enquiries. He is not unknown to Leonardo. It is important for me to know to whom I am indebted for saving my betrothed from drowning. Apart from rumours about him being the nephew of Lord Alistair Purnell—the Earl of Brinkcliff—the man remains a mystery and of no consequence. The only thing that is known for sure about him is that he is a common gambler.'

Robert spoke about Mr Purnell with such harsh censure that Lavinia felt compelled to rise to his defence. 'Really, Robert. You cannot hold that against him.'

'You know I consider gambling a weakness, Lavinia, and that I deplore it in any form—which gives me good enough reason to dislike Maxim Purnell. It is extremely galling to find myself indebted to a man of such poor character for pulling you out of the lagoon.'

'Then I feel I must apologise, Robert,' said Lavinia, her voice dripping with sarcasm. 'The next time I decide to fall into the lagoon I shall have to try and make sure that the person who is courageous enough to jump in and rescue me has breeding, good connections and background.'

Robert's eyes glinted hard at her through the eye holes in his mask. 'Don't be flippant, Lavinia. I cannot for the life of me understand what has come over you of late. Your behaviour is so out of character. It does not become you.'

Immediately contrite, Lavinia averted her eyes. Robert was right. What was happening to her? Why, whenever she was alone with him of late, did she feel a temper she didn't know she possessed come to a simmering boil?

'And, seeing that you are so interested in your rescuer,' he went on, 'it would appear that Maxim Purnell was at a ridotto last night—gambling, of course; by all accounts he lost heavily.'

Lavinia knew that a ridotto was where people went to indulge in gaming. Since the authorities had banned public gaming because it was the cause of so many bankruptcies of Venetian families, it still went on throughout the city in private places—palaces, wine shops and coffee houses—frequented by the very men who had made it illegal. For some reason she could not explain, she had not told Robert about her encounter with Maxim Purnell at the mask shop. Now that he had told her about Mr Purnell's losses at the ridotto, she wondered if it had anything to do with him not being at the ball.

Feeling disappointed and deflated, she took a glass of champagne from the tray of a passing waiter, an action which Robert observed with a frown of disapproval.

'That is your third glass of wine, Lavinia,' he commented with reproach. 'One glass is usually considered sufficient for a lady. I have noticed of late that you have acquired a taste for alcohol.'

Lavinia smiled coolly, refusing to let him intimidate her. 'That's right, Robert,' she agreed. 'I find champagne so refreshing—especially in this climate.'

'Nevertheless, Lavinia, I do not like to see my future wife quaffing liquor like a sot.'

Lavinia's eyes opened wide with burgeoning annoyance mingled with amusement. 'Robert! I drink no more than any other woman here tonight—in fact, much less. And I will remind you that I am not your wife yet and have no intention of being thirsty.'

Robert was cut and angered by the jibe. He stared hard at her through the eye holes in his black half-mask, but he was prevented from saying anything else—at that moment Valentina appeared beside them in an elaborate brocade gown and a huge feathered head dress. She enquired if they were enjoying the ball, and Robert was obliged to smile and utter polite words. Lavinia knew how much the effort was costing him.

Valentina, who had strong features and dark Italian skin, was a tall, statuesque woman in her early forties, having lived on the mainland until her marriage to Leonardo when she had come to Venice. Her fluent English could be at-

tributed to her sharp and clever mind and the many English
merchants she met through her husband's work.

Robert secretly thought her unfeminine and disapproved
of her outspokenness and independence of spirit, but Lavinia liked her sense of fun and no-nonsense manner, and
she strongly suspected that Valentina did not possess a high
opinion of Robert. But on this occasion Valentina was determined to try and make him smile, and after much persuasion she managed to get him on to the dance floor.

The music had slowed to a waltz to allow the dancers to
catch their breath, and Lavinia was standing watching
Daisy in her shimmering red dress and her rather boisterous
partner, when a man's voice spoke softly in her ear, making
her heart beat rapidly.

'Dance with me, Lavinia.'

Startled, slowly she turned and looked at the tall masked
man who had spoken to her and knew who it was immediately. Maxim's clear blue eyes pierced her own. He was
dressed in one of the most common disguises, La Bauta—
perhaps the most frightening and sinister of all. It was com-
prised of a black silk mantilla beneath a black tricorne hat,
the long mantilla covering his wide shoulders. A white
bauta mask covered his face, startling and eerie and spectral
in its whiteness, the upper lip prominent to allow for eating
and drinking.

Without waiting for Lavinia to reply, Maxim took her
hand and drew her into the dance and into his arms, sliding
his hand around her minuscule waist and holding her close
to his firm body, closer than was proper, she thought, but
she could not have objected if she had wanted to. Feeling
as if she were in a pleasant dream, she placed her gloved
hand in his and looked up at him as he whirled her round
with a relaxed grace, trying to imagine the expression on
the handsome face behind the mask.

'You look ravishing,' he murmured, feeling her close and glad that he'd decided to attend the ball after all.

Maxim's late arrival had nothing to do with the fact that he might be bemoaning his losses at the ridotto the previous evening—which was what Lavinia had suspected. Realising the futility of pursuing a woman who could never be anything more to him than someone he had met in Venice, a woman who was betrothed to someone else, Maxim's indecision about attending the ball at all was more to do with a well-developed instinct for self-preservation. The warmth of affection he was beginning to feel for Lavinia Renshaw, after only two meetings with her, was too disconcerting for his peace of mind, and he knew it would be sheer folly to pursue an affair that was doomed from the start.

But intending to leave Venice shortly and knowing the ball would be his last opportunity of seeing her, Maxim's resistance had wavered and he had found himself drawn to the ball as if he were a puppet and she were pulling the strings. He was attracted to her by the sincerity in her gaze, sensing that her charm and personality was unlike any other woman he had known. She had a distinctive beauty of which she seemed totally unaware, and a natural femininity which remained unflawed by self-interest. But Maxim's instinct told him that he must be wary, otherwise he would find himself drawn deeper into something over which he would have no control.

'I have been watching you for quite some time,' said Maxim, 'and think, perhaps, that you should have come to the ball as Columbine.'

'Columbine! But she was—'

'A flirt,' he told her softly on a teasing note, his eyes twinkling down into hers through the eye holes in his mask.

Lavinia cocked her head sideways, looking up at him.

'Are you not afraid that I might be affronted on being compared to such a character?'

'No. Typical of Columbine's character—who flirted outrageously with Harlequin, by the way—you show supreme intelligence and charm in the presence of such madness and sheer stupidity which surrounds you tonight.'

'Do I?' Lavinia laughed, entering into the spirit of his light banter. 'Nevertheless, if you have, as you say, been watching me for some time—and I have to say that I am disappointed that I am so easily recognisable despite the trouble I have taken to disguise my identity—it cannot have escaped your notice that Robert, the man I am to marry, is dressed as Harlequin.'

'I have noticed—and I would recognise you anywhere,' he murmured, looking down at her upturned face, 'despite the wig you are wearing—which makes you look adorable. Besides, I only had to look for the mask to know who was behind it. I have also observed that you do not flirt with your betrothed as one would expect a woman to flirt with the man she is to marry.'

'But surely to flirt means to show romantic interest without having serious intentions. Believe me, Mr Purnell, Robert is not the sort of person who would appreciate anyone flirting with him.'

Before Lavinia knew what was happening, Maxim had deftly danced her through some long net drapes on to a balcony, drawing her away from the light and standing close beside her near the balustrade. Warning bells began ringing inside her head, telling her of the impropriety of being on the balcony alone with this man Robert deemed unsuitable because of his unsavoury vocation, but she felt far too happy to object and refused to listen to them.

Appreciating the feel of the cool air on her face, Lavinia watched as Maxim removed his mask so that she could see his face, feeling her heart do a somersault when his handsome features were revealed to her. He boldly stared his appreciation until Lavinia had the distinct feeling that his imagination went further than the thin material of her gown. She stood quite still when he reached out and traced her mask with his fingers.

'I'm happy to see you did not return the mask to the shop.'

'Did you think I would?'

'It did occur to me. But the risk was well worth taking.'

'I did not tell Robert. I—I know I should have—but he would have been angry, knowing I had received a gift from a man other than himself.'

'Then it is time Robert began to appreciate the woman he is to marry and started paying her attention and showering her with expensive and exotic gifts,' Maxim accused, his unfathomable eyes locked onto hers.

Having taken the time to observe Robert Feltham, a man he recognised, having seen him on occasion in London although they had never been introduced, Maxim found it difficult to understand why someone as young and lovely as Lavinia could consider marriage to a man who had no sense of humour and was old enough to be her father. Feltham was also a man who had nothing to recommend him in either character or manner when dealing with others.

Maxim's attack on Robert caused a hot, embarrassed flush to mantle Lavinia's cheeks. 'He—he does buy me things,' she said, making a feeble attempt to defend the man she was to marry, a man she held in the highest regard and of whom she was extremely fond. 'But he has worked too hard to attain his wealth and the position he holds in society to squander his money on anything he considers frivolous and unnecessary. I know the mask I am wearing must have cost you dearly—and it has not escaped my notice that it has acquired an added sparkle from when I tried it on in the shop.'

'You deserve only the very best, Lavinia. I assure you that the jewels are not fake.'

'No. I didn't think they were. Which is why, when the evening is over, I should return it to you at your address. It—it's beautiful, but far too valuable. You really shouldn't have given me such a present,' she said helplessly, recalling his huge loss at the ridotto the evening before. 'I'm sure you can't afford it.'

Maxim's dark brows snapped together above angry eyes and his jaw tensed. Clearly it was the wrong thing to say and she felt she had offended him. After all, it wasn't for her to say what he could and could not afford.

'I think that's for me to worry about,' he said tersely.

Embarrassed and ashamed for speaking with uncharacteristic bluntness, she drew a fortifying breath. 'I'm sorry. I imagine you are going to tell me I was rude to say that.'

'You were. I am not a pauper, and if I give anyone a gift I expect them to accept it gracefully and not raise ridiculous objections. You do want to keep it? You do like it, don't you?'

'You know I do,' she said quietly.

Maxim sighed, placing his hands on her shoulders and looking down at her seriously. 'Then what's the problem? Lavinia—I would be mortally offended if you were to return it to me. It is a gift—from me to you. Accept it as such. When I see how beautiful it looks on you it was worth every penny—and I will know that every time you look at it you will think of me.'

'Yes—I will—and thank you,' she whispered. 'I shall keep it always.'

When he dropped his hands she turned and looked down into the small, high-walled garden below, discernable from the light shining from the many windows of the palace. A pale crescent moon hung in a cloudless sky that was littered by myriad stars. A wisteria vine had escaped its prison garden and trailed out of control over the rusticated walls, and budding jasmine and honeysuckle gave off a heady, intoxicating scent which rose up to where they stood on the balcony.

Lavinia asked herself why she suddenly felt nervous being alone with Maxim, and to her consternation found the answer. It was because he encroached too closely upon her, and because she was afraid he would come closer still.

They stood in silence for a moment, and she knew he was as aware as she was of the combustible nature of their relationship. It was disturbing, an awareness that was uncomfortable. This was only the third time they had met and already Maxim had established himself in her mind, and she was troubled by her own susceptibility. She had thought herself immune to any man, but Maxim Purnell had infected her with a fever of his presence.

'What are you thinking?' Maxim asked after a moment.

'I was thinking how lovely both the night, and the scent coming from the flowers in the garden below are,' she answered truthfully.

'And are you enjoying the ball?'

'Immensely,' she laughed. 'I've never in my life experienced anything like it. It's all so unreal—like living a fantasy.'

'Venetians are illusionists and fantasists, entwining the past, the present, and the imagined—which is the concept of the Carnival. Artifice and manipulation are all part of their heritage, and they thrive on it.' He paused, looking at her appraisingly as she gazed into the garden below. 'Have you any idea how lovely you look tonight?' he murmured.

There was a soft, caressing note in his voice which

should have caused Lavinia to take flight, but instead she merely looked at him inquiringly and smiled.

'If I do then it is more to do with the peacock's plumage I wear and the spell the Masquerade has cast on me than anything else. Believe me, I am exactly the same woman you plucked from the lagoon.'

He laughed, his strong white teeth flashing in the dim light, and Lavinia realised that when he did that he seemed much younger than his twenty-eight or twenty-nine years.

'I cannot argue with that—although as I recall, there was more to see of you when I plucked you out of the water,' he replied, his voice threaded with intimacy.

A warm flush crept beneath Lavinia's mask and through her veins when she remembered how he had been forced to tear her dress before placing his hands on her bare flesh. 'I think you recall too much,' she chided gently, smiling up at him obliquely.

'And I promise not to embarrass you by referring to it again. Tell me, is this your first visit to Venice?'

'Yes.'

'And what impression has it made on you?'

'Nothing I have heard or read about it equals the magnificence and wonderful reality.'

'I agree. People come from all over the world to see Venice—to dress up in Carnival clothes, to wear masks, to gamble…to fall in love,' Maxim murmured, his gaze dropping to her lips, wanting to crush her in his arms, to lose himself in her sweetness.

'With Venice?' she asked, watching his gaze drop to her lips, feeling her senses mounting to dizzying heights.

Maxim smiled, studying her closely, seeing her eyes shimmering behind the mask. 'If not with Venice, then with themselves—or each other.'

Lavinia lowered her eyes, the physical content of the last

few moments playing havoc with her emotions. 'W-when I first arrived I was disturbed and overawed by its sheer beauty.'

'You make it sound like a love affair,' he murmured.

Lavinia looked at him inquiringly and felt her eyes held by his. A tingle ran down her spine. There was something in their depths, something in the way he was looking at her which seemed to carry a message—if only she could understand it.

'Do I?'

'Yes.'

She flushed, never having experienced the sort of love affair he spoke of. 'Yes—I—I suppose it must.'

'You do not look like a young lady in the full flush of love.'

'Nevertheless, Robert—Mr Feltham and I are to marry as soon as we return to England.'

Maxim gave her a lengthy perusal before saying, 'Do you love him?'

Lavinia stared at him, momentarily at a loss to know what to say, for to tell him she loved Robert would not be true—at least, not in the way Mr Purnell would interpret the word love. But then, that kind of love she could not envisage, and since her meeting with this man, she doubted if what she had once felt for Thomas Dorsy could have come anywhere close.

'Robert is a good man—a man of honour and well respected within the circles in which he moves.'

'I am sure he is. But that was not what I asked you.'

Lavinia sighed, lowering her gaze. 'No. I know that. But I prefer to keep my feelings where my betrothed is concerned to myself,' she said quietly.

'And you care enough about him to marry him?'

'Yes, I do.'

'Then what are you doing out here with me?'

Lavinia stared at him, at a loss to know how to react or what to say in answer to his pointed question. 'I—I don't know,' she replied desperately, noticing how warm and sensual his gaze had turned, how relaxed he was.

'Have you—a woman betrothed to another man—not considered the impropriety of being out here alone with me?' Maxim asked calmly, his eyes beginning to glint with amusement.

'No—as a matter of fact, I haven't,' she answered nervously.

'I'm pleased to learn that, like myself, you do not allow convention to dictate your every move,' he murmured, raising his hand and gently touching the side of her jaw with the backs of his fingers.

'But I do,' she replied, feeling her flesh burn beneath his touch, realising that a gambling man must find the rules of social etiquette, which so governed her life, extremely tiresome. 'I come from a conventional family, Mr Purnell, who believe in all the important things such as honour and integrity, doing the right thing and behaving in a proper manner.'

He arched a sleek black brow quizzically. 'And truth?'

'But of course. There has to be truth.'

'Then why didn't you tell your betrothed of our encounter yesterday—and that I sent you the mask?' he persisted.

Lavinia stared at him, aware of how close he was to her. She could feel her body beginning to tremble, and the infuriating thing was that he was perfectly well aware of the effect he was having on her as he sought to tie her in knots about her dealings with Robert.

'How do you know I haven't told Robert about our encounter?'

'Because if you had you would have returned the mask.'

A lazy grin swept over his handsome face, and the force of that white smile did treacherous things to Lavinia's heart rate. 'Admit it, Lavinia. Admit that you are here with me because you want to be. Because you find yourself irresistibly drawn to me—as I am to you. Is that not so?'

Lavinia looked at him, despite her desire not to, not for the first time finding herself at a loss to understand him. 'No—of course not. You—you make me feel uneasy when you speak to me like this—and look at me the way you are doing now. There is nothing between us.'

'Isn't there?'

'No—and I have given you no reason to suppose there is.'

'There I must contradict you. You didn't return the mask. The mere fact that you kept it told me how you feel.'

'Please do not speak to me like this,' Lavinia implored helplessly. 'I don't understand you. I don't understand what it is you want.'

Lavinia was too innocent and naïve not to let her emotions show on her face, and for a long moment Maxim's gaze held hers with penetrating intensity. The clear blue eyes were as enigmatic as they were silently challenging, and unexpectedly Lavinia felt an answering thrill of excitement. The darkening in Maxim's eyes warned her he was aware of that brief response.

'I think you do, Lavinia,' he murmured.

For a moment Lavinia was thrown into such a panic she could not think coherently. He was standing so very close that she suddenly wanted to escape, to return to the others. And yet, at the same time, she could not move, and she allowed Maxim to draw her against his chest, her eyes wide open as he bent his head and placed his mouth over her own, plucking the breath from between her parted lips, his mouth warm and searching.

They both felt the sudden excitement of physical contact. Lavinia had never been kissed in her life, and she could not have imagined how pleasurable it could be. Too innocent and naïve to know how to hide her feelings, she followed his lead and instinctively yielded her mouth to his, and the moment Maxim felt her response his arms tightened around her, circling and possessive, desire, primitive and potent, pouring through his veins.

Holding her hips pressed to his, he could feel the slender body beneath the column of white silk tremble against his as waves of pleasure shot through her. Raising his hand, he caressed the nape of her neck, his lips leaving hers and tracing a line down the column of her throat, his breath warm on her flesh, before finding her mouth once more and tasting the wine-flavoured softness of her lips.

To Lavinia, absolutely seduced by his kiss, what he was doing to her was like being wrapped in a cocoon of dangerous, pleasurable sensuality where she had no control over anything. Not even herself. She shivered with the primitive sensations jarring through her entire body, feeling herself pressed to the hard muscles of his chest.

When Maxim at last pulled his mouth from hers he drew a long, shuddering breath, meeting her gaze and seeing that her eyes were naked and defenceless. His tanned features were hard with desire, and, aware that someone could appear at any moment, he knew that he must keep their passion under control.

Lavinia trembled in the aftermath of his kiss, unable to believe what had happened and that she desperately wanted him to repeat the kiss that had stunned her senses with its wild sweetness. Maxim was still holding her gaze, and she looked with longing at his lips.

'Don't look at me like that unless you want me to kiss

you again, Lavinia,' he murmured huskily, his eyes dark with passion.

With her heart beating hard against her ribs, slowly she raised her eyes to his and, leaning forward, again boldly touched his mouth with her own, feeling her breath sucked from her body as, unable to resist what she so innocently offered, he clamped his mouth on to hers once more, causing the blood to pound in her head and her senses to reel as her mind retreated down an unknown, forbidden path, plunging her into an oblivion that was dark and exquisitely sensual.

Drawing a shattered breath, and out of sheer self-preservation, an eternity later Maxim raised his head, astounded by the passion that had erupted between them, astounded that this woman had the ability to make him lose his mind so completely.

'Don't, Lavinia,' he murmured when she swayed against him. 'We have to stop this. Someone may come on to the balcony at any moment and then where would we be?'

Lavinia's senses were drugged as she stared at him bemused, her eyes large and luminous. As reality began to return and she came back to full awareness—of her surroundings, with the sound of music and laughter returning to her ears, she was shocked by the explosion of passion between them, shocked by what she had done. What had happened surpassed anything she had ever known, but Maxim was right. It must stop. She stepped back.

Making a sound that was a cry of mingled shock and fright, Lavinia was scarlet faced beneath her mask, wide eyed and trembling like a jelly. 'This—this is madness.'

'You voice my thoughts exactly.'

'It—it should not have happened. I—I must go. Robert will be looking for me. Oh, dear,' she whispered in sudden panic, 'what have I done? If—if we return separately, no one will know we have been out here together.'

Maxim stopped her, putting his hand on her arm as she was about to pass, seeing that her lovely eyes behind the mask were apprehensive and deceptively innocent. 'Wait,' he said gently. 'Calm yourself first. Don't let him see you like this.'

'Like what?'

'With your eyes aglow with passion and your lips trembling.' He smiled down at her, touching her cheek gently.

'He—he will think I have been dancing.'

'If dancing makes you look like this, then you should dance more often.'

'With most of my face hidden behind the mask he will be deceived.'

'Disguises are meant to deceive, Lavinia.' He frowned. 'You are not angry with me, are you?'

'I am not angry,' she replied quietly, meeting his penetrating gaze. 'Only afraid of what might happen as a consequence of this night.'

Maxim put out a hand and took a step towards her.

'No,' she cried with a hint of anger. 'Do you enjoy inducing feelings in me that can come to nothing?' She thrust his hand away and whirled from him violently. 'I must go,' and then she was gone, her white dress seeming to melt as she went through the curtains.

Maxim let out a deep breath and stood for a moment looking after her, then he turned his back and stared in moody contemplation at the garden below. He became lost in a deep reverie which was broken by the sounds from the ballroom beyond, and when he finally left the balcony some minutes after Lavinia, he had reminded himself harshly that he was technically involved with another woman who had borne his child

Lucy, whose very existence demanded his absolute and undivided attention. The child deserved better from him than this stupid preoccupation he had suddenly acquired for Lavinia Renshaw, a woman he hadn't known existed until a few days ago, a woman who was bent on marrying another man, a man Maxim would calmly and unhesitatingly like to tell to go to hell.

With her equilibrium shattered Lavinia slipped back into the ballroom, feeling like an adulterous wife returning to her husband and extremely conspicuous after what she had done. Moving through the crowd she tried to calm herself, ashamed of the weakness she had just displayed to Maxim Purnell. It was ridiculous, she told herself. This was only their third time of meeting and he had already gone much further than she should have allowed.

No decent, upstanding woman would have done what she had just done, she thought with bitter self-revulsion. No, indeed. Any moral, respectable, God-fearing twenty-year-old would not have gone out on to a balcony alone with a man, allowed him to kiss her like that and, worse, enjoyed the experience. She was horrified and afraid of the feelings unfolding inside her.

Eventually she located Robert and found herself looking at him in a way she never had before. The ugly truth of it was that she wasn't attracted to him—she never had been and never would be. Instead, she was attracted to Maxim Purnell, who had fascinated her from the moment she had opened her eyes to his after he had pulled her from the lagoon.

Robert was standing with the Eveshams and Julia and Daisy, who was flushed and breathless from dancing. Lavinia was immensely relieved that no one seemed to notice she had been missing. With her heart still racing, she glanced towards the balcony, just in time to see a tall figure dressed in black and wearing a white bauta mask emerge and become lost in the crowd.

After that the ball lost its glitter for Lavinia, and the rest of the night passed in some kind of haze. Before she knew it it was over. With dawn peeping on the horizon, amid what seemed to be a flotilla of boats all leaving the palace, they were ferried back to the Scalini house.

From the moment Lavinia had left Maxim on the balcony at the palace she had been living on a razor's edge. It was time for calm reflection; standing on the balcony of her room on the upper floor of the splendid old house, she lifted her face to feel the early morning Adriatic breeze cool her burning cheeks. Gazing out over the rooftops of Venice towards the Lido Channel, she could see the sun rising like molten gold on the horizon, bringing with it the cry of sea birds.

The night's events and what she had done swept over her in a wave of horror. At the mere thought of how she had almost thrown herself at Maxim Purnell, her fingers trembled and she was forced to draw a deep, uneven breath. It was as if the magic of the masquerade had cast a spell on her and made her behave totally out of character, for she would never have behaved in such a bold manner in Gloucestershire.

It was obvious that she had not been thinking clearly. Coming to Venice was a fantastic adventure, plunging her into a world so very different from the one she knew, and what had happened at the ball was beyond anything she could have imagined before—but it could not continue like that. She could not go on living in a world of dreams and letting her emotions get in the way of her common sense.

A sudden noise coming from the room next to hers—

Julia's room—dragged her from her melancholy thoughts. Glancing curiously towards the balcony only a short distance from her own, she strained her ears, certain she had heard voices followed by the sound of grunting and moaning. The French window which opened on to the balcony was open, for she could see the fine net curtain billowing out as it was caught and tugged by the gentle breeze.

Lavinia thought she could hear low voices, but then she was unsure. It sounded more like a groan. The unusual noises made her think that perhaps Julia was ill and that she might be in pain and needing help. Draping a robe over her nightdress, she left her room and padded towards her sister's, finding the door had been left off the catch. Listening carefully, she heard Julia's muffled laughter and a man's voice, who seemed to be urging her in subdued tones to be quiet.

Curiosity and a sudden need to know the identity of the man her sister was entertaining at this hour, when Lavinia thought everyone in the house but herself would be sleeping off the exertions and excesses of the ball, made her move closer to the door, knowing instinctively who she would find there. She dreaded having her suspicions confirmed, but she had to know.

Her stomach was trembling as she soundlessly pushed the door open and stepped inside, and for a moment she was transfixed with horror. The room was large and in the centre was an ornate bed draped with blue silk, but what she noticed right away was Robert and Julia standing beside the rumpled bed.

Chapter Four

Robert had his back to Lavinia and the sight of his nakedness, of his almost skeletal body and bare buttocks, held
her riveted. Her footsteps had been muffled by the thick
blue carpet, so neither of them had heard her enter. She
watched as Robert's arms wrapped themselves around Julia, who wore a bright red and yellow silk robe which gaped
open at the front to expose her large, pendulous breasts.

Rigid with horror, Lavinia stared at the appalling spectacle of Robert kissing Julia with such violent passion—the
kind of passion she had thought him incapable of feeling—
that she quickly realised that the groans she had heard were
of pleasure, not pain. Watching in mesmeric silence, she
saw Robert almost devour Julia's lips, before bending his
head and placing his mouth over the hard nipple moving
tantalisingly before him. Julia, a willing supplicant, laughed
deeply in her throat. Winding her braceleted arms round
her lover's neck and closing her eyes, she threw back her
head to stress the curve of her heavy breasts. Unbeknown
to Lavinia, she had already tasted the pleasure of ardent
love.

Lavinia's mind reeled as she sought some explanation
that might excuse their conduct, telling herself that things

were not always what they appeared to be, but there wasn't one. She felt physically sick with the force of the pain that attacked her. How could they? How could Robert, with his pettishness, his temper, his insufferable arrogance all directed at her, behave so disgustingly?

Feeling a rush of bitterness, she clenched her hands so tightly that her nails bit into her palms. Experiencing the full impact of Robert's treachery, anger leaped in her and she had a longing to hurl herself across the room and batter them both. Drawing a deep, silent breath, she shrank back in the doorway, wanting to get out of that room and never have to look upon either of their faces again. Managing to force her shaking limbs to move, she left the room as silently as she had come, and all she could see in her mind's eye was the love scene she had just witnessed.

Entering her room, she closed the door. Tears came into her eyes and she had to swallow against the constriction in her throat as fear for her future fought with her rage. She had been so stupid. How dare they do this to her? she accused silently with sweeping scorn, believing what her eyes had seen. There could be no excuse. They were both guilty of betrayal. Engulfed by tears of anger and misery, by her own ineptitude and her inability to control her own life, she flung herself on to the bed, sobbing wretchedly. Never before had she lost control of herself as she did then. Her normally quiet serenity and innate composure had been shattered.

When she could cry no more she went on to the balcony, feeling utterly drained and exhausted. But, she thought with calm reflection and with bitter self-reproach, how could she attack either Robert or Julia on a moral level when she was guilty of the same? Had she not betrayed Robert in her thoughts and by kissing Maxim Purnell at the ball?

Desperately needing to sort things out, she went over the

events of the night; no matter how hard she tried, she could not get past the incontrovertible fact that everything was changed. Coming to grips with Robert's treachery, she faced the knowledge that the future they had planned together was over. She could not marry Robert now. But what could she do? Her natural honesty and pride urged her to a confrontation and a final settling of accounts with him, but she couldn't. Not yet.

However, Julia forced her hand when she came to her room shortly afterwards, still dressed in her garishly coloured robe, which was wrapped around her voluptuous body. It was as if she wanted to flaunt what had happened earlier between herself and Robert in the face of his betrothed.

Lavinia's face was ravaged with weeping, but otherwise it was expressionless. She looked at Julia hard. 'What are you doing here?' she asked coldly, her mind torn between disgust and sheer astonishment at Julia's effrontery.

Julia moved to stand before her. Suspecting that the movement she had seen in the doorway of her room when she had been entertaining Robert had been Lavinia, she had come to gloat. Her face was transfigured with the joy of flinging the searing truth in the face of her pretty little sister at last.

'Why so hostile?' Julia asked, her penetrating eyes studying Lavinia in detail. 'Dear me, Lavinia. You do look quite dreadful. What's the matter? Too much champagne at the ball?'

Lavinia glared at her, no longer fearful of a woman she now knew hated her. The virulence of that hatred washed over her. 'I know what is going on between you and Robert, Julia. Don't insult me by denying it. I went to your room earlier and saw the two of you together.'

Julia saw the mask replaced by an expression of contempt.

'I have no intention of denying anything. I have no reason to,' she retorted flippantly.

'Was that the first time he has been to your room?'

'No.' Julia laughed. 'Of course not. Our affair began shortly before your father died—when I was in London,' she boasted shamelessly, uncaring how much the knowledge of it would hurt her sister. 'Good Lord, Lavinia. What do you expect from a man of Robert's years? Would you have him live the life of a eunuch?'

If Lavinia had known what a eunuch was she might have replied, but she hadn't the remotest idea, and she wasn't going to show her ignorance by asking.

'He would have married me,' Julia continued, 'but I have no money—and to Robert money is an important and necessary commodity. You know Robert's type. They marry only for prestige and money—and look elsewhere for sexual fulfilment.'

'I am beginning to realise that.' Lavinia's lip curled scornfully, the contemptuous way Julia spoke increasing her anger.

'That was when he became aware of your legacy. It was just what he wanted. So don't be concerned,' she jeered. 'I might be the one he wants in his bed, but you are the one he will marry—a quiet little virgin bride with an even greater attraction of thirty thousand pounds, rather than an impoverished widow—thanks to your father.'

'My father left you generously provided for—which is more than your husband did and more than you deserve,' retorted Lavinia scathingly, recalling the time when her father had been seriously ill and Julia had taken herself off to London to enjoy herself, callously leaving others to care for him.

'You were no blood relation to my father, which is why he left the bulk of his estate to Edgar and myself. After our mother died and knowing how ill he was, you hoped he wouldn't live long, didn't you, Julia—confident there would be something in his will for you when he died. How disappointed you must have been when you discovered how little he had left you—how little he cared for you.'

With her hands on her hips Julia glared at her. 'I was. But I was always miserable when I was around him. And now you have found out about Robert and me, it is something you will have to learn to live with.'

Lavinia stared at her, as if her ears were deceiving her. That Julia thought that she would still marry Robert after this would be laughable if it were not so serious or so sordid. Robert didn't love her, she knew that, but she had hoped he felt some fondness for her. But she now saw the cynical calculation and the cold-blooded way in which both he and Julia had insultingly played upon her innocence.

'No. I will never accept it. It is not possible.'

Julia was surprised and her eyes became wary. 'You mean you will not marry Robert?'

'Never.'

Momentarily silenced, Julia could see that Lavinia's face was ghost white, the turquoise eyes which she had always envied as hard as ice and as cold, and she knew that she meant it. Suddenly she could feel her own world beginning to crumble and that it was not to her advantage to have given Lavinia an insight into how things were between herself and Robert.

She had always believed the substance of Lavinia's make-up to be nothing stronger than milk and water, and that she was meek, malleable and submissive to the will of others. Suddenly finding herself confronted with Lavinia's blazing contempt, Julia was beginning to realise she was made of sterner stuff. If Lavinia did not marry Robert, he would certainly not marry her, and would look elsewhere for some other gullible woman to marry with a fortune. And then where would she be?

'I think we should discuss this with Robert,' Julia said.

'I have no intention of confronting him with this. Not yet, anyway. I am too disgusted. Marry him yourself, Julia. After all, you are more his age than I,' she retorted scathingly.

Julia's features became ugly. 'Don't you think I would marry him if he asked me? But he won't. He never will.'

'Then you'll just have to go on being his mistress,' Lavinia taunted, the cold mask she had worn when Julia had entered her room settling back into place. Her dismissive words were of confident contempt.

'I am aware that when Robert finds out about this he is going to be extremely angry, but the situation is of his making—and yours. Understand this here and now, Julia. I will never marry Robert, and neither will I return to live at Welbourne House with you in it—which, unfortunately, is still your right. What matters to me now is what I do with my life. I will shape it to my own design without any interference from you or Robert. Now please leave my room. I have nothing further to say.'

Beside herself with rage, Julia left the room, leaving Lavinia staring at the closed door long after it had shut with a final click.

Deep in thought, Lavinia considered her situation and what she must do for the best. That was when she thought of Maxim Purnell. In her present terrible plight, he was the only person who could help her. But would he want to?

Would he marry her?

He might, she thought with a cool calculation born out of desperation—for thirty thousand pounds. If, as Robert had told her, he had lost such a large sum of money at a ridotto, then he might be tempted to marry her if he knew so much wealth would come his way.

Within half an hour of Julia leaving her room, and feeling as though she had been born anew as a result of some extremely painful form of gestation, Lavinia calmly slipped out of the house and into the quiet streets without anyone seeing her.

On reaching his apartment after the ball, Maxim picked up some letters of business correspondence awaiting his attention. Perkins, his valet, who also doubled as his secretary, had brought them to his attention before he had left for the ball, but he'd put them aside, feeling that they could wait. Now he flicked through them, observing from the many different addresses scrawled across them that they had been following him around Europe for the past two months. He browsed through them absently until he came to one missive on which he recognised the handwriting.

It was from Alice.

After hurrying through the narrow streets to the house where Maxim was staying, Lavinia was admitted by a servant and shown to his apartment on the upper floor of the house. Tentatively she went towards the rather forbidding-looking door. As she stood before it, a wave of doubt swept over her, causing her to hesitate, to question what she was doing, but then she took a deep breath and squared her narrow shoulders, reminding herself that in her weakened and helpless state he was the only person who could help her.

Taking the bit between her teeth and vibrant with hope, she knocked on the door, waiting for what seemed to be an age. Eventually she heard a sound from within and the door was thrown open.

'What is it?' came an irate voice which Lavinia recognised immediately and almost sent her scurrying back down the stairs in fright. 'I told you I did not want to be—' Maxim stopped when he saw Lavinia standing there. Their eyes met and locked for a moment, Maxim's opening wider and wider, experiencing astonishment and incredulity, before brusquely recollecting himself. 'You! What the devil…?'

Apart from a towel wrapped around his narrow waist he was stark naked, bringing a soft gasp to Lavinia's lips and causing her cheeks to flush scarlet. Shocked to the depths of her virginal innocence, she was unable to take her eyes off his strong, muscular body, so eternally savage, proud and golden—and not one bit as puny as Robert's, which had been exposed to her earlier. Her carefully sheltered upbringing had not prepared her for the sight of a near-naked man of Maxim Purnell's splendid physique.

'I—I—forgive me. I had to see you—but I can see you do not look too happy.' Nothing had prepared her for the cold reception she received.

'Please,' he said brusquely, stepping aside to let her pass. 'Come in.'

At a glance Lavinia was struck by the spaciousness and splendour of the lavish apartment. The shutters had been opened to allow the bright morning sunlight to pour through, highlighting the gilt-stuccoed ceiling and the rich elegance of the furniture. Fragile porcelain figurines reposed on polished surfaces and marble stands, along with an impressive range of expensive Venetian blown-glass objects—all the different kinds of glass which Venetian craftsmen had been producing for centuries and for which Venice was famous. They told Lavinia that this apartment must belong to someone who was extremely rich, and who must be a very good friend of Maxim's to allow him to stay here.

Maxim closed the door behind her.

Pulling herself together, she looked at him and said, 'I had to see you. It is fortunate that I remembered where you live.'

'Is it? Why? What do you want to say to me that is so important? You must have excellent reasons for pursuing me here.'

Maxim was unconcerned that she had arrived when he was about to take his bath, and that he'd only had time to wrap a towel round his waist before answering the door, fully expecting it to be his valet. Picking up a robe from the back of a chair, he thrust his arms through the sleeves and secured it with a belt round the middle, before whipping away the towel from underneath.

Nervously Lavinia stared at him in silence, acutely and embarrassingly aware that he was completely naked beneath the thin robe that rippled on his athletic body when he moved. He was mocking her, making her mission appear trivial, making her wish she hadn't come. His eyes were cold, his face rigid, all emotion withheld by an iron control. What had happened between her leaving him on the balcony at the palace and now? Did he regret what had happened between them? With a painful effort she tried to suppress her disappointment. If she wanted to accomplish what she had set out to achieve, then she must cast off her pride and humble herself.

'You have taken a scandalous chance—risked compromising your reputation—by coming here,' Maxim said harshly, regarding her without anger but with a terrifying firmness and a hard gleam in his eyes.

'Yes—I know.'

Lavinia swallowed nervously. This was too much. How could she begin to tell him the reason that had brought her to his apartment to see him when he looked at her like that? So much had happened that she was overwhelmed with emotions.

'Well?' Maxim asked, his voice frank and unemotional as he tried not to let his mind dwell on this beautiful girl with a face like an angel and her large turquoise eyes shining with innocence. It struck him how very feminine she was, with the gold treasure of her hair, drawn from her face by a narrow band of blue ribbon, tumbling down her back like a silken curtain. Wearing a dress of summer blue, the skirt full with a tight waist, Lavinia was unlike anyone he had ever seen. The neckline was modest, the sleeves ending at her elbows with a delicate froth of white lace caressing her lower arms.

In silent, helpless protest Lavinia averted her eyes from Maxim's sternly handsome face as they glazed over with tears. How could he be tender and passionate one minute, and then cold and hard and unreasonable the next? Agonisingly aware of her mistake in coming here, she realised she must go. It was imperative that she got out of that room and away from his presence. With great difficulty she swallowed hard, keeping her head lowered so he would not see her tears.

'Forgive me,' she whispered. 'I can see my presence irks you. I should not have troubled you. If you don't mind I would like to leave.'

Abruptly she crossed the carpet to the door and he followed with all the stealth of a panther. When she was about to open it his hand pressed firmly on the wood, preventing her from doing so.

'No,' he said on a gentler note, looking at her downcast face, seeing for the first time how distressed she was, how tired and tense. Something stirred in the region of his heart. 'You came to say something. You must tell me what it is before you leave. Come. Tell me the purpose of your visit.'

Lavinia shook her head. 'No. I can't. I made a mistake.'

'You can't say that until I know what it is.' On a sigh he placed his hands on her shoulders and turned her round to face him. 'Lavinia, look at me.'

Unwillingly she met his eyes, and he could see the pain moving in their glorious, liquid depths. He also recognised desperation when he saw it, and for some unknown reason Lavinia Renshaw was extremely desperate about something.

'What is it?'

'I came to ask if you would marry me,' she told him at last.

Maxim was silent, looking at her hard, incredulously, as though she had suddenly changed before his eyes. Lavinia was making an offer, he realised, with quiet courage and no games. His expression became grim, and he could almost hear the funeral drum-roll of his heart.

'No.'

The word was uttered without anger, but was none the less cold and final.

Very quietly Lavinia turned her face away and her heart sank. Had he exploded with fury and injured vanity she would have understood it better than this deadly quietness which frightened her. With despair she saw the end of all her hopes of persuading him to marry her.

'This is plain speaking,' he said.

'Necessity drives me to it.'

'Rather that than to know you came here out of inclination.'

'I am not inclined to do anything out of inclination.'

'I am glad to hear it.'

'And you refuse?'

'Precisely. I'm not in the market for a wife. I don't know what has prompted you to come here and ask me this, and I am flattered. What man wouldn't be—to be propositioned by a beautiful woman?'

'It was presumptuous of me, I know.'

'Yes, it was,' he answered, moving away from her and standing by a round table in a haughty pose, very stiff and upright, with a suggestion of arrogance which came naturally enough to him. His eyes remained fixed on her face without the trace of a smile to soften their steely expression.

'Oh, please,' she whispered, unconsciously moving towards him, profoundly embarrassed, unchecked tears beginning to run freely down her face. Until that moment she wouldn't have believed she could feel more humiliated than she already did. She wished the ground would open up and swallow her. 'You have no idea how difficult this is for me. Please don't mock me.'

'I'm not. I realise something traumatic must have occurred to make you come here and ask me to marry you. At least tell me what it is.'

Lavinia swallowed hard, wiping away the tears with the back of her hand in a childlike gesture that had Maxim delving into the pocket of his robe for a handkerchief and handing it to her, trying not to let her anguish and the dampness clinging to her sooty lashes and tear-bright eyes weaken him.

'Robert has deceived me. He has betrayed me with my sister.'

Maxim nodded. Everything was becoming clear to him now. 'I see,' he said coldly. 'And what does that make you? Isn't it hypocritical of you to react like a hurt and angry child whose favourite toy is broken, when you are guilty of the same?' he reminded her cruelly.

His remark was like a slap in the face, but she had to concede it was true. 'Yes, I know,' she answered wretchedly, her tears having ceased.

'After all, I do not remember you trying to fight me off,' he said pointedly, trying to thrust away the poignant memory of how she had melted in his arms lest it weakened his resolve to have anything further to do with her. 'You let your ardour run away with you then. How do you know it wasn't the same for Robert and your sister? Anyway, how do you know they are having an affair? And if they are, why isn't he marrying her instead of you?'

'Because Julia is my half-sister, on my mother's side, and quite penniless. Robert will not marry any woman who does not bring with her a generous dowry. I—I caught them together in her room. It—it was dreadful. I cannot marry Robert after this, and I cannot live at Welbourne House— my home in Gloucestershire—with my sister either. I have nowhere else to go and I don't know what to do.'

'So you thought you would come here, hoping I would provide you with the solution to your dilemma? Am I right?' Maxim demanded.

'Yes,' she admitted. She could almost feel the effort he was exerting to keep his anger under control.

Maxim's eyes glittered with a fire that burned her raw when he looked at her, and his voice was deadly calm when he spoke. 'When and if I decide to marry, I prefer to do the asking myself.'

'I—I thought that after—'

'What?' he jeered, ignoring the way the colour drained out of her soft cheeks as he continued with deliberate brutality. 'That because we kissed—because we are attracted to each other—I might be swayed?'

'Yes.'

Maxim's eyes narrowed and his jaw clamped with grinding resolution as he stood looking down at her, trying to ignore the mute appeal in those large, luminescent eyes, seeking refuge in his anger. 'Then I'm sorry. Life isn't like that. I have kissed many women I have been attracted to, but that doesn't mean to say that I wanted to marry any of them.'

Lavinia was conscious of a sudden surge of anger, realising just how stupid and naïve she had been in turning to this arrogant and unfeeling man for help. How dare he treat what had happened between them so casually, as if the kiss was insignificant and meant nothing at all. She was ashamed that she had been such a willing participant. But perhaps this was nothing out of the ordinary and he was used to kissing ladies all over the place. And perhaps ladies accepted his kisses in their stride. After all, she thought bitterly, how would she know? Gripping her hands tightly by her sides, she regarded him coldly.

'I do not have your experience, Mr Purnell. Apart from yourself, no other man has kissed me,' she told him with simple honesty, giving Maxim further insight into just how truly innocent she was.

'Nevertheless, you were misguided to think I would marry you. You must understand that I can't marry you.'

She gasped as a sudden thought occurred to her. 'You— you are married? Is that why?'

'No.'

His dark face was inscrutable, but Lavinia saw something flicker behind his eyes. 'Then you are in love with someone else?'

'No. But it makes no difference. I will not marry you.'

Mortified and humiliated, Lavinia nevertheless managed to lift her chin a notch and look at him directly. 'Not even for thirty thousand pounds?'

Maxim's entire face instantly became hard, shuttered and

aloof. His brows snapped together with brittle anger and a feral gleam appeared in his narrowed eyes as they locked on hers with angry disgust. 'Now you do insult me,' he said, his voice so controlled that Lavinia felt an icy chill sweep down her spine. 'I cannot be bought, either. And what makes you think you are worth thirty thousand pounds?'

Lavinia gasped, her humiliation complete. 'Now it is you who insult me,' she flared, a fresh surge of anger rising up inside her like flames licking round a dry log, furious with herself for being stupid enough to think he might help her.

'If you have so much money then what you do should not be a problem. You can live where you choose or buy yourself another husband—which shouldn't be too difficult. You have other assets to your credit besides thirty thousand pounds,' he ground out with suave brutality, his insolent, contemptuous gaze raking over her.

Maxim's jibe, savage and taunting, flicked over Lavinia like a whiplash. Stung to anger by his harsh words, hot colour flooded her cheeks and her soft lips tightened as she exerted every ounce of her control to keep her temper and her emotions in check. 'I can't. The money is a legacy left to me by my father. It will not be made available to me until I am twenty-five—unless I marry.'

'I see. Then if you don't find some other fool to marry, it would seem you have a long wait ahead of you.'

'Are you telling me you are a fool, Mr Purnell?'

'To have become involved with you I must be. Don't you think you're taking a huge risk asking me to marry you—knowing nothing about me? Tell me. What exactly do you know?'

'Very little. I know you are a gambler—that you gamble with large sums of money—'

'And sometimes lose,' he told her.

'Yes, I know that.'

'No doubt Robert told you,' Maxim drawled sarcastically, with heavy emphasis on Robert's name and without taking his cold and merciless eyes off her. 'Did he, by any chance, tell you that I lost a large amount of money at a ridotto the other evening?'

'Yes.'

'Which gave you reason to suspect I might be in dire need of some more?'

'Yes.'

'And yet, knowing this, you are prepared to risk your thirty thousand pounds? How do you know I won't marry you and stake the whole lot on one game of cards.'

'I don't. I can't say that I approve of gambling on cards—'

'There are many other forms of gambling besides cards,' he cut in coldly, giving her a look that was a hundred times more deadly than his anger had been a moment before. 'And isn't what you are proposing a gamble? You took a chance that what happened between us at the ball might have put me into such a state of passion that I would fall at your feet.'

'I did not,' Lavinia burst out, blinded with wrath and humiliation, her anger in full spate—an anger she hadn't realised she was capable of. She was beginning to realise that all was lost, and yet now she was glad he had refused her, glad she had been saved from marrying this cold and unfeeling man, this stranger. The mere thought of tying herself to him for the rest of her life was fearful.

'I realise that I have gambled and lost and that there is nothing left for me to say other than I am sorry I asked you,' she continued furiously. 'I have no experience, you see. I may seem stupid to you, but when you kissed me I had no idea I was nothing more than an amusing diversion.

Forgive me. I should not have come here—I realise that
now. You have made it quite clear. I will trouble you no
further. Good day to you, Mr Purnell.'

Lavinia turned abruptly and moved towards the door,
holding her head high as she tried to preserve what little
there was left of her pride. Maxim Purnell did not deserve
that she should abase herself for him.

When Lavinia turned from him Maxim cursed silently
beneath his breath. He wanted to tell her to stay, to draw
her into his arms and kiss her as he had done at the ball;
if he had not received Alice's letter reminding him that he
had been away too long and that he had a duty towards his
child, he might have yielded to Lavinia's request, might
have let her persuade him, and enjoyed doing so. But his
absolute responsibility was to Lucy and he couldn't change
that, but when he looked at Lavinia his conscience was torn
one way, his feelings another.

'Wait,' Maxim said, reaching out and taking hold of her
arm.

Lavinia turned, surprised by the expression in his eyes.
It had a yearning quality, nostalgic almost, as if he was
crushed by some scarcely discernible problem, but she was
too angry to be moved by it. Her eyes frosted over. 'Kindly
take your hand off my arm,' she seethed. 'Don't touch me.'

Maxim dropped his hand. A cynical smile twisted one
corner of his mouth and his blue eyes remained unwarmed.
'What do you mean to do now?'

'That is none of your business,' she replied coldly.

'Then my advice is that you forgive Robert his dalliance
with your sister and marry him. Better the devil you know.'

Lavinia turned her head and glared at him. 'I don't want
your advice. I don't know what I'll do. But I'll find some
way out,' she said fiercely. 'I will find a way out of this
without you or Robert.' She took a step forward but hesi-

tated, looking back at him. 'I find myself beginning to regret your prompt action in jumping in to rescue me after I
fell into the lagoon. All things considered, it would have
been best if you had left me where I was,' she said viciously, and meant it.

Lavinia left him then. I hate him, she seethed silently,
repeating the words over and over all the way back to the
Scalini house, hoping the fury and the passion would convince her that all those other emotions didn't exist. Her
heart twisted agonisingly in her breast, telling her she could
not possibly survive the humiliation of Maxim's brutal rejection. But her mind told her coldly that she would.

Left alone with a raw ache inside him, the vexing tide
of anger which had consumed Maxim began to subside.
His mind was locked in furious combat with the desire to
go after Lavinia and the urge to forget her, but he knew
the latter was impossible. Perhaps it was because she was
as unlike Alice as it was possible to be. Everything about
her threw him off balance. Lavinia's mere presence resur-
rected emotions he thought had died when he had seen
Alice for what she was.

Her proposition pounded inside his head, combining with
the torment of his own harsh rejection. He saw her as she
had been when he had pulled her from the lagoon, and how
lovely she had been at the ball, filled with innocent, unselfish passion when he had drawn her into his arms and
kissed her. He realised just how devastated she must have
been when she had discovered that Robert was having an
affair with her sister, understanding the inexplicable anguish she must have been through, and how she had humbled herself by coming to him—to ask him to marry her.
And like a heartless idiot he had shunned, scorned and humiliated her, which she had not deserved and for which he

despised and reproached himself with a virulence that was unbearable.

Lavinia had stirred his desire as no other woman had succeeded in doing for a long time, so, unable to leave things like this between them, after he had bathed and dressed he walked to the Scalini house.

Chapter Five

When the maid came to tell Lavinia that Mr Purnell was waiting in the salon to speak to her, her first reaction was to refuse to see him, but, realising it would cause considerable speculation in the household if it became known she had turned him away without receiving him, she smoothed her hair and her skirts and went down to the salon.

With his hands clasped behind his back, Maxim stood looking down at the canal. Despite her firm resolve to remain calm and unmoved by him, Lavinia felt her heart give a sudden leap. He turned on hearing her enter, and she saw his face change when his eyes met hers across the room.

Lavinia stood for a moment in the doorway as if she had no wish to be alone with him. And then, with her head held high, she closed the door and calmly moved to stand in the centre of the room, finding it impossible to greet him with any degree of casualness after the harsh words they had exchanged just a short while ago.

'I don't know what you hope to achieve by coming here, Mr Purnell,' she said frostily. 'I think everything has been said between us.'

'Has it?' he asked, his voice echoing in the large white and gold salon.

'Yes. And I must thank you for being so frank with me.'

'I had to come. We can't leave things like this between us.'

Without emotion, Lavinia stood perfectly still as Maxim came closer. There was an aura of calm authority about him. His expression was now blank and impervious, and he looked unbearably handsome. The sight of his chiselled features and bold blue eyes never failed to stir her heart.

Maxim stood gazing down at her, looking deep into her eyes, observing with sorrow that the pink bloom he had adored so much had gone from her cheeks, and that there were faint purple smudges beneath her eyes, which told him that she'd had very little sleep, if any, since returning from the ball. The lovely face was as white as alabaster, and her eyes glittered through tear-damp lashes.

What was it that attracted him to her? he asked himself. Her sincerity? Her gentleness and purity, of both body and mind? Was it her smile, her touch, that set the blood pounding in his veins like an inexperienced youth? Ever since his feelings for Alice had died he had thought himself immune to such weaknesses as love and passion—and yet Lavinia affected him deeply.

Maxim was seized by a passionate longing to protect and revere this lovely young woman who had crept into his heart. He ached to treat her as she should be treated, to tread the hesitant steps of courtship and woo her as she deserved, but it was no good dreaming of what might be. He saw that she was looking at him frankly, openly, and with a dispassion so chilling that he was intensely moved by it, and yet he sensed that beneath it all was a heartbreaking dejection.

'You've been crying,' he said quietly.

'My state of health need not concern you.'

'But it does. I feel that I am responsible.'

'Please don't flatter yourself.'

'I don't. It was not my intention to cause you pain, and I could not leave Venice without putting things right between us. I owe you an apology. It was wrong of me to speak to you so harshly. I apologise for my boorish behaviour. I said things to you of which I am deeply ashamed.'

'Ashamed, Mr Purnell!' Lavinia exclaimed with a hint of sarcasm. She had been sorely wounded and was determined not to make this easy for him. 'I am certain there is nothing for you to be ashamed of. And as for apologies—don't you think it's a little late to withdraw anything you said to me?'

'Nevertheless I do apologise—and I shall not be happy until you tell me I am forgiven.' He smiled crookedly at her, willing her to respond, but there was no answering spark in her eyes. 'When I returned to the apartment after the ball, I received a letter from someone who never fails to rouse my temper—and your proposal was the final straw. I quite understand how hurt you must have been when you discovered what was going on between your betrothed and your sister.'

'I doubt it,' she replied coldly.

'Believe me, I do,' he murmured, his words full of meaning and his expression suddenly so sombre that Lavinia thought that maybe he did, but she would never know the truth of it.

'It—it was wrong of me to approach you,' she said tersely. 'It was extremely stupid of me. I see that now.'

'Why did you come to me?'

'I thought I made that clear. I confess that at the time I knew of no one else who could help me. You were my one and only hope—and I deceived myself most shamefully into believing you would want me. I now realise my mistake and how foolish I was. I did not realise that when I

ran from Robert I might be about to unite myself with another as unworthy as he,' she said scathingly, unfairly, carried away by her own anger, and by an almost physical
need to convince Maxim Purnell that she didn't want him.
'But it need not concern you, Mr Purnell. I shall return to
England and consider my situation there.'

'And in the meantime?'

'In the meantime nothing is changed. I will not marry
Robert, a man who can see no further than my legacy and
has no feelings for me. I will not barter myself for security
or money. It is degrading—which is something you have
taught me,' Lavinia said with deriding cynicism, a proud
light shining in her eyes as they held his. 'There has to be
more to marriage than that.'

Maxim raised an eyebrow inquiringly, the corner of his
mouth twisting wryly. 'Such as love?'

'I can't answer that—never having known the kind of
love you speak of. I strongly suspect that love is a contra-
diction of emotions which should be given freely and has
nothing to do with marriage.'

'And desire? Passion?' he asked, regarding her closely,
his gaze narrow and assessing.

'At least desire and passion are honest emotions.'

'And all consuming,' said Maxim.

'And I would say that there speaks a man of experience,'
she said coldly. 'But I would think those kind of emotions
are not as consuming as love. I would also say that when
passions are spent they are easily appeased and forgotten,'
she remarked drily, referring to the brief passion that had
been ignited between them at the ball, a passion they both
knew would have flared into something more and run out
of control had it not been checked. 'I strongly regret what
happened between us last night. Believe me, Mr Purnell, I

am not the kind of woman to go around kissing just anyone.'

Maxim's firm lips twisted in a morose smile, while inwardly admiring her perception even in a state of shock. 'I
hope not. But a face behind a mask can be deceptive—and
you were so beautiful at the ball—so very beautiful,' he
said, his expression softening, his gaze lingering on her
lips, remembering what it had felt like to kiss them.

Lavinia gave a hard, contemptuous laugh, stiff with pride
and anger, the humiliation and the hurt she had suffered at
his hands never far away. 'And the opportunity was beautiful, was it not? The Carnival atmosphere of the ball—the
revelry—the excitement. Just like the passion that flared
between us it was enchanting while it lasted—but with the
dawn I realised that the magic was just an illusion.'

'It needn't be.'

'Yes, it does. But I have much to thank you for. You
see,' she said, her eyes shooting turquoise sparks of anger
and not wavering from his, 'from now on, if I ever find
myself in a similar situation, I shall be too distrustful, too
much on my guard against men's wiles, to allow myself to
be deceived by charm, soft words and a handsome face. So
now, Mr Purnell, you can leave, knowing that you have at
least achieved something. You can leave Venice and forget
you ever met a stupid woman who quite shamelessly threw
herself at your head.'

Halted abruptly in the midst of this unpremeditated outburst of feeling, Maxim wanted to shake her. He knew she
was playing a part, that behind the hard expression and glib
words, the real woman, the warm and passionate Lavinia,
was still to be found. His ill-considered treatment of her
earlier when he had vented his fury on her had driven the
tantalising creature he had kissed at the ball to the bottom
of the lagoon, and replaced her with this angry young

woman who was being extremely careful at keeping him at arm's length.

Unable to prevent himself, Maxim reached out to touch her, taking her arm and pulling her towards him.

'That I can never do,' he said, drawn by the depths of the bewitching turquoise eyes looking into his and by the softness of her quivering lips. Forgetful of where he was and mastered by a passion almost beyond his control, he took her face between his hands, his clear blue eyes penetrating as they probed hers. Desire was in his own, and something more, something so profound that it held Lavinia spellbound.

'You little fool. I came after you because I was deeply touched by your distress and couldn't help myself,' he said fiercely. 'I don't want to hurt you. I care about you. I do care what happens to you. Deeply.'

Like a magnet Maxim's eyes were drawn to her mouth, and he became lost in the exciting beauty of her.

'Please, Maxim—don't,' she whispered, recognising the desire in the smouldering depths of his eyes. 'This is not a game.'

'Pity. It's just getting interesting.'

Before Lavinia could guess what he meant to do she was caught in his arms, and with her head reeling she found herself imprisoned against him. After all that had been said between them she could not let this happen. She struggled furiously when he bent his dark head and his lips took possession of hers, yet, despite her frenzy to escape, there was little she could do.

Maxim kissed her with such accomplished persuasion that gradually she melted in his arms, finding his mouth so warm after the chill she had endured. Maxim had awakened her to love at the ball, but she had been denied its fulfil-ment—not that she knew what fulfilment was, only being aware that she wanted him to go on kissing her, to feel his hands on her body, as she had seen Robert do to Julia, and observed the pleasure they gave and received from each other. She offered Maxim her lips, responding and yielding to his kiss where she should only have received.

A whole range of uncontrollable feelings were induced in her by his kiss, and her eyes fluttered closed when she felt a stir of immense pleasure sigh through her tired body. All she was conscious of was Maxim's mouth on her own, kissing her with commanding strength and passion, becoming aware of his hand stealing up the back of her neck beneath her hair, imprisoning her head. He deprived her of thought, leaving only feelings, and they filled her with such a sense of languorous pleasure that she seemed to be floating.

There was a sound behind them but they paid little heed, but then Maxim tensed and wrenched himself away from her, breathing heavily. Dazedly Lavinia looked up at him in surprise, but he wasn't looking at her. His eyes were directed at the door. Turning her head she looked round, and to her horror there stood Mrs Lambert, white-faced and in a state of shock, and Julia, her eyes blazing fiercely. Beside her was Robert, his expression one of absolute horror, his cold, malevolent eyes fixed on both herself and Maxim. The Eveshams were also there, with Sophia looking on with vicious amusement on her plain face.

With guilt-stricken shock Lavinia gasped, startled, her face flushed, her eyes glowing and her lips soft and moist from Maxim's kiss. Quickly she took hold of herself. At any other time the situation would have been one of extreme delicacy and she would have been swamped with shame at being caught in such a compromising situation that would be sure to ruin her reputation, but the scene she had witnessed earlier between Robert and Julia had been

far more shocking than what Robert now witnessed between herself and Maxim. The explosion of anger and hatred that shot through her when she met the eyes of her
betrothed was almost beyond bearing. Robert had betrayed
her, degraded her and for that he would pay.

Sir John and Lady Evesham melted into the hallway,
taking a reluctant Sophia with them, realising it was best
to leave Robert to deal with the unenviable task before him.

Robert was visibly trembling with rage, and when he
spoke there was a deathly sickness in every note. 'What is
the meaning of this? We cannot deny what our eyes have
seen. Sir,' he hissed, glowering at Maxim, 'have the decency to take your hands off Miss Renshaw. She is my
betrothed.'

Robert's angry statement told Lavinia that Julia hadn't
told him about the scene between them earlier when she
had come to her room.

'How dare you compromise her!' Robert exclaimed, beside himself with fury, casting a severe, critical eye over
Lavinia. 'Your disgraceful conduct and the impropriety of
such wanton behaviour disgusts me, Lavinia. Don't you
dare insult my intelligence by telling me that this is not
how it looks.'

Lavinia took a deep breath, feeling Maxim's arm tighten
about her protectively.'

'The situation is exactly how it looks,' Maxim said
coldly, favouring Robert with a long, withering look.

'Robert,' said Lavinia, aware of Mrs Lambert's absolute
astonishment and that Julia, who hadn't an inkling who this
ravishingly handsome man was she had found kissing her
sister, was glowering from her to Maxim as if she wanted
to throttle them both, 'I don't believe you've been introduced. This is Mr Maxim Purnell. Mr Purnell, Mr Robert
Feltham.'

'I don't think there is any need for introductions,' seethed Robert, flexing and unflexing his hands by his sides in vexation.

'No,' said Maxim, eyeing Robert with cynical contempt. 'There isn't.'

'Lavinia, go to your room,' Robert ordered. 'I'll speak to you alone when this overbearing scoundrel has had the decency to leave the house.'

'I think not,' Maxim said, his voice like steel and a murderous expression on his face. His mouth was tight, his eyes flashing dangerously, his icy anger far more intimidating than any show of hot rage. 'I regret to inform you, Feltham, that Miss Renshaw is no longer betrothed to you,' Maxim told him coldly.

Two high spots of colour appeared on Robert's thin cheekbones, the rest of his face was chalk white. He glared at Lavinia. 'What's this?'

Calmly Lavinia went to stand in front of him, her eyes on a level with his. If he expected her to cringe and cower then he was going to be disappointed. She gazed at him coldly, showing not the least fear. 'What Mr Purnell has told you is the truth, Robert. I have taken it upon myself to end our betrothal. I am not going to marry you.' Her eyes slid to Julia, finding it hard to believe that this woman, who was looking at her with so much hatred, was her sister. 'I thought Julia would have informed you of this.'

'Informed me? Be so good as to explain what you are talking about.'

'I thought she would have told you about my going to her room earlier and finding the two of you together. I saw you, Robert.'

Robert looked dumbfounded. 'Saw me? What did you see?'

Lavinia's smile was one of absolute contempt. 'Do you

really want me to tell you that in front of Mrs Lambert, Robert? Very well. I saw you with Julia,' she accused him angrily, thrusting her face closer to his, thinking she must have been out of her mind ever to have considered marrying such an obnoxious man. 'I saw you kiss her, caress her—as lovers do. I heard her sighs and groans—and your own, Robert. Would you like me to go on?'

Lavinia's disclosure brought a gasp of shock and outrage from Mrs Lambert. 'No,' she cried, looking from Robert to Julia in absolute horror and disbelief. 'Julia! What Lavinia is saying cannot be true. Tell me it isn't.'

Julia looked at her aunt, showing no shame for what she had done, and she certainly wasn't about to deny it. 'I can't, Aunt. It is true.'

'Oh—you wicked, wicked girl.'

Absolutely enraged, the strength of Robert's temper could be vicious when roused. Lavinia's exposure wounded his vanity, and the anger and hatred burning from his eyes when he rounded on her made Lavinia think he was actually going to murder her right there.

'You sneaking little slut. So, you saw me with Julia, did you? And was what you were doing with him any different?' he hissed, pointing a quivering finger at Maxim. 'You women are all the same. You look so pure, so innocent, but underneath you're nothing but a pack of bitches on heat—which is how you should be treated.'

With fury blazing from his eyes he raised his hand to strike her, but Maxim stepped forward, grasping Robert's arm in mid-air in a vice-like grip, his expression savage as he halted the physical threat to Lavinia.

'If you value your life, I wouldn't do that if I were you,' he warned, the words delivered in a cold, murderous voice, his eyes like dagger thrusts boring into Robert's. 'If you lay one finger on her I'll break your neck.'

Rubbing his arm when Maxim released it, Robert seemed to freeze, his mind registering the physical threat in his voice, his small eyes searching his granite features. Maxim Purnell was a man who seemed to operate control at all times, a man who brooked no argument from anyone, and his look forced Robert to step back.

'You can't threaten me,' he said, remaining defiant, not quite recognising the depth of Maxim's fury, but Lavinia saw the taut rage emanating from every line of his powerful frame, causing a trickle of ice-cold fear to run down her spine as she had her first insight into the violent forces he kept leashed inside him.

'No?' Maxim inquired, with a sardonic lift to one dark brow and a dangerous edge to his voice. 'I meant every word I said. If you so much as touch her I will kill you—which is something I would not regret. Perhaps I should tell you that Miss Renshaw is now betrothed to me. I came here to ask her to be my wife and she has consented. Is that not so, Lavinia?' he said, his voice so soft and tender that it would have fooled anyone into believing that he loved her, but it did not fool Lavinia.

The memory of his rejection was still too fresh and raw in her mind. He looked at her, smiling into her stunned face, willing her to speak the words he wanted her to speak, and she complied, unable to do anything else when he looked at her like that.

'Yes,' she acknowledged quietly, holding his gaze. 'Yes, I have.'

'But you can't,' wailed Julia petulantly, coming to life at last when she saw her own world beginning to crumble about her ears. 'Lavinia is my sister and not yet twenty-one. She cannot marry anyone without my say-so.'

Lavinia turned on her, speaking with contempt. 'Because you could never hold a rightful place at Welbourne, you have always been resentful of Edgar and me, showing both of us nothing but contempt all your life—so spare me your sisterly concern now, Julia,' Lavinia scorned, speaking with a deadly calm. 'Besides, I shall be twenty-one very soon. What you and Robert have done—what you intended going on doing even when he married me—I find disgusting and deplorable. I can only thank God that I found out before it was too late.'

'Nevertheless I know my rights,' hissed Robert, desperation not far away as he saw Lavinia's legacy slipping away from him. 'You are betrothed to me and I don't intend letting you get out of it so easily. I can sue for breach of promise.'

'Then do so by all means,' said Maxim, not two feet away from him, looming over him, smiling an absolutely chilling smile, his clear blue eyes gleaming with a deadly purpose. 'But I would strongly advise you not to make an enemy of me, Feltham. If you do I will crucify you. I'm a powerful man, with powerful friends, and I'll happily destroy you if you so much as bring a breath of scandal to Lavinia's name. She is under my protection now, not yours. I would advise you to remember that she is to remain in this house until I leave Venice. She will accompany me, of course—as my wife. I shall arrange for a special licence for the ceremony to take place right away.'

Robert fixed his cold eyes on Lavinia, purposeful and menacing. 'You naïve little fool,' he hissed acidly. 'You have no notion of what you are letting yourself in for, have you, tying yourself to a disinherited, impoverished gambler? Go ahead. But don't say I didn't warn you. The legacy your father left you won't last beyond his first game of cards.'

With these parting words, his face distorted and ugly almost beyond recognition, Robert saw something so terrible in Maxim's metallic eyes that he abruptly left the room without further discussion. Julia followed him, leaving Mrs Lambert in some distress, finding it difficult to know what to say.

'I am so very sorry, Lavinia, dear,' she said softly, her expression pained. 'I had no idea that anything of this nature was going on. Julia and Mr Feltham! Oh, dear. It's all come as such a shock.'

'It's all right, Mrs Lambert,' said Lavinia gently. 'Try not to worry about it. Perhaps it's happened for the best. Robert and I were never suited—and I can't for the life of me imagine why I thought we were.'

'But—but you? You and Mr Purnell,' she said, looking from one to the other, remembering how he had so gallantly come to Lavinia's rescue when she had fallen into the lagoon. 'You are not even acquainted. Don't you think you ought to get to know each other a little better before committing yourselves to something as serious as marriage?'

'There's no time,' said Maxim gravely, beginning to wonder what he had committed himself to by announcing to everyone that he and Lavinia were to be married.

'Very well,' said Mrs Lambert, turning to go. 'Just as soon as Valentina and Leonardo are awake, I shall inform them of everything that has occurred—and in the light of such disgraceful conduct from Robert and Julia, carrying on like that in their house, I cannot blame them if they insist on them leaving and finding somewhere else to stay. Oh, dear—and Daisy must be told. But she never did trust Robert,' she said, shaking her head at the whole sorry business and going out of the room in a flurry of skirts.

Left alone with Lavinia, Maxim knew he was in trouble and cursed himself for a fool. Everything was ruined, he thought bitterly. Everything he had hoped to accomplish where Lucy was concerned had been dashed because he

couldn't keep his hands off Lavinia Renshaw—but he recalled that when he had kissed her, he had not been thinking of either Lucy or Alice.

Lavinia had the power to drive Alice from his mind, but
thoughts of his daughter gave him sharp pangs of conscience and he felt guilty of betrayal. When Alice discovered he had married someone else, she would try removing
Lucy from him as far as possible. He hadn't meant for any
of this to happen, and he could see no way of extricating
himself with honour. Too late, he knew he shouldn't have
come. The danger had been too great. He should have
stayed away and tried to forget he had ever met the lovely
young woman he had plucked from the lagoon, but he had
been unable to prevent himself going after her, being drawn
to her like metal filings to a magnet. What had happened
was the fruit of his own folly and there was no escape.

In the cool, calculating manner which he adopted whenever he was dealing with a business transaction, he realised
he would have to draw up fresh plans which would prove
satisfactory to Lavinia; whatever was decided, he felt a
deep sense of responsibility towards her. Her problems
were pretty desperate, that was obvious, and she had no
defences against the world as he knew it. It was important
that she was protected from men like Robert Feltham, and
her reputation must be preserved. However, he was unprepared when she turned on him angrily.

'Now see what has happened because you couldn't keep
your hands to yourself,' she cried accusingly, her voice
trembling with fury. 'How dare you force yourself on me
like that?'

'Why?' asked Maxim smoothly, gazing down at her and
noting the telltale flush on her cheeks and the soft confusion
in her deep blue gaze. 'Because you can't help the way you

feel every time I do? You melt in my arms as though you belong there.'

'But I don't. We both know that,' she told him, mentally struggling for some way out of a situation which seemed doomed to end in further pain and humiliation for her whatever happened. Silently she stood looking at Maxim. The tension she had been under since she had taken it into her head to go to his apartment had sapped her strength and she began to tremble. With a sigh he moved behind her, putting his hands on her shoulders and gently massaging her neck.

'Stand still,' he commanded softly when she was about to protest. 'You'll find this soothing.'

Obediently Lavinia did as she was told, trying not to think of his cool fingers on the back of her neck as he gently worked at the knotted muscles that were making her head ache.

'Are you all right?' he asked, feeling her begin to relax. 'I can feel you trembling.'

She nodded, swallowing hard. 'Yes. But if you had kept your hands to yourself none of this would have happened,' she said softly, falling silent as he continued to massage her neck, and she knew he was thinking of those few passionate moments prior to Robert entering the room. 'It was very noble of you to tell them you came here to ask me to marry you,' she said on a calmer note, 'but you don't have to hold fast to what you promised. You shouldn't have said it.'

'I know I shouldn't. But the fact remains that I did.'

'And do you mean to keep your word?'

'Yes,' he said. 'Yes, I do. Besides, seeing that I was the one who kissed you, I felt duty bound to save your reputation. After being caught red-handed with you in my arms,

I had no choice but to rescue you from the scandal that would be sure to ensue and follow you to England.'

'I didn't ask you to.'

'I know.'

'You are not obliged to marry me, and I certainly don't expect you to. You can reconsider,' Lavinia said, closing her eyes with a sense of ease and well-being, feeling the tension beginning to melt from her body as his firm fingers continued massaging her neck.

'I won't. But listening to you now, I am beginning to think you are trying to dissuade me,' he said softly, his mouth so close to her ear that Lavinia could feel his warm breath on her cheek. 'Have you forgotten so soon that it was you who asked me to marry you? Don't tell me that you've changed your mind.'

'I don't know. What prompted you to say it?'

'Because I couldn't bear hearing the pompous jackass speak to you like that—bullying you in that appalling manner.' He stopped massaging her neck and turned her round, looking down at her steadily. 'And like all bullies he stepped back when confronted with a superior strength.' Maxim smiled crookedly. 'But I meant what I said. I will marry you, Lavinia. You obviously need looking after by someone. But I have to attach a condition—which we must discuss first.' His voice had an ominous ring to it.

Perplexed, Lavinia looked up at him, suddenly wary. 'A condition? What do you mean?'

'We will discuss it, but not now—not here.' Maxim noticed how tired and weary she looked, how pale, and that she was struggling to keep her eyes open. 'When did you last go to bed, Lavinia?'

She shook her head. Sick and weak, she looked at him. 'So much has happened that I can hardly remember. It was the night before the ball, I think.'

'I thought as much. I order you to go to bed and get some rest. Afterwards you must return to my apartment and dine with me. We will talk then. But this time you must not come alone. I am sure Signora Scalini can spare a maid to accompany you. Do you understand, Lavinia?' he asked when he saw her eyelids begin to droop.

She nodded, looking up at him in defeat, too tired to argue at that moment. The glow of the sun coming in through the open shutters lit up her magnificent eyes, and Maxim succumbed to the impulse which was tormenting him. He kissed her long and passionately, before letting her go.

After Daisy had been told every detail about what had happened and finally left, Lavinia was at last able to think about Maxim, about his character and the way he looked. There was a certain insolence in the way he moved and in the way in which he lifted his proud, dark head. Vigour emanated from him with a vibrancy which set his eyes alight, and softened what might otherwise have been too much darkness in a face that was forbidding in its strong masculinity. Beneath his calm sophistication was a man with many diverse and complex shades to his nature which most men lacked. Hidden deep inside was an innate amusement, watchful, mocking, and a keen perception of his own infallibility.

There was also the fact that he was a gambler. At any other time she would have said that to consider a man with this failing for a husband was absolute madness but, like the gambler *he* was, this was one time she would have to take a chance, even if she risked losing everything.

Chapter Six

Thrown into a turmoil of agitation about returning to Maxim's apartment, Lavinia dressed with care in an oyster satin gown, her only adornment being a single strand of pearls around her throat. The purple and gold of the evening sky was sinking into the lagoon when she arrived at his apartment by boat. She was accompanied by one of the maids, who Maxim immediately sent back to the Scalini residence with the message that he would see Miss Renshaw home himself.

Lavinia gave him a scandalised look, at which he smiled that devastatingly lazy smile of his.

'I think it is permissible for two people who are betrothed to spend a little time alone together.'

Maxim had dressed for dinner in snug-fitting grey trousers and dark green coat, with a grey silk waistcoat and white silk shirt. His black hair gleamed and fell casually over his forehead, giving him a youthful look, and his clear blue eyes set off the deep tan of his skin.

Taking Lavinia's hand, he escorted her inside the apartment, thinking how poised she was, and that her beauty was breathtaking as she moved serenely beside him. This young woman who had captured his senses was lovely—

so pure, so virginal—and he was certain that what he saw was a mirror image of what was within. He was achingly aware of how difficult it would be telling her what he had decided.

The candleglow enhanced the beautiful furniture and brought out the rich hues in the Venetian glass objects and the paintings on the walls, creating a warm, intimate atmosphere.

'Do you feel better now you have rested?' he asked.

'Yes. I didn't realise how tired I was.'

'I hope you're hungry. Perkins has been slaving away in the kitchen all afternoon.'

Lavinia gave him a querying look. 'Perkins?'

'My butler, secretary and cook.' He laughed. 'Perhaps I should call him my general factotum. But whatever he is, he has become indispensable to me. He knows all my idiosyncrasies and is sensitive to my every mood.'

Lavinia was surprised to learn he had a butler, having thought him to be in Venice alone. But somehow it seemed appropriate that he had someone to look after his needs. She couldn't imagine Maxim Purnell washing and ironing his own shirts and polishing his own boots.

Maxim seated her at the circular table over which was draped an exquisite cloth of snow-white Burano lace. It had been laid to perfection with silver and crystal, which sparkled in the light. He poured a light, sparkling wine into long flutes and Perkins—a serious-looking man of middle years—appeared with the food. It was delicious and cooked to perfection, and Maxim proved to be the perfect host.

'This is a lovely apartment,' Lavinia commented. 'Have you been in Venice long?'

'No. A few days, no more. I've been travelling Europe myself for the past two months, and I am now on my way back to England.'

'And has your visit to Europe been for business or pleasure?' Lavinia queried, keen to know a little more about
the background of this perplexing man. 'I would have
thought you were past the age when gentlemen came
abroad on the Grand Tour to expand their knowledge.'

'Unfortunately that is so. My reason for coming was
mainly business—but it has not been without its pleasurable
moments,' he murmured, his eyes coming to rest meaningfully on her face. 'Especially in Venice.' He smiled when
he saw a soft flush mantle her cheeks and she lowered her
eyes to her plate.

Lavinia sensed that his candid mood did not extend to
discussing more about himself. His evasive tone told her
that.

'The apartment belongs to a friend of mine who is in
Rome just now. Whenever I come to Venice—which is not
all that often—I stay with him and his wife.'

Over the meal neither of them mentioned the marriage
proposal, the talk being mainly about Venice and the other
cities Lavinia had visited in Italy, and during the conversation Maxim asked her about her home in Gloucestershire,
quietly observing how her eyes clouded and that she
seemed to withdraw into herself. He was curious.

'Did you have a happy childhood?'

She sighed, wistful. 'When I look back I suppose some
would say it was somewhat neglected—despite belonging
to a wealthy family. My father was a landowner and a
successful businessman,' she explained.

'How was your childhood neglected? In what way?' he
probed gently.

'Oh—I was well taken care of, fed, clothed, and edu-
cated,' she told him hesitantly.

'You went away to school?'

'Oh, no. Nothing like that. Edgar, my brother, was sent

away. He's seventeen now and finishing his education at Oxford. I had a governess.'

'And what was she like? No,' he said, smiling with humour, 'wait. Let me guess. Let me give you my impression of what I imagine a governess to look like. I imagine her to be at least a hundred—terrifying to look at, who rarely speaks of anything other than the rudiments of education and stands over her pupils like some grisly prophet of doom while they work at their lessons.'

'Good gracious.' Lavinia laughed, her laughter sounding like the purest water on glass to Maxim—cool and crystal clear. 'I could not imagine a worse fate than being taught by a governess like that. Miss Leigh was strict but she was not terrifying. She was at Welbourne House for eight years, and was rather elderly—at least that's how she always seemed to me—but she was certainly not a hundred.'

'I was jesting,' Maxim murmured, his eyes twinkling mischievously, strangely unwilling to let her stop talking about her past.

'I know that,' Lavinia smiled in response. 'I remember her as being a strict disciplinarian and an extremely clever woman. Everything she did was carefully thought out and controlled. She was also a robust woman, who was never ill and hated weakness in others. But she was kind to me and a good teacher. She taught me all I know. I have much to be grateful for where she is concerned.'

'And your mother? She is dead, I take it. What was she like?'

A profound sadness clouded Lavinia's eyes, which did not go unnoticed by Maxim, and his curiosity about her childhood deepened.

'I—I never spent much time with my mother—in fact, I can only remember her absent-minded smile whenever she came to the nursery, or on the rare occasions when I was taken downstairs and her eyes would alight on me. Oh, she—she was never unkind, but she was absolutely devoted to my father and focused all her attention on making him happy.'

'But he was not her first husband.'

'No. My mother married my father and came to live at Welbourne House after the death of her first husband—Mrs Lambert's brother. When I came along I think I got in the way of things. I always felt remote from both my parents. Most of my childhood was spent upstairs in the nursery. I can't remember my father ever touching me—although I suppose he must have when I was little. Both my parents were vague figures on the perimeter of my life,' she told him quietly.

'You must have been very lonely.'

'Yes—I was,' she confessed, meeting his gaze. It was one of pure absorption, urging her to confide her innermost secrets, which she found strange, for she had never told anyone how unhappy she had been as a child, not even Daisy. 'My life was as cloistered as a nun's and sometimes I felt as if I were suffocating. It was my parents' indifference towards me that hurt the most.

'When Edgar came along, his arrival drew their interest because they now had a son and heir.' Lavinia looked down at her hands to hide the pain she always felt when she recalled her parents' joy when Edgar had been born. 'They adored Edgar—everyone did,' she whispered quietly, remembering that there had never been any love left over for her. 'They worshipped him. He became the centre of their lives.'

'Are you close to your brother?'

'Yes—very. I wasn't jealous of him or anything like that.'

Maxim nodded, understanding her pain. 'And Julia? Forgive me but I could not help noticing the enmity between the two of you when I saw you together earlier.'

They exchanged a smile. 'You are very perceptive,' said Lavinia, 'but then it wasn't too difficult, was it? Julia and I have never been close—not like sisters should be. She always felt that she never belonged at Welbourne, you see, and always resented Edgar and me. When we were children her behaviour towards both of us was extremely harsh. Fortunately, she spent most of her time with her aunt, Mrs Lambert, in London, until she married.'

'And her husband?'

'He was killed in a riding accident. Unfortunately for Julia, he left her without a penny and a mountain of debts—most of them settled by my father, who never had much time for her. But he promised my mother before she died that he would always take care of Julia and, despite the way he felt about her, he was not a man to go back on his word. After that she came to live at Welbourne House—and there she will remain until she finds herself another husband.'

'Which is the reason why you will not go back to live there,' Maxim stated quietly.

'Yes. After what she has done, nothing will induce me to reside under the same roof as her again.'

'That I can understand. And Daisy?'

'I regret that Daisy and I didn't meet until we decided to come on this trip to Europe. She's a lovely, warm person. It would be difficult for anyone not to like her.'

'It seems to me that you have had a somewhat lonely childhood at Welbourne House. Were there no other children?'

'No. When Edgar went away to school, it was left to the servants to entertain me. They were kind in their own way, but they were too set in the way of the house to understand an adolescent girl. Looking back, I can see that Cook was my saviour.'

'Oh?' Maxim smiled. 'And what memories do you have of Cook? Happy ones, I hope.'

'Yes. I'm sure I must have got under her feet, but she never sent me away when I visited her while she worked. My happiest memories are of sitting in the rocking chair in the kitchen beside the huge open range, where she used to do all the cooking for the household, and she would tell me stories of her youth. She was married to a sailor who used to sail all over the world, and she would tell me such wonderful and colourful stories of the foreign places he visited—stories which, looking back, I am sure she added extra spice to, embroidering them to make them sound more interesting and exciting to a little girl eager to listen.'

'She must have been a wonderful person.'

'Yes, she was,' she murmured, slanting him a soft smile. 'I remember going to bed at night and lying awake, reliving those stories and imagining myself being transported to all those exotic places she had told me about.'

Maxim listened silently, thinking what a strange and lonely child she must have been, and how she must have yearned for children of her own age.

'So, with the absence of parental interest, and no companion other than an ageing governess and the cook, I can well see what you mean by a neglected childhood.'

'Yes,' Lavinia said gravely, meeting his gaze. 'I suppose it could be described as one of the most unloving and miserable a child could have. But when one is living it, it is not apparent. It is only when it is over that it becomes clear. If I am blessed with children of my own, I shall make quite certain that they do not suffer as I did.'

Maxim listened to her with sympathetic understanding. He himself had been raised in a household with so much love and laughter that he could not imagine being a responsibility grudgingly accepted.

'And has there been no romance in your life, Lavinia?' he asked with the hint of a smile, his eyes fixed warmly on her own. 'No young squire to sweep you off your feet? Discounting the obnoxious Mr Feltham, of course.'

She flushed softly beneath his probing gaze, thinking of Thomas Dorsy and how bright and handsome he'd looked in his uniform when he'd waved her farewell to go to India with his regiment. 'Yes—I admit there was someone—once,' she confessed.

'Tell me about him?'

'Oh, there's nothing to tell really,' she said, her voice soft with memory. 'His name was Thomas Dorsy.'

'From Welbourne?'

'Yes. His father was an old and intimate friend of my family. He was also an eminent lawyer in Welbourne. He wanted Thomas to follow in his footsteps—but Thomas had ambitions of his own.'

'And was he handsome?'

'Very—and he had the merriest, warmest laugh, and the bluest eyes and fairest hair this side of heaven. To my romantic, seventeen-year-old imagination he was Apollo and Lancelot all rolled into one—a thousand times more wonderful than all the knights of King Arthur's round table. No legendary hero could compare.'

Maxim was surprised to find himself resenting and thinking jealously of the young man Lavinia had known before. 'He sounds like the answer to every maiden's prayer. And what happened to this prince among men?'

The question seemed to discomfit her. As if stalling for time she looked straight ahead, fighting a sudden mistiness in her eyes. She waited a moment before answering, and when she did her voice was low, almost a whisper. 'He was a soldier. He—he was killed in some skirmish or other in India.'

'I see. And would you have married him if he hadn't been killed?' asked Maxim quietly, knowing she hadn't loved this young soldier—having told him herself when she had come seeking him out at his apartment earlier that she had never been in love.

'Yes, I think so. There was an understanding between us that we would become engaged when he returned to England.'

'India is a long way away. It could have been years before he returned. What if you had met someone else in the meantime?'

'I don't think so. Thomas expected to be away for less than three years, and I was just seventeen when he went away. His parents grieved terribly over his loss. He was their only child, you see. It was shortly after that when I met and became betrothed to Robert.'

At that moment Perkins—a dark and pensive man of few words—came in to take away the dinner things. Maxim stood up, walking round the table and taking Lavinia's hand.

'The night is warm so come and sit on the balcony for a while—not too long, though. The mosquitoes tend to be keen close to the canals. They hang like a net curtain on the waterfront. Have you been bitten?'

'No. Although I've fared better than Daisy. She seems to be susceptible to bites and stings from every insect imaginable,' she told him, realising that he had smoothly gleaned from her an exact picture of her life, right up to the moment she had been flung into the canal, and yet his own life still remained a mystery to her.

Settling herself in a chair across from him, she breathed deeply. The air was heavily perfumed with the heady smell of lemon-scented magnolias trailing over the balustrade, and hyacinths filling the terracotta pots on the balcony. A sleepy, almost dreamlike atmosphere prevailed over Venice both day and night, as though life lived beyond the weathered walls was somehow set apart.

Using her fan to waft away the tiny insects which came to annoy her she relaxed, content to gaze out over the little canal and up into the star-strewn sky, to listen to the music floating on the air from the many cafes in the squares, and conscious of Maxim's watchful gaze—alert, waiting, and more than ever before she was aware of him as an attractive man as she studied his handsome profile, and how effortlessly he could turn her bones to water.

At length Lavinia broke the silence between them, broaching the subject uppermost in both their minds.

'Before you left me this morning, you said there were conditions to be discussed. What did you mean by that?' she asked, looking across at him. Having removed his coat and neck cloth, his white shirt was partly open to reveal the strong muscles of his throat. A wave of sleek raven hair slanted across his forehead, and his eyes, darkened in the dim light, were full of decision. Propping his ankle on the opposite knee he fixed her with a studied gaze.

'It seems to me that your options are limited, and that a husband is the only possible solution to your problems,' he pointed out, sounding terribly businesslike, Lavinia thought. 'Do you agree?'

'Yes.'

'The way I see it you are desperate to break away from the people you know, and you cannot do that unless you have money, and to acquire your legacy before you are twenty-five you must marry.'

'That is correct—but it sounds rather mercenary when you put it so bluntly. However, the money will naturally be my dowry—and I do realise that a marriage based on such unfortunate and shaky foundations as ours is going to take some working at.'

'That's just it, Lavinia,' Maxim said, looking at her directly, not a muscle of his handsome, authoritative face showing any expression. 'It isn't going to work.'

She looked at him in puzzlement. 'But—I don't understand.'

'You will after I have explained. You will be considerably relieved when I tell you that I do not want your money.'

Lavinia was becoming more bewildered by the second. 'What are you saying?'

'That I will marry you and then—for reasons of my own—petition to have the marriage declared void when we return to England.'

Thrown off her balance, Lavinia stared at him uncomprehendingly. 'Oh—but—I—I don't understand.'

'I'm sorry. I'm not being very subtle, am I? It has to be this way.'

'But—on what grounds?'

'Non-consummation. What else?' Noting that she looked quite bewildered Maxim looked at her quizzically, his brows drawing together in an inquiring frown. 'You do know what that means, don't you, Lavinia?'

She flushed, looking down at her hands in her lap to hide her confusion. 'Yes. Yes—of—of course I do,' she uttered hesitantly, not entirely sure that she did, but so embarrassed that nothing would have induced her to admit it. Her sexual innocence and lack of knowledge regarding the male species had her puzzled. 'But—but why?' she asked, suddenly aware of all the magic disappearing from the night. This wasn't how she had thought it would be—what she'd expected—how she'd wanted it to be. Any romantic plans she'd had were being demolished by him.

'I can't tell you. But that is how it has to be,' Maxim said, having decided not to tell her about Alice or Lucy, knowing she would refuse to go through with the ceremony if he did.

The biggest problem would be telling Alice because, once Julia and the Eveshams returned to England, the scandal about him being caught in a compromising situation with Lavinia and then making her his wife would be bandied about in every assembly room and drawing room in London. It was inevitable that Alice would hear of it from Sophia Evesham, the two of them being friends, and he could imagine her fury. But once she learned he was to seek an annulment, he had no doubt that she would be mollified.

Maxim had every confidence that it wouldn't be too difficult securing a decree of nullity. It could only be obtained by an Act of Parliament and could take up to three years. The cost of a private Act and the related proceedings would be expensive, but not impossible to secure—if it was proved that he and Lavinia had lived apart and that she was as pure as she was now. He would have to make sure that he kept his hands to himself, which would be no simple matter, for she had absorbed his attention completely from the moment he had plucked her from the lagoon.

A tension had sprung up between them and Lavinia rose quickly, standing close to the balustrade and looking down into the dark water of the canal, turning her face away from Maxim's probing eyes in an attempt to hide her feelings, which were pinned to her face for him to see. But she could feel his eyes watching her, his blue gaze seeing and interpreting with great skill.

Trying desperately to hide her shock, disappointment and

dismay, Lavinia was oblivious to the boats going up and down with their passengers. There was no room in her vision or her heart but this one vast disappointment. A host of conflicting emotions were tearing round inside her head, and all of a sudden nothing made any sense. With a painful effort she fought to dominate her hurt and disappointment and accept this blow that fate had dealt her, aware of Maxim's eyes scrutinising her from where he sat. The silence between them grew uncomfortable, despite the noise of the city, and she felt as if she was waking to a nightmare from a happy dream. How stupid she must seem to him, how naïve and gullible.

Stiffened by pride, her only feelings being of anger and hurt pride, her voice was quiet and taut when she spoke. 'Tell me, Maxim. For what reason did you say you would marry me?'

She turned and looked at him, and Maxim peered at her, frowning. Her lovely eyes held a feverish glitter, and he saw that her expression had hardened and that her slight smile was full of irony.

'I am not so foolish as to think you have fallen head over heels in love with me—and I am grateful that you made no false declarations as such,' she said icily, a cold hand clutching at her heart.

'No, I have no intention of doing so.'

'At least you are honest.'

'I told you that I feel responsible for the way things have turned out for you. In the eyes of everyone you will be painted a scarlet woman—a shameless wanton, with no moral standards. You have broken all the rules that govern respectable society.'

'And Robert?'

'Robert's affair with Julia will not be made public, so you will be the one vilified and shunned, not Robert. I recognised the Eveshams when they arrived to witness our rather intimate embrace, and I know that Sophia is renowned for her spite. On returning to London she will make quite sure that your humiliation is complete. So be content when I say that I am willing to marry you. Let that be enough.'

With eyes blazing Lavinia moved towards where he still sat. There was a nonchalance in the way he looked up at her, which fed her anger. 'What? And be grateful? How dare you pity me!' she cried, her voice shaking with fury, feeling that her humiliation was truly complete.

Maxim rose, her reaction to his terms of marriage and the look on her face wrenching his heart.

Lavinia turned from him and strode quickly across the room, hot, angry tears welling up in her eyes. 'I would like to go now. I'll find my own way back.'

'Lavinia, wait,' he ordered, striding after her. Taking her arm, he spun her round.

She wrenched it from his grasp and glared at him. 'Get off my arm—you—you arrogant, insensitive brute. Let me go.'

'I will not let you leave until you have heard me out,' he said, his hands locking on her shoulders. In the glowing light his face was suddenly grim, his dark eyebrows drawn together in a straight line. 'You're going to listen to me if I have to force you to listen. Stand still, damn you,' he said when she struggled to free herself from his grasp.

She flared up. 'Why?' she cried, her colour high, her eyes ablaze. 'Why should I listen to you? This is madness. All of it. I haven't known you a week and already you are turning my life upside down. I don't even know who you are—and I don't think I want to any more. I find your conditions humiliating and insulting, and I have no wish to hear more. At heart you are no better than Robert and I want nothing from you. Nothing—do you hear?'

'Devil take it, Lavinia,' Maxim shouted in angry frustration. 'All I have done is ask you to marry me—out of concern, not pity.'

'I am quite capable of leading my own life without you. I'll find someone else to marry me,' she announced recklessly. 'For keeps. It shouldn't be too difficult.'

'I don't believe you,' he said flatly. 'Who will you find at such short notice? Another pompous little rat like Robert, who can see no further than your legacy? Oh, yes,' he sneered, 'there will be plenty of men like that ready to jump into his shoes.'

'And why should you care? I am not yours and never shall be.'

'All right—I admit it. I curse the day I became involved with you—but, like it or not, I am involved and I want to help you.'

'I want no favours from you,' she flamed, meeting his gaze squarely, astounding him by the violence of her outburst. 'You—you vile clod,' she lambasted him uncharacteristically, not given to flinging abuse at people and unable to think of a more appropriate word just then.

Maxim arched a sleek black brow, one corner of his finely chiselled mouth quirking into something that looked suspiciously like a grin to Lavinia. '*Clod!* Come now, Lavinia. That's damned unflattering to say to a man who will very likely be staking a great deal to get you out of a fix.'

Lavinia's expression remained wary and antagonistic, and it was then that Maxim saw the pain behind the anger and defiance in her lovely eyes.

'There you go again,' she said scathingly. 'Do you have to gamble on everything?'

'You stubborn little fool,' he murmured, sensing a softening in her attitude. 'I may be a gambler, but I am also a businessman—and I happen to be extremely good at both.'

'And I bet you are acquainted with all the gaming halls in Europe,' she accused with angry derision.

Despite the intended insult in her words, Maxim grinned, feeling extremely tolerant, thinking how lovely she looked with her colour up and her eyes sparking fire. 'Intimately,' he agreed.

'But I thought you lost a lot of money at a ridotto the other night,' she asked, her eyes full of uncertainty.

'What? Enough to make you suspect that I might have put myself in Queer Street and readily jump at the chance to seize your legacy by marrying you?' He grinned. 'No. Although it was enough for it to be noticed and talked about. I don't normally lose such large amounts, but the ridotto was the night after I met you. For some reason which was not obvious to me at the time, I couldn't concentrate. My fingers were all thumbs and I made mistakes.'

Despite her anger, Lavinia was secretly flattered to learn that he had been thinking of her, and yet at the same time appalled that he had lost a large sum of money. 'I hope you are not blaming me for your misfortune at the tables.'

'I wouldn't dream of it,' he laughed. 'Now, what do you say? Will you marry me—and be willing to let me petition for a decree of nullity when we return to England and you have obtained your thirty thousand pounds? Will you allow me to help you?'

'I still don't know why you should put yourself out for me in this way. I am nothing to you.'

Maxim wanted to shake the stubbornness out of her. 'I am doing this because I happen to care about you, damn it—and because I care what happens to you. I am willingly offering you a solution to your problems.' And creating more for myself, he cursed silently because, if she agreed, it would be interesting to see how long he could remain detached from the marriage.

'Have you the remotest idea how humiliated I shall feel when my husband has our marriage declared void? And what will happen to me then?'

'You will have your thirty thousand pounds to begin a whole new life.'

Lavinia sighed, folding her arms across her chest and thoughtfully moving away from him. The truth of what was happening struck her with awesome finality. She had been shamed and humiliated by Robert beyond endurance and beyond decency, and now here she was, faced with an annulment to her marriage to Maxim before it had even taken place. The very idea revolted her. It was immoral. Her mind revolved in a maddening spiral as she struggled to come to terms with it, because she could see no other option open to her.

'Well?' asked Maxim after several patient moments of watching her pace up and down, waiting for her response, her lovely face set in lines of indecision.

Lavinia stopped pacing and looked across at him, meeting his gaze squarely. He spoke in a businesslike manner, his voice and his expression unemotional, his heart a chilling quagmire of considered assessment, and she was sickened to think that ever since that first moment when he had plucked her from the lagoon and she had opened her eyes and gazed into his, he had seemed to be the incarnation of every romantic hero throughout history, with a disturbing ability to reduce her to the state of a quivering jelly.

Here she was, considering uniting herself with the most handsome man in Christendom, and yet she had never felt more lonely and despairing in her life. The arguments against marrying him rolled back and forth like an endless flooding tide. He pitied her like he would a whipped cur, and he would play his role as saviour heartily, but he did not want her for his wife. Having been the one to seek him out and ask him to marry her she had little to be proud of, and it goaded her to think that if she accepted his offer she must rely on him for his support.

As dearly as she wished to hurl an angry refusal in his face, she restrained herself, hardening her mind. She was about to embark on a meaningless alliance with a man whom she believed was sincere in wanting to help her, but in the end he would want rid of her. And yet he was offering her freedom. Yes, she thought, at least she would have that, and then she could take charge of her own life. Fate had dealt her a cruel blow, but she need not be the victim of circumstance.

She looked at him steadily, her face showing no trace of emotion as, with her head high, her pride and self-respect all that she had left, she answered him.

'Yes. Very well,' she said stiffly. 'I will accept the marriage as only a temporary affair—a marriage in name only—to be annulled as soon as my father's lawyer has released my legacy. I have nothing to lose and much to gain. Misfortune placed me at the mercy of Robert, and I have little liking for the bargain between us—but it is clear that my future lies in financial independence sooner rather than later.' After all, she thought cynically, where had honesty and fidelity got her in the past? 'However, I would like to make a pact. I have conditions of my own.'

Maxim arched an eyebrow inquiringly. 'Which are?'

'That you make no attempt to kiss me again. You will not touch me. You will keep your distance. Is that understood?'

'Perfectly. I was going to suggest it myself.'

In this, as in everything else, Maxim was firmly committed to accomplishing his goal, and he was determined to avoid any further confrontation with her. It would only complicate matters, and he didn't need any further complications. But despite his words and his determination not to allow her to venture too close, he could not resist one last urge to tease. He lowered his eyes and moved to where she stood close to the open balcony, an infuriating amusement dancing in their depths when he paused in front of her.

'But don't tell me you didn't enjoy my kisses,' he said softly, tormenting her senses, his eyes settling on her softly parted lips, 'because I won't believe you.'

Lavinia averted her eyes at the flippant way he referred to something which to her had meant so much. He obviously found it amusing, but she wasn't laughing. She would like to tell him that it didn't mean anything to her either, but she would be lying, and with his infuriating ability of seeming to know exactly what she was thinking, he would know it too.

'Why did you kiss me if you were not serious?'

He shrugged. 'It's a normal physiological reaction in the male species when confronted by a beautiful woman. And I am a keen appreciator in the beauty of women,' he said softly.

Lavinia turned away as heat coursed through her. With her newly acquired knowledge she believed him. The amusement in his blue eyes to something that was so serious to her was unbearable.

'But I cannot deny that I am strongly attracted to you, Lavinia,' he went on, his voice having taken on a note of gravity. Coming to stand behind her, he placed his hands on her shoulders and turned her to face him, looking deep into her eyes. 'In that I am sincere—and if it were at all possible I would not be speaking of petitioning for a decree of nullity.'

A slight, cynical smile touched her lips.

'Why do you smile?'

'I was thinking that for the time we will be together before we are free will be like a masquerade—only without the magic. Rather like a Carnival of Love which turns into a tragedy once the mask is removed.'

'I'm sorry, Lavinia. That's how it has to be. But it need not be a disaster. After a brief encounter—sometimes at first sight—which is what happened between us, the attraction—passion or desire, call it what you like—is as real and as potent as an attraction that develops over a long period of time. I do not like these conditions I have imposed on you, but there are important matters in England that forbid me to enter into a serious and lasting relationship with you—unless, of course, circumstances change and we find ourselves drawn together and mutually agree not to part.'

That was something Lavinia refused to let herself hope for. Swallowing hard against a lump that had risen in her throat she nodded, wondering what could be so important that he was being forced to put a brake on their emotions like this. 'Please don't torment me with words, Maxim,' she begged. 'This is difficult enough for me to handle.'

'I won't,' he promised, his voice filled with finality. 'Of course, if these conditions are not agreeable to you you can still draw back,' he told her. 'What I am offering you is a way out of your predicament.'

'I know. I am grateful—and I am moved by your concern for my well being and future happiness. But you must admit that the circumstances are unusual.'

'I do admit it. Do you object?'

Lavinia shook her head. 'No. All I ask is that you explain it a little more.'

'What do you want to know?'

'How will you secure a decree of nullity to our marriage?'

'Through the Ecclesiastical Courts. They have the power to release parties from the marriage bond on grounds of non-consummation or if the parties are too closely related by blood. Divorce of a valid marriage has to be obtained by a private Act of Parliament, which must be preceded by a separation in the Ecclesiastical Courts. It will be tedious and extremely costly, but I shall take care of that,' he said, aware that the procedure was so expensive that only the wealthy could avail themselves of it. 'It could also take the best part of three years—but I shall see that you get your thirty thousand pounds long before that so you can begin a new life.'

'And you are willing to do that—for me?'

Maxim looked at her, a grim smile touching his mouth. 'Yes. If I had exercised any decency, any restraint over my ardour, I would not have shamed you and made a spectacle of you in front of your relatives and friends.'

'What will my life be like when I am married to you—until I am free, that is? Shall I live with you—in your house?'

'You may live precisely where you choose to live—but not with me. You will be perfectly free. Knowing your circumstances, might I suggest that you go and live with my aunt at Thornhill Farm in Kent until you decide what to do. It's where I was brought up and I think you will like it there. However, I shall ask you to keep the fact that you are my wife to yourself. Apart from Aunt Ursula—who has always been like a mother to me and has a right to know what is happening beneath her roof—for the time being no one else must know.

'It could complicate matters for me,' he said, for he didn't want Alice finding out about his marriage to Lavinia at the risk of incurring her fury, knowing that she was more than capable of denying him access to Lucy. It was inevitable that she would find out some time—when Lavinia's sister and Sophia Evesham bandied it about London on their return—but it would suit him if she found out later rather than sooner. 'Do you understand?'

'Yes. Thank you.'

'Is there anything else you want to ask me?'

She shook her head. 'No. I—I think I would like to leave now.'

'Of course. I will escort you back in the boat.'

'No,' she answered, her voice sounding sharper than she intended. 'If you don't mind—I would rather you didn't.'

Maxim nodded, understanding. 'Very well. As you wish. I will ask Perkins to accompany you instead.'

'Thank you, but I can go back by myself.'

'No. I insist.'

Returning to the Scalini residence, to her surprise, Lavinia found that she was at peace with herself now that her decision had been made to enter into this strange marriage with Maxim Purnell. She felt glad that she had agreed to it. In fact she thought, with cold logic, that it would have been madness to have rejected a match which guaranteed her the chance to live her own life as she chose to live it, while leaving her fully her own mistress. All things considered, things hadn't turned out badly after all.

The scent of wisteria with cascades of delicate mauve blossom was heavy on the night air. Shadows and poles and slowly sinking steps punctuated the sepulchral stillness on the empty canal as the boat drew close to her destination and, apart from the gentle lap of the slick, black water against the walls on either side of them, Lavinia was struck by the silence. The canal was enclosed and dark. Above,

there was only the sky, with its disquieting shadows, beyond which lay the dawn. She bent her head backwards
and glanced up at the Scalini residence, to see Robert looking down at her from the balcony of his room, which
caused a shiver to pass down her spine.

Lavinia and Maxim were married in a quiet ceremony at
a little church buried within the heart of Castello. The only
people present were the Scalinis, Mrs Lambert and Daisy,
and Tom Player.

Tom looked on in puzzlement. Maxim had explained to
him the reasons why he was marrying Lavinia Renshaw
but considering he had been contemplating marrying Alice
when they had last spoken—after he had paid his uncle a
visit on his return to England to reconcile matters between
them—it all sounded a bit of a muddle and rather strange
to him. Tom had grave misgivings about the whole affair,
and he didn't think Maxim would find it as simple as he
thought, annulling his marriage to this lovely young woman
who came out of the church on his arm as his wife. To his
mind she was everything Alice wasn't, and when he saw
the glances Maxim cast her way, he very much thought that
he was already halfway to being in love with her.

After being severely chastised by Mrs Lambert, Robert
could not be persuaded to do the honourable thing and
marry Julia. Intending to return to England, he left Venice
the day before Lavinia's marriage to Maxim. Mrs Lambert
and Daisy were to remain for a further two weeks in Venice, and Lavinia was deeply sorry to say farewell to both.
However, she promised to call on them when they returned
to their home in London just as soon as it could be arranged.

Angered by the whole affair and humiliated by Robert's
treachery, Julia was to remain in Venice with them. On

coming back to England, she would return to live at Welbourne House. Unfortunately, her aunt declined to offer her a home with her and Daisy in London, and she had nowhere else to go. Her aunt also thought that living in close proximity to Robert in Gloucestershire might bring him to his senses, and that in the end he would do the honourable thing and marry her.

It was hard for Lavinia to leave Venice, and as the coach rolled on towards the Alps, with a feeling of nostalgia she vowed she would return to the splendid city, a city wedded to the sea and sitting sedately like a grande dame in her golden crown, with her jewel box wide open to the sun. Like a visiting lover she would return.

Chapter Seven

After a long and tedious journey through Europe Maxim and Lavinia arrived at Thornhill Farm, a rambling old farmhouse on the outskirts of the village of Rotherfield in Kent.

When the coach stopped before the front door, Maxim looked at Lavinia, knowing how nervous she was about meeting his large family. 'Try and relax,' he said softly. 'Though you may find living at Thornhill different from your own life in Gloucestershire, remember that these are hard-working, exceptional people. Since the death of my own parents, Aunt Ursula and her family have given me invaluable care and assistance to achieve my goal in life. I am extremely fond of them all, and savour their love and their friendship. You'll like them, I promise you.'

Lavinia smiled at him nervously. When she stepped from the temporary haven of the coach, she would be stepping into a new world, and she would feel very much a foreigner in it. Seeing her hesitation, Maxim got out and put up a hand to help her down.

'If you are ready, Lavinia.'

She nodded, lifted her resolve, and took a firm hold of her courage and his hand.

A tall, handsome woman in a plain black dress came out

of the house to meet them, smiling broadly, and behind her Lavinia saw what she could only describe as a sea of beaming faces of adults and children alike. Maxim was immediately enfolded. It was clear to her that they had all been waiting for his arrival, and the manner in which all the children squealed with delight and threw themselves at him in a flurry of arms and legs, told her that they worshipped him.

Never having seen people greet each other with so much joyous abandonment, the happy scene brought tears to Lavinia's eyes. She blinked them aside when Maxim took the tall woman's arm and drew her towards where she stood beside the coach.

Ursula Metcalf had been a widow for five years. Maxim's mother had been her sister. She had four children, two boys and two girls, all of them grown up and married, and all had provided her with grandchildren, eight all told.

'Aunt Ursula, this is Lavinia. I told you all about her in my letter,' said Maxim, looking at his aunt pointedly.

Ursula met his gaze and nodded, understanding that he wanted no one other than herself to know about his marriage to this lovely young woman, and why. 'Welcome to Thornhill, Lavinia,' she said with a gracious smile, looking down into the wide, innocent eyes. 'I do hope your stay will be a happy one. Did you have a pleasant journey?'

'Yes—thank you,' Lavinia replied, finding it difficult hiding her nervousness.

'And has Maxim told you anything about us?'

'A little,' she answered, glancing at Maxim with wide-eyed uncertainty.

Ursula laughed chidingly. 'Is that all? Well—I can see we must remedy that. Come and meet some of the family,' she said, putting a gentle arm around the younger woman's waist and drawing her forward.

'Some?' gasped Lavinia, unable to believe there could be more.

'Yes,' laughed Ursula. 'My sons, Ben and Will, are mending the fences in the far pasture. It will soon be dark so they'll be along shortly. And whenever it's time to eat they always arrive on time,' she smiled pointedly. 'We have a meal ready for you. I am sure you must be famished after your long journey from Dover.'

Lavinia was introduced to children and adults alike, trying to make a mental note of all their names, which, being so many, was no easy matter. Ella and Marion, Ursula's daughters, were married to Paul and Michael respectively, and both were dark and extremely pretty. Margaret, a small woman with auburn hair and an open, warm and friendly face, was Ben's wife, and Stella, who she suspected was the quietest of them all, was Will's wife. Ben, the eldest, lived at Thornhill with his family, and the others lived in their respective cottages close to the farm.

All the children eyed Lavinia with a great deal of interest, and with all the curiosity a stranger produced—especially when the stranger appeared on the arm of Uncle Maxim, who quietly thought her poise and loveliness was breathtaking as she moved amongst them.

The atmosphere inside the house was warm and welcoming, and if anyone was curious about Lavinia's relationship with Maxim, they made no comment and accepted the situation for what it was. They also accepted her, fussing and wanting to please, and Lavinia knew it was not out of conventional politeness, but because this was as they were. When Ben and Will appeared, two well-built young men, the thickness of their girths telling Lavinia that they were overfond of indulging their appetites, they all became seated at the huge table groaning with food in the parlour, where tonight the whole family was assembled for the evening meal in honour of Maxim's presence.

As the meal progressed with much gaiety, Lavinia was entertained throughout in a manner she had not thought possible, and in this relaxed and congenial atmosphere she soon began to feel her nervousness evaporating like the steam from the kettle simmering away on the huge open range. She sat among the family, quiet and shy but at ease, comfortable—studying each and every one of them, and meeting Maxim's unwavering eye every now and then when he looked to see how she was coping with it all.

Ursula, who presided graciously over this happy gathering with a good deal of pride, observed these exchanges and took particular note of how Maxim's features would soften each time they caught his wife's glance, and she smiled quietly to herself. One of her many attributes was intuition, and her intuition told her that her nephew's preoccupation with Lavinia in Venice, and his gallant attempt to befriend her, would lead him along a route he had not bargained on. Maxim thought he would be able to put her out of his life as effortlessly as he seemed to negotiate his many business deals, but Ursula knew it would not be that simple.

After the meal when the families began drifting off to their own homes close by, Maxim settled his gaze on Lavinia.

'I'm afraid that I must be on my way, too.'

Lavinia's eyes flew to his, her heart plunging despairingly. 'You're not staying?'

'No.'

'Maxim has his own house, Lavinia,' Ursula explained, and the sharp, secretive look she cast her nephew did not go unnoticed by Lavinia, but she was too dismayed to read anything into it just then.

'Oh! I—I didn't know. I—I thought—'

'What? That he lived here at the farm? No, my dear. Maxim hasn't lived here for years—although he still looks on Thornhill as his home, don't you, Maxim?'

'You know I do, Aunt,' he confirmed, his eyes shifting with a glowing fondness to the older woman, before bringing them back to Lavinia. 'Walk with me to the carriage, will you, Lavinia?'

Silently she walked beside him out into the night, blinded to her unfamiliar surroundings by the acute disappointment that swamped her, conscious only of the fact that he was to leave her. Perkins was already inside the carriage, waiting with his usual calm aplomb. Maxim paused, his face poised over his wife's, mysterious in the shadows.

'Have you far to go?' Lavinia asked, searching his eyes above her own. They had been together for so long that she was already feeling the wrench of their parting.

They stared at each other in a struggle that racked them both.

'No. I live nearby.' He read the consternation and recognised the worry in her eyes. 'You will be all right here, Lavinia. Ursula will see to that,' he said, soothing her fears as much as he was able.

'Yes—yes, I know.' He seemed the embodiment of unquestioning authority as he stood there, and she wanted to tell him she would miss him, that she thought she was falling in love with him, but that wasn't part of their arrangement—and she clung to the arrangement made between them as a shield.

But deep inside her things beyond her control were combining to make her feel helplessly drawn to him, like his kisses in Venice, which had made her body vibrate to his touch. But she didn't fool herself into believing it had been anything deeper than pure, common, indiscriminate lust that had prompted those kisses, and that to a man as handsome and virile as Maxim, she must be one of the most uninteresting, unattractive women he'd bothered with in his entire life.

Lavinia had married him knowing all that it entailed and that he was never going to make any undying declarations of love to her, and she knew not to ask him for more than he could give. When she had her legacy she would quietly disappear from his life, while trying to keep as much of her heart intact as she possibly could.

Deftly, Maxim took her slender fingers within his and lightly brushed a kiss on them, genuinely reluctant to be leaving her, which would have surprised, delighted, and given Lavinia reason to hope had she known this. Releasing her hand, he climbed up into the carriage, and Lavinia watched it disappear down the dark narrow lane until it was out of sight, though she could still hear the rattling of the wheels passing over the uneven road. All of a sudden she was swamped with desolation, but then she felt an arm placed gently about her waist and turned to find Ursula beside her, smiling down at her with understanding.

'Maxim will soon be back. He'll more than likely ride over some time during the next week or so.'

'Why does he not live here with you any more?' Lavinia asked, her curiosity about Maxim and his mysterious lifestyle beginning to get the better of her.

'Because he likes to be completely independent—but not too independent,' Ursula chuckled softly, 'otherwise he would not have chosen to live within easy reach of Thornhill.'

'And his mother was your sister?'

'She was. We were very close. She died two years after her husband—a man she adored. Her death was a terrible thing to me—and to Maxim. Simply terrible it was.'

'And was Maxim their only child? He's never mentioned any brothers and sisters to me.'

'Yes he was—and it soon became evident to everyone that he was an exceptionally gifted child, with the amazing ability to learn quickly. He had a thirst for knowledge that left my own children standing—which was why he was sent away to receive the education he deserved. But as you have seen for yourself tonight, Lavinia,' Ursula said, smiling down at her in the dim orange glow shining through the open doorway, 'he did not lack for company as he was growing up. Now—come along inside. I imagine you're tired after your journey. I'll show you to your room.'

Lavinia allowed herself to be taken back inside and up to the room which had been prepared for her, and as she snuggled in bed beneath the feather quilt, she gave a great deal of thought to Maxim and his warm and wonderful family, finding herself looking forward to her first day in this new and strange environment.

Two days later Maxim presented himself at the Winstanley residence in London, where, since his departure for Europe, Alice had resided with Lucy and her stepmother. Caroline Winstanley was an extremely wealthy woman whom Alice's father, George Winstanley, had married two years before his death. Maxim was only slightly acquainted with her, but well enough to know that she had little liking for her stepdaughter.

Being the only one at home, she received him in the drawing room.

'Alice is not at home at present, Mr Purnell,' she told him, seeming pleased to see him.

'I'm sorry. I thought I'd surprise her,' Maxim replied, meeting the direct and intelligent brown eyes of Caroline

Winstanley, a small, slim and still-pretty woman, with dark hair peppered with grey and calm features.

'I am expecting her back soon, so if you would like to wait I will order some refreshment.'

'Thank you. Whilst I am waiting perhaps I might see my daughter.'

'I know how eager you must be to see Lucy after so long an absence, but do you mind if I talk to you first? There are certain matters I would like to discuss with you.'

Maxim would have preferred to see his daughter, but his sense of unease and sharp instinct told him that Mrs Winstanley had something on her mind that troubled her. He settled himself in a chair, calmly waiting for her to speak, knowing before she opened her mouth that it concerned Alice.

'You've recently returned from the Continent, I believe,' she said by way of conversation as the maid fussed around with a tray of refreshment.

'Yes. I've been in both France and Italy. With the growing unrest and open insurrection seeming more than likely to be transformed into revolution in France, with a great deal of my money invested over there, I felt compelled to put my affairs in order.'

'I agree that it's all extremely worrying. All the time we get news of disturbances in the French provinces. I do believe the peasants have a grievance and that their want of bread is quite desperate. I can well imagine how the nobles and clergy are all dreading the ideas of liberty which are afloat,' Mrs Winstanley said, handing Maxim a cup of tea and looking with irritable impatience at the maid hovering by the table. 'Thank you, Jenny. That will be all for now.'

When the maid had closed the door behind her, Mrs Winstanley lost no time in coming to the point, her eyes fixed on Maxim's expressionless face. 'I'm glad Alice isn't here because I wanted to speak to you privately. It does concern you, after all.'

Her faint intonation of warning set Maxim on edge. He became guarded.

'What is it? Would I be correct in thinking that it concerns Alice.'

'Yes,' she replied, confirming his suspicion. 'I do not like raising indelicate matters—and I'm sure you will think I'm speaking out of turn—but I cannot be quiet on this subject.'

'Mrs Winstanley,' said Maxim, placing his cup on the table in front of him and leaning forward, resting his arms on his knees. 'I don't think there is anything you can tell me about Alice that I don't already know.'

'Perhaps not. It's just that if you have come here to agree to her terms and heal the breach with your uncle—in which event Alice will agree to marry you—I do hope you know what you're doing.'

Maxim smiled grimly. 'So do I.'

'Ever since she became aware that you are the Earl of Brinkcliff's heir, she has become obsessed with the idea of the title. To rise from simple origins to become her Ladyship, Countess of Brinkcliff—to be envied and admired and to enjoy all the power and privilege that goes with the title—is the summit of her ambition.'

'I know that,' Maxim replied, hiding his thoughts behind a coolly polite façade.

'And yet you will still agree to do as she asks—no, demands—even though it goes against your own judgement?'

Maxim frowned, his expression grave as he considered her question. There was a time when he had been in Italy, when he had seriously contemplated returning to England and becoming reconciled with his uncle and marrying Alice, to try and salvage something out of their relationship for Lucy's sake. The trouble was, he had never expected his decision to be beset by anything as powerful and consuming as Lavinia Renshaw. For the first time in his life he was at the mercy of his emotions, when reason and intelligence were powerless.

'Ever since Alice learned she was to bear my child she's been determined to penalise me because I refused to give in to her every whim—to seek a reconciliation with my uncle. I do realise that if it is the only way I can have Lucy with me, then eventually I must seriously consider her demands—unless I decide to seek legal custody in the courts, which is something I shrink from doing.'

'And if not, then you will make Alice your wife—knowing what she is like? No,' Mrs Winstanley said when he was about to interrupt. 'Please, hear me out while there's time. You know her character—and, much as I hate to admit it, the truth is that she is her father's child,' she said with bitterness. 'Unfortunately I was misled by my late husband before our marriage. I learned very quickly that he cared less for me than he did for my money. Had he lived, I have no doubt that he would have fleeced me of every penny.'

Having known George Winstanley, who had been a small shipping merchant of moderate means, a man of dissolute character who had sought his pleasures in brothels and gambling dens—which was where he met his end in a brawl after being accused of cheating at cards—Maxim knew that what she said was the truth.

'As you—and no doubt the whole of London—will remember,' she continued, 'he came to a bad end—and badness will come out—which is obvious when one looks at his daughter. I can only pray that Lucy has not inherited her mother's bad blood.'

Maxim winced, his eyes turning to blue ice, but he remained still and silent as he let her continue.

'Oh, Alice is beautiful, yes—but her behaviour is quite shocking. There are depths which I am only now beginning to perceive. You probably think I should not be speaking like this about my husband's only child, but I feel I must. I know her mother tried raising her as best she could but, being an only child, she was much favoured by her father, who overruled her mother's discipline. Alice is ambitious and greedy—and the most immoral young woman I know.'

Maxim listened to her quietly. He knew she was telling the truth, but still he waited, knowing there was more to come. Mrs Winstanley would not have gone to all this trouble if it was merely to refresh his memory as to Alice's character.

'Immoral? Kindly explain to me what you mean by that?' Maxim glanced towards the door, thinking he heard a footstep out in the hall, but he thought no more about it as Mrs Winstanley went on.

'She is not normal. Alice brings degradation and destruction to all who come under her spell.'

'That's harsh speaking, Mrs Winstanley.'

'And not without foundation, I do assure you, Mr Purnell. It is my belief that she was born wanton—dangerous, even—and she seems to go out of her way to shock people.'

'Then why do you remain in the same house as Alice?'

Perched straight backed on her chair, Mrs Winstanley gave him a direct, meaningful look. 'You have a daughter living in this house, Mr Purnell.'

Maxim's face tightened. 'What are you saying? That Lucy is not cared for?'

'That is precisely what I am saying. Alice spends all her time shamelessly gallivanting about London on the arm of an assortment of men with disgraceful reputations. Often she does not come home until the next day and frequently brings one of them with her. Her present, most ardent, admirer is Sir Francis Newbold—another is Claude Lauriston, the Comte de Chemille, who is presently in London. They are both dissolute gamesters, and quite infatuated with her. But it is the French comte who, I might add, is almost twice her age, and has proposed marriage to her. Are you acquainted with him?'

'I am, although he cannot be counted among my friends.'

'He intends returning very soon to his château in Normandy if things remain as they are over there. The implications of this could prove disastrous to yourself if you do not agree to Alice's terms.'

Mrs Winstanley searched Maxim's features, expecting a reaction, but there was nothing, except for a muscle that began to twitch in his jaw at the mention of the Comte de Chemille.

Inside Maxim seethed. The mere thought of Alice's name in connection with this man—a blackguard, wild and with the reputation of a sewer rat—sent his temper soaring, but not out of any feeling or concern for Alice. She could associate with whomsoever she damned well pleased, just as long as she kept them away from Lucy. However, Maxim had reason to be alarmed. In her determination to marry well, Alice might decide to accept the Frenchman's offer of marriage if he did not marry her himself.

'I take it you have no liking for the Comte de Chemille either, Mr Purnell.'

'None. Strip away his fine title and you are left with nothing. It is because of his indolent, arrogant breed, their determination to cling on to the old, oppressive feudal regime and their refusal to engage in trade, that France is crumbling. The Comte de Chemille is unconcerned that privilege has become a burden, that people starve because they cannot afford to pay the soaring food prices, that the taxes are intolerable.'

'Which, by all accounts, is why they are rebelling and refusing to pay the taxes—even going so far as to attack their lords' châteaux, and in many cases setting fire to them.'

'That is happening. In the wake of the peasants' refusal to pay dues, like many other aristocrats, Claude Lauriston may be returning to his château to reassert his authority. One obvious means would be to starve his villagers into submission by cutting down unripe corn—which, by all accounts, promises to be abundant this year after two failed harvests.' He smiled slightly. 'I'm sorry. These are matters I normally discuss with my business managers, not ladies whose houses I visit. Tell me about my daughter. How is she?'

'She is well enough—if somewhat withdrawn and quiet. She is not an outgoing child at the best of times, and is developing a somewhat nervous disposition.'

'And is Alice not concerned about this?'

'Alice is not concerned about anything other than her own needs, Mr Purnell. She has little to do with her daughter,' Mrs Winstanley told him bluntly. 'Lucy is often sent to stay with her sister in Surrey because she doesn't want to be troubled with her. Miss Sharp—the nurse she employs to look after her—has sole charge and the responsibility that goes with it. Alice tolerates Lucy—so long as she gives her no trouble.'

'And Miss Sharp? What is she like?'

'Middle-aged—and terribly strict. I do the best I can, Mr Purnell, but Alice resents my interference in what she frequently reminds me is the nursemaid's domain. I may be her stepmother—who, I might add, pays for most of her extravagances since her father left her with very little money—and while I am aware that I occupy a position of some influence, where Alice's favour is concerned it is nothing but a fragile flame.'

Maxim's mind acknowledged what Mrs Winstanley was telling him, and for some reason Lavinia's face intruded into his memory. He recalled her telling him of her own upbringing, of how she had been a responsibility grudgingly accepted by her parents—neglected and unloved, spending years in virtual solitary confinement while attention had been lavished on her younger brother. Maxim had seen for himself the forlorn look in those wonderful eyes of hers, and had been moved and saddened by it. There was no way on God's earth that he would allow the same thing to happen to his daughter.

'My advice to you, Mr Purnell, is to obtain custody of Lucy through the courts. It will mean accusing Alice of being an unfit mother, but it will be worth it if it will remove the child from her influence. You must forgive me if I mention your uncle in this instance—it is not my wish to interfere or to offend you, you understand—but perhaps if the two of you were to become reconciled, your position as the next Earl of Brinkcliff would become much stronger and carry more influence with the courts.

'You must realise that if you don't agree to marry Alice, there is every possibility that she will marry the Comte de Chemille and take Lucy with her to live in France. In which case, access will be difficult for you—and if revolution does break out, the consequences could be dire.'

Maxim tensed, having already thought of this himself. He nodded thoughtfully. 'Yes. I do realise that, Mrs Winstanley, and I must thank you. I appreciate you telling me this.'

At that moment they both looked towards the door when it opened. Alice stood there, poised and as beautiful as

Maxim remembered, but there was a hard, feral glitter in her green eyes when they came to settle on her stepmother.

'Thank you for entertaining Maxim for me, Caroline. But, as you can see, I am home now, so please leave us,' she said, dismissing her stepmother as she would a servant.

Without haste Caroline stood up and looked at Maxim, who had also risen and towered over her. 'Goodbye, Mr Purnell,' she smiled. 'It's been nice to talk to you.'

Maxim nodded, his face grim as he watched her go out, leaving him alone with Alice. His eyes became riveted on her, and she almost cringed before him—almost, but not quite.

'This is an unexpected pleasure, Maxim. Your trip to Europe was satisfactory, I trust? I see you so rarely these days,' she complained petulantly.

Maxim raised a dark eyebrow. 'I wasn't aware that you wished my company. However, you do not look surprised to see me, Alice,' he said, suddenly remembering the furtive footsteps he had heard out in the hall earlier. 'You have several faults, but I did not realise that listening at doors was one of them.'

Alice did not deny that she had overheard some of what her stepmother had been discussing with him—although not the last part when Caroline had told Maxim to become reconciled with his uncle, in the hope that, as the future Earl of Brinkcliff, his position to obtain custody of Lucy through the courts would increase his chances considerably. Knowing this, Alice's vicious, scheming mind would wield an indiscriminate blade.

Alice sighed somewhat wearily as she sauntered purposefully towards him, a petulant droop to her bottom lip. 'I do hope you're not going to believe what she says, are you? I'm not nearly so wicked as she wants you to think. Caroline has detested me since the day she married my father. Sometimes I really do wish she would take up with someone else and leave.'

'And what would you do without her money to finance your extravagant lifestyle, Alice? Your father left you little enough to live on for you to enjoy yourself in the manner to which you have become accustomed.'

'Now you are being unkind,' she pouted, lowering her eyes and running a finger slowly up his chest. There was a hardness to his voice which made her uneasy.

Having dressed with care earlier to go for a carriage ride through St James's Park with Sir Francis, with her lavender silk dress cut revealingly low and her full breasts swelling invitingly over the top, knowing just how lovely and irresistible she looked, Alice stood close beside him. Maxim's appreciation of beautiful women had once assured her success, but now she had a distinct feeling that it was not going to prove as easy as she expected.

Maxim admired her beauty; indeed, what sighted man would not. She had skin as white as alabaster, hair as black as midnight and a figure to rival Venus. The soft blend of her sultry perfume enveloped them both in an invisible cloud, and when she gazed at him, her lips parted in that self-assured smile of invitation he remembered well, a smile which at one time would have sent his senses spiralling and the blood pumping rapidly through his veins.

Alice was all temptation and he had denied his body such pleasures for many months, but he made no move to touch her. She made Lavinia seem like an angel. He saw a hard gleam in the depths of her slanting eyes, a gleam that belied the soft feminine allure. It wasn't attraction he saw, but a cold-hearted calculation that turned his blood to ice.

'If you listen to Caroline's malicious lies it will ruin everything. I heard what she was saying about Sir Francis, Maxim—and I must tell you that he means absolutely noth-

ing to me. He merely keeps me amused. However, Claude
Lauriston, the Comte de Chemille, is quite another matter…' she preened '…and it is true that he is besotted with
me and has proposed marriage.'

'And you have become well acquainted with the Comte?'

'But of course. After all, a woman needs an escort.' Alice's eyes narrowed and glittered. 'Do you see him as a
threat?'

Maxim's face tightened with distaste. 'No. More of an
inconvenience.'

'Maxim,' she reproached, pretending offence by his
harsh tone, 'you have to trust me. It's important that you
do. Please don't think I'm the sort of person Caroline accuses me of being. Of course I have gentlemen friends—
and I flirt a little bit. I admit it. But now you are back I
shall devote all my time to you. What are your intentions?'

'You mean, are they strictly honourable?' he returned
imperturbably. 'I haven't come back with my tail between
my legs, if that's what you were hoping.'

'No,' she said icily. 'I can see that. Perhaps you would
like Lucy and I to return to live with you at your house in
Grosvenor Street?'

'No, Alice. Lucy, yes. Not you. I've had three years to
consider my intentions where you are concerned, but that
is in the past. My prime concern now is Lucy. She is my
present and my future. That I have not lost sight of,' he
assured her.

'And you have made up your mind that I have no place
in your future?'

'Yes,' he answered calmly, knowing his answer would
not have been so firmly spoken had his life not become
enmeshed with Lavinia's. He wondered how Alice would
react if she knew he was already beginning to look forward
to a future that included the woman he had married, know-

ing Lavinia would be as surprised as he was by the revelation.

However, he wasn't ready to reveal his marriage to Alice
unless he had to. The Lamberts and Julia intended extending their time in Italy for a further two or three weeks, and
the Eveshams were not expected back in England for at
least another month, so he was confident that their secret
was safe for the time being.

Alice's eyes glittered like shards of glass. 'And if you
think I'm going to let you take Lucy and cast me off like
a soiled bedsheet, then think again, Maxim. You will leave
me with no choice but to marry Claude.' She tossed her
head haughtily. 'I have a fancy for him, anyway.'

Maxim's look was bordering on contempt. 'Come now,
Alice. This is me you're talking to—the man who knows
you too well. I don't believe you have a fancy for anything
or anyone except furthering your ambition.'

Sensing that she was in danger of sliding further down
the ladder, Alice tried to soften her features. 'You are the
one I am bent on marrying, Maxim—the father of my
child.' She pressed herself against him and threw back her
head to give him the full benefit of her beauty, a calculating
expression in her eyes and a sly smile curving her lips.
'Come now—you do still want your daughter, don't you?'

'Damn you, Alice,' he said fiercely. 'You know I
wouldn't be here if it weren't for Lucy.'

'I don't believe you. You do care for me—and I can't
help thinking of you. I care for you more than you realise.'

'If you cared for me you wouldn't give a damn about a
title.'

'But if we marry you must see it's important. It cannot
be ignored.'

'You ask too much. You must realise by now that I will
not be pushed, cajoled or manoeuvred into anything by you

or anyone else. From the moment you made yourself available to me you have worked to this end. How galling it must be for you, when I refuse to succumb to your demands as you expected I would,' he said coldly.

'Yes, it is, but it isn't too late,' she persisted. 'The first step to respectability would be for you to marry me.'

'No,' he said, and there was a cold finality in his voice that struck Alice hard. She winced, seeing cruelty in his merciless stare. 'I will not be manipulated or gulled into marriage. The truth is that you would be a pitiful excuse for a wife and I want none of it. You no longer interest me. You're spoiled, demanding and irrational. If I were to marry you our lives together would be a mess—my own a nightmare.'

Undeterred, Alice tilted her head back a little further, her body touching his. 'Kiss me, Maxim,' she murmured in an attempt to weaken him.

With a glower of contempt he shoved her aside. 'Stop it, Alice. You've already used every feminine ploy in existence on me, but it won't work,' he growled, making a deliberate attempt to alienate her by moving away.

'You had no objections before Lucy was born, as I recall.'

'You were undeniably appealing—to me,' Maxim pronounced, his gaze mocking, 'and how many others? You, Alice, are promiscuous and a slut.'

Alice's eyes narrowed viciously. Deep inside she was simmering with rage that he dared to cast her off like a common whore—and that he firmly refused to be drawn on the subject of his title. Ambition burned in her. During the last few years many noblemen had propositioned her to become their mistress, but only the French comte had offered her marriage.

Claude was no longer a young man and certainly nowhere near as handsome as Maxim. Nor could his wealth come anywhere close. Money was important to her, but more importantly she wanted position—and Maxim could give her both. His stubborn determination to remain alienated from his uncle added to her frustration. She had broached the subject many times, confident that he would weaken one day, but this time she sensed there was a change in him. She could feel her position in his life slipping away and she didn't like it. She recalled the day when she had given birth to his daughter and how she had cursed because she had not given Maxim a son. If she had, her power over him would have been considerably greater.

'And I suppose you're going to accuse me of being an unfit mother after listening to Caroline's spiteful outpourings.'

'You're an unnatural mother. A cat would be a better mother than you. Whatever differences there are between us, Alice, I will not permit you to destroy Lucy's happiness. Good Lord, do you think I'm going to stand by and watch her being influenced by you—to grow up and associate with the kind of riff-raff a decent woman would not be seen dead with? I'll do whatever it takes to secure her future. I want the best for her, which is why I think she will be better off living at Rotherfield with me.'

Alice clenched her fists by her sides and glared at Maxim hard. 'No. Never. Lucy is my daughter. She stays here with me.'

Maxim looked at her, his stance menacing. 'Spare me your concern, Alice. You've no love for Lucy. Ever since she was born you've scarce looked at the child. You've resented her since birth because she wasn't the son you desired—which would have made your hold over me even greater. Nevertheless, I have a right to see my daughter and I would like her to come to Kent for a few days. I hope you have no objections to that?'

'Lucy!' she sneered. 'That girl is all you care about. If you want to play nursemaid then go ahead. I'll send her down to Rotherfield with the woman I employ to look after her.'

'Thank you. And now may I see her? After all, she is the reason why I came.'

At three years old Lucy was everything Maxim could have wished for in his daughter. He always treasured the time he spent with her. She was his child, his blood was in her veins, and she had her being because of him. She was an intelligent, raven-haired little bundle of high spirits, whose blue eyes sparkled with trust and light—at least they had, before he'd left England. Now, as he entered the nursery and saw her in a green linen and lace gown and starched cap perched on her glossy curls, playing quietly by herself with some wooden bricks, the heartbreaking void in her wide eyes wrenched his heart.

He coolly acknowledged the nursemaid, who was sewing at a table close to the window. She rose when he entered and bobbed a little curtsey. 'It's all right, Miss Sharp. Attend to your duties. I'm here to see Lucy. Lucy?'

On hearing his voice Lucy's head jerked up, her eyes seeking his. His own glistening with emotion, after placing a long beribboned box on the table in the centre of the room he immediately swept the little girl up into his arms.

'Papa!' she gasped, as she was caught up in an emotion-ridden embrace.

'Hello, princess,' he murmured, his lips pressed against her soft cheek. 'I hoped you'd be downstairs to welcome me.'

'Mama doesn't like it when I go downstairs,' she said quietly. 'I have to learn to be good and not to make noise.'

Anger flowed hot through Maxim's veins, which he contained with effort.

'Have you come to take me home?'

'Not yet, princess. Not today. Papa has things to do. But in a day or so you're coming to my house in Kent to stay for a while. Would you like that?'

'Ooh, yes. Will Mama come too?'

'No. Just you and Miss Sharp. I want you all to myself. Now, give me a kiss, and, if it's a really nice kiss, maybe I'll find a present for you.'

Lucy immediately obliged. Flinging her arms about his neck, she kissed his cheek resoundingly.

'Let's see what we have here,' said Maxim, sitting at the table and cradling her on his knee. 'I've brought you a very special present all the way from Venice.'

'Venice? Is that a long way away?'

'Very,' he laughed. 'It's a beautiful town in Italy, full of enchanting palaces and built in the water. One day I'll take you there and show you.' Holding her lovingly, he helped her little fingers untie the ribbon and pull the lid away.

'Oh, Papa,' she gasped, her eyes big and round with delight when she saw the exquisite china doll lying on a bed of white satin. It had glossy blond curls and was dressed in a gown of silver and white lace, and came complete with petticoats and more gowns, and all the paraphernalia necessary to complete the wardrobe of a lady of quality. 'She's beautiful.'

'I think so too. What will you call her?'

This was an important decision for Lucy to make. She thought hard for a moment, and then said decisively, 'Angel—because that's what she looks like.'

'I think Angel is a very nice name, Lucy,' Maxim agreed, clasping her in a hug.

Maxim's return journey to Rotherfield Hall was spent in indecision, but by the time the carriage passed through the tall iron gates, he knew he would not, could not, form any kind of union with Alice. A vision of Lavinia's glowing eyes and entrancing smile drifted into his mind—his wife in the eyes of man and God. He knew now that he was not prepared to let her go and determined to use every method of persuasion to make her stay. He smiled, already looking forward to it.

Chapter Eight

At Thornhill Lavinia wrote a lengthy, tactful letter to her brother at Welbourne House, explaining all about her decision not to marry Robert, and—making no mention of Julia—that their parting had been mutual. When she went on to tell Edgar about her marriage to Maxim, she was too embarrassed to write that her husband intended ending their union as soon as possible, so she left it out. Knowing Edgar, despite his youth he would be outraged on finding his sister being treated so abominably, and would appear at Thornhill and demand to know the reason why.

Lavinia settled down and enjoyed the life on the farm. She loved the close companionship of the other women, and found the children scampering about all over the place on their sturdy little legs adorable. She would play their simple games and, when one or another of them plopped themselves into her lap when they were worn out, read them stories, of which she had a multitude. Wide-eyed they would listen, enraptured. Their happy, smiling faces and spontaneous laughter often made her want to cry. Had she ever looked like that? she wondered poignantly. She didn't think so.

The way of life at Thornhill was delightful, and she knew

that when the time came for her to leave it would tear her apart. But she couldn't stay. She would have to face it eventually. But never had she felt so close to so many people—to a family; it made her realise how much she had missed as a child, and why Maxim, aware that her childhood had been starved of affection, had brought her here.

Lavinia had been at the farm for four weeks when she wandered into one of the small hay barns to look at the litter of six puppies Bess, the black and white collie dog, had given birth to three weeks before. Having found their legs, the puppies were tumbling about all over the place. Sitting contentedly in the hay she watched them, delighting in their antics. Counting only five, she frowned and began looking around for the one that was missing, having gone further afield to explore.

Hearing a soft mewling coming from beneath the hay she scraped it away from the wall. Seeing a hole in the stonework she knew immediately that the puppy had somehow found its way through and couldn't get out. With Bess looking on with a good deal of interest as she kept sniffing and whining at the small opening in at attempt to entice the puppy out herself, she drew the dog aside and put her hand inside, tentatively feeling around. Her fingers came into contact with all manner of debris, but she was unable to locate the small furry bundle.

Lying on her stomach to enable her hand to reach further into the hole, she breathed a sigh of relief when she felt it, but the little monster didn't seem to want to be caught and wriggled itself free. In exasperation she pulled her arm out, considering asking one of the men for assistance. Raising her head, a sudden gasp escaped her lips when she saw Maxim standing in the doorway silhouetted against the light behind him. With his arms folded over his chest and his shoulder propped casually against the door jamb, he was watching her with a lazy smile.

The anger caused by his visit to Alice was gone, gently alleviated by his journey to Thornhill and, to a greater extent, by his desire to see Lavinia, and the amusement he felt as he watched her lying on her belly in the hay trying to wrestle the puppy out of the hole in the wall. His lips quirked in a half-smile as he watched her trying to get hold of it, speaking softly as she tried to coax it out.

At first he had been sorely tempted to go and help her, but it would have deprived him of the pleasure of watching her from his vantage point by the door. Until that moment he had never thought so much pleasure could be derived in simply watching a woman who was oblivious to being watched.

'Maxim!' she gasped, aware of how she must look to him. She had been so engrossed in what she was doing that she hadn't heard him come in.

Maxim's gaze was long and sure, and Lavinia found herself unable to move as she feasted her eyes on his handsome face, thinking how casual he looked dressed in a loose white shirt tucked into cream-coloured breeches that hugged his narrow hips, and disappeared into brown leather riding boots. For the past month he had occupied all her waking moments and she had longed for the time when he would come to Thornhill, having hoped he would have done so before now.

Swallowing uneasily, she was disturbed by his sudden presence and the scorching heat of his perusal in the quiet stable smelling of warm hay. He was lithe, powerful of hard sinew and rippling muscle, his shining black hair falling in an unruly casual sweep across his forehead. The atmosphere was sultry, and tiny insects and dust spiralled in the thin shaft of light shining in through the small window festooned with cobwebs.

'Ursula told me I might find you here,' he murmured, moving towards her. He felt a sharp stab of discomfort as he admired the way she looked in the shimmering light lying in the hay. Her body spoke invitation with every graceful movement, and he allowed his eyes to wander in a drowsy inspection, savouring every facet of her beauty, unable to drag his gaze from the vision of her loveliness so temptingly displayed. Dressed in a simple pale blue gown, her hair spread loose about her shoulders with bits of hay sticking to the luxuriant golden tresses, he realised with a startling awareness how much he had missed her these past four weeks—and how much he wanted her.

'I—I didn't hear you come in,' Lavinia said, her face flushed from her exertions and her embarrassment at him finding her lying in such complete disarray. She was quite put out that he had been silently watching her and had made no effort to alert her to his presence. 'You should have made your presence known to me.'

'What! And deprive myself of the pleasure of watching you?' he murmured.

Reddening profusely beneath his deepening grin, Lavinia averted her gaze, considering it best to ignore his comment. 'One of the puppies has disappeared into this hole. I can feel it but it stubbornly refuses to come out.'

'Here, let me have a go.'

Sitting beside her in the hay and half-lying, he thrust his arm inside the hole, his expression one of studied concentration while he groped around. Suddenly he smiled and withdrew his arm, a wriggling pup covered in dust in his hand. After giving it a brief rub down and making quite sure it was unharmed, Maxim returned it to the others in the warm nest Bess had made for them in the hay, where she proceeded to lick it vigorously.

Kneeling and peering into the nest, her cheeks adorably pink, Lavinia reached out and gently stroked the velvety coats of the puppies huddling round their mother.

'Are you enjoying your time at Thornhill?' Maxim asked.

Lavinia turned her head and looked at him, tucking her hair behind her ear in a casual gesture that made Maxim's pulses leap. 'Yes—very much,' she answered, again focusing her attention on the pups, whilst remaining acutely aware of her husband's continued gaze where he sat close beside her in the hay.

'I thought you would,' he murmured.

After a moment Lavinia glanced up at him and caught him watching her. 'Maxim.'

'Yes.'

'Why are you staring at me?'

'Because I can't help it.' Lavinia smiled then, the first genuine, unrestrained smile she'd given him since entering the barn, and it had a radiance that made his heart quicken. 'And because you have a beautiful smile,' he said quietly, gently tracing the curve of her cheek with a stalk of hay. Driven to the brink of distraction, every nerve in his body was aware of her sensuality.

'Have you come to tell me we are to go to London to visit my father's lawyer, concerning my legacy?'

'If that is what you want—but when you hear what I have to say, you might agree with me that it is no longer necessary.'

'Oh! It all sounds very mysterious. What are you saying?' she asked curiously.

Maxim grinned, a wicked glint in his eyes. 'All in good time,' he murmured, raising his hand to touch her tumbled hair. He spoke softly, but there was something in his eyes, a softness, a glowing, that made Lavinia's heart beat wildly. Glancing at him from beneath her long, curling, sooty lashes, her smile stayed on him, and he basked in its warmth. 'What are you thinking?'

Lavinia sighed, hugging her knees and looking at him softly. 'I was thinking that life is so very strange. Everything can be so straightforward every day and all the people you know can be so predictable—and then, in the time it takes to blink an eye, everything can change.'

'You mean like tumbling into the Venetian lagoon,' he teased gently.

'Yes. Do you regret being on board the ship that day when I was thrown from the boat?' she asked him.

The serious look in her eyes, which were soft and limpid like two dark blue pansies, was Maxim's undoing. They were pulling him inexorably into their depths, and he wanted nothing more than to wrap himself in her sweetness. From the moment he had first laid eyes on her, all the days of self-denial, of wanting her, that he had lived through in frustration, had tested his restraint far beyond any limit. Surrendering to the call of his blood, he moved with unconscious thought and answered her question with his mouth, pulling her down into the hay and sliding his fingers into her wealth of hair.

'Maxim—please don't,' Lavinia begged, making a feeble attempt to push him away. 'No one's ever—'

'Hush, my love,' he breathed, his lips against her mouth, his eyes dark and sombre with passion. 'I know—I know,' and he placed his lips on hers, unable to tear himself away.

At that moment Maxim didn't care about their agreement or the consequences. His only desire was to hold her, to kiss her, to make her his wife in the true sense and to hell with the consequences, and the way she was responding, with such tender sighs, pressing herself closer, kissing him with a confidence and total lack of shyness that would have astounded her had she stopped to think, he knew she would take no persuading to forget their agreement either.

Lavinia moaned with pleasure when Maxim sucked the sweet breath from her mouth, telling himself to go slowly, to be content with whatever she was willing to permit, but desire so primitive and potent poured through him when he felt the length of her body moulded to the hardened contours of his own that he found it virtually impossible. Slowly her hand travelled upwards, over his shoulder to the nape of his neck, her slender fingers slipping through his hair. Maxim's mouth slid in a line from her lips to the soft flesh of her throat, venturing further to more tantalising ground.

With her head thrown back and the hay rustling softly beneath them, Lavinia gasped as his kisses progressed with a feathery lightness, but she was unprepared for the salvo he was about deliver to her senses when his hand slipped inside her bodice and drew her breast out, his mouth covering her nipple and beginning to explore with a feverish hunger. His bold tongue tormented and teased, and he was delighted when he felt the soft pink bud harden.

With a silent moan Lavinia was shocked at the things he was doing to her, but she was powerless to stop him. Her skin began to glow and tingle as his lips continued their sweet torture. They were moist, warm and gentle, kissing her brow, her cheeks, her lips, exploring boldly, and she felt her nipples begin to throb and swell and long threads of warmth begin to radiate from them. New sensations and heat went staggering through her as Maxim continued his assault, and it was all done with an intensity and absorption that had her trembling.

The fire that had been building inside her exploded into

flames. Beneath his caress her body, her breasts, were beginning to throb with a sweet pulsating ache as she continued to permit, to welcome and enjoy, the invasion of his
tongue as it flicked over her exposed flesh, and when his
mouth found her mouth once more, she parted her lips to
receive his kiss. What he was doing to her was unlike anything she had ever known. It was like floating on a cloud
of dangerous and terrifying sensuality, where she had no
control over anything.

A desperate need became a torment inside Maxim, and
he knew he had to stop now before he went too far. Deeply
touched by the exquisite sweetness of her surrender, he
dragged his lips off hers, his mouth hovering above hers,
bruised and moist after their kiss. He stared at her dewy
skin, at her eyes turned dark with passion, with a hunger
that almost made the notion of forgetting their agreement
and making love to her there and then in the hay seem too
inviting to resist.

Lavinia looked so very sultry and seductive, lying there
beneath his gaze, breathtakingly alluring, her lips curved in
a sublime smile. Half-lowering his eyelids, his gaze passed
over her with deliberate slowness, devouring every detail
of her, pausing at length on her lips.

'Dear Lord! You are too damned beautiful to be true,'
Maxim whispered, his lips nuzzling her ear, his voice thick
with passion. 'It's torture for me just to look at you. You,
my dear wife, are a brazen wench. I have been seriously
deceived. I thought you as innocent as a new-born lamb. I
knew as soon as I looked at you that you were something
special. Just how special I am now beginning to realise.'

Lavinia's soft perfume mingled with the warm-smelling
hay, sending his senses reeling. Once again his lips found
her throat, and the force of passion building inside him
threatened to crumble the wall of his restraint. Taking her

hand and gently placing his lips on her moist palm, he sighed before looking at her, his eyes smouldering.

'I have missed you.'

'Have you? I'm glad to hear it.'

'You do realise that this wasn't part of our agreement, don't you?'

'Yes,' she breathed, her huge dark-lashed eyes lustrous and warm.

Lavinia's skin had blushed to the colour of a soft pink rose—a flower well worth cultivating, Maxim thought as a leisurely smile lifted the corner of his mouth. 'I find seducing you extremely pleasurable. Despite our agreement, my dear wife, I find I cannot treat you with the impartiality I should.'

'Do you mean you regret our arrangement?'

'No. I will say that I have decided to take our marriage a stage further—that I have a far better arrangement in mind,' he said, his mouth returning to savour her lips. After an eternity he raised his head on a sigh. 'No matter what I said when I agreed to our marriage, my sweet, it does not change the fact that I want you.'

Much bemused, Lavinia looked at him, welcoming this change in him, but surprised and unable to understand it.

Maxim noticed her puzzlement and again placed his lips in the warm, soft hollow of her throat where a pulse throbbed just beneath her flesh. His hollow laugh held a trace of mockery. 'You see, I have become quite entangled in my desire for you, Lavinia. You have captured my attention like no other woman has in a long time.'

Lavinia leaned on her elbow, looking down at him. 'I am surprised.'

'Oh?'

Her eyes twinkled mischievously. 'I would not have taken you for a love-smitten swain.'

'Neither would I,' he chuckled, pulling her back down into the hay.

'Maxim,' she gasped. Sensing he was about to become carried away again she placed her hand on his shoulder and forced him back a little, despite his resistance. She looked at him in desperate appeal for him to stop kissing her so that she could make sense of all this. 'I don't understand what you are saying—what it means.'

He sighed. 'Are you so casual about the way you look—the way you are—that you are not aware of the effect it has on me? I am no saint, Lavinia. The very sight of you, the feel of you in my arms, knowing you are my wife, wrenches at my insides, twisting them so painfully that my whole body aches for release. My passion for you is hard-driven. I crave to have you as my wife—in my bed.'

Gnawing on her bottom lip, she gazed up at him. 'Are you telling me that you no longer want to end our marriage?'

'Do you?' he murmured, the warm light of desire in his eyes as he lowered his head, his kisses playing tantalisingly upon her lips.

'Please don't be evasive, Maxim.'

Lavinia sighed when he continued to kiss her. He was being quite impossible.

Hearing the plea in her voice, Maxim raised his head and smiled down at her. 'All right. I will tell you that lying here with you in my arms, feeling how willingly you respond to my attentions, makes me unwilling to release you. I know I am bound by our agreement made at the beginning, but it will be hard for me to break the vows we made to each other and before God.'

'I know,' Lavinia whispered. Having been brought up in the church, this troubled her also. She had been uneasy about the whole affair from the start.

'We gave our sacred vows to each other in church—that we would remain man and wife until death do us part. Even though our marriage has not been consummated—and we did not intend for it to be—are we not bound by our vows? I think those vows, made before God, supersede any agreement we made.'

Looking at him, Lavinia was bewildered by this sudden change in their situation. However, she welcomed it whole-heartedly. Warmth began to seep along her veins as she began to realise what it would mean to her.

Maxim cocked an eyebrow. 'Do you want to remain married to me, Lavinia? Answer me truthfully.'

Meeting his engulfing blue gaze, she looked at him steadily, loving him. He hadn't made any undying declarations of love, but he had told her that he wanted to take their marriage a step further, that he no longer wanted an annulment, when they would both be free to continue with their lives separately. The years ahead had suddenly taken on a rosier hue.

'Yes. I think you know I do,' she answered, feeling that she had given him the answer he wanted.

'You're sure?'

'Yes. And are you sure?'

'I knew it the first time I held you in my arms. You have belonged to me since I pulled you out of the Venetian lagoon. You belonged to me then—my body knew it even if my eyes didn't see it. I want you and need you. I don't want to lose you, Lavinia. I cannot, will not, let you go. I want what every man wants from his wife—for her to give him comfort and ease throughout the days—and nights—of their lives together.' His eyes twinkled with a hint of humour. 'Oh—and not forgetting children. Do you like children, Lavinia?'

'I had no experience with them until I came to Thornhill—but now I do. Your cousins' children are adorable. And—I think they like me.'

'According to Ursula, they think you're an angel.'

'You have been discussing me with Ursula?'

Maxim drew away from her and sat up, releasing a long breath. 'Yes. I was interested to know how you are settling down at Thornhill. It is important to me that you enjoy your time here—especially if you are to remain in Rotherfield as my wife.'

Lavinia sighed, savouring the word. 'Wife!' she murmured. 'I don't feel like your wife.'

'You will, my love.' A smile played on his lips, curving gently. 'Very soon.'

'You certainly haven't treated me like your wife.'

'And you know why. But everything will be different now. It's time to forget the past. It's time for you to begin living—with me.'

'So—my lord and master is to take me to his home?'

'Yes. But not now. For the moment you must remain at Thornhill.'

Feeling a sharp pang of disappointment, Lavinia sat up. 'Doesn't it mean we can give up the charade and tell the world that we are man and wife?'

Maxim frowned, the expression on his face suddenly guarded. 'No. We can't. Not yet. I ask you to be patient a little longer.'

'You—you don't regret what has just happened, do you, Maxim,' Lavinia asked tentatively. 'What we have decided?'

'Regret? No. It's just that it is worrying when I know it can lead to serious consequences for those involved.'

Lavinia was puzzled. 'Those? Who?'

There was a torturous pause. Maxim was faced with the inescapable fact that when Alice learned of his marriage to

Lavinia, her rage would be savage. He was afraid of the lengths she might go to exact her revenge, and strongly feared it would send her flying into the arms of her French comte. Her actions would be vicious in intent, monstrous in effect. But she would have to know. He would tell her himself at the first opportunity.

Lavinia was beginning to realise just how little she knew about this man she had married. She felt a stirring of resentment. 'Why, Maxim—does the idea of telling everyone I'm your wife not appeal to you?'

'It appeals to me very much. I'd like nothing better— but I can't. Not yet. Be patient, Lavinia. Be satisfied for now when I tell you that if the news that I have a wife is spilled too soon, it might prove disastrous to someone who is very dear to me.'

The sombre, bitter note in his voice penetrated Lavinia's mind, but she did not pursue the matter. No doubt as he drew her into his world these secrets would be revealed, as and when necessary, but until that time came she must be content.

Maxim peered into the nest. The six puppies were contentedly suckling Bess's teats. Smiling crookedly he looked round at Lavinia, his eyes warm and tender, his gravity of a moment before replaced by a gentle teasing. 'How does six appeal to you?'

'Six? Six what?'

'Children. See how proud and content Bess is with her litter.'

Lavinia flushed. 'And so will I be—just as long as it's one at a time.'

'On one condition,' he said.

'Oh?'

'That they all look just like you.'

'Willingly.' She smiled as he caught her up into his arms, causing her whole world to tilt once more.

When he was able to pull himself away from her Maxim stood up, casually brushing the hay from his breeches. Reaching down, he took Lavinia's hand and pulled her to her feet, yielding to the temptation again and wrapping her in his arms. His face was hard with passion, his eyes smouldering as once again his warm lips covered hers. Lavinia shivered with pleasure, her lips moving against his, unwittingly increasing his hunger. When he finally pulled his mouth from hers he drew a long, tortured breath, his gaze going past Lavinia to the door.

'We're going to have to stop,' he murmured. 'We have an audience.'

Slowly Lavinia's swirling senses began to return to the present. Turning and following the direction of Maxim's gaze, she saw the gaping faces of eight-year-old David and his five-year-old sister Mary, Margaret and Ben's children, standing in the doorway. Their eyes were as wide as saucers as they stared in wondrous awe at what they were doing, and before either Maxim or Lavinia could utter a word, they had turned and scampered off back to the house.

A lazy, seductive grin spread across Maxim's face. 'I think our secret is out.' Taking Lavinia's hand he drew her towards the door. 'Come along. We'd better follow them. I know Aunt Ursula will be delighted.'

Ursula was. Smiling knowingly, she looking from one to the other with approval as she smoothed down her pristine white apron.

Maxim laughed lightly. 'I can see David got here before us.'

'He did. And it's about time too,' she scolded gently. 'But I don't need a crystal ball to tell me what he saw happened. I suppose it's safe to assume the two of you have decided not to go your separate ways after all?'

'It looks like it,' Maxim replied, his arm sliding possessively around Lavinia's waist to draw her closer to his side. 'But I want it to go no further than the family for the time being. You understand that, don't you, Aunt?'

She nodded. Understanding why. 'You look happier than I've seen you, Lavinia,' she said softly, observing her pink cheeks and shining eyes.

'I confess I can't remember being so happy. Maxim has taken me by surprise,' she said, gazing up at him adoringly.

Ursula laughed. 'When Sir Galahad straps on his shining armour these things do happen. I wondered how long it would take you to realise you make an ideal couple.'

'You knew?' said Maxim.

'Women have a sixth sense about these things,' Ursula said, her eyes twinkling as she left them to go back to her work in the kitchen. 'Will you be staying for supper, Maxim?' she asked over her shoulder as she was leaving the room.

Maxim smiled slowly, his eyes settling on his wife. 'I will, Aunt—and perhaps breakfast.'

Chapter Nine

Later, when Maxim entered Lavinia's room, sensing her apprehension, he closed the door and slowly advanced towards her, his eyes never leaving hers. She waited passively, warily, for him to come to her, her heart pounding in her chest and feeling a strange fluttering in her stomach.

Looking down into her upturned face Maxim's fascinated gaze moved over her. Her shining wealth of golden hair tumbled about her shoulders, framing a face of heartbreaking beauty. Involuntarily, his gaze dropped to her mouth. It was a tantalising mouth, inviting. Seized by a passionate longing to protect, to treat with reverence his lovely young wife, he placed his hands on her shoulders, surprised when he felt the stiffness in her body and how it trembled beneath his touch.

'You're trembling,' he said softly.

'Yes, I know,' she admitted, her voice quivering nervously, his observation bringing colour to her cheeks. His touch was so light, and yet she could feel the strength in his hands. 'For the life of me I cannot think why.'

Maxim sighed and leisurely drew her into his arms. 'Neither can I,' he murmured, gazing down into her upturned face, the feel of her turning his blood to fire. 'Ever since we met I've been fighting against my need for you. You are so beautiful, Lavinia.'

Mesmerised by the silky smoothness of his voice, so filled with sensual promise, Lavinia melted against him. The warmth of his touch stole her breath, igniting a flame within her blood, and the intensity of his blue gaze held her transfixed. Its potency was intoxicating. Her senses became scattered, and she willingly let him wrap her in a crushing embrace and place his mouth over hers.

His kiss was just as exciting and devastating as ever, and she parted her lips to receive it. It was both fierce and tender, and unlike anything she had previously experienced. Curling his arm round her waist, his hand caressed her back, moulding her hips close. Lavinia was caught up in the stirring sensation his kiss always evoked, her arms sliding up his broad chest and fastening themselves round his neck.

Raising his head Maxim deftly removed her robe to reveal her white lawn nightgown. Instinct and the apprehension he saw in her liquid eyes made him hesitate about removing that as well. Lavinia didn't object when he lifted her up and carried her to the bed, but when he placed her on the sheets and stretched out alongside her, his long fingers beginning to pull her nightgown up over her knees, she jerked free.

'Maxim, please don't,' she begged.

Her obvious unease and confusion restored Maxim's sanity and made him relax his hold. Reaching to draw her back into his arms, she recoiled from his touch. He questioned her hesitation with a frown.

'Lavinia? What's the matter? It's not a human sacrifice I'm asking you to make.'

His words brought a flush to her cheeks and she averted her eyes. 'I—I know.'

Maxim reached out and took her chin, carefully turning her face around to look at him. 'Look at me.' Scarlet-faced, she raised her eyes. 'What is it? What do you think happens between a husband and wife when they go to bed together? Tell me.'

She looked at him, pain and bewilderment mirrored in her eyes. 'Forgive me, Maxim. I—I don't know what to do,' she confessed wretchedly. 'Or what you expect of me.'

At last Maxim knew what was wrong, the reason for her apprehension. He smiled, while mentally cursing her mother and her governess for not having told her what took place in a marriage bed. 'So that's it. For a start, Lavinia, I don't expect you to do anything. Didn't anyone ever tell you what happens between a husband and wife in bed?'

'No. You must think me very ignorant and stupid.'

'I don't. You are wonderful and sweet,' he said, looking across to where she lay, as if poised for flight. He sighed. 'Lavinia, come here and lay beside me. '

Slowly she did as she was told, lying in the crook of his arm. 'What are you going to do?'

'I'll show you.'

'Will it hurt?'

'Yes, but only the first time,' he murmured, planting a kiss on the top of her head. 'But believe me when I tell you that you are on the threshold of a great discovery. This delightful body of yours, my love, has some incredible surprises in store for you. I will only go as far as you want me to. You can tell me to stop any time you like,' he murmured leaning down and kissing her cheek, determined, despite his promise, that he would not stop until he had achieved what he intended. Nothing short of an earthquake was going to stop him making love to her now he'd started.

The soft seductiveness in his eyes and the velvety softness of his voice stilled Lavinia's panic and she tried to relax. Maxim bent his head and placed his mouth on hers, kissing her long and deep, having no intention of pulling back until he drew a response from her, even if he expired of unassuaged passion in the process. Somehow he was going to have to arouse her without becoming too aroused himself.

Slowly his hand travelled the length of her spine, moulding her hips and pressing her closer. Closing her eyes Lavinia shuddered against him. Fires were ignited inside her and Maxim drew a gasp of pleasure from her when his lips dragged themselves to her throat and down to her breasts straining beneath the thin fabric of her nightgown.

A moment later he rose and quickly removed his clothes. Lavinia gasped, fighting panic and drawing back at his maleness, from the sheer physical power of his body. He smiled at her reaction, stretching out once more alongside her, tenderly drawing her against his taut, tightly muscled body.

'Have you never seen a naked man, Lavinia?'

'No,' she answered.

'What do you think? Is it so bad?'

'No,' she whispered, looking into his eyes.

Maxim laughed softly. Lowering his head he kissed the soft flesh of her breast where her nightgown had parted, caressing the hard, rose pink nipple with his tongue. Slipping his hand down the length of her thigh, he slowly pulled her nightgown up and began to explore the soft, inviting contours of her body, so supple yet so firm. Hearing her gasp at the contact, he raised his head and looked at her. Her eyes fluttered open and he smiled, determined to be gentle. He would make her body sing with rapture before he was done.

But it was no easy matter ignoring the urgent heat and throbbing in his loins. Having no intention of relinquishing the territory he had gained, leaving his hand on her waist he claimed her lips once more, tasting her sweetness. There was a thoroughness to his kiss which ravaged Lavinia's senses—deepening and demanding, until a low moan of pleasure rose from her throat.

To Maxim's immense joy she arched against him, wrapping her arms around his neck and giving herself up to his caress. He gloried in her innocence, proud that no man had touched her like he was doing now, feeling a surge of tenderness for this lovely, unspoiled young woman who was his wife. Slipping her nightgown over her head almost without her noticing, at last the perfection of her body was laid bare for him to see.

Fighting back his rampaging desire, Maxim watched the reaction to his caress pass across her face as her body submitted willingly. His hands became more insistent and he gloried in her perfect beauty, placing a series of kisses over every inch of her exposed flesh, longing to bury himself in her but holding back.

Unconsciously Lavinia gasped in startled resistance when his hands and his lips became more daring and began exploring and caressing further. She hadn't realised how sensitive the small hollow in her throat, the flesh across her stomach and her breasts were until he kissed her, caressed her there. Effortlessly Maxim stopped her hand when, through a haze of desire, she saw her nakedness spread out before him and modestly tried to pull her nightgown over her, which drew a soft chuckle from him.

'It's too late for that, my love,' he whispered, renewing his wicked assault and kissing the taut skin of her stomach.

Lavinia's reaction was immediate and she gasped, the heat radiating from his body drugging her senses. His hands as they stroked her naked flesh were surprisingly gentle and hot against her skin. Maxim raised his head, and what Lavinia saw almost stole her breath away. Even if she intended fighting him, her physical resistance would be useless against his unswerving seduction. He would not release her until the vows they had made before God were securely tied in the physical, tender knot of passion.

In the soft candle glow his powerful body glowed bronze. His face was hard, his eyes dark with passion, and yet there was so much tenderness in their depths that Lavinia's heart ached. A startled moan of intense pleasure escaped her lips when his hot mouth enveloped her nipples as if he meant to devour them. Closing her eyes, she willingly gave herself up to the fierce stabs of pleasure shooting through her, wrapping her arms around him as though she couldn't bear to be parted, until she felt his hand travel down to the golden triangle between her thighs.

Maxim felt her resistance and raised his head. 'Lavinia, please,' he said huskily, his face taut with restraint. 'Trust me. Relax, my darling.'

Drawing a shuddering breath, she nodded, gasping when he continued his sweet torture, amazed by the sensual hunger that swept over her. Her skin felt incredibly sensitive and she felt hot all over, but this time it wasn't embarrassment. It was something else. Through a haze she looked into his face as he hovered above her, mutely inviting him to explore further. His fingers teased and toyed, and she yielded to the primitive, exquisite pleasure. Never had her body felt so many sensations all at once. It became a furnace, her limbs molten, and she clung to him, a pulsing, warm ache aroused deep within her, one that was unfamiliar and frightening, but she could not fight it.

Struggling not to break his control, Maxim could not believe Lavinia's ardour as she moved instinctively against him, and he realised with surprise and delight that his wife was a tantalising creature of intense passion and sensuality.

There was no fear left in Lavinia as she waited and longed for Maxim to take her, to do to her what she had dreaded. She didn't know what she wanted, but she was aching with unfulfilled need. Any resistance now fled as the voluptuous needs of her body soared and heat spread from her breasts to her loins. Her heart leapt and her breathing quickened with unbridled pleasure and combined terror when he covered her body with his own, drawing her hips beneath him.

Through the mist Lavinia saw the hunger, the tension, on Maxim's face, and for the first time she realised his own needs were as great, if not greater, than her own. Kissing her with urgent hunger, skilfully he built a desire in her so intense that she hardly noticed when he drove into her. Her body jerked and she gasped for breath, but the pain was short-lived. The magic didn't die and the pain turned to pleasure.

In the grip of a spiralling excitement Lavinia wrapped her arms around her husband when he seized her mouth in a plundering kiss. She returned it hungrily, expressing her love with all her heart and soul when they became one, straining to come closer, moving in unison. Her body began playing strange tricks on her as she was possessed by a delirium, a madness, which was warm and greater than anything she had ever imagined. It grew and grew, brimming over until she thought she was drowning in a sea of pleasure. Her body responded to Maxim as if she were another person—a wanton—and her senses soared until she thought she could endure no more. It ended in an explosion, and an oblivion of bliss claimed them both.

Utterly spent, Maxim rolled to one side, taking Lavinia with him. She lay with her head on his damp chest, the thick coils of her hair draped over them both. Limbs entwined, they lay together, neither of them moving or speaking until their hearts and breathing had slowed. Prey to a multitude of emotions, Lavinia sighed, aware of a sharp, sweet pleasure. Somewhere inside her a pulse still throbbed. She had not known it could be like this, and now she did Maxim would find her an eager, willing wife.

Maxim drew Lavinia's hair from her face and kissed her flushed cheek, feeling humbled by her beauty and her unselfish ardour. A surge of tenderness swept through him at her sweetness. She stirred in his arms and raised her face to his, her eyes like those of a wide-eyed kitten still dark with passion, her lips soft and vulnerable, her face one of pure tranquillity.

'How do you feel?' he asked, his voice gentle, his gaze so tender that Lavinia's heart contracted.

She sighed with contentment. 'Like your wife, and blissfully content,' she murmured, placing her lips gently on his chest.

'Did I hurt you?'

'I felt no pain, Maxim. Only pleasure.'

'And do you think you are going to enjoy performing your marital duties, my love? Are they as dreadful as you imagined they would be?'

Her lips quirked in a little smile. 'No. It was quite wonderful. Will it always be like that?'

'It will get even better—when I have taught you a thing or two.'

Her eyes widened. 'You mean there is more?'

'Much more,' he laughed, 'and I am convinced you will be an avid pupil. You leave me in no doubt about your inexperience, my love. Despite your wide knowledge of intellectual matters, your education in sexual matters is gravely lacking. Some things are impossible to simulate and the innocence of your body and mind is one of them. I am surprised your mother or your governess didn't instruct you as to what to expect.'

'My mother wouldn't have given it a thought, and I real-ise now that it was beyond my governess's comprehension that what she would consider to be an obscene act was necessary to ensure the continuity of the human race. No wonder I was watched before I went anywhere and every-thing I read was vetted first in case it corrupted my virgin mind.' Resting her chin on her husband's chest she gazed up at him. 'Tell me what I have to learn, Maxim.'

His hand came up to touch her tumbled hair, then he drew a caressing finger down the soft curve of her cheek. 'I shall have to teach you how to please me.'

'You mean I didn't?' she gasped, pretending offence.

He laughed deep in his chest. 'You did, you minx. But there's more. Much more.'

Wondering if he would like to show her, Lavinia moved her body provocatively against his, her lips parting in a heart-stealing smile. Even as she formed the thought Maxim read her mind, and he was acutely aware that his body was stirring once more with alarming intensity. Desire was there in his blue gaze, and something more. It was so profound that it almost stole Lavinia's breath.

'Don't you think you should try and get some sleep, my love?' he suggested huskily, secretly hoping she would say no.

She sighed. 'I'm not the least little bit sleepy, Maxim.'

Surrendering to the silent demand in his eyes, with her breasts brushing his naked flesh, Lavinia inched her way up to his mouth, lightly laying her lips on his. 'If I have so much to learn,' she breathed, 'when can I have my first lesson?'

In answer to her question Maxim rolled her on to her back and took control, his senses alive to every inch of her form languorously stretched beneath him. Their passion was all-consuming, bittersweet, ecstatic, ending in a pinnacle of pleasure.

Falling to sleep within the protective circle of her husband's arms, Lavinia had never felt so happy and content. With Maxim by her side she could not fail to continue to be so. She loved him. It was the truth, and she wanted to tell him that she loved him, but something held her back. It was important to her that she was loved equally in return, and Maxim had not told her he loved her. He had told her he wanted her and needed her. But that wasn't the same as love.

And besides, the annulment he had insisted on at the beginning of their marriage, and the casual manner in which he had told her it was no longer necessary, made her uneasy. Whatever it was that had made him enforce such harsh conditions must have been of a serious nature. Why had he changed his mind?

The following day Lavinia existed in a blissful state. Her happiness was full to overflowing. It was late afternoon and she had not seen Maxim since he had left her bed that morning. Sunlight spilled along the path on which she walked, so lost in thought that she didn't realise how far she had wandered from Thornhill. The day was warm and peaceful, and she could hear a stream tumbling along beside the path.

Tall trees cast their shadows across her way, and the leaves in a mosaic of glorious colours formed a canopy above. She sighed, content to be alone, to think of Maxim. Coming to the end of the path she paused, having reached a main thoroughfare. Wondering which way to go, she stood within the shelter of the trees pondering, seeing a carriage approaching. Looking straight ahead, her eyes focused on some tall wrought-iron gates, a huge weeping ash to one side of them. They opened on to a short, private drive which formed a circle in front of a magnificent three-storey house, built of golden yellow stone and enriched by splendid carving.

Unable to tear her eyes away she stared at it in admiration, for it was a house unlike any other she had ever seen. Its sheer size and grandeur told her that its owner was both powerful and wealthy. Lawns like velvet stretched beyond the gates, and she glimpsed a fountain spouting water high into the sky, before falling back to earth in a gentle, shimmering cascade. Flower beds and elaborately carved stone urns were brimming over with flowers, and a lake could be seen to the right of the house, with an island pavilion in the centre.

Drawn out of her reverie by the approaching carriage, curiously her gaze was drawn to its occupants. One of the women had striking features and shining black hair beneath a stylish, emerald green hat which matched her jacket. Two other women occupied the carriage. One she assumed would be the lady's maid, and the other rather elderly looking woman, dressed in plain black and holding a little girl on her knee, Lavinia thought would probably be the child's nursemaid.

Lavinia's presence was almost hidden from view by the thick foliage. She watched as the carriage swung in through the open gates, travelling halfway round the circular drive and halting at the bottom of a low, wide flight of stone steps. At that moment the great double doors of the house were opened by a footman from inside and a man emerged, going quickly down the steps to greet his guests.

Lavinia continued to watch in idle fascination. To her the perfectly groomed man was every inch an elegant, relaxed and poised gentleman, and evidently the owner of this majestic house. His dark blue jacket set off his broad shoulders, and his snowy white neckcloth emphasised his black hair and dark looks.

Suddenly Lavinia felt the pull of those looks, her eyes drawn to them like a magnet, feeling her body freeze when she recognised those chiselled features printed indelibly on her heart. Like a stone statue, unflinching, her eyes unblinking, she watched him open the door of the carriage and assist the woman in emerald green down the steps, feeling a stab of unbearable pain as the woman reached up and kissed his lips, smiling and looking incredibly beautiful.

Lavinia stared at the scene in ringing silence. Watching Maxim, her face lost what little colour it had. Unflinching, she saw him place an arm on the woman's waist, and Lavinia saw her look up at him and smile. Maxim bent his head to hear what she had to say, and what Lavinia took to be an affectionate gesture broke a hole in her emotional barricade.

Maxim moved towards the carriage, reaching inside and taking the child from the nursemaid. Over the distance that separated them, Lavinia saw his handsome face was full of laughter as the little girl flung her arms around his neck. With familiarity and affection Maxim held her in his arms and carried her up the steps. The woman's hand rested on his arm, and the group of people disappeared inside the house and from Lavinia's sight.

How long she stood there staring at the closed doors to that magnificent house she could never remember after that. It was the moment when her bright bubble of happiness had burst. Maxim's words when she had offered to return the mask to him at the ball hit her like a hammer blow—I am not a pauper, he had told her, and the words went on and on echoing through the tunnels of her mind. So, this was his. All of it. What an idiot, what a stupid, blind besotted fool she had been.

What he had done was underhand. He had deceived her. She should have known there was more to him than an amiable gambler. Oh, how dare he? she thought with a rush of unjust, angry pain.

Turning abruptly, she strode back down the path, unseeing. The sun which had shone so brightly had gone out of her day. Furiously she tried to face what she had seen. Before Maxim had come to Thornhill and asked her to be his wife in every sense, she would have had no reason or right to be angry because of their arrangement, but after last night everything was different. Rage, white hot and strong, coursed through her, bringing a suffering so excruciating as to be unsupportable.

How gullible she had been to let herself believe after his passionate kisses and soft words that he really did want her, for she now realised that his words had been hollow, his passion no different from the passion he might feel towards any woman he found himself in such confining intimacy with. Already she could feel the pain of her shattering loss.

Hurrying, stumbling back along the path which she had so recently walked with a happiness she could not conceive, now she saw nothing, heard nothing but the heavy pounding of her heart. Thankfully she managed to enter the house and go to her room without being seen, closing the door behind her and shutting her eyes tight, as though by shutting them she would shut out the reality of what she had just seen. But when she opened them again the sight was still there.

Who was the child she had seen—and the woman, beautiful, confident? Were they lovers? But Maxim had told her there was no one else in his life, and she had believed him.

And that house! That magnificent, beautiful house. Some instinct, perception—whatever—told her that the house was his.

Maxim had deceived her cruelly, but what mattered to Lavinia more than his obvious wealth and opulent lifestyle, which went hand in glove when one owned a house such as she had seen, was the woman and how much she meant to him.

Rage enveloped her and she clenched her hands. Damn him. This was all his fault. This whole sorry mess. If he had stuck to their agreement and kept his hands to himself they could have gone their separate ways. There was nothing to ease the raw pain of the misery she felt. Wanting answers to her questions she went in search of Ursula. Better to face the worst and have it over with.

Ursula was alone in the kitchen, stirring something in a large iron pot on the stove that was giving off an appetising meaty aroma. Looking up, she smiled when Lavinia came in. 'Hello, Lavinia. Back from your walk, I see.'

'Ursula,' Lavinia said, going and standing in front of her, unable to contain herself a moment longer, 'please tell me who owns the big house I saw at the end of the path which takes you away from the village—the one that follows the stream.'

Ursula stood up straight and stared at her. The look on Lavinia's face gave her an uneasy feeling.

'It belongs to Maxim, doesn't it?' Lavinia went on when Ursula didn't answer, her eyes large, her expression calm, whilst inside she was screaming. 'Please tell me. I have to know.'

Ursula nodded, wiping her hands down her apron. 'Yes. The house you saw would be Rotherfield Hall. But come, let's go into the parlour where we are less likely to be interrupted.'

'I knew it,' flared Lavinia when they had closed the parlour door behind them. 'I saw him, Ursula. I saw Maxim. He has guests—a woman, an extremely beautiful woman, and a child. Who are they?' she demanded, preparing herself to grasp the facts as Ursula presented them to her.

Ursula was looking at Lavinia intently, as though to assess the effect of the bombshell she was about to drop on her.

'The child you saw is Maxim's daughter—Lucy.'

Lavinia stared, her hands clenched by her sides, her knuckles white. 'His daughter?' The revelation was excruciating.

'Yes.'

'And—and the woman?'

'Is Alice Winstanley. Lucy's mother.'

Lavinia felt as though she was encased in ice. Every part of her was frozen as she forced her lips to ask the question that sprang to her mind. 'I see. Is she his wife?'

'No, my dear,' Ursula replied, her expression gentle, her voice full of concern. Lavinia's voice was a sound of pain and despair. 'You are his wife. I'm sorry, Lavinia. Maxim didn't intend for you to find out like this. He didn't mean to make you unhappy.'

As straight as a slender slither of steel, Lavinia turned and moved away from Ursula. A terrible, silent stillness descended on the room as she tried to digest the awful truth. At last she knew the reason why Maxim had insisted on an annulment to their marriage. It was to enable him to marry the mother of his child. Why he hadn't married Alice Winstanley in the first place she didn't know and had no wish to. She only knew that by walking in the direction of Rotherfield Hall she had blundered irretrievably into an appalling revelation

'How does he come to own such a magnificent house,

Ursula?' Lavinia asked, her voice strained, reluctant to ask about Maxim's relationship with the woman just then. It was much too painful. 'Did it belong to his father?'

'Goodness, no. His father owned a small sailing vessel and made his money carrying coal from Newcastle to London.'

Lavinia's lips curved in a wry smile. 'The house I saw today did not come from plying coal from Newcastle to London, Ursula.'

'No, you are right. Maxim bought Rotherfield Hall several years ago.'

'But—how? Is it true that he's the nephew of the Earl of Brinkcliff?'

'Yes, he is, but he made his money himself. Maxim and the Earl are estranged. His family is an old and noble one and Maxim is untitled by choice. It's a long and bitter tale, Lavinia—going back to before Maxim was born.'

'Will the title pass to the next in line?'

'There is no one else.'

'Why does Maxim remain estranged from his uncle?'

'Because he has been blessed with the same proud arrogance and indomitable will that has marked all the Purnell men before him. He cannot forgive his grandfather and the present Earl for turning their backs on his father and disinheriting him, because he dared to defy his own father and marry the woman he loved—a woman—my sister— the old Earl did not approve of. Oh, she was the gentlest of women, warm-hearted and so very lovely, which were the things that drew Maxim's father to her in the first place. But because she lacked the breeding required of the next Countess of Brinkcliff, she was considered to be most unsuitable.'

'Did Maxim's father ever regret turning his back on his inheritance?'

Ursula smiled. 'No—not for one minute. He was extremely happy married to my sister—making enough money for them to live on. From an early age it was clear to everyone that Maxim had been gifted with a superior intelligence. He learned fast and prospered. Through hard work and determination he owns ships that fly his flag, land both here and in America, where coal and gold are mined. He has amassed the kind of fortune some people can only dream of.'

Lavinia stared at her incredulously, finding the extent of Maxim's wealth impossible to take in.

'My own sons are more casual about life, content with what they have and unhurried about life in general,' Ursula went on, 'whereas Maxim has always been the guiding force. He has a brilliant mind for business and invests his money wisely—although this trouble brewing in France is causing him a good deal of worry. Having capital invested in businesses over there, shipping and such like, he went to see for himself the extent of the trouble.'

Lavinia continued to stare at her in dazed disbelief. Completely unaware of any of this, or the reasons which had taken her husband to Europe—to Venice, where they had met—she suddenly felt very stupid, dismayed and disappointed that he hadn't told her.

'I know Maxim can be a mite overbearing and intimidating at times,' Ursula went on in an attempt to soften her nephew's character, 'but it is not intentional. He works hard and demands too much of himself—and he expects others to have the same drive and determination.'

'But I had no idea he was so rich.'

Finding this difficult to believe, Ursula stared at her. 'He gave you no indication?'

'No, he didn't. It's all so ridiculous, don't you think?' she said with a bitter laugh. 'I thought he was a gambler—

a professional gambler, who makes his money going from one gaming hall to the next. How stupid and gullible I must have been.'

At any other time Ursula would have seen the funny side to this—Maxim, throwing his money away at the tables—but she could see how much Lavinia was hurting inside, knowing she was putting off the moment when she would ask her about Alice and Lucy.

'Believe me, my dear, Maxim thinks too much of his money to throw it away at the tables. Oh, I'm not saying he isn't averse to a game of cards or dice now and then, or that he doesn't enjoy it when he does, but he plays purely for enjoyment and is sensible enough to know when to stop. I suppose you could call him a gambler of sorts—thriving the way he does on taking risks on investments, driven by the thrill of the wager.'

Momentarily lost in thought, Lavinia recalled the time in Venice when Maxim had lost such a considerable sum of money at a ridotto to be noticed and gossiped about. Even Robert, who was averse to gambling in any form, had heard about it. But Lavinia felt an unexpected, melting warmth in her heart when she remembered how Maxim had explained that he didn't usually lose such large amounts of money, and how he had told her that it was the night after his meeting with her and he had been unable to concentrate on the game—implying that he'd been thinking of her.

Suddenly Lavinia brought herself up sharp, determined not to let thoughts such as these weaken her. Immediately she brought the conversation back to her husband's relationship with Alice and his daughter.

'What is Maxim's relationship with his daughter, Ursula? Is it a close one?'

'It is. Maxim worships her—and of course Lucy adores

him. It's unfortunate for them both that circumstances keep
them apart.'

'Circumstances? What circumstances, Ursula? Why
didn't he marry Lucy's mother? Was Alice married to
someone else?'

'No. Nothing like that. If you knew more about the situation, then maybe you would understand.'

'Will you tell me?' Lavinia asked.

'I'm sorry—I can't. Maxim has to be the one to tell you.
He will explain.'

Lavinia was conscious of a sudden surge of despair. In
the depths of her misery she recalled her own childhood,
of the child she had been who had desperately reached out
to be touched and loved by her own father. Unmoved by
her longing for affection he had driven her back with a firm
hand, and looked at her with eyes which had been unseeing.
As she grew older Maxim's daughter would experience
those same heartbreaking moments if she was denied the
presence and love of her father, and it was unbearable to
think that, because of her, it might happen.

A heavy guilt settled upon Lavinia. Maxim had been
prevented from marrying Alice by marrying her instead. He
should have told her. What he had done was unforgivable.
The burden he had placed on her was too hard to bear, and
it would be no easy matter pushing him into the arms of
another woman.

She took a long, quivering breath. 'If Alice is the mother
of his child then he has a duty to marry her. Surely his
daughter's future happiness and security is worth that. If he
had not met me in Venice he would have returned to England and married Alice, wouldn't he, Ursula?' she said
quietly.

Ursula shook her head. 'I believe so,' she answered truthfully. 'But like everyone else I do not know how Maxim's mind works. He is an extremely complex person.'

'Maxim should never have married me,' Lavinia said wretchedly. 'He should have told me all of this.'

'Would it have made any difference?'

'Oh, yes, Ursula, it would,' she cried, quite distraught. 'Were it not for me he would have married Alice. I know he would.'

'Lavinia—you are being too hard on yourself. Believe me, I know Maxim well enough to know that now he has met you, married you, he will never give Alice another chance. He is fiercely proud and accountable to no one. When she told him that she was to bear his child, she hurt and shamed him so much when she refused to marry him unless he adhered to certain conditions. I believe she killed all the feeling he had for her then.

'Before he met you in Venice, if he did think of returning to England and marrying her, it would be for Lucy's sake and for no other reason. If you are in any doubt as to what his feelings are for Alice—just watch his face when you mention her name. He will explain all this to you.'

'I cannot bear to think that everyone here has known about Maxim and Alice all along, that this was behind the knowing looks and secret smiles.'

'No one was being unkind, Lavinia. Maxim asked them not to mention either Alice or Lucy to you until the time was right for him to tell you himself.'

'I feel so stupid. Oh, Ursula, it's all so dreadful.'

'It needn't be.'

Lavinia stared at her. What was she to do? With cynical clarity she knew what she had to do, that she must leave Thornhill and any idea of happiness she cherished with Maxim. She had never realised so acutely as she did now how little she knew about him, and when she thought of what she had just discovered everything inside her recoiled from it with horror.

She could not bear to leave him, but she must. Every time he took her in his arms, kissed her, lay with her at night, she would be unable to put that other woman and her child out of her mind. And she would despise herself for keeping them apart. Her decision became an internal battle, but in the end her conscience overcame her sentiment. She shook her head wearily.

'It's a little late for that.' She softened suddenly, seeing the hurt, pained look in the older woman's eyes. 'I know you mean well, Ursula—and it is only right that you speak up for Maxim, but you must understand how difficult all this is for me. Maxim has a child—to a woman he is not married to. And he should be. It's a situation I cannot accept.'

'I think you might change your mind if you were acquainted with Alice,' said Ursula, sorrow pulling at her heart strings at the thought of Lavinia leaving Maxim.

'Maxim must have some feelings for her—his daughter is evidence of that. And while ever I remain married to him, I am preventing him from doing the honourable thing. Clearly he intended marrying her, otherwise he would not have insisted on an annulment to our marriage when I received my legacy—which I know he told you all about in his letter before we arrived in England. I cannot remain married to him knowing this, Ursula, and I am angry and deeply hurt that he didn't see fit to tell me.'

'But—you do love him?'

'Yes,' she admitted, giving her a sad little smile, feeling a hard lump at the back of her throat. 'I never thought it possible to love another human being so much. I love him so much it hurts. But I will not be lied to or deceived.

Maxim married me out of sympathy and pity—nothing more.'

'Lavinia, that is not so!' Ursula exclaimed. 'He married you with the best intentions. He cared enough to marry you at the risk of losing his child.'

'Then he should not have done it,' Lavinia cried wretchedly, biting her lip to hold back her tears, engulfed with anger, humiliation and her own gullibility. 'I didn't ask him to. It is an emotional burden too difficult for me to bear. Had I known he had a child whose mother hoped to marry him, I would never have agreed to become his wife. He should have been honest with me.'

'What will you do?'

'I'm going away—to London,' she said decisively. 'I have friends there—Daisy Lambert and her mother. You remember—they were the people I was in Venice with when I met Maxim.'

'And Maxim?'

Lavinia's expression was suddenly hard and decisive, her tone final. 'He will know where I am when he files the papers for a divorce.'

'Then take care, Lavinia. When Maxim discovers that you intend to leave Thornhill, his anger will be terrible. He's not used to encountering opposition from anyone.'

'Then it's time he was.' Lavinia's lips parted in a tremulous smile and her expression softened. 'Don't worry about me, Ursula. I'll be fine, really. I'll be all right,' she said with more determination than accuracy.

Chapter Ten

Choked by a terrible miasma of loneliness and depriva-
tion—feelings she recognised, having grown up with
them—Lavinia shut herself in her room, hoping that no one
would intrude. Yesterday she had been buoyed up with ex-
pectancy, but now, in the light of all this, her future, as
were her prospects, was bleak. With her mind on what Ursula had told her and her journey to London the following
morning, she became unnaturally calm, as calm as a block
of ice that has no warmth.

After undressing for the night and wrapping a robe round
her naked form—discarding with contempt the frilly nightdress she had worn the previous night—mechanically she
began to pack her clothes neatly in her trunk. It was her
intention to take one bag with her when she left containing
a few necessary items of clothing. She would make ar-
rangements to have her trunk collected later. When she
heard a knock on her bedroom door she went and opened
it, thinking it might be Ursula or Margaret, and was totally
unprepared to find Maxim standing there. His face was a
hard, chiselled mask, his brows drawn together in an ominous frown as he studied her pale face and strained features
before he spoke.

'May I come in?'

Lavinia stood aside and allowed him to enter, unable to do anything else. His words were cold, spoken without emotion, but she wasn't fooled. Maxim was in a fury. In silent dread she watched him move slowly, wordlessly into the room. Having removed his jacket and neckcloth he looked casual, and when he fixed his cold eyes on her she could almost feel the effort he was exerting to keep his temper under control. He was angry because she was leaving. Angry and unforgiving. Ursula had told her he had a vile temper, and she had a strong feeling that she was about to witness it for herself.

Trying to remain calm, Lavinia took a deep breath in an attempt to quell the quivering in her limbs and the gladness she felt on seeing him. No matter what lay between them, she could not stop loving him.

Maxim shifted his gaze to the open trunk. 'You are leaving.' It was a statement, not a question.

Lavinia shot him a mutinous, measuring look. 'Yes. What are you doing here, Maxim? Why have you come?'

Having moved into the centre of the room, he turned and looked at her. His face could have been carved from a block of granite, and there was a hard, ominous look in his clear blue eyes. 'You know why. When Ursula sent word to the hall to inform me that you intend leaving for London in the morning, I came to see what you are playing at.'

'Ursula should have left well alone.'

'Why, Lavinia? Why are you leaving—and without a word to me?' His voice was controlled, angry.

Lavinia's mouth was set in a tight, angry line, belying the passion of which it was capable. 'You know why, Maxim.'

'Do I? Tell me.'

'All right, I will,' she replied, tilting her chin with an air of defiance as she tried desperately to be composed, to still the trembling in her limbs as she faced the cold, dispassionate man in front of her. 'Although I am sure Ursula will already have told you.'

'She has. But I would like to hear it from you all the same. You are angry, I can see that.'

'And with good reason. When I was taking a stroll earlier, quite by chance I happened to come across a house—although being so enormous, it would be virtually impossible to miss—don't you agree, Maxim?' she said, her eyes locking on his and her voice laced with sarcasm. 'I had no idea who owned it until I saw a carriage carrying your guests arrive—and you came out of the house to receive them.' She smiled thinly, showing no sign of the hurt she had suffered, was still suffering. 'That was when I realised it was your home. You all looked very cosy to me—and it explains why you don't want me there.'

'You were watching?' he asked, thrusting his hands deep into his pockets and beginning to pace restlessly up and down the room with brisk, athletic strides.

Maxim would have thought he was incapable of feeling any angrier than he had at Alice's unexpected arrival at Rotherfield Hall, but the explosion of fury and foreboding he'd felt when his cousin Ben had arrived to inform him that Lavinia was leaving for London the following morning, and the reason why, eclipsed that. Clearly what she had seen and what Ursula had told her affected her more than he had imagined it would.

'Yes,' Lavinia replied in answer to his question. 'Although not intentionally. I wasn't spying, if that's what you think. Naturally I was curious when I realised that enormous pile I saw belonged to my husband—and more so when I saw him receiving and kissing another woman before my eyes.'

Maxim was moved to tell her that it had been the other way round, and that if she had looked more closely she would have seen that it had been Alice who was kissing him. But he allowed her to continue.

'She certainly displayed a proprietorial manner towards you, and you did not seem to resent that.'

'I had no idea Alice would decide to accompany Lucy. I certainly did not invite her.'

'Why didn't you tell me about Alice and your daughter?' Lavinia demanded, searching Maxim's granite features for some sign of remorse or guilt, but he gave her nothing but a hard stare that was devoid of all compassion and understanding.

'Would it have made any difference?'

'Of course it would,' she told him, two high spots of angry colour mounting her cheeks. 'Why weren't you honest with me? Despite the knock to my reputation in Venice when you were seen compromising me, knowing this, I would not have married you.'

Pausing in front of her his eyebrows shot up in sardonic amusement. 'But you did.'

'And I regret it. Bitterly,' Lavinia said coldly, purposefully. 'How I wish I could go back. Everything would be different.'

'Despite what you think, it was my concern and loyalty to you that prompted me to conceal the facts about Lucy and Alice. Damn it, Lavinia, I wanted to help you—fool that I was.'

'Yes, you were.'

His blue gaze was mocking. 'Do not forget that it was you who came to me first and almost begged me to marry you,' he drawled sarcastically.

'I did not beg,' Lavinia seethed with angry pride. 'Do you think I wanted to go to you and ask you to marry me?

That I liked doing it? How you must have laughed when I offered you my paltry thirty thousand pounds.'

'I did not laugh. I was deeply touched,' Maxim replied seriously.

'When I went to you that day I rejected everything I was brought up to regard as honourable and decent. I could see no other way of extricating myself from a situation that seemed irredeemable to me at the time.'

Maxim studied her, unable to believe her anger. Having left her that morning before she was awake, soft and warm after making love, he found it hard to believe that this virago, with her heightened colour and blazing eyes, was one and the same. She was a different woman to contend with than the serene Lavinia he had come to know. With a supreme effort he tried to rein in his temper, with little success.

'So you are running away to London.'

'I am not running away. I simply cannot stay here any longer. I'm making it easy for you. Everything is as it was when we married.'

Maxim moved closer to her, watching her, his eyes merciless and unflinching, an almost lecherous smile tempting his lips. 'Not quite.'

Knowing exactly to what he was referring Lavinia flushed and lowered her eyes in mute misery beneath his penetrating, relentless gaze. 'Nevertheless, the bargain we made still stands.'

'In the eyes of the law our marriage is legal and binding. Despite any agreement made between us, by any definition you are still my wife.'

'Nevertheless, it was an arrangement—a temporary arrangement.'

'To hell with the arrangement. I thought we both agreed that the arrangement we decided on when I came upon you in the barn was much more in keeping with our idea of marriage.'

'That was before I knew about Alice. Does she know about me?'

'Of course not.'

'Do you mean to tell her?'

'Yes.'

'How will she react, do you think?'

'Knowing Alice, she'll be furious. But that won't concern you in London.'

'No, it won't. Mrs Lambert and Daisy will have returned from Italy, so I shall stay with them until I have decided what to do next.'

'How do you intend getting to London?'

'I shall take the mail coach from Rotherfield in the morning.'

'That is not acceptable,' he snapped. 'I will not allow it.'

Lavinia stiffened. 'I do not recall asking your permission.'

Looming over her, Maxim looked formidable, invincible. 'Nevertheless you need it. Despite what was agreed between us at the beginning of our marriage, I am still your husband and don't you ever forget it. No matter what transpires between us in private, in public I expect you to behave as my wife. I will not have you travelling in a mail coach like any common traveller and that's the end of it.'

With her nails digging into her palms and her chest rising and falling with each furious breath, blazing anger leapt into Lavinia's eyes as she confronted her husband. 'And I recall you telling me that I am free to do as I choose, to live where I choose.'

'That was before last night,' Maxim said in a terrible, silky voice, his cold, threatening gaze pinning her to the spot. 'Things have changed between us. If you dare venture towards the coaching inn I will have you brought back, and you won't like what I will do. Do you understand me?'

Lavinia paled, flinching at the bite in his voice. This was a Maxim she didn't know. 'You wouldn't dare.'

Placing his hands on his hips and with his feet planted apart, he leaned towards her in an aggressive stance. 'Try me,' he warned softly. Although quietly stated, it had the undeniable ring of a threat to it. 'If you must leave I will send my carriage to Thornhill in the morning. But why you are making such a fuss about Alice is quite beyond me.'

'This is not just about Alice and you know it,' Lavinia argued. 'You should have told me. By making me your wife you have placed a burden on me that is like a stranglehold of guilt. How do you think I feel, knowing I stand between you and marriage to a woman who should be your lawful wife—a woman who is the mother of your child born in an illicit relationship?'

When these last words had slipped from her mouth there was a deep and dreadful silence, threatening and charged with a violent animosity. Lavinia felt the depth of Maxim's fury, saw the strained rage emanate from every inch of his powerful frame. At last he spoke, and when he did his voice was cold and lethal.

'You know nothing of Alice's character or the circumstances that have kept us apart.'

'Ursula told me—'

'Not everything.'

'Then why don't you tell me?'

Maxim stood in front of her, thinking of Alice. Someone as unworldly and naïve as Lavinia wouldn't recognise the type of woman Alice was—self-confident, sexually alluring to every man she came into contact with, never for a moment doubting her power over the opposite sex and her ability to control and manipulate them to her advantage.

All but himself. His face tightened, but his voice was ominously low when he spoke.

'I don't think that's any interest of yours. Besides—you have already made up your mind to leave Thornhill, so there seems little point. But what about us?'

'There is no us, Maxim.'

'And you believe that, do you?'

Lavinia nodded, her features strained, her eyes large and full of misery. 'I have to.'

'And are you going to ignore what we discussed yesterday—how it felt when we made love?'

Lavinia's heart twisted agonisingly in her breast, and her emotions told her she could not possibly survive the pain of it. She nodded, a lump of anguish and regret lodged in her throat.

'Yes, Maxim. That's where you made your mistake. You shouldn't have done it. You have a child—a daughter. I refuse to be the one responsible for keeping you from her. Don't you understand? I couldn't live with myself. If you have any conscience at all you will marry her mother— which is what you should have done in the beginning.'

Her words ignited a leaping fury in Maxim's eyes. 'And do you think me so contemptible that I didn't ask her to marry me?' he flared with much bitterness.

'Ursula told me that you did. You will have to ask her again when I am no longer your wife.'

'Alice had her chance to marry me and I will never give her another. There is nothing between us any more. I don't love her. I don't believe I ever have—and she has none for me. In fact, Alice is a first-class bitch whose ambition and constant scheming sickens me,' he said harshly. 'If you knew her you would know what I'm talking about. When I saw her in London recently I realised I didn't want her anywhere near me. That was when I made the decision to keep you with me as my wife.'

Lavinia tensed, humiliated beyond bearing. 'And I will not be kept like your servants and your horses,' she retaliated coldly.

'It was not my intention to keep you like a creature against your will.'

'I'm glad to hear it. You were so sure of yourself, weren't you, Maxim? You came to me like a man bearing a gift, quite unconcerned whether I cared for it or not. But this is not about decision making. It's about your high-handed attitude to assume what I might want. I gave up any idea of an annulment because you asked me to. You didn't consider, you just decided. When you came to me last night you stepped out of line and changed the whole nature of our relationship. You should have left well alone. I cannot stay with you knowing this. As far as I am concerned our agreement still stands and we must abide by it.'

Rage kindled in Maxim's glittering eyes. 'I may no longer want to.'

'Alice is the mother of your child,' Lavinia continued to argue fiercely. 'You should reconcile yourself with her and put your daughter before your own selfishness. What you have done is irresponsible. If you had exercised any decency and restrained your ardour—and I know to my cost how difficult that is for you,' she said with strong reference to what had occurred between them the previous night, 'you would not have found yourself in your present predicament.'

Maxim raised his eyebrows and looked at her in surprise, torn between anger and amusement. 'I cannot change the way I've lived my life until now—and I don't recall you complaining last night,' he said on a softer note, his gaze devouring her face.

His bold, glinting smile and the lazy mockery in his eyes almost proved too much for Lavinia. 'Yes,' she replied lamely, annoyed when she felt her cheeks flush beneath his penetrating gaze. The pull of his eyes was far worse to resist than the frantic beat of her heart. But only an idiot would have succumbed now. She had dared to speak her mind, to let him know how she felt. She must be resolute. 'You can be very persuasive, Maxim,' she conceded.

His finely sculpted mouth curled in a sneer. 'Thank you for that, anyway.'

'I thought you considerate in granting your affection to others—which was the case when you so valiantly rose to defend my honour in Venice—but to hear you vilify the mother of your child, to depict her as some kind of monster, makes me wonder what manner of man you are and if you are to be trusted at all. You speak of her with antipathy— why, I do not know and I have no right to ask. But it's disrespectful and cruel.'

Maxim's entire body stiffened and his metallic eyes snapped to her face. His expression hardened into a mask of freezing rage and they glared at each other, the fragile unity they had shared the previous night shattered. The warm threads that were being woven between them were broken. Maxim's anger made him carelessly cruel and his face became hard with grinding hostility. His voice had a dangerous, cutting edge.

'You, madam, don't know what you are talking about and have said quite enough. You forget yourself.'

His words rekindled Lavinia's receding anger and her eyes sparked like chipped ice. '*I* forget myself? You are the one to have deceived me and yet you have the gall to tell me not to forget *my*self!'

'You go too far.'

Frustration exploded within Lavinia. 'Do I, indeed! I

have shocked you, have I not? I have suddenly turned out to be a woman who is not afraid to speak out. Clearly you thought me too naïve and stupid to challenge you. I can see that you don't expect me to think and feel—that you want to do it for me.'

'And I can't see why you are making such a fuss about everything. Perhaps if Ursula had told you about the conditions Alice imposed on me you might understand.'

'Ha! Conditions were imposed on me too, as I recall. The two of you may not love each other, but it seems to me that you have much in common when it comes to proposing marriage. But it makes no difference. Forget your pride, Maxim. Make your peace with Alice. Isn't your daughter worth it? If you don't, you are going to have one very unhappy child.'

Somewhere in the dark caverns of Maxim's mind he slowly began to realise that Lavinia's concern for Lucy's well-being had been brought about by her own unhappy childhood, and that it was why she was hellbent on sending him into Alice's arms. But at that moment he was almost at the point of fury where reason and the ability to think clearly had left him. His features were like granite, the air thick with bitter confrontation.

'I don't like your tone, Lavinia. What gives you the right to sit in judgement?'

'I don't. I happen to be concerned for your daughter.'

'Concerned!' he repeated with insolent amusement. 'I wonder why.'

'Because, unlike you, I happen to believe that a child belongs with both its parents.'

His eyes raked her with a look of glacial scorn. 'Now why is it,' he mocked, 'that after being raised by parents who couldn't be bothered to give you the time of day, I find it strange that you are suddenly such an authority on what you think is best for *my* child. You know nothing. Until you do kindly keep your classifications to yourself.'

Raging furiously inside, Lavinia was incensed by his arrogance. He was cold, colder and harder than she had ever seen him, his face set and remote, watchful and guarded.

'Why—you arrogant, self-opinionated heartless beast,' she flared, breathing hard, her eyes sparking fire as the argument became a battle of unwavering wills. 'You know nothing about what my life has been like. It is precisely for that reason that I do know. I know what it's like to be ignored. I know how it feels to think there must be something wrong with you because you're unloved. So don't you dare treat me like some kind of imbecile.'

'I don't. Lucy is neither ignored or unloved.'

'No—she is more like some pampered pet who can be passed from mother to father while they argue their differences—neither of them doing what is right for the child,' Lavinia flung at him, throwing back her hair and glaring at her husband, who caught his breath, thinking he had never seen her so savagely beautiful. This malleable, tractable young woman he had met in Venice, was changing before his eyes. She was proving to be more volatile than he realised.

'Where are your priorities, Maxim?' she went on. 'Sacrifices have to be made for children. It appears to me that those sacrifices will cause you personal inconvenience—which is evidently too much to ask of you.'

'Damn you, Lavinia, and your narrow, blinkered view of life. You insult me and my intelligence most grievously. But understand this,' Maxim hissed, enunciating every word so they would be indelibly printed on her mind for all time. 'I will not marry Alice. I will never marry Alice. Marriage is not always a foregone conclusion to an affair.'

'I'm beginning to realise that,' she snapped, too angry to

quail before the murderous look tightening his face. 'You are a monster, Maxim. A cold and hateful monster.'

His eyes were like ice and cynical. 'You're right. I am.'

'And you have no heart.'

'Exactly,' he replied. 'And you will do well to remember that if you deceive yourself into believing otherwise. I am no poodle to be led by the nose. Alice made that mistake and will live to regret it.'

'I do not like your world, Maxim. You have a distorted view of what is right and decent. In your world it would seem that babies come before marriage. That is not acceptable to the order of things in my life. Maybe you are right and I do have a blinkered view on life, which I can only put down to my upbringing over which I had no control. But I am beginning to realise that perhaps it wasn't so bad after all. At least I was given good principles. I was also taught about decency and the difference between right and wrong—which appears to have been sadly lacking in your own education.'

'I wouldn't go on if I were you,' Maxim warned in a murderous voice, his voice hoarse in his throat, his fists clasped to his sides as he struggled to keep them from reaching out and throttling her.

Lavinia stopped cold, realising that she might have gone too far, but she was too angry to allow herself to be intimidated by him. They glared at each other, neither of them prepared to back down from the confrontation.

'I realise you must despise me for speaking to you like this, but I have to let you know how I feel. You should not have let me find out about Alice and Lucy by accident. You should have told me in the beginning.'

'There was no need if we were to seek an annulment.'

'There was every need,' Lavinia persisted.

Maxim's glare was deadly. 'Have you finished?'

Lavinia drew herself up straight, her face pale and steeled with a resolute, frozen look. 'Yes. I shall leave first thing in the morning. I am quite determined, so do not try to stop me.'

Maxim could almost feel her fury and anguish, but her resolution was firm, solid and unbreakable. Her mind was made up about leaving, he could see that. In the space of twenty-four hours she had developed a newly acquired confidence in herself that was lethal. His clear blue eyes turned to shards of ice.

'Stop you? I'll be damned if I will. Go to London and take your damn sermons with you. I'll even be here to carry your bags out to the carriage and wave you on your way.'

'Don't bother. I can carry my own bags. And where our marriage is concerned, it was never meant to be permanent and can easily be dismantled. I want a husband for life—not until the next woman who takes his fancy comes along.'

'And if I told you that you are the only woman I want?'

'How can I believe that when you have so skilfully hidden so much from me? If you can treat one woman so abominably, how do I know you will not do the same to me?' Lavinia accused, too demolished over his secrecy over this, trying not to dwell on how his eyes were flashing a brilliant, dangerous hot blue in his tanned face, or the snarling smile across his even white teeth, and the tangle of blue-black curls that tumbled over his forehead, making him look like a gypsy, wild and fierce, and so incredibly handsome that it wrung her heart. But she refused to be swayed.

'I have been unhappily deceived in your character,' she went on relentlessly. 'Because we can no longer have our marriage annulled you can go ahead and start divorce proceedings on the grounds of desertion, adultery—whatever you like—I really don't care, just so long as it is over and done with quickly. From what Ursula has told me and what I have seen, you are a wealthy man, Maxim—so wealthy that it makes my thirty thousand pounds seem like a mere tuppence. Use your influence—pull some strings. I'm sure you can manage that.'

Maxim didn't flinch. He merely looked at her with eyes that had frozen over before turning and going towards the door. But with implacable resolve he came back to her with confident, brisk strides, sardonic amusement curving his handsome lips, refusing to spare her. Towering over her, his smile was vicious.

'And what will you do if I refuse to file for a divorce? What if I decide not to let you go and keep you as my lawful wife—to share my board and my bed and bear my children?'

Lavinia stiffened, feeling the colour drain from her face. She didn't recognise the ominous glitter in those ice blue eyes. Behind his sardonic expression was a burning anger. 'You wouldn't do that, Maxim,' she whispered, automatically backing away from him towards the bed, overcome with an irrational fear, primitive and instinctive. Never had he looked so tall, so powerful, so coldly frightening.

'I might. I am tempted—especially when I look at you,' he said huskily, only a few inches away. As he let his admiring glance roam freely over her wealth of thick golden hair and slim, restless figure, he noticed she was wearing nothing beneath her robe. He arched a brow and smiled, meeting her gaze.

Reading the sudden glow in his eyes Lavinia was alarmed. The bed blocked her retreat so all she could do was face him. Her breath caught in her throat. If he touched her she would crumble, and after their harsh words which had settled everything between them, she could not allow that to happen. His obvious intention turned her into a trembling mass of rebellion and fear. Swallowing hard she gasped. 'Please don't do this. You can't.'

Maxim moved closer, his gaze focusing on her lips. 'But I can. I am your husband. I have every right. Why you want to torture us both in this way baffles me. Come, Lavinia, admit it. You want what I want.'

'No. Not any more,' Lavinia told him, which was not the truth. She would go on wanting him until the day she died. He was so close she could feel the heat of his virile body.

Maxim experienced a surge of triumphant satisfaction when he saw the flickering weakening in her eyes. 'Then prove it to me.'

Immediately he reached out and Lavinia jerked away from him, but he caught her and drew her closer, his arms going round her and holding her with a crushing force.

'Take your hands off me,' she ordered, infuriated by his obvious intention to weaken her resolve, which he knew he was capable of doing every time he took her in his arms.

'Not a chance,' Maxim whispered as she struggled against him.

All the days they had been together, of wanting her, of frustrating self-denial for the past twenty-four hours—Maxim's need for her had built up to such a pitch that he was almost beyond restraint. All he could think of was shattering her demureness and reserve and laying bare the woman of passion—a woman he had every right to make love to. Bending his head until his mouth found hers and forcing her lips apart, he began kissing her with fervency, determined to make her respond.

Lavinia held herself rigid, her determination not to yield as strong as his own determination to make her. She knew that he wanted her full cooperation, and that if she gave it, it would be more damaging to her pride and their relation-

ship than anything else. Tears gathered under her eyelids
and the world seemed to tilt around her and to retreat. She
fought the weakness, not wanting to be completely at his
mercy, but her body was already beginning to respond with
a gross miscalculation of her will.

Powerless to prevent what she knew would happen next,
she melted against him and returned his kiss with a silent
desperation and a fervour that betrayed her own longing,
crushing her soft mouth to his and almost moaning out loud
at the sheer pleasure of it. She wasn't made of stone. She
was flesh and blood, and her blood was on fire.

The moment she leaned into him and opened her mouth
in response, Maxim shoved her back on to the bed. Lavinia
gasped when he hurriedly tore off his shirt and trousers and
tossed them onto the floor. With a strength born out of fear
she turned and struggled to the other side of the bed, but
he reached out and caught her, bringing her back and rolling on to her, pinning her hands on either side of her head
as his own hovered over her, dark and satanic, desire raging
in his eyes.

'Please, Maxim, don't do this,' she begged as he lowered
his face purposefully toward hers. The previous night he
had been gentle and loving, but now he seemed to want to
hurt her. 'Not like this.'

He captured her protests with his mouth, kissing her with
a violence that stole her breath away, his fingers searching
the soft contours of her body beneath her robe, which had
fallen open. They cupped her breasts, teasing her hardened
nipples, moving down over her abdomen to the curling
mass of golden hair between her thighs, skilfully building
her desire.

Lavinia's trapped body writhed beneath him and she
tried to fight back the waves of pleasure that washed over
her, tried not to respond to the erotic onslaught to her

senses. She tensed every muscle in her body to resist the calculating, heartless things his knowledgeable fingers were doing to her, but sharp stabs of desire were shooting through her, melting her resistance, driving her insane with need and want.

When her body became pliant beneath his, Maxim felt a surge of triumphant satisfaction and found her lips once more, kissing her deep and moulding the full length of his body to hers, forcing her to become aware of his raging desire. With her eyes closed, Lavinia felt a warmth begin to seep through her entire body. It brought a soft moan of exquisite, mindless pleasure to her lips, and she kissed him with fierce desperation. Aching desire was building up to a crescendo and jarring through her body. Desperate for release, she wanted him inside her.

Maxim raised his head, his eyes dark with passion, watching her face. 'Tell me you want me, Lavinia. Say it,' he whispered, dragging his lips to her breasts and making small circles on her flesh with his warm tongue. Lavinia opened her dazed eyes and looked at him. Feeling her body tremble with uncontrollable need, Maxim saw the answer screaming at him in her liquid eyes and he smiled. But he held back. He had to hear her say it.

'Say it,' he repeated, covering her body with his own and provocatively moving against hers, deliberately keeping himself in check and controlling his burgeoning desire when she arched her hips.

The fire that had been building inside Lavinia threatened to explode. Unable to stand it a moment longer, the words he demanded to hear tore out of her in a tormented sob. 'Yes—damn it, Maxim. Don't torture me like this.'

The moment she surrendered he drove into her, bringing a moan of pure pleasure to her lips. She received him like an opening exotic flower, wrapping her arms around him and clutching him to her. They moved in unison, each giving the other maximum pleasure, the climax when it came erupting inside them both with spasms of pure bliss.

For a moment only their ragged breathing could be heard, and then Maxim shrugged himself free of her embrace and rolled off her, thrusting his arms and legs back into his clothes. Tucking his shirt into the waistband of his trousers, he looked down at his wife, trying not to dwell on how wounded she looked, how young and heartbreakingly lovely. Having pulled her robe over her naked form, she struggled to sit up, her eyes still dark and sultry with passion, her lips swollen and trembling.

Maxim's hard eyes raked her face. 'You see. Now can you deny that you still want me?' he jeered cruelly.

Clutching her robe beneath her chin with shaking fingers, Lavinia sat up and glared at him. 'Weren't you satisfied with the pain and humiliation you have already inflicted on me without doing that? I'll never forgive you for what you've just done, Maxim. Ever.'

With long strides he crossed towards the door where he turned, contempt twisting his lips. 'I shall make sure your thirty thousand pounds is made available to you within the next few days.'

The door slammed behind him with the cold finality of a death knell.

Trembling violently, all Lavinia's attention was focused on the closed door. Beset by confusion, she was unable to think or feel. She was unable to believe what Maxim had done to her. If he truly cared for her he would not have done that. In the tearing, agonising hurt which enfolded her, she was ashamed, after all her harsh words, at how easy it had been for him to expose the proof of her vulnerability.

She was, in fact, greatly disturbed. It was not what he had done. It went beyond that, and therein lay her confusion. How could she still want him, love him after that? But want him and love him she did. Looking at him standing in the open doorway afterwards, his carelessly thrown-on shirt open to the waist, his gleaming black hair all tousled and an intense look in those clear blue eyes, had shaken her with a desire so strong it frightened her. Remembering him like that was enough to make her forget and forgive anything.

Tears blinded her vision. Lowering her head, she wept for her inability to purge him from her heart, for her lack of will and with a fear for a love she was unable to control. In her fury and ravaged pride, she dashed her tears away and swore she would kill Maxim if he ever touched her again.

Tormented by his callous and cruel treatment of Lavinia and unable to drive out the memory of what he had just done, riding back to Rotherfield Hall Maxim's heart twisted with remorse and regret. She had told him she would never forgive him, and she was right not to do so. She must despise him, but not nearly as much as he despised himself.

Maxim was willing to concede that he had used her viciously, and he would send his carriage to take her to London in the morning. As for her request for a divorce—if she still wanted one, he would give it to her. With his jaw thrust forward and as rigid as granite, anger spurred him on, Lavinia's decision to leave him having put her beyond all limits of his tolerance. The sound of his horse's hooves pounding beneath him took on a deadly finality.

The following morning Maxim lost no time in acquainting Alice with the bare facts of his marriage to Lavinia, without disclosing his impending divorce.

Alice had come to Rotherfield because both Francis

Newbold and the Comte de Chemille were out of town. Feeling bored, she thought it might prove entertaining and diverting if she accompanied Lucy to Kent for a few days. Maxim could hardly turn her away. Besides, she had not been incapable of winning his regard once, and she was most anxious to have it now.

And now he had the gall to tell her he had married someone else.

Somewhere in Alice's brain a hot cauldron began to boil and immediately her imagination was seized. The door was blown right open to jealousy and revenge.

'You coward,' she blazed. 'You gutless coward. And you left it until now to tell me. Who is she?' she demanded in a hysterical tone, envious malice darting from her eyes. 'I demand to know who she is. And why isn't she here with you?'

'She isn't here because I want to settle the matter between us before I introduce her to Lucy.'

Jealousy, hot and fierce, suddenly sprang up inside Alice. 'Never. How dare you make plans for my daughter behind my back?' she spat, her voice shaking with suppressed rage. 'She has no right to even know her. Lucy is mine.'

'Lucy is my daughter too.'

'Who is she, Maxim—this woman you've married behind my back? I demand to know.'

'Demand all you like,' Maxim replied, his voice cold and contemptuous, his expression unmoved. 'You'll find out in time. You don't know her.'

'I'll make you sorry you did this.'

Maxim's forbearance where Alice was concerned was stretched thin, almost to the point of breaking. His eyes became brittle and there was a grim note in his voice. 'Do you dare to threaten me, Alice?'

Alice glared at him, committed to setting Maxim back

on his heels because he'd had the audacity to form a firm
and permanent union with another woman. 'If you like.
Now you are no longer free to marry me I will marry someone who is,' she flung at him savagely, knowing how
deeply Maxim would suffer when she took Lucy away from
him altogether.

'You heartless, scheming witch. Have you no sense of
decency?'

Fire shot through Alice's eyes. 'You're a fine one to talk
about decency. If you'd done the decent thing you would
have become reconciled with your uncle and married me.
Lucy would then have been able to live with her rightful
father. But where there is one there is always another.'

Her mocking tone scraped against Maxim's raw nerves.
'And who do you have in mind? Francis Newbold or your
French comte?' he ground out.

'The Comte de Chemille will do nicely. Claude has
asked me to be his wife so I will accept. He is returning to
France very soon. When he does I shall go with him.'

Maxim went white. 'Marry your French comte by all
means, but you will not expose Lucy to danger. I forbid
you to take her out of this country. Have you no concept
about what is happening in France?'

She shrugged. 'It will blow over in time.'

Savage fury ignited in Maxim's eyes. 'Blow over? You
fool, Alice. I've recently returned from France, where revolution is apparent in the minds of the people. In Paris
discontent is already raised to the point of rebellion, giving
rise to bloody riots which have to be put down by military
force. I will not stand by and let you take Lucy into that
hornet's nest.'

'Try and stop me,' Alice hissed wrathfully, turning from
him and flouncing towards the door.

'Oh, I shall, Alice. I shall pull out all the stops to prevent you. I shall get custody of my daughter. I swear I shall.'

'Never,' Alice hissed fiercely. 'You'll never have her. I'd see her dead first.'

'And that is precisely how she will end up if you take her to France.'

Grim-faced, Maxim held a tearful Lucy as she was leaving Rotherfield. She clung to him, her little arms gripping him tightly.

'Please let me stay, Papa,' she begged. 'I like it here. You promised to take me to the farm and show me the ponies.'

It was the first time she had been to Rotherfield Hall, and Maxim had hoped her stay would have been longer. But as things stood, it was best that she remained with Alice.

'I know, princess. But you must go back to London with your mama. I'll bring you back to Rotherfield before too long and take you to see the ponies. I promise.'

Maxim watched Lucy leave Rotherfield Hall with loving but worried eyes.

Chapter Eleven

Ursula arrived at Rotherfield Hall shortly after Alice had left for London. The silence inside the great house struck her and she sighed, shaking her head somewhat sadly. How often had she told Maxim that it was about time he settled down and filled it with his offspring. It was far too big for one man to rattle around in. Maxim was an exacting master who demanded that his house and estate, like his businesses, were run as smoothly as a well-oiled machine. Everyone who worked for him was in awe of this cynical, formidable master and strove to please him.

Mr Perkins came towards her, his expression a mask of aloof formality. He carefully guarded his position of trust at Rotherfield Hall, and performed all his tasks for Maxim with the faultless precision of a well-tuned orchestra.

'Is my nephew at home, Mr Perkins?'

'He is in his study, Mrs Metcalf.'

'And Miss Winstanley?'

Mr Perkins's eyes gleamed and there was a momentary crack in his rigid features. 'Miss Winstanley left with her daughter for London an hour ago.'

Ursula smiled smugly. Now *that* she found particularly encouraging, although she knew how disappointed and dejected Maxim would be feeling following Lucy's departure. The child hadn't been at Rotherfield Hall twenty-four hours before she had been whisked back to London by her mother. Alice's hasty departure could only mean that Maxim had told her about his marriage to Lavinia.

Deeply concerned by recent events, and having become extremely fond of Lavinia, Ursula could not let matters rest as they were. Remembering Maxim's actions over the years where his grandfather and his uncle were concerned, and how he'd succeeded in coldly cutting them out of his life as if he was not of their blood, Ursula knew he would do the same with Lavinia if nothing was done.

When Mr Perkins showed Ursula into Maxim's study, where he was going through a pile of correspondence, he rose from his desk in taut silence and strode towards the window. His expression was hard, his stance like that of a man being stretched beyond endurance by an internal struggle. It was plain that he was concerned about Lucy and already missing her, and he was also feeling betrayed and furious over Lavinia's leaving.

'Alice is threatening to marry her French comte,' he told his aunt, his voice strained, 'more out of spite than any tender feelings she might feel for the man.'

'What do you intend doing about Lucy? You can't let Alice take her to France in the present climate.'

'I don't intend to. Something has to be done to stop her.'

'Would you have married Alice on her terms if you had not married Lavinia?'

Maxim shook his head. 'No. I did consider it when I was in Italy, but when I saw her in London and listened to what Mrs Winstanley had to say concerning her behaviour, nothing could have induced me to tie myself to her for life.'

'So you made up your mind to remain married to Lavinia.' Ursula watched his face. Apart from a muscle clamping in his jaw, it didn't flinch when she mentioned his wife's name.

'Something like that.'

'And you expected Lavinia to go along with it—without any explanation?' Ursula asked, angered by Maxim's ruthless lack of emotion. 'Really, Maxim! That was too bad of you.'

Maxim regarded his aunt's angry face in dispassionate silence as she proceeded to berate him.

'That poor girl has suffered as much as you have. I cannot believe you can be so callous. Because Lavinia's heart is open she gives all of herself, holding nothing back. Don't abuse her goodness, Maxim. Have you given a thought about what's to happen to her when those people who saw you compromising her in Venice spread the gossip in London? No. I can see you haven't. You can't see beyond your own damaged pride. When it becomes obvious that you are estranged, that you have discarded her—'

'I haven't discarded her. Lavinia has discarded me.'

'Well—whatever. Your marriage to her was no secret. People will expect to see you together—will expect you to live together. How will you explain it?'

'I don't have to explain anything to anyone,' Maxim replied with cold indifference.

'Gossip and speculation can be cruel to an innocent like Lavinia.'

'Then she should have thought about that before she ran off to London.'

'You have no choice but to rescue her from that situation. You are her husband. It's your duty.'

'I strongly suspect I am the last person my wife would want to rescue her,' he ground out scathingly.

'I don't believe that. Lavinia doesn't deserve to be shamed. Her connection to you will make that innocent, lovely girl notorious—and that kind of notoriety isn't good. Nobody will want to have anything to do with her. How do you think she will deal with that?'

'Very well, I imagine,' Maxim replied, his voice devoid of concern. 'She told me in no uncertain terms that the agreement we made in the beginning still stands as far as she is concerned.'

Ursula looked at this cold dispassionate man she had known all his life with disbelief. 'It will be difficult having your marriage annulled after sharing her bed,' she said, her voice laced with uncharacteristic sarcasm.

Maxim's expression tightened. 'I'll file for a divorce as soon as I can get to London and see my lawyer.'

'On what grounds?'

'Desertion. Lavinia didn't have to leave. But in doing so she has given me irrefutable grounds for divorce,' he told his aunt with icy finality.

'I see. She will never endure the disgrace of being a divorced woman. That poor girl will be brought low by it.'

Maxim's mouth thinned to an angry line. 'Dear Lord, Aunt! Don't lecture me. Because of this marriage I've more than likely lost Lucy.'

'And Lavinia knows it. She's eaten up with guilt about that. If you can't understand why she's gone to London, I can. No woman would live with a man, knowing she stands between him and his daughter. You can't dismiss her from your life so casually, Maxim.'

'Yes, I can. I have the more pressing matter of Lucy.'

'No one can be that cold, that callous. Do you have to act so dispassionately?'

'What would you have me do?'

'You told me about your talk with Mrs Winstanley when you went up to London. If you want your daughter, take her advice. That Purnell pride and quick temper of yours is a bad combination, Maxim, and you are bringing a lot of grief upon your own head. There's also something else you should consider.'

'What?' he snapped, pacing up and down in restless fury.

Familiar with all Maxim's moods, good and bad, Ursula remained undaunted. 'If you want to gain custody of Lucy, it will be better having your wife with you instead of against you. Otherwise, while you're busy trying to convince the court that Alice is an unfit mother, they just might consider you to be an unfit father. Think about it, Maxim. You failed to marry the mother of your child, and you are in the process of divorcing your present wife after just a few weeks of marriage. What do you expect them to make of that?'

Maxim shrugged, thrusting his hands deep into his pockets and staring out of the window, his brow furrowed with a deep frown.

By no means done, Ursula went to stand beside him, looking up at his granite features, seeing a muscle move spasmodically on the side of his jaw. 'There's more at stake here than your pride and antipathy towards your uncle, Maxim. Your daughter depends on you—and so does Lavinia, if you did but know it. For them you must put aside your feelings and go and see your uncle. With Lavinia by your side, your Uncle Alistair behind you and some influential lawyers to fight your case, you might be able to wield enough power to prevent Alice taking Lucy to France and gain custody.'

Maxim's body went rigid and he stared at her in disbelief. 'Aunt Ursula! How can you tell me to go and see my uncle with a begging bowl in my hand after what he is guilty of where my father and mother are concerned—your sister, don't forget.'

'I don't. And you don't have to beg for anything. And

aren't you forgetting that it was your grandfather who was at fault who, by all accounts, deeply regretted doing what he did. I realise how deep your resentment for your grandfather goes, but he is dead. He did relent before he died. I still have the letters he sent, begging your father to return to Brinkcliff Hall. Your grandfather wanted to become reconciled so that he could formally make him his heir, but your father was as stubborn as he.'

'The same letters my Uncle Alistair has been sending to me over the years,' Maxim said scathingly, combing a heavy lock of black hair from his forehead with his fingers and restlessly resuming his pacing up and down the room.

'Yes. Your uncle is a very poorly man, Maxim, and he never wanted the position your father thrust on him. Perhaps it's time you gave a thought to what is to become of the estate when he dies. There is no one else. You are the next Earl of Brinkcliff and there's not a thing you can do about it.'

'I have made it plain to my uncle that I don't give a damn for the estate or the title.'

With a sigh of weary resignation Ursula turned to go. 'Maybe not. But your son might.'

Maxim ceased pacing and glanced at her sharply. 'I don't have a son.'

'No. But after staying at Thornhill the other night, what if Lavinia has conceived a child? I think you should give it some thought.'

Ursula left Maxim in a tormented silence. His mind was locked in furious combat at the thought of having to capitulate to his uncle, but he realised he could no longer remain distant if he meant to gain custody of Lucy. But it would be hard enough to relinquish his hatred without drawing the old man into his life as an ally to aid him with his case.

But Ursula had spoken sense. Everything she had said

was true. He realised it would benefit him enormously if the court saw that he had the full backing of the Earl of Brinkcliff—and his wife. He also realised that he hadn't a cat in hell's chance of gaining custody of his daughter with a divorce pending.

Thinking of Lavinia, he was torn between torment and tenderness. When his anger and pain had finally diminished enough and he could think more rationally, he reconsidered their estrangement. Despite what had transpired between them the previous night, with a defeated sigh and unable to lie to himself any more, he realised he didn't want a divorce, and he would be damned if he would give her one. And what if she was with child? He had messed up with Lucy and he had no intention of doing so again.

Recalling her agonised face when he had left her last night, how vulnerable and hurt she had looked, he ached with remorse. How could he have thought for one moment that he could live without her—that he could purge her from his heart and mind? In his fury last night he would have said he could, but now, in calmer mood, he knew it was impossible.

It mattered to him what happened to this beautiful, intelligent, foolish young wife of his. For the first time in his life he had found a woman who was rare and unspoiled, a woman who had succeeded in touching his heart, which was something all the other women had failed to do. He had no intention of letting her go, and this had nothing to do with his battle to gain custody of Lucy. He realised how much he loved Lavinia, and the truth of his admittance didn't really surprise him.

Recalling how severely she had taken him to task over his assumed neglect of his daughter, a smile tugged at the corners of his lips. Her severe dressing down and chastisement over his lack of moral standards had angered him beyond words, but secretly he loved her for it. She was a deeply concerned young woman, to whom strong principles and a high regard and respect for marriage and the rearing of children mattered—a woman who expected the same moral principles from others.

A new sense of urgency banished the anger and frustration that had clouded his thinking since Ben had arrived at Rotherfield Hall yesterday to tell him Lavinia was leaving and why. Resigned to what he knew he had to do if he was to bring some order back to his life, he sat at his desk and began drafting a letter to his uncle.

Lavinia travelled to London alone in Maxim's impressive coach drawn by a team of four handsome horses. She took little notice of the many people milling about both inside and outside the inn where they stopped for refreshment and to rest the horses. It was when she was about to resume her journey that her eyes were drawn to a coach that seemed familiar. It had just pulled into the inn yard and the occupants, three women and a child, were making their way inside the inn. One of the women paused and stared at Lavinia.

Sensing the woman's eyes on her, Lavinia hesitated as she was about to climb inside the coach and half turned in her direction, instantly recognising the beautiful woman with black hair and exquisite features she had seen Maxim receiving at Rotherfield Hall.

It was Alice.

Lavinia's heart almost stopped completely, and then began to pound. For a moment she was unable to move. Their glances caught and locked. An icy chill trickled down Lavinia's spine when she looked into those eyes. They were as hard and ruthless as those of a cat watching its prey.

Why had Alice left Rotherfield Hall after so short a visit?

Lavinia asked herself. Was it because of her? Had Maxim told Alice about his marriage? If so, having recognised Maxim's splendid midnight blue coach, Alice would know who she was—and when Alice's savage glare ripped across the yard and tore into her, Lavinia knew that she did.

Lavinia's gaze was irresistibly drawn to the child, Maxim's child, whose features were so incredibly like his that it wrenched her heart. She was dark haired with clear blue eyes and a small dent in her chin. Lavinia detected a sadness about her. Her eyes were red, which told Lavinia that she had been weeping. Raising her eyes to Lucy's mother, she saw her eyes were narrowed as she stared openly. Alice made no attempt to conceal the pure, unadulterated hatred and contempt she felt for her rival. Her look was so venomous that it would have reduced a lesser woman to ashes. Tearing her eyes away from Lavinia, she grasped Lucy's hand and dragged her inside the inn.

Lavinia climbed into the coach, deeply affected by the brief encounter. She felt sick and cold and trembled inside, and she was engulfed by a kind of repugnant horror after seeing the mother of Maxim's child. She was convinced that she had been looking on a woman who believed she had been cruelly wronged and was bent on revenge. And the child had looked so unhappy, so sad. Had she been crying because Alice had taken her away from her father?

With time for reflection, she turned her thoughts to Maxim and questions began to plague her. He had told her he had no intention of marrying Alice once their marriage was ended, and if this was so, how could he hope to live close to his daughter? Ursula had told her how much he adored the child, so surely he would want to play a part in her upbringing. Did he hold his uncle in such contempt that he would rather forfeit living with his daughter than become reconciled? And Alice? Was she so dreadful that he could not bear the thought of being close to her?

If so, Maxim's reasons for not marrying his former mistress might be justified. He had told her Alice had made conditions before she would agree to marry him. What were those conditions? They must have been harsh for a man as proud as Maxim to refuse to agree to them when he was so devoted to his daughter.

Had she been too harsh on him? Lavinia asked herself. When Ursula had told her about Alice and Lucy she had been too ready to form her own conclusions and judge Maxim, knowing nothing about his reasons for not marrying Alice. She should not have done that. She should have believed in him. After the kindness and consideration he had shown towards her in Venice, she should have known he would not shirk from doing what was right by his daughter without good reason.

Swamped with misery she suddenly wanted to tell the driver to turn the coach around and return to Rotherfield, to throw herself on Maxim's mercy and beg his forgiveness. But when she recalled how cold and implacable he had been when he had left her room at Thornhill, and how readily he had agreed to a divorce, she knew he would not welcome her back.

When Lavinia arrived in London and presented herself to Mrs Lambert and Daisy at their house in Stratton Street, they were overjoyed to see her again, but their delight soon turned to confused shock when she told them she and Maxim were to divorce. Feeling that she owed them an explanation, Lavinia told them the reason why they had parted—about Alice and Lucy—requesting them to keep the whole shameful business to themselves for the time being. She refrained from telling them about the conditions

Maxim had imposed on her before their marriage. It all seemed so sordid and humiliating now.

She heard nothing from Maxim, but true to his word he made the thirty thousand pounds from her father's legacy— or his own account—available to her immediately.

She had been in London for two weeks when, after much persuasion and dressed in a satin gown of cobalt blue, she accompanied Mrs Lambert and Daisy to the theatre. They were escorted by Mrs Lambert's bachelor brother, an elderly gentleman who frequently escorted his sister and Daisy to social events.

It wasn't until the curtain had come down, and the actors had retreated backstage during the interval, that she allowed her eyes to idly scan the audience in the auditorium. It was filled with noise and laughter and people moving about to pay courtesy calls on their friends, who received their visitors in their boxes with all the dignity and grace as if they had they been at home.

Lavinia's gaze was idly drawn to a tall, silver-haired, elderly gentleman occupying a box with three other gentlemen across from them on the tier below. She was about to look away when the elderly gentleman rose along with the others to acknowledge a woman who had just entered their box.

Bending forward in her seat better to see, Lavinia's eyes became riveted on the scene and a sick paralysis gripped her when she recognised Maxim as one of the gentlemen occupying the box. The woman was Alice Winstanley, beautiful and vivacious in a sumptuous gown of scarlet and silver lace, her black hair gleaming, her red lips parted in a wide smile of sensuality. When Lavinia saw Maxim introduce her to his friends, and how Alice's fingers wrapped themselves with a possessive familiarity round his arm when she leaned closer and spoke to Maxim, a pain like she had never experienced before almost severed her heart in two.

Unable to tear her eyes away she saw Alice throw back her head and laugh hilariously at something one of the gentlemen said to her, taking a seat among them when the next act of the play began. It was at that moment that Maxim, seeming to sense himself being watched, glanced up at her box and saw her. Across the distance their eyes locked, but then Lavinia looked away and leaned back in her chair, and her husband's view of her was mercifully obliterated by Daisy.

Never before in all her life had Lavinia felt so agonisingly, unbearably jealous of another woman as she did of Alice Winstanley at that moment, or as angry as she was with Maxim. She may have given him her blessing to become reconciled with the mother of his child, but how dare he subject her to the painful, humiliating spectacle by parading his mistress in public so soon after his break up with her?

She gulped, swallowing down the tears that accumulated in her throat and threatened to choke her. Resisting the urge to get up and leave the theatre, she sat through the remaining acts of the play in a haze, deaf to the words and blind to everything going on about her, her only conscious thought being that her husband was close by, dancing attendance on his mistress.

Daisy, noticing her friend's strained profile beside her and sensing that she was not paying attention to the play, leaned towards her. 'Lavinia, are you all right? You're not ill, are you?' she inquired softly.

'No. No—I'm quite well, Daisy,' she replied with a weak smile, preferring to keep what she had seen to herself. 'I have a slight headache, that's all.'

Afterwards, being jostled from every direction by people

standing around discussing the play as they awaited their carriages, Maxim stood in the foyer of the theatre, having become temporarily separated from his uncle who had paused to speak to an acquaintance. About to move towards the door where it was less congested, and hoping to see Lavinia before she left the theatre, her presence having taken him wholly by surprise, he halted as his gaze came upon her, standing alone near a tall pillar. She was collecting the attention of most of the men in the foyer—and to his chagrin he had to concede that, dressed in a cobalt-blue satin gown which set off her slender figure to perfection, she warranted such admiring regard.

All his attention became focused on the cool, slim features of his young wife and his brows drew together in a frown. Where he had left her with anger at Thornhill, after discovering just how strong-willed, stubborn and infuriating she could be, he now perceived an air of seriousness about her. She displayed none of the frivolity that was present in all the other ladies present, and there was an intent directness in her gaze as she surveyed the scene about her that told Maxim she was finding it all disconcerting.

Perhaps what had transpired between them on her last night at Thornhill had stripped all humour from her, for she was as cool and aloof as an ice queen, being forced to attend an event she found distasteful. He silently cursed the rift he had allowed to form between them, and Alice's unexpected arrival at his box and her determination to remain for what was left of the play, for he would have liked to have escorted his wife to the theatre himself.

With cool composure Lavinia watched Maxim approach, her eyes fixed on the stony, chiselled set of his features. It unsettled her, especially when those blue eyes locked on to her own and moved with exacting slowness over every part of her. It was only two weeks since she had last seen him, but she had forgotten how brilliant and clear his eyes were. In a strange, magical way they seemed capable of stripping her soul bare. Every fibre of her being cried out for him, but her insulted spirit rebelled.

It was all she could do to face his unspoken challenge and not escape to the confines of the carriage waiting to take them home. There was a change in him, subtle, but still it was there. What it was that had brought it about she had no way of knowing, but little by little the realisation dawned on her that this man was a man she did not know. He appeared able to hold himself aloof and apart from everyone, and yet with his mere presence, dominate the scene around him as he did now.

They stood and looked at each other, each conscious of the anger, the passion, the argument and the strife of their parting at Thornhill.

Having admitted the truth to himself that he loved Lavinia, unable to imagine his future without her at his side, Maxim was eager to reach out to her, to feast his eyes on her again, but something about her stiff manner halted him. He gazed down at her pale face, looking deep into her entrancing turquoise eyes, and he felt himself overcome and gripped by the same coldness that flowed out of her.

But if he had looked deeper into her bright eyes, he would have noticed that they were sparkling with suppressed tears of pain and humiliation; from the moment she had seen him with Alice in the theatre when she had become agonisingly aware of his presence, she was unhappy beyond words, and felt as if she were dying slowly and painfully inside. Even so, she would not humble herself at this man's feet, and pride—abused, stubborn, outraged pride—straightened her back and brought her head up high as she met her husband's steady gaze.

'I did not expect to see you here, Lavinia?'

'Why shouldn't I be?' she replied, her voice strained. 'I enjoy the theatre as much as anyone else.'

'I trust you enjoyed the play?'

He addressed her as if she were a mere acquaintance, his voice cool, matter of fact, and Lavinia's pride ached for some assuaging vengeance. 'Yes, thank you,' she lied tersely, vividly aware of the crisp, familiar scent of his cologne.

'You are staying with Mrs Lambert and Daisy, I understand.'

'Yes. They have been very kind.'

Maxim nodded, regarding her coolly. 'I shall call on you. Maybe tomorrow. You will be there?'

'I might be—but then again, I might not,' she said with a mocking smile. 'I might be driving in the park with Daisy. But you needn't put yourself out, Maxim. There is nothing to discuss.'

'On the contrary. There is much we have to settle between us.'

She arched her delicate brows. There was a saturnine twist to his mouth which made Lavinia want to lash out at him. She seethed inwardly. Didn't this arrogant, infuriating man know just how much he had hurt her, shamed her in front of all these people, by appearing in public with his mistress? His mistress! The mother of his child! These few words stung Lavinia like so many wasps. These people at the theatre tonight may not know who she was now, but they soon would when their divorce became common gossip.

'Was I mistaken? I thought we ended that discussion at Thornhill,' she said with a little defiant toss to her head, refusing to let him see how wretched she felt.

'Then yes, you were mistaken. The argument is far from settled yet.'

Her eyes narrowed. 'If all you want to do is argue, Maxim, then I would appreciate it if you keep away from me.'

Leaving her mother talking to some friends, Daisy came to stand beside Lavinia, greeting Maxim politely, who responded in kind. She smiled brightly in an attempt to banish the crackling iciness between these two, but to no avail.

Maxim fixed his eyes on his wife. 'I am here tonight with some friends—'

'I saw,' Lavinia snapped.

Maxim raised his brows at the angry rebuke, knowing full well she was referring to Alice, but this was neither the time nor the place to explain his former mistress's presence in his box or argue the matter. 'We are to go on to my club to dine, otherwise I would invite you to join us,' Maxim told Lavinia.

'Then I would have to refuse. I have an engagement of my own that I have no wish to break,' she lied, favouring him with a slightly mocking, sweet smile, unable to help herself and wondering why she felt the need to make him jealous. 'Goodbye, Maxim.'

Maxim thrust down the feeling of pique of being brushed off like a mere servant. Watching his wife sweep out of the theatre with Daisy, he was angry, but he could not resist moving towards the door and watching the view of her proud head, swaying skirts and trim back as she climbed into the carriage, the lanterns casting their shifting light upon her lovely face.

Settling herself beside Daisy, Lavinia found it equally as hard to resist glancing back at her husband, and she was startled to find his brooding gaze locked on her with a frowning intensity. As the carriage moved off she released a trembling breath and steadied her nerves, watching the buildings they passed, but in her mind she saw only a startling pair of clear blue eyes.

Having returned from Europe and hearing from Mrs Lambert when she came to call on her mother that Lavinia was staying with her and Daisy in Stratton Street, Sophia Evesham, as plain and uninteresting as Lavinia remembered, paid them a surprise visit a week after their trip to the theatre. She was aware of Lavinia's marriage to Maxim Purnell in Venice and was eager to know if the rumour was true, and that there really was a rift between them already. She had also come to impart some malicious gossip which she hoped would put Lavinia's back up, unaware that Lavinia had borne witness to every humiliating detail.

Lavinia was unprepared for the renewed jealousy that exploded inside her when Sophia calmly mentioned the theatre incident that the whole of London seemed to be gossiping about. However, despite being in a state of acute misery, with her heart plummeting to the very depths of despair, she was determined not to expose her anguish to this vituperative female who had the nerve to call herself Daisy's friend. She forced herself to hide her annoyance and smile under Sophia's penetrating inspection and unflinching hauteur.

'It was Mama who told me that you have not taken up residence at Mr Purnell's house in Grosvenor Street, and that you are staying with Daisy and her mother. There's nothing wrong, I hope, Lavinia, between Mr Purnell and you. I heard that he left London a week ago.'

Having secretly hoped that Maxim would call on her as he had said he would, and feeling worse than ever knowing he had left London without so much as a note, Lavinia looked at Sophia with a cheerfulness she was far from feeling, folding her hands sedately in her lap.

'Wrong? Of course not. Maxim has pressing matters of business to take care of at Rotherfield, that is all. I expect him to return to London and join me soon,' Lavinia told her, smiling sweetly, hoping God would forgive her this small untruth, but she had no intention of giving Sophia anything to crow about. And as for Maxim owning a house on Grosvenor Street—that was another surprise, she thought bitterly.

'Rotherfield?' chirped Sophia. 'How strange?'

'What is so strange about that?'

Sophia shrugged, the glow of triumph brightening her eyes. 'I heard that he has gone to Oxfordshire with his uncle, the Earl of Brinkcliff.'

Lavinia gave her a tolerant, brittle stare. 'Then he must have changed his mind.'

'Rumour has it that he was at the theatre with him on the night he was seen with his former mistress, and that they have become reconciled.'

'With his uncle, or Miss Winstanley?' asked Lavinia, her soft voice heavily laced with sarcasm.

Sophia gave an annoyingly grating laugh. 'Why, his uncle, of course. Although…gossip has it that he has mended the breach with them both.' Perceiving that her information had hit its mark, she prattled on about other things.

Fortified by her anger Lavinia forced herself to smile and listen, giving nothing away, and only when Sophia had gone did her fragile serenity slip.

'Oh, Daisy!' she whispered wretchedly, her pride well and truly battered. She couldn't bear it. Not when she loved Maxim so much. 'Maxim left town without coming to see me. How could he?'

'Take no notice of Sophia, Lavinia,' said Daisy in an attempt to placate her, while wanting to strangle both Sophia and Maxim Purnell with her bare hands for causing

Lavinia so much misery. 'Don't let her upset you. She's just jealous because she'll never be able to catch a man like Mr Purnell.'

The Eveshams were giving a ball and they were all invited. However, not inclined to go out into society after her experience at the theatre, Lavinia immediately declined the invitation, which brought an exclamation of disappointment from Daisy as she was about to write an acceptance.

'How can I possible attend a ball, Daisy, when I'm estranged from Maxim? I have no intention of putting myself forward as an object of ridicule.'

Daisy remained adamant. 'Of course you can. Besides, Lavinia, no one knows about your divorce yet. It's early days.'

Lavinia paled at the mention of her divorce. 'How can you be so sure? Don't forget that Maxim has recently been seen in public with his former mistress, so it may already be common knowledge.'

'I doubt it. Divorce is nothing to be proud of and not the sort of thing one bandies about. In any case, surely you don't intend hiding yourself away until after it's all over. Divorces are rare and it could take at least two or three years before it becomes absolute. Besides, apart from the theatre incident, you haven't seen Maxim since coming to London. Despite what Sophia said, perhaps he thinks you are both making a mistake and wants you back. That may have been his reason for wanting to see you—before you so firmly put him off.'

Lavinia shook her head sadly. 'I didn't mean to. I was just so angry and hurt that he would shame and insult me by parading his former mistress in front of me.'

'But how was he to know you would be there?'

'It makes no difference. After what happened between

us he won't want me back. Maxim isn't like that. He's
sterner and more unbending than I ever thought. Besides,
I'm the one who insisted on a divorce, not Maxim. You
don't know him like I do, Daisy. He'll never give me another chance. I no longer exist for him. I realise now that
I should never have left him like that.'

'I know, and it was foolish of you, Lavinia. I'm sure the
two of you could have worked something out if you hadn't
got so angry. Your regrets are written all over your face.'

'You're right,' Lavinia acknowledged honestly. 'But I'm
just going to have to accept what's happened and learn to
get on with my life.'

'Yes, you must, and you can begin by attending the Eveshams' ball with me.'

'Honestly, Daisy, I don't think I can face anyone at present—especially not Lady Evesham. I still cringe when I
remember the look on her face when she came upon Maxim
kissing me in Venice—and the malicious amusement in Sophia's eyes.'

'Sophia is only jealous because after all the money her
parents lavished on her debut and the trip to Europe, she
failed to attract a suitor. Whereas not only were you betrothed to Robert, but you also managed to secure the attentions of the extremely handsome Mr Purnell.'

'Nevertheless, Daisy, if everyone has somehow got wind
of my estrangement from Maxim, I couldn't bear the shame
of it. How they will gloat. Any decent, unattached bachelor
will certainly not want to dance with me, and by the end
of the evening I will be a social outcast.'

'All the more reason why you should go. Brave it out,
Lavinia. You won't be alone, and by London standards it's
only going to be a small gathering.'

'But think of the gossip, Daisy.'

'It's a most unfortunate affair and bound to be much

talked about. If your divorce is already common knowledge, then you'll have to face it sometime. Better to get it over with and stem the tide of malice. Contrary to what you think, Lavinia, your success will be greatly increased by your impending divorce to Maxim Purnell.'

'In what way?'

'Any woman who has managed to ensnare a man of his standing and reputation—which I'm only just becoming aware of myself, never having heard of him before he jumped into the Venetian lagoon to rescue you—and then files for a divorce, is bound to become an object of curiosity.'

'My marriage to Maxim, which is to be followed so soon by divorce, may assure me social possibilities, but not necessarily respect,' said Lavinia on a sigh.

'You have not been properly introduced into London society so everyone is bound to want to know everything there is to know about you—and a woman as lovely as you will always cause comment and speculation.'

'And being my first ball, Daisy, I really should be accompanied by my husband. I am certain that if Maxim hears about it he will be furious.'

'Good. It might give him something to think about when he learns his wife is no meek and supplicating young thing who intends hiding herself away from the world in shame and mortification. I intend making sure that you look your best for the ball and have every gentleman in London kneeling at your feet before the night is out. If that doesn't pique your husband's pride and bring him back to London when he learns of your success, I shall be most surprised.'

'That is insane, Daisy. If he'd wanted to see me he would have called before he left London. I'm sure he must despise me.'

Daisy's smile held a touch of cynicism. 'If he does then

at least he feels something for you. If news of your divorce has not come out, then you must say that Mr Purnell has pressing matters of business to attend to at Rotherfield and that he hopes to join you in London later. There's nothing unusual in that.'

'Sophia says he's gone to Oxfordshire with his uncle, not Rotherfield.'

'Ignore what Sophia says. She isn't important. You must pretend everything is all right between you and Mr Purnell until something happens to rock the boat. You'll find it easier to live with. My instincts tell me you will be a success and by the next day all the rage—and my instincts are never wrong.'

Taking her courage in both hands Lavinia gave in, but she was uneasy.

Chapter Twelve

The night of the ball finally arrived. Lavinia spent more time over her appearance than usual, having the maid sweep her hair up into intricate, tantalising curls, threaded through with golden ribbon. Her gown was a dream of gold chiffon, with a provocatively plunging bodice displaying more of her swelling breasts than she thought was proper, but Daisy didn't appear to think so. With a twinkle in her eye she smiled with undisguised approval.

'You look splendid, Lavinia. I can't wait to see everyone's faces when you are announced at the ball. But Mother is going to have a fit and order you back to your room to change when she sees how low your bodice is. Here, wrap your stole around your shoulders and don't take it off until you reach the Eveshams.'

Lavinia was unaware that no sooner had society digested the news that Maxim Purnell had married in Europe, when it was followed by his wife's arrival in London without him and that she was to attend the Eveshams' ball. Rumour also had it that she was a dazzling beauty and that she and her husband were not in accord. His presence at the opera in the company of his former mistress had been duly noticed, giving rise to a good deal of interest and speculation.

Entering the doors of the Evesham residence—a large country house on the northern outskirts of London—Lavinia had never felt more terrified in her life. Memories of the last ball she had attended evoked poignant memories, for it had been in Venice and Maxim had swept her off her feet.

The three ladies were escorted by Mrs Lambert's brother. Against a background of music and laughter they were received by Sir John and Lady Evesham, with Sophia standing mute and aloof by their side. After exchanging polite pleasantries they moved off towards the ballroom, where long French windows with velvet drapes opened on to a terrace and extensive grounds. Daisy smiled at her friend.

'There you are, you see,' she said quietly, observing the tension on Lavinia's face, thinking that she looked like a lamb about to be slaughtered. 'That wasn't so bad, was it? Since their return from Europe, the Eveshams have lost no time in spreading the gossip about you and Mr Purnell. Lady Evesham has told me that everyone has been bombarding her with questions about you, and are curious to know why you are in London alone after only a few short weeks of marriage. Already the gossips are talking of a split between the two of you.'

'But no one knows for sure, do they?' asked Lavinia in alarm.

'No. It's no secret that your husband has a daughter, and everyone expected him to marry Alice Winstanley eventually. His European marriage to you is a mystery they will hasten to excavate. However, no one knows about your separation so relax and enjoy yourself. You are by far the most beautiful woman here tonight, and already everyone is glancing your way.'

Lavinia smiled softly, holding her head high and ignoring the stares as she injected some confidence into her movements. 'They can stare and whisper all they like, Daisy,' she replied courageously, fixing the most ravishing smile on her face. 'I'm not going to let it bother me.'

Daisy smiled at her approvingly. 'Good for you. By to-morrow morning you will be a sensation.'

Moving past huge flower displays and liveried footmen balancing glasses of wine on silver trays in the huge blue and white foyer, they entered the glittering ballroom. Chandeliers dripped their sparkling crystals over the heads of couples dancing to the strains of a waltz. It was a magical scene, of colour and movement.

Feeling she was under inspection, Lavinia had noticed how heads turned her way when she had been announced, which was followed by a buzz of speculative conversation. Despite her assertions to Daisy that she didn't care what people thought about her, she was painfully self-conscious of everyone devouring her with eager interest.

Recalling what Maxim had said to her in his anger on the night they had parted, that no matter what transpired between them in private, in public he expected her to behave as his wife, she was determined to abide by that and do nothing to dishonour his good name. With her head held high and a smile pinned to her face, she moved among the throng, determined that no one looking at her would know how miserable and lonely this mysterious stranger was in their midst, and that her heart was as dead as a stone and as cold as ice. How they would gloat, Lavinia thought bitterly, when they discovered her secret.

She went through the motions of being introduced by Mrs Lambert to people of note, talking and laughing at the right time, protected by an invisible shell that nothing could penetrate. A crowd of young gallants was already forming about her, and she collected her thoughts sufficiently to respond politely to their compliments and to look as if she was enjoying the ball, allowing one of them to lead her on to the dance floor.

From the gallery looking down on to the ballroom, Maxim's eyes were drawn to his wife. Determined to bridge the gap that was widening between them the longer they remained apart, he had returned from Brinkcliff Hall with his uncle to make his peace with Lavinia. Having arrived in town just two hours ago, he had gone directly to call on her, only to be told on arriving at the Lambert residence that she was attending a ball at Sir John Evesham's house.

On discovering that in no time at all his wife had flagrantly launched herself into society, Maxim had experienced a sharp jolt of displeasure. Firmly ordering the servants to have Lavinia's clothes packed and dispatched posthaste to his own residence in Grosvenor Street, he immediately set off for the Eveshams' ball.

And now as he stood and watched her, for the first time in his life Maxim experienced an acute feeling of jealousy which caught him completely off guard. It was a feeling he found decidedly unpleasant. Frowning with furious displeasure, he considered her *décolletage* to be too revealing, the neckline cut so low as to intrigue and tantalise her admirers. He could not bear to see other men vying with each other with infuriating persistence to dance with her, coveting her, to watch the admiration and appreciation in their eyes as they followed and devoured her every move, leaning forward to allow their eyes to delve into her bodice.

She was like a young queen holding court. The loveliness of her smiling face was flushed with dancing and the champagne she drank between dances, and when she moved her slender, though softly rounded form floated with a fluidity and grace over the floor in a swirl of chiffon, the tips of her gold satin slippers visible as her feet darted to and fro in step to the music. In the simple elegance of her golden ballgown, chosen to blend with the soft warmth of her skin and hair, Maxim's breath caught in his throat as he watched the irresistible curve of her lips and the brilliance of her magnificent turquoise eyes as she gazed at her partner.

And yet there was something remote and detached in the attitude of this dazzling creature. Observing her closely as she engaged in light-hearted repartee, he saw there was something mechanical in the smile pinned to her face. The love, the warmth and the passion that he had roused in her and had flourished, had become frozen into this beautiful effigy.

But he had never seen her look so provocatively lovely, so regal, glamorous and bewitching—and she belonged to him. Lord, how he'd missed her. He ardently yearned to hold her in his arms, to feel her warmth, smell her hair, her flesh. The yearning was like an obsession in his blood. It tormented him all the time. An ache was growing inside him. Never had he felt anything like it, and Lavinia and Lavinia alone could assuage that ache, with her lips, her body.

Unable to endure this torture a moment longer Maxim turned on his heel. His only thought was to get to her and inject some warmth back into her, to take her in his arms and send her persistent suitors packing.

People were still arriving and Lavinia was with Daisy talking to a group of boisterous gentlemen when the butler announced Lord Stannington. The name was unfamiliar so Lavinia took no notice. It was only when the voices around her became hushed and she felt Daisy clutch her arm that she looked at her, following the direction of her gaze towards the entrance of the ballroom. She paled, overcome with shock. Unable to move, her eyes became riveted on a tall gentleman fastidiously tailored in black evening attire. It was Maxim, just as supremely powerful and splendidly and unbearably handsome. When she saw him she felt such a pang of longing and need that she wanted to run to him and fling herself against him.

His commanding presence was awesome. During the time they had been apart she had hoped she had managed to conquer the debilitating effect he always had on her senses, but his potent sexual magnetism was like a palpable force. How tall he was, how lean and muscular, and how her blood stirred at the sight of him. How had she allowed him to do this to her? She was scandalised by the stirrings inside her that the mere sight of him commanded, and she resented this hunger, this need, that held her captive to her emotions.

Lavinia watched him as he talked to Sir John and Lady Evesham. He looked so relaxed, and he spoke to them with such lazy good humour that she could hardly believe he was the same relentless, rage-filled man who had forcibly clasped her to him and made love to her at Thornhill one month ago. It was as if he were two people: one she loved and admired, and one she feared and mistrusted—and, she reminded herself, with good reason.

'Maxim!' she whispered. 'What on earth is he doing here, do you think, Daisy?'

'More to the point, what's he doing calling himself Lord Stannington?'

'I have no idea. I know Maxim cares nothing for titles and that he is estranged from his uncle, the Earl of Brinkcliff. Perhaps they have become reconciled, which would explain his use of the title—being the Earl's heir. What will he do? Do you think he will ignore me? Oh, Daisy— I couldn't bear it if he did that.'

'He won't. Your husband is not the sort to make a scene—and my guess is that he wouldn't be here if you weren't.'

Lavinia was calm as could be to everyone around her, but her heart was pounding and she seemed to have trouble catching her breath. Maxim turned and caught her gaze, and with hope and disbelief springing to her eyes, she watched him cut through the groups of people with deceptive casualness, briefly acknowledging those he recognised, many a feminine eye following him as he advanced towards her.

As he came closer a knot began to form inside Lavinia's chest. He was politely frightening, his eyes like ice, and he bore down on her with the predatory grace of a stalking beast. The music had ceased and people were talking among themselves, but Lavinia was aware that everyone's attention was riveted on them, eager to see what would happen when Maxim Purnell reached his wife.

Holding her gaze, Maxim's eyes were silently telling Lavinia that for the sake of appearances they must both behave as though everything between them was in accord. He had such strength, authority and incredible drive that he would be in control of any situation.

When he stood in front of her he looked searchingly into her eyes, taking her hand and raising it to his lips. 'This is a pleasant surprise, Lavinia. I hope you are enjoying yourself.'

'Yes, thank you, Maxim,' she replied, favouring him with a honey-sweet smile, sensing that behind his chiselled features and air of calm he was furious.

Smiling faintly he swung his gaze coolly over the disappointed faces of the group of young men gathered around her. 'Please excuse us. My wife looks excessively warm after her exertions on the dance floor. I'm sure she will be glad of some fresh air.'

Taking her elbow in a firm grasp, his free hand resting possessively in the small of her back, he guided her towards

the French windows somewhat less than gently. A few gentlemen met his eye and, recognising the challenge in his
gaze, they turned away. Maxim propelled his wife from the
safety of the house on to the terrace, not speaking until
they were far enough away from the eyes and ears of everyone, and then he turned, fixing her with the full blast of his
fury.

'What do you think you're playing at by coming here?
Are you deliberately trying to provoke me?' he demanded
with hot, unreasonable anger, the barbs of jealousy pricking
him to a painful depth.

'Provoke you?' his wife replied, her eyes wide as she
feigned a look of innocence, determined not to let him draw
her to anger and cause her to lose her fragile grip on her
emotions. 'Why on earth should I do that? We are estranged, Maxim.'

He stepped close, towering over her, and Lavinia almost
retreated from those fierce eyes. But she steeled herself and
stood her ground before his accusing glare.

'I assure you, Lavinia, that I will have you behave with
more dignity and in a manner more befitting your station
than you seem concerned about. You are still my wife and
you will behave accordingly.'

Lavinia's heart was breaking, but she gave him a ravishing smile. 'I haven't forgotten, Maxim, and there are all
sorts of things I remember about being your wife. And
don't worry. I will do nothing to embarrass you—and I
sincerely hope you do nothing that will embarrass me.'

His eyes narrowed in question. 'What do you mean by
that remark?'

She shrugged her slender shoulders. 'What I say.'

'Suppose you tell me why, the minute you are out of my
sight, you forget how to behave.'

'My behaviour is quite in order—which cannot be said

of your own. I find your manner unreasonable and insufferable.'

He glared at her. She was right. His manner was unreasonable and insufferable, and he didn't even begin to understand it. His blazing gaze was drawn to and froze on the beautiful swell of her petal-soft breasts above the golden bodice of her gown. 'And do you have to display yourself so wantonly to the entire male population of London? How dare you come out in public alone—in that dress.'

Lavinia flinched at the cold, ruthless fury in his eyes as they raked over her. Bravely she tried to hold on to her composure and stop herself exploding. 'I see nothing wrong with my gown. I think it's extremely pretty. And I hardly think you have the right to dictate where I go and what I shall wear under the circumstances. Really, Maxim, if you brought me out here for no other purpose than to berate me, then I shall go back inside.'

Torn between the urge to lash out at him or burst into tears, she made a move to pass him, but his hand locked on her wrist. 'You will stay here and talk to me. I will not have you making a scene, Lavinia. Consider the meal everyone will make when they see there is disharmony between us.'

'Like you considered my feelings when you came to London and paraded your former mistress at the opera for everyone to see?' she flared accusingly, her eyes sparking fire. Bringing the matter out into the open at last, she wanted to fling her hurt in his face. 'How dare you do that to me? Have you any idea how shamed and insulted I felt when I saw you together that night?'

Her words brought Maxim up sharp and he stared at her. He realised that she had seen Alice come to his box that night at the theatre, and the foolish young woman had drawn her own conclusions. Lavinia looked so young, so

vulnerable, facing him with those mutinous, appealing turquoise eyes locked on to his, that his anger was defused.
His senses were jolted into life by the elusive, perfumed
smell of her. Half-smiling, half-frowning, he looked into
her eyes. 'I stand rebuked, but that I can explain.'

'I don't want to listen to your lame excuses.'

'Yes, you do,' he said, grasping her arm and forcing her
to look at him when she spun on her heel to walk away.
'When I came to London shortly after you left Thornhill,
it was to see my lawyers and my uncle. I was with him at
the opera the night Alice was there. She came to our box
to be introduced and it was impossible to remove her without causing a scene. Unfortunately, her visit was long
enough to be noted and set the theatre alight with rumours
of a reconciliation. Please believe me when I tell you that
nothing could be further from the truth.' He smiled, suddenly, his eyes gently teasing, his voice quiet. 'But why all
the fuss, Lavinia? I thought that was what you wanted.
Wasn't that why you left me?'

'Damn you, Maxim!' she flared. 'Did you have to do it
so publicly?'

'I do assure you that it wasn't intentional. I would not
have done that to you. And when I told you I was to go
on to dine with acquaintances at my club afterwards, it was
the truth.' His eyes narrowed, glinting mockingly down into
hers. 'Which cannot be said of your own supper arrangement that night. You implied that the company would con-
sist of other men. Were you trying to stir my jealousy by
retaliation, Lavinia?'

'Retaliation? How amusing. Do not judge me by your
own behaviour, Maxim, or feel you have anything to explain,' she said caustically.

'I don't. I merely thought you would like to know. And
the reason I didn't call on you at Mrs Lambert's before I

went to Oxfordshire with my uncle was because after your cold reception at the theatre, I considered it best, for the time being at least, to avoid any confrontation that might end as our last meeting did.'

Lavinia's eyes flew to his in blazing fury. 'Whenever we happen to meet in the future, Maxim, it will *never* end like that one, and I would appreciate you not mentioning it again. It is a night I have no wish to recall. Why are you here, anyway?'

'Lavinia,' he said impatiently, taking both her arms and looking down into her lovely face. 'I am here for no other reason than to see you.'

Her ire was ill suppressed as she ground out between clenched teeth, 'You could have done that the last time you came to London, but you chose to ignore me.'

'I have just explained why I didn't come to see you. I did not ignore you. I am here now because there are things we must discuss—that have to be understood between us.'

'I understand perfectly well how things stand between us, Maxim,' she said, turning away.

Maxim moved to stand close behind her, not touching, but near enough to prevent her moving past him without coming into contact with him. 'I'm sorry you were hurt,' he murmured. 'Whatever may be going through that pretty head of yours, Lavinia, I have no desire to return to Alice, and I had no idea she would come bursting into my box at the theatre.'

Lavinia smiled softly to herself, her instinct telling her that his initial anger had been caused by his jealousy on seeing her surrounded by so many admiring young males, and that despite everything, he did still want her. The knowledge warmed her, and made up for a good deal of his abominable treatment of her. But threads of anger still coursed through her, and she had no intention of letting him off lightly.

Over her shoulder Maxim gazed down at the seductive swell of her breasts and he ached to caress the womanly softness of her, to embrace her and ease the lusting ache at the pit of his belly. Strange lights danced in her golden hair, and her slender shoulders gleamed with a creamy soft lustre. The heady allure of her perfume mingled with her womanly essence, filled his head, stirring and warming his blood.

Lavinia turned and faced him, almost overawed by his nearness, and trying to break the contact he was beginning to stir inside her. She didn't move as he ran a finger along the curve of her lips, trailing it down the column of her neck and along the smooth, velvet curve of her shoulder and down her upper arm. It was a soothing caress that awoke tingling answers in places she tried to ignore. The betrayal of her body aroused vexation in her. His touch burned her flesh and seared into her heart, reminding her how deeply she still loved this insufferable man. It was a hard fact for her pride to accept, especially when they were to divorce.

Maxim lifted a brow as he regarded his wife, and she read in their depths and the heat of his stare what he had in mind. Calmly she met his gaze.

'Cool your ardour, Maxim,' she warned. 'This is neither the time nor the place and most certainly not part of our agreement.' Trying to regain her composure she struck a stubborn pose, the look in her eyes as she silently met her husband's sardonic gaze one of pure mutiny. 'Please excuse me. It's becoming decidedly chilly out here all of a sudden.' Jerking her arms out of his grasp she turned from him and walked quickly back into the house, unaware of his infuriating smile of admiration as he watched her go.

To her husband at that moment, Lavinia was the epitome of a stubborn, prideful woman. Yet for all her fire and spirit she displayed none of Alice's viciousness.

An expression of disappointment crossed Daisy's face when she saw Lavinia enter the ballroom alone. Taking her hand, she drew her to one side, but was prevented from asking what had occurred on the terrace when she became aware that people were looking their way.

Glancing up, Lavinia saw a smiling Sophia bearing down on her, accompanied by an extremely beautiful woman with raven black hair. Immediately she had a premonition of disaster. The woman was Alice Winstanley, Maxim's former mistress and mother of his child, and she watched, sick with dread, as she moved serenely towards her. Oh, why did Alice have to be so devastatingly provocative and beautiful in a rich, burgundy-coloured gown and the body of a goddess? she thought despairingly.

There was a tension as everyone waited to see what would happen when Maxim's mistress came face to face with his wife. Choosing that moment to reappear through the French windows, Maxim saw what was about to happen and sensed Lavinia's distress. Determined to save her from being shamed and humiliated in front of everyone, immediately he made his way to her side, taking her hand and linking it through his arm. She glanced up at him, gratitude in her worried eyes, glad of his support as she watched Alice come closer.

The room began to rock and tremble beneath her, and she was sickened to think this woman knew what it was like to be loved by Maxim, to have her naked body caressed by him, to know how devastating and drugging his kisses could be—for their bodies to be linked as one.

Sensing what she was feeling, Maxim reassuringly squeezed her fingers, which were linked through his arm.

He didn't look in the least perturbed that they were about to be confronted by Alice, but the look he bestowed on Sophia, who was taking a malicious delight in a situation entirely of her making, was murderous.

Alice halted in front of them, bestowing on Maxim a smile dripping with charm, whilst eyeing Lavinia like a hostile cat. She had no qualms about meeting his wife, in fact, she was obviously out to relish her rival's embarrassment and humiliation.

'Alice!' said Maxim with a lazy smile. 'As usual you look lovely. No doubt you will have all the gentlemen at your feet before the night is over.' He turned to Lavinia. 'Permit me to introduce to you my wife, Lavinia.'

Normally a man would not introduce his wife to his mistress in polite society, but there was no way Maxim could avoid doing so without making a scene.

Alice's beautiful brows rose slightly when her eyes met Lavinia's. Myriad emotions washed over her face, none of them pleasant. Lavinia returned her stare steadily, trying not to look disconcerted or intimidated. She was aware of every man and woman in the room secretly looking at them with eyes that glittered, above mouths that curled with amusement. She loathed every one of them, furious that, out of sheer spite, Sophia Evesham had put her in this position. Fortified by her anger and her husband's support, she looked directly into Alice's eyes with a quiet, dignified composure which made Maxim proud.

'I'm pleased to meet you, Miss Winstanley.'

'Likewise,' Alice answered, her tone insincere and lightly contemptuous, her look insolent. 'I've been hearing a great deal about you.'

Lavinia gave a delicate lift of her brows. 'So soon? You surprise me, Miss Winstanley. I arrived in town a month ago, and this is only my second appearance in public.'

Alice laughed, a harsh, abrasive sound. 'Gossip is always plentiful in London. That's one thing you can depend on.' She shifted her gaze back to Maxim. 'You really must call some time, Maxim. It's shameful the way you neglect our daughter. You have no idea how much she pines for you.'

Maxim's eyes were like shards of ice. 'Yes, I do. It is my intention to call tomorrow. I trust you will be at home, Alice. There is a matter of some importance I have to discuss with you. Lucy is well, I hope?'

'A little dispirited. But it's nothing a visit from her father won't cure. I'll look forward to your call,' she said with a satisfied smile curving her lovely lips, making sure Lavinia understood the claim she had on Maxim.

In spite of herself, Alice's resentment and jealousy began to rise as her eyes flickered once more over the woman at his side, hating her. She was overawed by Lavinia's cool self-assurance, her casual, confident beauty, and contemptuous of Maxim's open admiration of his wife. She threw Maxim a glare that might once have moved him. Now he was frankly amused. She was hot, suddenly, trying desperately to control her temper for fear of being made to look a fool.

'Excuse me,' she said haughtily, snapping open her fan and using it with verve. 'I am promised for the next dance and I can see my partner looking for me.'

Lavinia and Maxim watched her move on in a relieved silence, the tension beginning to relax between them.

'Thank you, Maxim,' Lavinia murmured. 'I couldn't have endured meeting her alone.'

He smiled down at her, squeezing her hand. 'I dare say you'd have coped admirably.'

The musicians chose that moment to play a waltz and Maxim smiled, a slow, lazy white smile that melted Lavinia's heart. He might be mercurial, unreasonable, demanding and impossible, but he still made her heart sing.

'Every other gentleman here tonight has danced with you. I think it's high time you danced with your husband. Come, dance with me, Lavinia,' he murmured, his voice as soft as it had been on that other occasion when he had asked her to dance at the masquerade in Venice.

Mesmerised by the seductive invitation in his voice, Lavinia let him draw her on to the dance floor, abandoning her waist to his encircling arm. It was as steady and firm as a rock. Maxim was a superb dancer and moved with a lithe, athletic grace. He whirled her into the dance and she seemed to soar with the melody. She gazed at her husband admiringly, liking the way his superbly tailored black coat clung to his splendid shoulders. His face had lost some of the tan he had acquired in Europe, but it was still darker than any other man's present, and combined with his gleaming black hair, his pristine white shirt and neckcloth stood out in sharp contrast.

Maxim felt her tremble and bent his head, giving the impression to all watching that he was paying his wife an intimate compliment. 'We have an audience. Hold your head up, Lavinia. Look into my eyes and smile. Let them see that we are a devoted couple.' He arched a satirical dark brow. 'You may even flirt with me a little if you so wish.'

Lavinia looked at him, utterly confused by his sudden appearance and not knowing what he wanted of her. Had he come because he cared, because he'd missed her and was unable to live without her? Was he sorry for what he'd done and come to make amends? Dozens of questions invaded her mind. There was so much she wanted to ask him, so much she wanted to say to him.

Unable to understand him she searched his sultry eyes,

suddenly resenting his easy arrogance in assuming that she would be ready to fall at his feet as if nothing untoward had happened between them. Not at any price would she consent to be treated so. The fact that she had been full of remorse over their parting and her harsh words about his lack of responsibility where Alice and his daughter was concerned, and had considered returning to Rotherfield and throwing herself on his mercy, while praying at the same time that he would come to her and take her in his arms and alleviate her suffering, went out of her mind as her pride came to the fore.

'And if I don't?' she said stiffly in response to his remark.

Maxim saw rebellion beginning to stir in the depths of her glorious turquoise eyes. 'Pretend.' His arm tightened about her waist, forcing her into an awareness of his lithe body. He was perfectly well aware of the effect it always had on her when he held her in his arms, knowing how easily he could bring her to submission.

'I can't pretend, Maxim. Besides, Daisy says that it's unusual for a woman to flirt openly with her husband.'

'I don't give a damn what Daisy says,' Maxim said through gritted teeth, his earlier jealousy on seeing every man in the room undressing and devouring her with their lust-filled eyes still simmering beneath the surface of his calm façade. 'Look at me like you've been looking at all those other doting swains who've been clinging to your side all evening like limpets to a rock—or have you used up all your smiles on them?'

'Of course not, but at least they were civil, their remarks flattering.'

'Every man resorts to flattery when there's something they want from a beautiful woman,' Maxim growled.

'Don't be deceived when they shower you with pretty compliments and speeches. They're all after only one thing.'

'Nevertheless, they were full of charm, every one of them, and told me I'm the most beautiful woman at the ball tonight. What do you think, Maxim?' she asked with mock innocence, looking up at him with her head cocked on one side, her eyes calmly watching for his reaction to her challenging question.

Maxim was furious that so many men had been drooling over his wife, but he swallowed his chagrin and smiled charmingly down at her with half-shrouded eyes.

'What can I say? As your husband I must agree with every one of them.'

'Must? Maxim, I don't want you to feel you must agree with them just to humour me.'

His brows arched in ironic amusement. 'I'm not humouring you. I meant it. You are by far the loveliest woman here—but don't let the compliment go to your head.'

She smiled, satisfied. 'I won't.'

'Now tell me what you're doing here. Not content with attending the ball alone and making yourself conspicuous, you have to make me appear ludicrous by flirting with every man present?' His clear blue eyes held hers, full of accusation. 'Well? What have you to say for yourself?'

With an effort Lavinia retained her composure as they moved over the dance floor, aswirl with couples moving gracefully to the music, lovely and melodic.

'Nothing. When you're in this mood, whatever I say in my defence will be futile. For a start I wasn't flirting. I was merely being polite. And I wouldn't call attending a ball to which I've been invited making myself conspicuous. Besides, I could hardly wait for you to escort me, seeing that we are estranged. What would you have me do? Go slinking around as if I've disgraced myself? We may be divorcing, but that doesn't mean I have to make an outcast of myself. What are you doing here, Maxim? I—I thought—'

'What? What did you think? That I would calmly sit back and allow you to walk out of my life? May I ask what your admirers talked to you about?'

'You may, but I will not tell you.'

He nodded, studying her beneath half-lowered lids with tranquil amusement. 'Do I have reason to call any of them out?'

She smiled, her eyes glowing with repressed laughter. 'Several. But with so many, you would be hard pressed to beat them all.'

'Don't count on it,' Maxim replied, spinning her round with unnecessary force.'

She laughed. 'Maxim, please slow down. You swirl me round so fast I'm beginning to feel quite dizzy.'

'You've drunk too many glasses of champagne.'

She was indignant. 'No, I have not.'

'Yes, you have—four—or was it five?'

His smile was amused and slightly mocking which annoyed her. 'You were watching me?'

'Yes. I had nothing better to do.'

'You could have sought me out earlier.'

'What? And deprive all those besotted swains of the pleasure of your company? You've made quite an impression and, regardless of your marital state, you must prepare yourself to be pursued,' he teased lightly.

'And here I was thinking I would be safe in London,' she quipped.

Maxim caught her gaze, his eyes narrowing seductively. 'Safe? Safe from me? From loving me?' he murmured, his warm breath fanning her face. He smiled infuriatingly at the bewilderment in her eyes. 'What have you told every-one?'

'Nothing,' she replied, totally bemused by his behaviour and wondering what he was leading up to. 'Apart from Mrs Lambert and Daisy, no one knows we are estranged—that—that we are to divorce, if that is what you mean. I must thank you for being so prompt in making the money accessible to me. I have decided to look for a small house somewhere in London.'

'There's no need. There will be no divorce.'

Lavinia's eyes widened in amazement. 'But—I don't un-derstand. What are you saying?'

He smiled down at her, his gaze dropping to the tantalis-ing creamy swell of her breasts exposed above the bodice of her gown, a sight that had enraged him earlier, and one in which he now took lustful delight. She looked incredible, ravishing, he thought, and he was determined to adorn that slender neck with the finest jewels in the kingdom before too long.

'You heard me, my sweet. I don't want a divorce. I have no intention of letting you out of my sight ever again. This last month has been the longest month of my life and I don't intend enduring another like it.'

Lavinia stared at him, reeling from his incredible con-fession. Afraid to hope, and unable not to, she gaze up at him, her knees quaking so badly that she feared she would stumble.

'Have you considered the consequences of a divorce, Lavinia?'

'The consequences for whom?'

'You. It will certainly be unpleasant.'

'I would imagine divorce is always unpleasant.'

'With a scandalous divorce suit hanging over you, you will become the object of everyone's attention.'

'Surely that applies to both of us?'

'Hardly. Don't forget that I would be the one divorcing you on the grounds of desertion, and it would do you nothing but harm. You would be ostracised by decent society. Could you endure the severe censure and disgrace the stigma of being a divorced woman would bring you?'

'I—I don't know, Maxim. I haven't really thought about it.'

'You will become notorious in a way you do not deserve. What would you hope to gain?'

'My freedom.'

His eyes probed hers. 'And do you want to be free, Lavinia? Of me?'

Lavinia searched his face, feeling her heart turn over exactly the way it always did when he looked at her like he was looking at her now. She saw the glow in his half-shuttered eyes kindle slowly into flame, and deep within her, she felt the answering stirrings of longing, a longing to feel the tormenting sweetness of his caress, the stormy passion of his kiss, and the earth-shattering joy of his body possessing hers. 'No.'

'Thank God for that,' he murmured huskily, impatient for the dance to end so he could whisk her away and make love to her. 'As an experienced man of the world I never would have believed that I would fall victim to a beautiful, innocent young woman who firmly refuses to yield to my authority and blithely incurs my displeasure by leaving me. You, my love, have the power to amuse, enchant, bewitch and infuriate me as no other woman has done before. I only hope that you have been as miserable as I have been.'

The tenderness in Maxim's eyes warmed Lavinia's heart. 'Yes, I have,' she confessed, feeling the music possessing her as her body moved to the melody, melting into his.

'You did miss me?'

Gazing up at him she was happy to see his eyes were serious and devoid of his usual arrogance. She wanted to tell him that she had missed him more than she would have believed possible, that she had missed his presence, his quiet strength, the laughter they had shared and his lazy smile, and the way he was looking at her now.

'Yes,' she admitted softly. 'When I left you everything suddenly seemed so empty and meaningless.'

Maxim's lips curved in a soft, satisfied smile and tenderness washed through him at the sincere honesty of her reply.

'I was too hasty in my judgement, Maxim. I'm sorry. I was upset and hurt that you didn't tell me about Alice and Lucy.'

'I understand that now.'

'Do you?'

'Yes. I should have told you. It was wrong of me not to, I realise that now. I don't blame you for being angry. I want to explain everything to you, Lavinia, but not here. I don't deserve you,' he murmured. 'You're so perfect. When the music ends I have no intention of remaining to dance attendance on dozens of elderly ladies and utter meaningless platitudes for the next few hours. We will make our excuses to Sir John and Lady Evesham and leave soon afterwards.'

'But—we can't, Maxim. It would appear rude.'

'Yes, we can. We'd better leave before I hurl you down on to the floor and ravish you in front of all these people. Do you want to make a scene?'

'No, of course I don't.'

'Then do as I say.' His smile was lazy as his eyes settled on her moist lips with hungry ardour. 'I can think of more pleasurable ways of spending an evening with my wife. In private.'

Hot colour burned Lavinia's cheeks and she ground her teeth with indignation when she recalled the last time she had experienced the kind of pleasure he was talking about. Determined not to let him off lightly for what he had done to her on her last night at Thornhill, she stared defiantly into his eyes, her body stiffening against his as he whirled her over the dance floor, her step matching his with admirable precision.

'Yes, I'm sure you can, Maxim. But I seem to recall that your interpretation of pleasure is not mine. I have every reason in the world to despise you for what you did to me.'

Looking down at her, Maxim's sharp eyes didn't miss a thing, including both her suppressed ire and her nervousness. His expression softened. 'You're right, and I apologise. I realise that some form of atonement for my behaviour towards you is in order.'

With great difficulty Lavinia had to stifle a smile, for despite his words to the contrary, there was a complete absence of contrition on his face.

'I behaved very badly,' he admitted, 'but you did drive me to it.'

Meeting his impertinent gaze Lavinia gasped. The arrogance of his last remark was so typical of him that she almost laughed.

Maxim smiled softly, a warmth entering his narrowed eyes. 'I don't recall you protesting too strongly at the time, either.'

Swamped with embarrassment Lavinia's flush deepened attractively and she averted her eyes, wishing he wouldn't taunt and torment her in this infuriating manner. 'Please, Maxim. Do we have to discuss these things in the middle of the dance floor with everyone looking at us? Have you no shame?'

He grinned, his eyes alight with devilish amusement.

'None whatsoever, my love. But I do agree. I think we should retire to discuss this in private.'

Panic suddenly gripped Lavinia. 'But this is all so sudden. I can't leave with you just like that, Maxim. I came with Mrs Lambert and Daisy. I must return with them. Perhaps we can meet and discuss things in the morning.'

His face hardened. 'No, Lavinia. We leave together.'

The sudden bite in his voice made Lavinia stiffen in his arms. 'You cannot always expect me to bow to your authority, Maxim. I must have time to think about this.'

'I have given you four weeks. Isn't that long enough?'

'A—at least let us stay for the buffet.'

'We'll eat at home if you're hungry.'

Lavinia longed to defy him, but she didn't dare. The music ceased and he led her off the floor.

After making their excuses to their hosts, Maxim escorted his wife out of the Eveshams' residence, aware as he did so of the regret on the faces of several unattached males. He met their eyes with a look that threatened to slice every one of them into pieces if they dared approach her.

Chapter Thirteen

Like every other residence in Grosvenor Street, Maxim's town house was an imposing building. The door was opened by a footman and they stepped into a high, spacious hall with a white marble floor. Lavinia could not restrain an exclamation of approval, which brought a smile to Maxim's lips.

'Goodness, Maxim! You've certainly done well for yourself. Having seen Rotherfield and now this, you have all the trappings of an aristocrat.'

He grinned. 'I knew you would like it.'

Lavinia looked at him steadily. 'Am I so predictable, Maxim? Were you so sure I would come?' she enquired.

'Naturally,' he replied.

'Conceited of you,' she said lightly with a little smile tugging at her lips.

'Life has made me that way,' Maxim retorted.

'Yes—I can see that,' she remarked, looking around her. 'A house such as this is most appropriate for Lord Stannington—the future Earl of Brinkcliff,' she said with a teasing light in her eyes.

An ironic smile twisted Maxim's lips and he scowled. 'I'm glad you think so,' he replied absently.

Lavinia frowned. 'For a man who will one day inherit an earldom and all that goes with it, you don't look too happy about it.'

'I'm not. It makes me damned uncomfortable if you must know. Does it bother you being Lady Stannington—knowing that one day you will be a countess?'

'I confess that I find it extremely daunting, but I think I shall be able to live with it. Ursula told me about your estrangement from your uncle, so I can only assume you have healed the breach and become reconciled.'

'Yes. Ursula pressed me into it. I'll explain everything to you later.' His gaze narrowed on her smiling lips. 'Does the promise of a coronet and all that goes with it make me more desirable as a husband, Lavinia?'

She looked at him steadily. 'Do you seriously think those things matter to me, Maxim? I'm not interested in grand estates or riches. Nor am I interested in a coronet—only the man who wears it.'

'Some women would settle for nothing less,' he said, thinking of Alice.

'I'm not some women. When did you see your uncle?'

'I had a meeting with him three weeks ago here in London.'

Lavinia was still hurt to know he had been in London and hadn't tried to contact her after their encounter at the theatre, but said nothing.

'Come along, let me show you to your bedchamber,' he murmured, eager to be alone with her.

They went up the elegant curving staircase to the landing where they had adjoining suites. Maxim disappeared into his own, stripping off his jacket as he went and leaving Lavinia alone with a fresh-faced young maid. The room was extremely grand and tastefully furnished. the overall colour scheme being midnight blue and ivory. 'My name's

Betsy, my lady,' said the maid, bobbing a respectful curt-sey. 'Lord Stannington has employed me to be your personal maid.'

'Has he now!' said Lavinia with a wry smile on her lips, her eyes making a sharp assessment of the gowns Betsy was in the process of unpacking from a large trunk. Recognising them as being her own, she felt a stirring of resentment that Maxim had impudently ordered them to be brought from Stratton Street without first speaking to her about it. 'I'm sure we will get along very well, Betsy—' she smiled '—and I must thank you for unpacking my things.'

Betsy helped her new mistress out of her clothes and into a white satin and lace nightdress. She had just finished fastening the tiny buttons at her throat when Maxim strode through the connecting door into the bedchamber, wearing a mulberry-coloured dressing robe and filling the room with his presence.

Casting Betsy a glance of dismissal, he went towards his wife, impatient to have her in his arms after so long. 'Thank God we are alone at last,' he murmured, drawing her close.

Lavinia saw the darkening in his eyes and stalled his kiss by placing her hands on his chest and looking up at him, still annoyed with him for taking the liberty of having her clothes brought here without her say so.

'What is it, my love?' he asked, feeling her hesitate.

'Maxim! When you came to London, were you so sure I could be persuaded to return here with you that you immediately ordered my clothes to be packed up at Stratton Street and brought here?'

'I was,' he murmured, drawing her hair aside and nuzzling her ear with his warm lips.

Lavinia sighed. 'You're impossible.'

He relinquished her ear and grinned. 'We've already agreed that. Are you complaining?'

She looked at him, loving him. 'No. Nothing you do surprises me.'

'Are you still hungry?'

She saw the need, the intensity of his longing, reflected in his eyes, and her stomach quivered in anticipation of what was to come. 'No. Not any more. At least—not for food.'

'Good girl. That's what I like to hear.'

The desire darkening his eyes and the raw emotion in his voice made Lavinia hesitate and draw away from him. 'Maxim, wait. There are things to discuss first?'

'They can wait until morning. We have better things to do just now.'

'Indeed?'

'Yes,' he said, catching her upper arms and pulling her towards him. 'I'm going to love you, Lavinia.' He saw the wary light in her eyes, knowing she was remembering the last time he had made love to her, forcing himself on her. 'I'm not going to hurt you. I give you my word. I would never hurt you, not intentionally. I want to give you the world.'

'I've already told you that I don't want the world. It's not important to me. Why did you come to London, Maxim?'

'Because you matter to me a great deal. Dear Lord,' he breathed, gathering her into his arms, his senses intoxicated with the smell of her scented flesh. 'I've missed you. These past weeks have been hellish. I want you. I need you so much.'

At last his mouth covered hers in an endless, drugging kiss, and his arms tightened around her. Lavinia's heart quickened with pulsating pleasure. Drawing her towards the

bed Maxim's questing fingers unfastened the tiny buttons
at her throat, pushing her nightdress off her shoulders and
letting it fall in a circle about her feet.

Catching his breath his eyes beheld the beauty of her.
His fascinated gaze moved over her, having forgotten just
how lovely she was. Her skin was as smooth as alabaster,
her shining hair tumbling over her shoulders, her brows
delicately arched and her sooty lashes thick and curling.
Her eyes were like luminous turquoise jewels, her mouth
vulnerable, soft, and begging to be kissed.

Loosening the sash of his robe and shrugging out of it,
Maxim drew her down on to the bed. He intended to make
amends, to give her so much pleasure that she would forget
that last time—and as Lavinia moaned beneath him, her
body craving satisfaction, she didn't care about that other
time.

Later there was satiation and only the sound of their
breathing. Lavinia had no basis for comparison, but in bed
Maxim was a magnificent lover, both demanding and ful-
filling. There was a carefully controlled brutality in his
lovemaking, yet there was patience and tenderness and passion. And yet, he might make love to her, but that wasn't
the same as loving her.

The relief she felt now he had decided he no longer
wanted a divorce was immense, and she smiled into the
dark, knowing that even if she still insisted on one, his
indomitable will would prevail against any argument she
might raise. She accepted that their future was together, and
matters concerning Alice and Lucy must be discussed and
worked out in a sensible and adult manner. But when the
image of Alice invaded her mind, and that of his child, she
was troubled.

The following morning, eager to join Maxim for breakfast, Lavinia hurriedly bathed and dressed in a lemon silk

gown with a modestly scooped neckline and long sleeves, tying a matching sash about her slim waist. After Betsy had brushed her hair until it shone, she arranged it beautifully into thick curls about her head.

Glancing through open doors into rooms as she went downstairs, Lavinia saw the house was furnished to suit Maxim's excellent masculine tastes. A footman standing in the hall opened the door to the dining room and she stepped inside, seeing Maxim already seated at the far end of a long, extremely grand, mahogany dining table with at least a dozen highbacked, dark green velvet chairs on either side, and two elaborate crystal chandeliers hanging above.

Immediately he rose and came towards her with long strides, looking superbly handsome in tight grey breeches and a shirt of thin white lawn. His hair was brushed back and glossy black, but an errant wave threatened to fall over his forehead at any minute. Arrogance and authority was stamped all over him, but Lavinia was not intimidated by it. As usual there was a strength and vigour about him that brought a warmth to her cheeks, but this morning it seemed more pronounced. He reminded her of a healthy animal trapped in a cage, deliberately restraining his energy.

Enfolding her in a tight embrace, Maxim kissed her lips before standing back and peering with a warm tenderness into her glowing eyes. 'You look wonderful,' he told her. 'Not too tired this morning, I hope.'

She smiled warmly, the pleasant smell of his spicy cologne wafting over her. 'If I am I shall have to blame you,' she teased.

Taking her hand he led her down the length of the table, pulling out a chair across from his own. 'No need to stand on ceremony when there's only the two of us. I'm glad you decided to join me for breakfast. I hoped you would.'

'Thank you. I'd love some coffee,' said Lavinia, smiling at an aloof looking footman who was standing to attention like a soldier close to a large dresser containing platters of food and holding a welcoming pot of delicious-smelling coffee in his hands.

'As long as you don't upset the chef by not eating,' said Maxim. 'André is very efficient and being French, he is extremely temperamental and takes it as a personal criticism if anyone refuses to eat.'

'What! Even you?'

'Even me,' he grinned, spreading a napkin over his knees.

Breakfast was a feast of fluffy scrambled eggs, mushrooms and crisply curled bacon and toast in silver racks, all washed down with fresh coffee. The footman came and went, leaving them alone for most of the time so the two of them could converse in private. Despite her earlier concern as to how deeply Maxim cared for her, Lavinia had never felt so happy and contented. She drained her cup and smiled at him, thinking how relaxed he was. When they had finished eating and their plates had been cleared away, he dismissed the footman, asking him to leave the coffee pot as they would probably want another cup.

Maxim sighed, gazing across at his wife, watching the morning sunlight turn her hair to silver and gold, while he relished her beauty and the keen intelligence in her wonderful turquoise eyes. 'Dear Lord, I've missed you. Do you realise that this is the first morning of our lives together as husband and wife?'

Meeting his gaze Lavinia smiled softly. 'Yes. I find it all rather strange but I suppose I'll soon get used to it. But when you came to London three weeks ago, you could not have been missing me all that much, otherwise you would have come to see me after our encounter at the theatre.'

'I have already explained all that. Besides, my time was taken up with legal matters. Not only did I meet with my lawyers and my uncle, but also with my business managers to discuss the alarming events in France. Unfortunately my investments over there are suffering because of the present crisis.'

'I see. How did your uncle receive you?'

'Like the prodigal son.' He grinned. 'He was not as I imagined him to be. In fact, he bears a strong resemblance to my father and myself. Unfortunately, he is not a well man so he has been unable to enjoy life as he would have wished to—but he did accompany me to the theatre the night Alice decided to introduce herself to him.'

'I think I recall seeing him. Is he a tall, silver-haired gentleman?' she asked.

Maxim nodded. 'He also told me that he never coveted the title and all that it entails, and that it was the worst day of his life when my father left. Did Ursula tell you about the family feud?'

'Yes—at least some of it.'

'Uncle Alistair told me that my grandfather was wrong to treat my father as he did, and quickly came to realise his mistake when he disinherited him for going ahead and marrying the woman he loved.'

'Why, after all this time, did you decide to go and see your uncle, Maxim?'

'Out of necessity rather than any aspirations I might have for the estate.'

'Why? What do you mean—out of necessity?'

Maxim looked at her steadily. 'One of the reasons I went to see him was for my daughter's sake. Alice is planning to marry a French comte and has threatened to take Lucy with her to France. I would not agree to it at any time, and especially not in the present climate. It is my intention to gain custody of Lucy through the courts, and I shall find it that much easier if I have my uncle's backing. I mean to use his influence to block Alice taking Lucy out of the country. I have contacts in high circles, but my uncle's contacts are even higher. His influence and opinions carry much weight with people who count.'

Something cold was beginning to wrap itself round Lavinia's heart. A feeling of impending disaster seemed to crackle in the air. 'I see. What were the conditions Alice insisted upon before she would marry you, Maxim?' she asked quietly.

'That I became reconciled with my uncle. Alice is a stubborn, selfish woman—and fiercely ambitious. Her eyes were firmly fixed on the grand title that would become mine when my uncle dies—should I bow to her demands and become reconciled with him, that is. Alice's greatest ambition—or perhaps I should say obsession—was to become the Countess of Brinkcliff, and she would not have me without the title.'

'I see. And you refused to concede to her demands, even though doing so would give you custody of your daughter?'

Maxim sighed, absently tracing the rim of his empty coffee cup with his finger. 'I would be lying if I said I didn't consider it—which was the reason why I insisted on an annulment to our marriage. But when I returned to England and saw Alice in London, when I was reminded how vicious she is, how cold and ruthless she can be to obtain what she wants, nothing could induce me to tie myself to her for the rest of my life. Besides, I had made you my wife and already cared for you deeply. My growing need for you made me vulnerable, and it was becoming increasingly difficult to think of parting from you.'

Lavinia was encouraged by his words, spoken softly and with sincerity, but how she wished he had included the

word love. 'How confident are your lawyers about you
gaining custody of Lucy?'

'Very. With my uncle's influence, some good lawyers to
present my case, and you by my side, I am confident that
I will be able to wield enough power to sway the courts in
my favour.'

Lavinia sat very still, not liking the thought that was
forming inside her head. Sitting across from her Maxim
looked so relaxed, with a natural elegance that she admired.
And yet, she had an odd feeling that behind his calm exterior there was a power, a forcefulness, carefully restrained
but waiting. And she had a curious feeling that if she should
say one wrong word, make one false move, one mistake,
he would unleash that power on her. The first tendrils of
fear coiled in the pit of her stomach.

'I can see how it would harm your case considerably if
it became known that you were considering divorcing your
wife,' she said quietly, her voice strained.

Maxim looked at her, his expression hard, sensing her
withdrawal. 'It would be devastating, which is one of the
reasons why I cannot allow that to happen. I want to present
a settled picture to the courts. It is important that you and
I are seen to have a loving, harmonious relationship.'

Bitter resentment wrapped itself round Lavinia like a
steel band. So that was it. She saw it all—how his mind
had worked with cold, mechanical precision as he had
formed a strategy to gain custody of his daughter. He had
come to her for Lucy's sake and nothing else. The hurt
went so deep she wanted to lash out at him. With heartbreaking clarity, all the pieces of this complex puzzle were
beginning to fall into place. The whole picture presented to
her was gruesome in every degrading detail. A rock settled
on her heart where just a short while ago love had dwelt.
She looked back at her husband through eyes of horror,

disbelief and dismay, stony-faced, gullible, stupid and na-ïve.

'You—you were using me all along. When you said you wanted me, that you needed me, they were all lies.'

'No. I have never lied to you, Lavinia. I meant every word I said.'

'What am I, Maxim? Some tender morsel expressly prepared for your enjoyment to take at your leisure?'

'Now you are being ridiculous.'

'Please don't make it worse. This isn't fair. Using me to induce the courts into granting you custody of Lucy—without speaking to me about it first—is—is wicked.'

'It's not like that.'

'Yes, it is. How dare you do this to me? Without consulting me about this, or considering how I might feel, you sought me out and seduced me into your bed because I am a necessary tool in your struggle to obtain custody of your daughter.'

The atmosphere inside the room was quiet. The muscles in Maxim's jaw tightened. He was fuming, and yet he was very much in control of himself and determined to remain that way. He tapped his fingers on the polished surface of the table, his eyes like blue shards of ice as they held hers.

'I admit it. I do need you if I hope to gain custody of Lucy. I can't present a good case if I'm in the middle of divorcing my wife.'

'Thank you for being honest,' she replied icily.

'I need you, Lavinia. Lucy is going to need you.'

Unable to sit still a moment longer Lavinia pushed back her chair and stood up, glaring at him, her eyes alight with bitter, angry condemnation. 'And her mother? Does she not love and need Lucy? For heaven's sake, Alice is her mother, Maxim. You cannot shut her out of her daughter's life. Do you expect her to stand by and watch you take

Lucy from her without a fight? Your attitude towards her
is criminal and I will have no part of it.'

Like a python uncoiling itself Maxim rose from his chair,
flinging his napkin down and placing his knuckles on the
table in front of him. He leaned forward, his shoulders
squared, his jaw set with implacable determination. He emanated restrained power and unyielding authority Lavinia
had always been aware of and feared in him, but she would
not be intimidated by him now.

'That is sentimental rubbish. Let me tell you something
about Alice you don't know. In short, she is a slut, whose
name over the past two years has been linked with an assortment of licentious and depraved men she did not think
twice about taking to her bed. She has used every feminine
ploy in existence to bring me to heel, but it didn't work.
She is also an unfit, unnatural mother, who has no love
whatsoever for her daughter and considers her a nuisance.

'Ever since Lucy was born she has hardly looked at her,
resenting her because she was not the son she hoped for—
which would have made her hold on me complete. When
she learned of my marriage to you, she swore to avenge
herself and she will—using Lucy as her weapon of destruction if she is not stopped. Now do you see why I want
Lucy here with me?'

Lavinia nodded, appalled by what he had told her. 'Yes,
I can.'

'You should. In fact, Lucy's upbringing is a scenario not
unlike your own, and it is my intention to remove her from
her mother's irresponsible care before it runs full term and
she is ruined by it.'

Instantly the colour drained from Lavinia's cheeks leaving them ghastly white, but her eyes were so dark they
might have been black. Her stiff face was set.

'Please don't make it worse than it is. You take a lot for

granted, Maxim. If you think I am going to move into your home merely to protect your interests you are mistaken.'

Icy blue eyes cut back at her, fierce anger knitting his brows. 'Have you an aversion to helping me bring up my daughter?'

'Of course I haven't. I am sure she's a lovely child and will receive all the love you are capable of giving. But she is not my daughter and you must do it alone,' she said, immediately regretting those last few words spoken in anger and not meant. But it was too late to retract them now. 'I shall return to Stratton Street as soon as I have ordered Betsy to pack my things.'

Maxim's face darkened, but his eyes were a brilliant, dangerous blue. 'Like hell you will. You're staying with me and you're going to co-operate and maintain a supportive image. Damn it, Lavinia, you can't run away every time we argue.'

'You're right, I can't, so I shall make quite sure this is the last time,' Lavinia countered, her voice ragged with emotion as she fought to contain her anger, feeling the fragile unity they had shared since the ball beginning to slide down the slippery slope of clashed wills. 'I must congratulate you. What you have done is a brilliant tactical move on your part. But how could you ruthlessly use me to manipulate things until they happen the way you want them to—if you really cared for me, Maxim, you would not have done this. You deliberately deceived me.'

Maxim turned white. 'Now it is you who insults me. I have an aversion to deceit and would never stoop so low as to use it,' he hissed, clamping his jaw together as he fought to bite back his wrath.

'You've misled me and that's the same thing,' Lavinia cried brokenly, feeling emotionally battered and as if her heart were being torn to pieces. 'I will not live with a man who walks all over people to get what he wants. I'm sorry, Maxim. I am grateful for everything you did for me in Venice, but after this I owe you nothing.'

'No? I disagree. I have given you many things. Let me itemise them,' he said with icy calm. 'I gave you my protection when you needed it, and my name. I also made you my wife in every sense of the word and introduced you to my family and my home. For this I expect you to stand by me on this one, important issue.'

'No, Maxim. You don't expect. You demand it of me.'

No longer casual and relaxed, Maxim was tense, like a panther preparing to spring. He moved round the table towards her with slow, deliberate steps. Looming over her, he forced her rebellious gaze to meet his, cold and implacable. When he spoke his voice brooked no argument.

'If you want to convince yourself that I have deceived you, then do so, but you will do it here in this house. When I made up my mind not to divorce you, not for one moment have I considered letting you go. And if I had, do you think after what passed between us last night I would ever consider it again?'

'Has it not occurred to you that you cannot keep me here by force?'

Maxim's brows arched. 'It has, and I hope it does not come to that. I will not tolerate you doing anything that will jeopardise my daughter's safety. I want your word that you will co-operate with me on this.'

Lavinia's emotions were at war within her. She tried to think objectively, knowing how important Lucy was to Maxim. And if what he said was true, that Alice was thinking of marrying a Frenchman and taking Lucy with her to France, a country that was on the brink of a violent, bloody revolution, then Maxim was right to do everything within his power to try and stop her.

And if she returned to live with Mrs Lambert and Daisy while Maxim remained at his house in Grosvenor Street, everyone would be correct in their assumptions that things weren't right between them. Gossip alone would undoubtedly damage his chances of keeping Lucy in England. She could not do that to him or Lucy.

She nodded. 'Very well, Maxim. You have it.'

Relief flooded his face. He stared at her for a moment longer and then moved away from her with lazy deliberation and poured himself another cup of coffee. Lavinia was infuriated to see he was smiling, a satisfied male smile. He had won, as he had known all along he would. She stood her ground a moment longer, glaring at him with a hard, cold anger that seared through her body, before turning and crossing towards the door. He stopped her with his next words.

'I told you I had more than one reason for going to see my uncle. Aren't you interested in hearing what it was?'

She turned and faced him, the length of the room stretching like a mile between them, waiting for him to speak.

'It occurred to me after you left Thornhill that you might be with child. If so and you bore a son, I realised I had no right to deny him his inheritance. That was when I wrote telling my uncle that I would see him.'

Lavinia stared at him incredulously. 'You—you did that?'

'Yes.'

Her eyes glittered with rage at this final outrage to her intelligence. 'Then I'm sorry to disappoint you, Maxim. There is no child.'

'Maybe not now. But there might be—after last night.'

Fuming, Lavinia left the room, trembling with a rage that possessed her with a hard, merciless force all the way to her room, but if she had looked back, she would have seen that there was neither triumph nor satisfaction on Maxim's face, only an aching gentleness and regret in his compelling eyes.

Left alone an unpleasant and extremely worrying thought was beginning to form in Maxim's mind, one which, until now, he had not considered. Was it possible that Lavinia did have an aversion to helping him bring up Lucy, despite what she had said to the contrary? One heard tales about stepmothers who couldn't stand the sight of another woman's offspring—a child not of their body—and would refuse to have anything to do with them, especially when their own arrived.

In the space of a second the realisation that this might apply to Lavinia stunned him. His body became taut, his face a hard, grinding mask, his hands clenching and un-clenching at his sides as he tried to bring his feelings under control. Was the sweet drift of happiness he had felt on finding Lavinia again and becoming reconciled under threat once more? Dear Lord, he prayed in twisted torment, don't let me have to choose between my wife and my daughter.

During the following two days it was as if Maxim and Lavinia existed in opposing camps. Maxim went about his business as usual and Lavinia spent some of her time vis-iting Daisy and familiarising herself with the servants and the running of the house. Mealtimes were to be endured, with neither she nor Maxim prepared to give an inch—until Lavinia could stand it no longer.

Tonight they were to dine with Maxim's uncle, the Earl of Brinkcliff, at his town house in Brook Street, and she was determined to make a concerted effort to somehow put things right between them before they left the house. If it meant unconditional surrender on her part, then so be it.

She loved Maxim too much to carry on in this ridiculous fashion.

As she dressed with great care for the evening ahead in an extremely fetching cream satin gown, she found herself thinking of Lucy, which she was doing a lot of late as her thoughts became less disjointed and she began to think more rationally. Maxim was hurting, tortured that he might lose his daughter, and Lavinia's heart constricted when she realised that she might have given him the impression that she didn't want the child to have a place in their lives together. That this might be behind his cold attitude towards her melted her heart. Oh, what a fool he was if he thought that.

When she was ready she went downstairs to find him. Having heard him come up to change she knew he would be waiting for her.

'Where is my husband, Mr Perkins?' she asked when she encountered her husband's secretary in the hall.

Mr Perkins cast a disgruntled look at the closed study door, wishing his master would cease behaving like a cross-tempered tyrant and come to his senses. 'In his study, my lady. Would you like me to tell him you're ready?'

'No, thank you,' she replied, heading for the closed door, quaking inwardly at the forthcoming confrontation with her husband. 'I'll do that myself.'

Without knocking she opened the door and went inside, having to repress a smile when she saw Maxim working at his desk, a quill in one hand and his dark head bowed over a column of figures. Having dressed for dinner with his uncle in a charcoal grey suit with a sapphire blue waistcoat and white shirt, he looked unbearably handsome. He also looked annoyed when he looked up and saw her. His eyes did a quick sweep of her body, lingering briefly on the neckline of her gown, and Lavinia was glad she had chosen to wear a gown with a less revealing bodice than the one she had worn for the Eveshams' ball.

'You work too hard, Maxim,' she said, giving him a brave, tremulous smile, seeing how his shoulders stiffened at the sound of her voice.

'I enjoy working.'

'Yes, I can see that.' When he made no move to rise and cast his eyes down once more to the column of figures, she moved closer to the desk. 'How do I look?' she asked, trailing her fingers absently along the edge of the mahogany desk. 'Do you like my dress? Is it suitable for dinner with your uncle, do you think?'

A wry smile touched Maxim's lips and cracked his granite features. 'I expect so.'

Distracted, he raised his head and studied her from beneath sceptical raised brows, unable to prevent his eyes moving over her shapely form and appreciating the subtle scent of her alluring perfume, which settled over him like an invisible, unrelenting net. His gaze became riveted on her lovely face, the softness in her large eyes and the delectable curve of her soft lips. With a sigh he put down his quill and stood up, her beauty and sensing that she was trying to make peace between them neutralising his anger.

'You seem to have acquired a remarkable collection of gowns, Lavinia.'

'Yes, I have. When you made the money accessible to me, Daisy and I went shopping.'

He arched a sleek black brow. 'I see. You haven't spent all of it, I hope,' he said drily. 'I would hate to think I've acquired an extravagant spendthrift for a wife.'

'Of course I haven't,' she replied, smiling sweetly when he looked ready to argue. 'I hope you will credit me with more sense than that. But, equally, I would hate to think I have acquired myself a miserly husband.'

Unexpectedly an answering smile tugged at Maxim's sensuous lips. He cocked a dubious brow, amazed at the spirit of this woman he had married. He perched his hip on the corner of his desk in front of her, taking the weight on one foot and slowly swinging his other leg, his arms folded across his chest, lazy mockery lighting his eyes.

'So—when you arrived in London and presented yourself in Stratton Street, you weren't pining away for me after all.'

Lavinia's expression suddenly turned solemn and she drew a tortured breath, knowing that if she said the wrong thing he would use it against her. 'I was, Maxim. I was pining. In fact, if you must know, I was quite wretched. I told you how much I missed you at the ball.'

All Maxim's senses collided when he saw the invitation in her imploring eyes. 'You have a very peculiar way of showing it.'

'And you, Maxim, make it almost impossible for me to do so.'

His eyes flickered over her and Lavinia's heart leaped with joy when she saw a warmth and a softening in his eyes, and that he wasn't going to fight her. Instead of suffering in silence she should have approached him in the beginning.

'Come here,' he murmured, his gaze dropping to her moistened lips.

Desire surged through him as she moved closer, heating his blood, as it did every time he imagined her in bed on the other side of the connecting door to their rooms. His body's relentless craving to appease his desire for her had almost driven him insane, and it was pride and pride alone that had prevented him from shattering that door and joining her in her bed. Forcing his hands to reach out and pull her into his embrace, he crushed her against his chest and held her tightly to him, as if he would never let her go.

'Remind me to punish you most severely for putting me through hell. You, my darling, are the most exasperating woman alive.'

'I agree,' she murmured, her lips close to his, her eyes as dark and languid as a warm, moonless night. 'But you do like me a little bit, don't you, Maxim?' she coaxed teasingly.

'More than a little bit, you minx.'

'How much more?'

'I'll show you,' he breathed, unable to resist her a moment longer, wanting to taste the sweetness of her lips, to feel her closeness, the fullness of her breasts pressed against his chest. His mouth locked onto hers hungrily, his kiss searing her lips, and she returned his kiss with a smothered moan of joy. Twining her arms around his neck, she pressed herself close, glorying in his embrace as he deepened his kiss, his arms sliding up and down her back as he moulded her closer to him.

'You little fool,' he murmured when he finally tore his mouth from hers, unable to relinquish his hold on her as he feasted his gaze on her long lashed, turquoise coloured eyes, turned languid and solemn with emotion. 'Do you know what you have done to me? Do you know what you have made me suffer? Do you know what I have been through these past two days? I thought I should go mad. Never do that to me again, Lavinia.'

Leaning back in his arms she looked up at him, loving him, revelling in the simple joy of being held in his arms. 'Do you know why I said what I did, Maxim? Why I was angry?'

'Tell me.'

'Because I was hurt and disappointed. I have always

known you to be a man who goes after what he wants, yet the method you have used to win me seems somehow less than honourable. I truly believed you had come to London because you were suffering the same sense of loss as I was. Can you imagine how humiliated I felt when I discovered you had come simply to use me in your custody battle over Lucy—that in your arrogance and conceit you had planned to bring me here to make love to me, knowing perfectly well the effect you always have on me and how easy it is to bring me to submission.'

Shame washed over Maxim in sickening waves when she told him how much he had hurt her. 'I'm sorry if that's what you thought, but in the beginning it wasn't like that. When I made up my mind not to consent to a divorce, it had nothing to do with my custody battle over Lucy. When you left me I was crushed. I could not imagine the rest of my life without you and I was so frightened of losing you, Lavinia. You have become a part of me—like my flesh and blood. I love you. I love you so much. May God help you if ever you run from me again,' he warned fiercely.

Lavinia trembled looking deeply into his eyes, thinking the sound of his voice saying he loved her to be the sweetest sound in the world. Maxim saw it in her eyes, felt it in the way her body melted in his arms, the emotional impact his declaration had on her, and he smiled down at her upturned face.

'You, my darling—you wonderful, infuriating woman,' he went on, his tone husky and deep with desire, 'are the only female alive who is capable of driving me to the point when I am tempted to throttle you or to make love to you until we both expire. You have become such an essential part of my life that I would be desolate without you—and after what occurred between us over breakfast when you argued so forcefully, I envisaged having to decide between you and my daughter. Do you want me to give up all claim on Lucy?'

Lavinia was swamped with shame and her heart contracted painfully when she realised she was right in thinking she might have given him reason to ask that awful question. 'No. I would not ask you to do that. I would never ask you to sacrifice someone you love.'

'Then what is it you want from me?'

'Only that you talk to me, Maxim. There must be honesty and frankness between us. What happens to Lucy does affect us both, you know.'

'And you will be willing to make her a part of our lives together—even when our own children come along?'

'More than willing,' she told him softly, his question telling her that she had been right and that it was this that had been troubling him all along. 'Lucy is your daughter, Maxim. How could I fail to love her?'

'Even if her father is an insensitive brute with a list of shortcomings stretching from here to eternity, with no other thought than to seduce my wife into bed in order to induce a suitable response to my demands?' he chuckled tenderly, sliding his hands seductively down her spine and pressing her closer.

'Maxim!' she laughed. 'I am astounded at your unprincipled determination to get what you want and your absolute lack of contrition. Have you no shame?'

He grinned, a warm glow igniting in his half closed eyes. 'Apparently not,' he answered, his lips claiming hers once more.

So lost were they in their kiss that neither of them heard the carriage halt in the street outside, or the opening of the door when someone was admitted into the hall, only pulling apart when Mr Perkins entered with his usual expression of aloof formality. Maxim glanced at him, his arms still around Lavinia, unaware of the surge of relief that almost cracked his diligent secretary's countenance on seeing everything was back to normal between his master and his wife.

'What is it, Perkins?'

'Mrs Winstanley is here to see you on an urgent matter, my lord.'

Maxim released Lavinia instantly and his face became a frozen mask. 'Send her in.'.

Chapter Fourteen

The small, dark haired woman swept into the room, her manner agitated, her expression anxious. 'Please forgive my intrusion, but I had to come,' she said quickly.

'Mrs Winstanley, this is my wife, Lavinia. Lavinia, Mrs Winstanley is Alice's stepmother,' Maxim told his wife by way of explanation, trying to stem the tide of terror already searing through his veins, his instincts telling him that Caroline Winstanley was the harbinger of grievous news.

The two women looked at each other, Mrs Winstanley inclining her head politely. Lavinia sensed from her taut expression and anguished eyes that whatever had brought her to this house tonight was a matter of extreme importance and of a serious nature.

'Excuse me,' said Lavinia softly, beginning to move towards the door. 'I'm sure you would like to speak to my husband in private.'

Maxim placed his hand on her arm, halting her. 'No, Lavinia, don't go,' he said, his voice raw with emotion. 'I would like you to stay and hear what Mrs Winstanley has to say.'

She looked at him. His face was tense, but seeing a softening, a pleading in his eyes, she nodded and stood quietly with her hands folded in front of her, waiting for Mrs Winstanley to divulge the purpose of her unexpected visit.

'I have been out of London for two weeks, visiting my sister and her husband in Surrey, Mr Purnell,' she said, ignorant of his reconciliation with his uncle and that he was now addressed as Lord Stannington. 'When I returned I discovered that Alice married Claude Lauriston yesterday and has gone with him to France. I'm so dreadfully sorry.'

Something exploded inside Maxim, shattering his emotions from all rational thought. He stared at Caroline Winstanley as though she had taken leave of her senses, shrinking from asking the question that was uppermost on his lips, but knowing he must. 'And Lucy?'

'She—she has taken Lucy with her,' she told him quietly.

Savage fury ignited in Maxim's eyes. Never had Lavinia seen a face of such dark, menacing rage as his was at that moment—rage at his own weakness and inability to have prevented this happening after all his efforts. For the first time in his life Maxim tasted bitter defeat. His fist came crashing down onto the polished surface of the desk, sending papers fluttering to the floor, the sound vibrating about the room and crashing against the walls as his formidable anger grew.

'Dear God, I'll make her pay for this. I was so close to stopping her—a week at the most. Damn her to hell. She knew what I intended when I became reconciled with my uncle. Knowing I had married someone else, she knew I had healed the breach for one reason only—that I intended to wield enough power to sway the courts in my favour to obtain custody of Lucy. The bitch. The conniving, amoral bitch. This is the revenge she planned when I refused to marry her. I should have foreseen it.'

'She—she did leave you a note,' said Mrs Winstanley, fumbling in her reticule and handing it to Maxim.

He took it and broke the seal, his eyes scanning Alice's untidy scrawl. His face went white. 'Good God!' he exclaimed when he had finished reading.

Lavinia went to him instantly. 'Maxim! What is it? What does it say?'

His tortured eyes locked on to his wife's. 'That she will grant me custody of Lucy for a settlement of one hundred thousand pounds.'

Lavinia was stunned, shocked. 'You—you mean she thinks so little of her daughter that she will sell her to you—as—as though she were a parcel?'

Maxim's eyes were like blue chips of ice, his lips twisting with contempt. 'I tried telling you what Alice is like, what she is capable of. Now do you believe me?'

She nodded slowly, trying to comprehend what this was doing to Maxim. 'Yes—yes, I do. But it's obscene.'

'Claude Lauriston belongs to the French aristocracy,' Mrs Winstanley explained quietly to Lavinia, 'but he is impoverished. He is also past his prime. Having a beautiful wife by his side will boost his ego no end—not to mention replenishing his family coffers should your husband agree to Alice's demands. He has no desire to be saddled with Alice's illegitimate daughter, so her demands do not surprise me in the slightest. He is a greedy man and as amoral as she is. I have no doubt that he put her up to it.'

'And will you give her what she asks, Maxim?' Lavinia asked, unable to imagine the sheer magnitude of the sum Alice demanded.

'The money means nothing to me. I will not argue over the amount when Lucy's safety is at stake.'

This was stated firmly and without emotion, bringing home to Lavinia the sheer magnitude of her husband's wealth. A hundred thousand pounds would be like a drop in the ocean to him. 'What will you do?' she asked him in some confusion.

'I have no choice but to go after them,' Maxim answered, his voice harsh with urgency, his face white and tense with anxiety and pain.

'But—but they will have left England for France by now.' Suddenly, realisation of what he intended doing made Lavinia's heart slam against her ribs. 'Maxim! You can't go to France.'

'I have to, Lavinia,' he said with a cold, controlled calm, sitting at his desk and hurriedly writing a note. That done he strode to the door, throwing it open and handing the note to Perkins who was hovering outside in case he was needed. 'Have this delivered immediately to my uncle and instruct one of the grooms to have my horse saddled while I change,' he commanded. 'I want to be away from here and on my way to Portsmouth within the next half hour.'

Maxim mounted the stairs two at a time, leaving his wife to show Mrs Winstanley out. Overwrought, she then hurried after him with the hope of dissuading him from embarking on his reckless, foolhardy venture, pacing up and down as he changed his clothes, watching as his valet silently put items of clothing that he might need into a small leather bag.

'Maxim, please don't go,' she begged, fraught with anxiety. 'People are being killed all the time in France.'

'I know. And it's precisely for that reason why I must go. Try not to worry, Lavinia,' he said, deftly fastening his shirt buttons. 'The peasants' grievances are against their ruling lords, not a visiting Englishman.'

'But the revolts are taking place with hysterical savagery—with violent men wandering all over the countryside.' She followed him to a chair where he sat to pull on his boots. Putting her hands on the arm of his chair she knelt beside him, her voice anguished, her wide eyes full of appeal. 'Please listen to me, Maxim. They won't care who you are if they think you have money they can steal. And why would the Comte de Chemille return to France now—at this time, with wholesale looting and the burning of châteaux? Why hasn't he remained here in England where it's safe?'

Maxim's finely chiselled lips twisted with grim irony. 'Perhaps the Comte de Chemille has had a touch of conscience and is concerned about his family holed up in his château in Normandy. He has a younger sister and brother, I believe, from his father's second marriage. Neither of them are married. He will want to keep the mob at bay if he can.'

Lavinia sat back on her heels. 'You seem to know a great deal about the Comte de Chemille, Maxim.'

'I was afraid that something like this would happen so I made a point of finding out as much as I could about him, other than what I already knew—that he is a blackguard, a gamester and a drunkard—a man who has never bothered to hide his contempt for the industrious lower classes. Like every other nobleman in France he thought his lands, his feudal dues, and a hundred other things that maintain his indolent, arrogant breed, would last forever.'

'Then why did he not find himself a noblewoman to marry? Why sully his ancient line with the blood of a commoner?'

'The answer is simple. He is impoverished, and what better way of maintaining his châteaux, his stables and his dissolute lifestyle than by marrying a woman who was my mistress and bore me a child. Whatever else he is, the Comte de Chemille is no fool. He knows what I am worth, and through Alice he will also know how much Lucy means to me and that I am seeking to obtain legal custody

of her through the courts. He is confident that I will pay
dearly for my daughter.'

'The man is a monster,' Lavinia said, getting to her feet
when Maxim rose to put on his jacket. She watched in
horror when his valet opened a long leather box and handed
him two pistols, which he shoved into his belt ready to
defend himself if need be, ramming home to her the enor-
mity of what he was about to do. In speechless horror she
looked at his face, which was rigid and sterner than she'd
ever seen it before, and she was frightened.

'Please don't go, Maxim,' she whispered, her eyes wide
with fear. 'I'm so afraid that you'll become caught up in
the insurrection and not come back. It's dangerous to be
even known as an associate of anyone who has fallen out
of favour. If the people should decide to take direct action
against the Comte de Chemille and you are seen going to
his home, you will be assumed guilty by association and
will be shown no mercy.'

Maxim raised his head, his eyes burning into hers. 'Don't
you think I know that, Lavinia? Which is why I must get
Lucy back. What kind of father would I be if I sat back in
the comfort of this house and let the mob attack her—a
defenceless child? I would despise myself. How much respect would you have for me then?'

Grasping his bag and enveloped in a long black riding
cloak, he turned from her and strode out of the room. Hurriedly Lavinia ran after him down the stairs and into the
street, where a groom was waiting with his horse—the poor
animal having no notion of the gruelling journey ahead of
him. Maxim would stable him in Portsmouth and hire another when he reached Le Havre. After securing the bag to
the saddle he turned and swept his wife into his arms. Lavinia closed her eyes and a sob broke from her. She clung

to Maxim with all her strength, feeling his arms holding her tightly, his breath on her neck.

'Forgive me, Maxim. Please forgive my weakness—my selfishness. I am so afraid for you, that is all. You are right to go and I am so proud of you. I wouldn't expect you to do anything else, and I would be disappointed in you if you didn't go to save your daughter. But please take care,' she implored desperately. 'If anything should happen to you I couldn't bear it.'

'I will,' he said, his voice raw with emotion. 'I promise you I will.' With his mouth close to her ear he tightened his hold. 'I love you, Lavinia. Be brave, my love. I will soon be back—with Lucy.'

'I love you, Maxim. Please come back safe. Both of you.'

He stopped her mouth with a kiss, infusing into it all the passion of his love for her, and then he released her and flung himself onto his horse's back, galloping along Grosvenor Street and into the night.

In her agony of their parting, the sense of what had happened scarcely penetrated Lavinia's mind, and she stood in the street looking into the darkness which a moment before had swallowed up her husband. She hardly noticed when a coach came to a halt outside the house and a tall man with silver hair stepped out. He came to her and touched her arm, and only then did she look at him, with tears coursing down her cheeks. Understanding her anguish, the Earl of Brinkcliff placed his arm about her shoulders and took her back inside the house.

'So,' Alistair said, when Lavinia had dried her tears and they were seated across from one another in front of a cosy fire, 'you are Lavinia—Maxim's wife.' He was not unaware that there had been an estrangement between his nephew and his lovely young wife or the reason why, and he was happy to discover they had reconciled their differences. She really was a lovely, captivating young woman.

'Yes,' she said softly, responding to his warmth with a smile.

The Earl of Brinkcliff was almost as tall as Maxim, and his features bore a startling resemblance. There was also that same proud arrogance that marked Maxim, and his eyes held an alert sharpness she had expected in such a powerful man. Despite his gaunt look and deeply grooved face, in his mid-fifties Alistair Purnell was still a striking-looking man. She wondered why he had never married, thinking that perhaps it might have something to do with his ill health.

'I apologise for my behaviour earlier. I don't normally cry like that in the street.'

'It's not every day your husband rides off at a moment's notice to set sail for a country where revolution is about to explode at any minute. Believe me, my dear, I do understand,' Alistair said, a warm tenderness glowing in his eyes. 'I hope you don't mind me coming here, only I know how deeply Maxim cares for his daughter.'

'I'm glad you came. I couldn't bear being on my own just now. Besides, I'm sorry we had to cancel dinner. I've been so looking forward to meeting you.'

'Thank you. Poor Maxim. This has come as a terrible shock to him.'

'I do so hope he takes care,' Lavinia said quietly.

'Don't be afraid. I am sure he'll be all right. He's sensible, and I'm immensely proud of him—proud that he's my nephew. You know, I've followed his amazing progress since my brother died. My only regret is that we didn't meet until recently—when he decided to accept what is rightfully his. Oh, I know what urged him to do it, but I was happy to receive him whatever the reason. I've waited for this for longer than I care to remember. I look forward to receiving you at Brinkcliff Hall. The old place has been empty far too long.'

Lavinia found herself thinking of Ursula and her large, happy brood of children and grandchildren at Thornhill, and she realised how lonely this man must have been all these years at Brinkcliff Hall, devoid of his family. Alistair was watching her, and did she imagine it or was there a pleading in those sharp grey eyes? Whatever he gave Maxim, it was less than what Maxim could give him—a lonely man in need of the freedom to die with absolution and in the warm embrace of his family.

'I shall look forward to it,' she smiled.

'Thank you, Lavinia. Maxim has told you the cause of the estrangement between us?'

'Yes.'

He shook his head solemnly. 'It was an unfortunate business. When my father disinherited my brother, he realised he had made the biggest mistake of his life. He tried to repair the damage, but my brother—stubborn and stamped with the same Purnell pride as most of our forebears—refused. Not being in the best of health I didn't relish taking on the role of the next Earl—but I don't think I've made too bad a job of it,' he chuckled softly, his grey eyes twinkling with humour lightening his features.

'And how are you now?' asked Lavinia, having noted his breathlessness, his gaunt, grey face and slightly stooped back.

'Since Maxim came to see me my health has never been better. However,' he said, rising with the help of a walking cane, 'I tire easily—so if you will forgive me I will leave you now. And try not to worry, my dear,' he said, noting how worried she looked and seeing the fear for her husband lurking in her lovely eyes. 'Maxim will be all right. I'm sure of it. You'll soon have him back in London with his daughter.'

'I don't intend waiting in London,' Lavinia told him calmly, having made up her mind what she would do.

'Oh?'

'Mr Perkins is to leave in the morning to await Maxim's return in Portsmouth. I shall go with him.'

'Is that wise?'

'I think so. I couldn't bear the suspense of waiting here in London. Besides, when he arrives in Portsmouth with Lucy after a long ride across France followed by the channel crossing, the poor child will need me.'

'Yes, my dear. You are quite right.'

Having reached Normandy, it was the glow in the midnight sky that Maxim saw first as he rode through dense wood. A sickening dread gripped his heart as he watched it grow redder and brighter the closer he got. He urged his horse into a gallop when a huge flame leaped up into the sky quickly followed by another. The closer he got the higher the flames became, and when he at last emerged from the darkness of the trees, his eyes became riveted on the horrific spectacle spread out before him.

Death and destruction wreaked by the mob surrounded the once-beautiful château of the Comte de Chemille. Some still danced and laughed like wild, crazy savages, drunk on blood and the Comte's wine. Burning torches were still clutched in their hands, some brandishing knives and axes, anything that would serve as a weapon. The blood-soaked bodies of loyal servants littered the ground, and the magical beauty of the flower gardens had disappeared beneath trampling feet.

The château was a blazing inferno, the fire feeding greedily on the precious treasures it housed, the flames penetrating higher and higher into the night sky. The heat was intense. Smoke smarted Maxim's eyes and burned his nostrils, and the noise was like the huge, angry roar of an enraged beast. Above it all could still be heard the agonising screams of those who hadn't got out of the château and were being incinerated alive, and those who managed to escape the scorching, searing heat were set upon and slain by the mob.

Maxim stared transfixed at the horror confronting him. Suddenly there was a thunderous crash of falling timbers as part of the upper floors gave way, sending a fountain of sparks upwards. Their work done, the mob began to disperse. The awful truth that his daughter might have perished in the blaze entered Maxim's soul and panic clutched at him.

Feeling it safe to do so when the last of the mob had disappeared, flinging himself out of the saddle he began searching among the dead and dying scattered over a wide area. In the midst of all this carnage he singled out a woman lying in a pool of blood face down, the fine quality of her emerald green silk gown distinguishing her from the rest. The expensive material was torn and muddied, and her hair was spread out on the grass like a shining black halo. Quickly he went to her, going down on one knee and gently rolling her onto her back.

It was Alice.

Her chest rose and fell in shallow gasps, and he thanked God she wasn't dead. When he touched her hand her eyes flickered open. They became dilated, her mouth a crimson slash across her face whiter than death and already the texture of wax. When her eyes became focused on Maxim she grimaced. It was obvious that she was in great pain and close to death.

'Maxim! You should not have come,' she managed to gasp, and seemed to gain sustenance from his presence.

'Did you think to escape me?' he said gently. Hardened as he felt towards her, there was no longer any anger in him, only an immense pity which welled up from the bottom of his heart for this woman he might have married. 'Did you think I wouldn't come to France and find you at the risk of my life?' He would have raised her, but with a feeble movement of her hand she stopped him.

'Don't, Maxim. It's too late. I know I'm dying.' Her sigh which followed her words gave an impression of extraordinary resignation.

'Lucy? Where is Lucy? Dear God, Alice, don't tell me she is dead.' The acute anguish and pain he felt that this might be so was almost too much for him to bear. Mercifully, Alice's next words brought him immeasurable relief.

'No. She is safe. When the mob came some of the servants escaped into the woods. Lucy is with them. Look for her, Maxim. Find her and take her back to England. You will find her at a village a mile north of here. She is with a family by the name of Laurens.' She closed her eyes as she fought for breath, and a froth of blood appeared at the corner of her mouth. 'Would you have given me the money, Maxim? Would you have bought your daughter?'

'Yes, I would. You know that.'

'Then she is fortunate. She has a place in your heart I could never have,' Alice said, the effort to speak almost too much. Her smile was cynical. 'I never thought I would be envious of my own daughter.'

'Alice—' Maxim uttered, knowing he should hate her, but in these final moments of her life he couldn't. He was unable to go on because a hard lump appeared at the base of his throat, shutting off his words. Tears formed in his eyes and glistened. She saw them and smiled.

'You weep for me,' she whispered, 'after what I have done? How odd.'

'Not really, Alice,' he managed to say, taking her limp hand in his own. 'I know you will die—as we all do in the end. I weep for the small miracle we created, what we once had, what we might have had, if your ambition hadn't got in the way.'

'I know that. I learned my lesson too late. I wanted you to honour me with riches, titles and everything I've always dreamed of, and I became a victim of my own greed—but,' she whispered, a sudden gleam entering her eyes, 'I did become a countess, didn't I, Maxim?'

Maxim swallowed hard, unable to answer.

'I wanted to hurt you because you spurned me. I regret that—and I do not ask your forgiveness for what I have done. Poor Claude. He died trying to defend his château. They are all dead—as I shall be soon. But I'm not afraid of dying—and it's better I go now before I'm old and undesirable.' Her smile was beautiful. 'When you think of me, Maxim,' she whispered with great difficulty, the dazzling brilliance of her green eyes falling on his face for the last time, 'I shall be forever young.'

Beyond speech, she fell silent and gazed at something beyond Maxim. Her eyes glazed over and she breathed her last.

Leaving her lying where she was, his heart almost too heavy to support, Maxim mounted his horse and rode north, towards the village where Alice had told him he would find Lucy. He found her with a servant woman, and with her tiny, warm body nestled close to his beneath his cloak in front of him on his horse, he rode back towards Le Havre.

The following day when Maxim embarked on the Channel crossing to England with his daughter, it was Tuesday, the fourth of August 1789, and it was the dawn of a new revolution in France. Later that night the National Assembly made sweeping reforms, demolishing the feudal regime and all the burdens which had oppressed the people for centuries, making sure it would be impossible for them ever to be reintroduced.

In mounting tension and sick with worry, Lavinia waited three days in Portsmouth for Maxim to return to England. Fate seemed to be taking a malicious pleasure in making her wait. Reports about what was happening in France arrived with every vessel, and were so worrying that she was frightened her husband would not come back.

She was constantly under Mr Perkins's quiet, watchful gaze, for Portsmouth was a busy port with ancient buildings crammed against each other, all fighting for space. It teamed with all manner of disreputable characters of every conceivable shape and colour—beggars and half-naked street urchins and drunken, bell-bottomed sailors who had not seen land for months, poured out of the many taverns and liquor shops bellowing their curses, with hard-faced, gin-sodden women hanging on to their arms, willing to allow any perversion in exchange for the price of more gin.

With her cloak wrapped tightly about her, Lavinia walked along the quay, gazing at the masts and rigging of the merchant ships anchored in the Portsea dockyard, flags and bunting dancing gaily in the breeze. Not one vessel moored without undergoing her close inspection.

Unaware of the sounds, sights and scents that surrounded her, in her solitude she gazed out to sea, watching the bow of a small vessel plowing its way through the green-brown water. It moored not far away from her and she watched with no particular interest, having seen so many come and go in the last few days. It wasn't until she saw the tall figure of a man with a bundle in his arms step on to the deck, that all her senses were jolted into awareness.

Her relief was enormous and her eyes became riveted on him, unable to believe that it was Maxim, but it was. His unshaven face looked haggard beneath the shadow of his hat, and the small bundle in his arms was Lucy. Wild with joy her heart soared, but her recent succession of hope, fear and grief, had taken its toll of her resistance. At first she was frozen, and all she could do was stand and watch as he climbed ashore.

It was then that her body came alive and she was running, tumbling headlong into his one outstretched arm. For a long moment they clung together, a bewildered Lucy trapped between them. Lavinia felt Maxim's lips on her brow, her cheeks, and she was too deeply moved for speech. After what seemed like an eternity she pulled away and looked up at him and smiled, her eyes moist with tears.

'Thank God you're back, Maxim,' she whispered, gazing anxiously into his pain filled eyes. They were bloodshot, his lids heavy, stark evidence of his nights without sleep.

'Alice is dead, Lavinia.'

His eyes were like windows through which Lavinia could see the unspeakable horrors he had witnessed in France. She wanted to know what had happened, but she wouldn't ask him, not now. There would be time for that later.

'I'm sorry, Maxim. Was it very bad?'

He towered over her, his lean, hard face full of torment as he remembered how Alice had died. 'The worst.'

'Tell me later. I can only think of one thing at the moment—that we're together. You're alive, and we'll never be parted again. I couldn't bear having to wait for you in London so I came to Portsmouth in the carriage with Mr Perkins. As soon as you and Lucy are rested we can leave.'

Lavinia looked at the little girl clinging to Maxim like a

small, frightened shadow. She was an extremely pretty child in a sad, resigned kind of way. Her black hair had a blue sheen and fell in gentle waves about her oval face, which was pale and delicate. Her pale blue eyes fringed with sooty black lashes were replicas of Maxim's, and she was looking at him pensively. Shifting her gaze, Lucy glanced at her out of the corners of her eyes and Lavinia smiled softly, gently touching her cheek, hoping to put her at ease.

'Don't be afraid, Lucy,' she said. 'I won't hurt you.'

'It's not you she's afraid of, Lavinia. It's the upheaval. She's confused about everything that's happened and doesn't understand it.'

'I know. Perhaps Lucy and I can make friends on the journey to London.'

Lucy's face was serious, her eyes searching Lavinia's intently. Lavinia sensed that she hadn't known much kindness in her short life—only that shown to her by Maxim. And he was right. Lucy was confused about everything that had happened to her, and she didn't understand the significance of this strange woman's relationship to her father. But her presence and her soft words had a comforting effect on her and she smiled, her soft pink lips opening like a tiny rosebud.

From Rotherfield Hall Lavinia often walked over to Thornhill with Lucy, strolling hand in hand down the lane where she had walked the day she had first seen her step-daughter—the day she thought her life had ended. How wrong she had been. She and Maxim were together now. Alice and the awful events leading up to her terrible death in France were in the past, and Lavinia had found a great joy in getting to know Alice's daughter.

They had recently returned from Gloucestershire where

they had been visiting Edgar, feeling free to do so now
Robert had finally done the honourable thing and married
Julia and she no longer resided at Welbourne House. Edgar,
who was a fine young man, who admired Maxim and his
business acumen enormously, had finished his education
and was excited about continuing in his father's business.
He was also looking forward to taking his brother-in-law
up on his offer on how best to invest his money.

Thinking of her brother Lavinia smiled, looking forward
to the time when he would visit them at Rotherfield. Lavinia loved Rotherfield Hall, with its elegant rooms and
beautiful grounds, a house into which Welbourne House
would fit a dozen times over. She was so proud to think
that Maxim had achieved so much through his own en-
deavours, although she was still having difficulty coming
to terms with his vast wealth. When he had to go to London
on business he always took her with him. He would show
her off like a precious jewel, wanting her to enjoy the position of prestige she was entitled to—being the wife of the
next Earl of Brinkcliff.

Sometimes when she stole a glance at him and realised
she bore his name, a sharp thrill would shoot through her.
He never ceased to amaze her. He was so sophisticated, so
elegant and full of charm, but he was forceful too—a power
held in restraint, and a man with a strong sense of his own
infallibility, a man with many diverse and complex shades
to his character.

He was also a man who was meant to dominate, and he
often found it irritating that the gentle, naïve young woman
he had plucked from the Venetian lagoon, a woman who
had been ignored as a child and had been reared in a sheltered, austere environment, had a mind and will as strong
as his own and had not been born to be dominated. The

way it looked it was evident the two of them were not likely to lead a docile life.

But whatever their differences—which they always overcame in the nicest possible way—their love was undisputed. They knew they were meant to be together, and the joy and happiness they found in each other was complete.

Today, ten months after Maxim had brought Lavinia to live at Rotherfield Hall, the sky was pale blue and cloudless, with the gentlest of breezes blowing over the paddock at Thornhill. Almost the whole family had come to watch Lucy make friends with her new pony, a little bay mare which had been passed on to her from David now he was too big to ride it himself. David was nine years old now, and Lucy adored him.

In fact, Lucy adored everything about Thornhill. Having so many children to play with was a new experience for her, and after her initial shyness had worn off, she had surprised everyone by responding to all the fuss and attention with a startling vitality, which poured from her like heat from the sun. She was such a happy, bright child, and charged with energy. But her inquiring mind, the playful devilment in her nature and the teasing light in her eyes, reminded Lavinia so much of Maxim.

Having lifted her into the saddle, Maxim leaned on the fence, watching with a look of immense pride as David led her round the paddock, laughing along with everyone else when an arrogant flock of geese was sent cackling out of the way of the pony's hooves, causing Lucy to give vent to a peal of happy laughter. Leaving Ursula's side, Lavinia went and stood beside her husband, placing her arm around his waist when he drew her close.

'Who would have thought she could look like this,' murmured Lavinia, her eyes fixed lovingly on her stepdaughter. Lavinia loved her as she would a child of her own, and

Lucy returned her love a thousand fold. She was such an affectionate, pretty little girl, with her black curls and the determined thrust to her round chin.

Maxim looked down at his wife, his eyes as clear and blue as the sky above, crinkling with a smile. 'She is quite amazing, isn't she?' His gaze became intent on Lavinia's upturned face, her free flowing hair gilded by the sun's rays. He was impressed and intrigued, and would never cease to be amazed at some new character of this woman he had married. With each day's passing, their knowledge and understanding of each other increased. 'Lucy adores you, you know that, don't you? It's wonderful what you've done for her.'

A slow flush crept delightfully over her cheeks. 'She's done a lot for me too. Look at her, Maxim. She's as pretty as a picture and as merry as a magpie on her pony.'

'So she is. I am fortunate to have been so blessed,' he sighed, his arm tightening about her shoulders, his gaze dwelling warmly on her upturned face. 'What more could a man want.'

'What more, indeed,' Lavinia said, with a glow in her eyes.

She said it in such a way that Maxim smiled softly, knowingly, having suspected for a while, from the dreaminess in her eyes and the fact that he had never seen her look more beautiful, that she had something on her mind, that there might be something she had to tell him.

'Lavinia, have you something to tell me that I should know about?' His voice was warm with love and humour.

Lavinia's lips curved in a sublime smile while her eyes grew dark and sultry. 'Only that I am with child.'

There was an unusually bright glitter in Maxim's eyes when he took her in his arms, and he had difficulty swallowing. 'Thank you,' he said, his voice low and husky.

Drawing back and seeing a sheen of tears in her eyes, he cradled her face gently between both his hands, gazing down into their misty turquoise depths. 'Are they tears I see in your eyes, my love?'

'If they are then it is because I am so happy.'

With a laughing sigh Maxim pulled her back into his arms, hugging her tightly. 'Do you remember what you said to me in Venice when we agreed to marry?'

'Remind me,' she whispered, her cheek against his throat, his chest warm and hard beneath the thin fabric of his shirt.

'When you agreed to those ridiculous conditions I imposed on you regarding our marriage, you told me it was like a masquerade which would lose its magic when the mask was removed.'

'Yes, I remember.'

'Well? Has it?'

Leaning back she tipped her head up to him, her eyes aglow with love. 'No. And the Carnival of love is not such a tragedy after all.'

* * * * *

The Viscount's Bride
by
Ann Elizabeth Cree

Ann Elizabeth Cree is married and lives in Boise, Idaho, with her family. She has worked as a nutritionist and an accountant. Her favourite form of day-dreaming has always been weaving romantic stories in her head. With the encouragement of a friend, she started putting those stories on to paper. In addition to writing and caring for two lively boys, two cats and two dogs, she enjoys gardening, playing the piano, and, of course, reading.

Chapter One

Chloe glanced at the clock on the mantelpiece and jumped up from the chair. She should have met the others in the drawing room five minutes ago. Her attention had strayed from the article concerning the scarcity of grain in Europe to an article about Madame de Staël's death and she had found it so interesting she forgot to watch the clock.

'Does Justin know you hide away in his study to read his journals?'

She whirled around, heat rising to her cheeks. Brandt, Viscount Salcombe, stood in the doorway of the study, an amused smile at his mouth. She stifled a groan. Of all the people to find her, why must it be him? 'I am not hiding away. I had something I...I needed to read.'

'From the *Gentleman's Magazine*? Could it not wait until after the assembly or did you hope to bring up one of the topics during the evening?'

Since that was exactly what she intended, her flush only increased. 'How ridiculous!' Why must he always plague her? And make her feel so young and silly? 'Is it not time to leave for the assembly?' she asked pointedly.

'Yes, which is why Belle sent me to find you. It was

fortunate Mrs Keith noticed you were here as Belle failed to inform me that you might be in the study reading Justin's journals.'

'There is no need to mention that.' What if Belle or worse, her husband, the Duke of Westmore, questioned why she had developed such an interest in agriculture?

'Very well, I will keep your secret on one condition.'

'What is that?' she asked cautiously.

'That you agree to stand up with me tonight.'

Stand up with him? 'I…'

His mouth curved. 'Or I will mention to my cousin or Belle your interest in farming.'

He would probably do so just to annoy her. 'Very well,' she said ungraciously.

'Then I suggest you put it back in its place. Unless you plan to bring it with you.'

'You may tell Belle that I will join you in the drawing room very shortly.' She was behaving childishly, not at all as a proper young lady should towards someone she disliked, but she did not seem to be able to treat him with the cool politeness she desired. That he seemed to find her a source of amusement only irked her more.

She set the journal on the pile of magazines on the desk. She prayed Brandt would keep his word and say nothing. What if Belle or Justin should guess that she intended to marry Sir Preston? They would need to know some time, but she preferred that to be after Sir Preston had…

'By now, Belle will undoubtedly think I've abducted you.'

She marched to the door and cast him a cold look as she passed him into the hall. Her mood was not improved as she climbed into the carriage and seated herself next to Belle, only to find Brandt seated next to Justin and across from her. Her time at Falconcliff visiting Belle, who was now the Duchess of Westmore, had been marred by this man's arrival yesterday.

The month and a half she had been in Devon had been idyllic. For the first time in ages, she had felt a sense of freedom; her guardian, Arthur, the Earl of Ralston, and his plans to marry her to the highest bidder far away. She had been recovering from a severe bout of influenza when she first arrived but the sea air and her increasingly longer walks had helped recover her strength. As had her happiness at being with Belle, Belle's husband, Justin, and baby Julian, now nearly six months old. Their neighbours had welcomed her. And she had decided to fall in love with Sir Preston Kentworth, whom she was certain was beginning to return her regard.

Everything was perfect. Until yesterday.

She cast a dark look at Brandt as he talked easily with Justin and Belle. He was Justin's cousin and certainly there was a resemblance. Both were tall, broad-shouldered, dark-haired men possessing an arrogant confidence. Justin, with his cool reserve, was considered the more handsome, but she knew from the London gossip that many women considered Brandt, with his disarming charm, equally attractive. His father's scandalous death two years ago only added to his desirability. His lack of wealth did not seem to deter them one whit as there were rumours he was well on his way to recovering the fortune his father had lost.

He would undoubtedly charm all of the ladies in the neighbourhood just as he had charmed the London women during the Season. She only hoped he would not leave a trail of broken hearts behind him since he was unlikely to stay in a village as slow as Weyham for very long. At least she was immune to him. She supposed he was handsome, but she did not like overly handsome men. And he was too tall as well. She preferred men who did not hover over her, making her feel helpless as if they might overpower her. Another point in Sir Preston's favour, for she could actually have a conversation with him without straining her neck.

Chloe glanced out of the carraige window and saw they had arrived at the assembly rooms. An assortment of carriages already stood outside the square building.

The rooms had been built half a century ago when Weyham had been a modestly popular seaside resort. Only a few visitors frequented its pleasant beaches now, but the weekly assemblies continued to be popular, often attracting guests from the neighbouring towns.

Inside the small entry hall, Belle allowed the men to go on ahead. She halted and turned to Chloe. 'I know you do not particularly like Brandt,' she said in a low voice, 'but please try not to allow your feelings to show so clearly on your face.'

'I am sorry. It was just that he always teases me so. Was it really so obvious?'

Belle smiled rather ruefully. 'Yes, I fear so. At one point you were fixing him with a most fierce look.'

'Oh, dear.' She knew Belle's fondness for the cousin Justin considered a brother. 'I promise I will try to be very civil. I am to stand up with him tonight.' She hoped that would make Belle feel better.

'I will not ask how that came about.'

She should probably not mention blackmail. She gave Belle a vague smile. 'I suppose we should join the others. But do not worry.'

'I know you have a kind heart, but I hope you will consider extending it to Brandt. He is really not so terrible. And he will not be leaving very soon.'

How disappointing. 'I will.' She followed Belle in, intending to put Brandt completely from her mind. They were joined by Mrs Heyburn, the local squire's wife. Chloe only half-listened to the conversation as she looked around the room, hoping to find Sir Preston. She finally spotted him standing with a group of men in one corner.

She excused herself from Belle and Mrs Heyburn and started across the room, then hesitated as the men burst into loud laughter, most probably over one of the Squire's boisterous hunting jokes. It was one thing to approach Sir Preston when he was alone, but quite another when he was with friends. It was just that he needed rather a lot of encouragement. He was shy about dancing and did not seem comfortable asking anyone to stand up with him.

Before she decided what to do, Lydia Sutton bounded up to her. 'Chloe! Why did you not tell me Lord Salcombe was coming!'

'I did not know until last night, when he arrived unexpectedly,' Chloe said without much enthusiasm. The last thing she wanted to do was discuss him.

'He is so dashing. And a rake, is he not? My friend, Harriet—she is Lady Harriet Pumphries, the Marquis of Lawton's daughter—wrote he was nearly called out by Lord Bixby for trifling with his wife.'

'It was only a rumour as Lord Bixby does not seem to care who flirts with his wife. If anything, Lady Bixby was flirting with him. Or attempting to,' she said, distracted by the sight of Sir Preston leaving the ballroom. She hoped he was not going to the card room.

'Chloe! How could you say such a thing!'

Lydia's squeal of enjoyable horror brought Chloe back to the conversation. 'I should not have repeated such gossip. I pray you will not say a thing to anyone.'

'Of course I will not.' Lydia fanned herself as she looked about the room. 'Do you know if he plans to dance at all?'

'I really cannot say. He did not dance very often in London.' Or engage in any of the scandalous behaviours his reputation warranted. Instead, he had been rather aloof, which only added to his overall attraction.

'I hope he will.' Lydia's attention had strayed again. 'I see Mrs Clifton is wearing her new London gown. How I wish I could persuade Mama to take us to town for some new gowns. But she says there is nothing in London that we cannot procure from Madame Dupré. And there is Emily. Really! One would think she would realise how atrocious lemon is for her complexion. But then she never knows how to go on.'

Chloe glanced in Emily Coltrane's direction. She stood in one corner of the room, her broad face wearing its habitual scowl as if she wished to warn everyone away. Lydia was right, her yellow gown only emphasized her sallow skin and mousy hair. Despite Emily's evident and puzzling dislike for her, Chloe could not help but feel sorry for her.

Lydia shut her fan. 'Lord Salcombe is dancing with Lady Haversham. He dances very well, does he not?'

Chloe glanced in his direction just as he held out his hand to Marguerite, Lady Haversham, who was the wife of their nearby neighbour. She smiled at something he said and Chloe looked away. She really must escape from Lydia, not only to find Sir Preston, but because she did not want to spend the evening discussing Brandt. 'I suppose so. Lydia—' she began, but before she could say more Gilbert Rushton sauntered up.

He grinned. 'Good evening, Lady Chloe, Lydia. I saw you over here looking out at the crowd and then chatting madly and wondered who was the subject of such animated speculation.'

'We were merely commenting on how well Lord Salcombe dances,' Lydia said.

Mr Rushton glanced at the dancers. 'He does indeed. Certainly Weyham is much enlivened by his presence. Should I add to the speculations concerning Lord Salcombe?'

'I must…' Chloe began. She was beginning to think she would never escape.

'I never pay the least attention to gossip,' Lydia said primly.

'But this concerns all of us.' Mr Rushton paused for effect. 'There are rumours he is Waverly's mysterious benefactor.'

'How splendid!' Lydia said.

Chloe's stomach lurched, all thoughts of Sir Preston gone. 'That is impossible!'

He cocked an eyebrow. 'Why?'

'Because…' Because she could not fathom where he would find the funds. But more than that, he was the last person she wanted in the old stone house she had fallen in love with the first time she saw it. As forlorn as it was, with its overgrown gardens and crumbling stone walls, the house still maintained an air of solid dignity. Its old neglected chapel with a tiny walled garden was the most romantic thing imaginable, along with rumours of secret passages that led from the house to the chapel and even to the sea below. She had been delighted when, shortly after her arrival in Devon, workmen began repairs to the roof and walls. The identity of the buyer remained unknown, although conjecture as to whom he might be ran rampant in the village. 'It is not the sort of house he would like at all. I am certain you are wrong.'

'You appear quite adamant that he should not live there.'

'I am certain it is not that! Chloe just does not want to know that we have guessed. But do not worry, we will not say a thing!' Lydia beamed at her.

'I do not know anything at all.' What if Lydia decided to repeat the rumours and mentioned Chloe? 'I really must find Belle.'

'But you are coming to my house tomorrow, are you not? Remember, we are to practise the dances for the Haversham ball. Sir Preston will be there and Tom and Emily Coltrane as well as Mr Rushton,' Lydia added, looking hard at Mr Rushton.

'I fully intend to be there. But for now I must keep my appointment at the card tables,' Mr Rushton said. He executed a neat bow and sauntered off.

'So, you will be there, will you not, Chloe? Do you not recall that you promised to show Sir Preston the waltz?'

'Oh, yes.' How could she possibly forget when she spent as much time as possible reading about farming so that she might impress Sir Preston with her newly acquired knowledge? In fact, she planned to take the opportunity tomorrow to discuss a new breed of sheep she had read about. 'I must go.' She started to edge away.

'Do you think Lord Salcombe would come?'

'Lord Salcombe?' She stopped and stared at Lydia. 'Most certainly not. I am sure he would find such entertainments too dull.'

'But he might not. We could ask him. Or perhaps you could ask him since you are related and you must know him very well.'

'I really do not know him well at all. And we are only related through marriage and hardly even that.' For Belle was only her sister-in-law through her first marriage to Chloe's half-brother, Lucien, although she thought of Belle as her sister.

'But will you ask him?'

'Perhaps,' Chloe said vaguely. The image of him among the young people of the neighbourhood practising dances boggled her mind. And most certainly she did not want him watching her with his sardonic gleam while she attempted to discuss sheep with Sir Preston. 'I really must go.'

She was thankful that, at that moment, Henry Ashton appeared to solicit Lydia's hand for the next dance. After promising she would most certainly be in the Sutton drawing room tomorrow, Chloe finally made her escape.

Sir Preston still had not reappeared. He was probably in the card room. She had just reached the edge of the assembly room when she heard her name. She turned and found Lady Kentworth, Sir Preston's mother, at her side. Her heavy face creased in a smile. 'My dear Lady Chloe! How delightful it is to see you. How charming you look? Is that a new gown? You had it made up in London, I have no doubt. There is nothing quite as stylish here in Weyham.'

'Yes, it is from London.' She managed a smile. Lady Kentworth's effusiveness always overwhelmed her. Although she was all that was friendly, something about her small eyes and thin mouth made Chloe cautious. But perhaps it was only a natural desire on her part to avoid offending a potential mother-in-law.

'Have you seen my son? I believe he is in the card room. I do hope he can be persuaded to dance at least one of the dances. Perhaps with you, since you and he have become such particular friends.' She did not give Chloe a chance to reply and chatted on for a few more minutes in her loud voice before finally declaring that she thought she might play a hand of cards. Somehow, Chloe found herself entering the card room with Lady Kentworth, who insisted she must greet Sir Preston. Chloe wanted to cringe. She only hoped Lady Kentworth would say nothing about a dance.

The card room was small and stuffy, the tables crowded together, and her embarrassment increased as Lady Kentworth marched her across the room. Several people glanced up as they passed, including Lady Haversham, whose look of sympathy rendered Chloe even more mortified. Then she wanted to run when they stopped by Sir Preston's table. Two other men sat with him. And one of them was Brandt.

But it was too late. Lady Kentworth was already speaking. 'Ah, Preston, here is Lady Chloe.'

The men looked up. Heat stained her cheeks when Brandt's gaze fell on her. 'Lady Chloe. Have you come to join us? Or did you wish to remind me of our dance?'

The dance? She had completely forgotten about it. 'I merely came to…to watch the games. I must be going.'

'Perhaps Lady Chloe might like to play a hand. Sir Preston has been instructing her, you know,' Lady Kentworth announced.

'No, I really must go.'

Sir Preston turned around to look at her. His pleasant, square face lit with a smile. He stood. 'No need to hurry off. Be glad to have you play a hand. Blanton, here, has to do his duty on the dance floor.'

Blanton rose and bowed in her direction. 'My wife won't give me a moment of peace until I do the pretty with her.' He pulled the chair out. 'The chair is now yours.'

He walked off. Chloe restrained herself from following. 'I do not think…'

Mr Rushton smiled at her. 'No need to be shy, Lady Chloe. Kentworth claims you are a most promising pupil.'

'Most certainly is,' Sir Preston said kindly. 'Promise we won't ride roughshod over you.'

'But...'

'See, you have no need to worry,' Lady Kentworth said. 'Sit down, Lady Chloe.' She gestured to the chair, her tone brooking no argument. Chloe sat in the vacated seat to Brandt's right. Lady Kentworth beamed. 'Very good. I see Sylvie Compton in the corner. I promised I would play a game with her.' She bustled away.

Chloe hardly knew where to look. 'I really do not wish to play.'

'Afraid you'll be badly trounced?' Brandt inquired with a wicked gleam.

'Of course not,' she snapped and then remembered she was supposed to be a novice. 'That is, I expect to be badly trounced.' That did not sound any better and the open amusement in his face only flustered her more.

'Whist, then. Salcombe can partner you,' Mr Rushton offered. 'Even up the odds.'

Brandt? She glanced at him. He returned her regard, his expression bland. 'Lady Chloe would undoubtedly prefer someone else.'

He didn't need to make it so obvious he didn't want her. She lifted her chin. 'I rather thought Sir Preston could be my partner.'

Sir Preston looked startled. 'Er, honoured, of course, but may not be the best partner. Salcombe is more skilled.'

Now, she understood. They thought she played so poorly that she would need Brandt to make up for her skills. 'I am certain we will do fine.'

She would have to be completely blind not to miss the look that passed between the three men. 'Er, no doubt,' Sir Preston said.

But they could hardly be blamed. Until a month ago,

she had rarely played card games except with her most intimate friends. And even then, she refused to play for stakes. She had not intended to play in Devon at all, but at an assembly a month ago, Sir Preston had noticed her watching one of the games. Assuming her reluctance to play was due to her lack of ability, he offered to instruct her. He had been so kind she could not refuse, nor had she the heart to correct his impression. It was then, as she watched his blunt, kindly face while he explained the rules of commerce, she decided he was exactly the sort of husband she wanted. After that, as he continued to instruct her, his pleasure in her progress had only increased her conviction he was the man she wanted to marry. However, her happiness was marred by knowing she was deceiving him. Worse, she found feigning ignorance increasingly difficult and keeping the competitiveness she so hated in herself at bay.

'Then that is settled.' Brandt picked up the deck. 'Whist? Or do you wish something else?'

'Whist, if you please.'

He shoved the cards towards Sir Preston. 'Since Sir Preston is seated to my left, he will shuffle the cards and then you will cut them,' he told her.

She bit back the urge to tell him she knew that perfectly well. She cut the cards and then Brandt dealt the hand and turned up the trump. The game began.

It did not take more than a few plays to realise the three men were indulging her, Brandt most of all. When he did not play a card she suspected he had in his hand and let her win a trick, she suddenly was tired of her pretence. On her next play, she won the trick. As she did the next one. Rushton started and glanced at Brandt, his brow raised. And when she took the next trick as well, she could almost feel the atmosphere change. The single-minded concentration she had not felt for an age took over and she forgot everything but wanting to win. She would prove to Brandt she was not the silly chit he thought her.

They played three rounds and, in the end, she and Sir Preston triumphed. She looked at Brandt, taking no pains to hide the elation she felt. 'We have five points.'

There was silence. She realised the three men were staring at her. 'Indeed you do,' Brandt finally said. She could not read his expression at all.

'Good God!' Rushton exclaimed. 'Appears your lessons paid off after all, Kentworth.'

'Brilliant!' Marguerite exclaimed from behind her. 'No one ever beats Brandt at whist. Or most other games for that matter.' Startled, Chloe saw Marguerite and several others had gathered around them. She wanted to sink in her chair, but she forced herself to look at Sir Preston who appeared stunned.

'Splendid, Lady Chloe,' Sir Preston said. 'Never thought…well, had no idea last time we played.'

'Must have you give me a few pointers, Kentworth,' Squire Heyburn boomed. 'Another round, Salcombe? A match between you and Lady Chloe. I, for one, will place my money on Lady Chloe. What else have you been teaching her, Kentworth? Piquet?'

'I do not think…' Chloe began.

'Come, Lady Chloe,' Mr Rushton said. 'Just one more hand. Such skill should not be allowed to languish.'

'Although I always find there is a great deal of luck in cards. And some are much more lucky,' Emily Coltrane said with the cool, disapproving stare she always bestowed on Chloe.

Everyone turned to look at Emily whose neck coloured to a dull red. Her brother, Thomas, gave a disgusted snort. 'Hold your tongue, Em.'

'Ah, but it depends on whether you know how to take advantage of the opportunity presented to you,' Brandt drawled.

'Most certainly Lady Chloe does,' the Squire boomed. 'Come, now, one more game.'

Come, Chloe, just one more game. Suddenly, she was back in the dark, dank study at Braddon Hall, her half-brother, Lucien, smiling at her in his charming way, his voice cajoling, as he urged her to play another hand against one of his half-drunk friends. Refusal was impossible, for then the dazzling smile would disappear from his face, replaced by a cold sneer that frightened her. And so she would play again and again until he sent her back to her bedchamber where she would tumble into bed, only to fall into a sleep filled with nightmarish images.

'Chloe?' Marguerite's worried voice jerked her out of her trance. Chloe rose, her sense of victory completely vanished. She wanted only to escape. 'I would rather not. At least not now. I am certain Emily is quite right. It was only luck.'

'There is one way to find out,' Mr Rushton said. 'Be glad to partner you this time.'

'No, I cannot!'

Everyone stared at her, the astonishment on their faces at her outburst making her feel even more wretched.

Brandt stood. 'Another time, perhaps. Lady Chloe has promised me a dance.' He turned to her. 'I will escort you back to the ballroom.' He held out his arm.

She took it, hardly knowing what she was doing. Marguerite smiled, although her face still held concern. 'A splendid idea. I've no doubt Chloe would much rather dance than spend the evening in a stuffy card room.'

'Of course, of course,' Squire Heyburn said. 'Can play again some other time.'

Chloe nodded and managed a smile. Brandt led her to the ballroom where a country dance was in progress. He released her arm and looked down at her.

'Where did you learn to play cards like that?'

She started. 'Sir Preston taught me.' Even to her own ears, she sounded as if she were lying.

'Apparently his skills as an instructor far exceed his skills as a player. I've never seen anyone make such progress in so short a time.'

'I was merely lucky tonight.'

'Of course.'

She suspected he did not believe her at all. 'I…I have no doubt if I play again I will lose quite badly.'

'You underestimate your ability. You are uncommonly talented.'

'If I am, then it is a talent I would prefer not to have!' she burst out, then wished she had bitten her tongue at his startled expression.

'It is nothing to be ashamed of,' he finally said. 'I doubt you are planning to exploit your talents at the gaming tables.'

Her head spun for a moment and she felt almost sick. 'No,' she said faintly.

He stared at her. 'I did not mean to overset you.'

'I…I am not overset.'

'You look as if you are about to swoon.'

'I am not.'

'You are. Forget the dance. You need to sit down.' Before she could protest, he tucked her arm more firmly through his and guided her through the chaperons clustered along the edge of the room and to a small anteroom off the ballroom. Two very elderly ladies, one of whom appeared to be napping, occupied the two chairs near the mantelpiece, but several vacant chairs lined the adjacent wall. He led her to one of them. 'Sit down. I will send Belle to you and then fetch you a lemonade.'

She looked up at his rather grim face. 'There is nothing wrong. I...I suddenly felt very warm.'

'Then there is even more reason for you to sit. And if I discover you have moved, I will have no compunction in carrying you to a chair.'

She gasped. 'I beg...' But he had already stridden off.

Belle appeared a few minutes later, her face worried. 'Chloe, what is wrong? Brandt said you almost swooned in the ballroom.'

'I really did not. He is exaggerating.'

Belle took the chair next to her, her concerned gaze going over Chloe's face. 'What happened?' she asked gently.

'Noth...' she began and then stopped. 'Oh, Belle, I did the most dreadful thing. I played a game of whist with Sir Preston and Mr Rushton and Brandt. Sir Preston was my partner and...and we won.'

Belle was silent a moment. 'That does not sound so dreadful.'

'It was because I have been pretending I knew nothing about cards and Sir Preston has been instructing me and I never meant anyone to find out. I had not meant to play but Sir Preston invited me and Lady Kentworth insisted that I should so I finally agreed. I could see that Brandt...that is, all of them felt very sorry for me and intended to give me a few hands, which made me angry. Instead of pretending, I...I wanted to prove to them I was not as stupid as they thought after all. And then I was very sorry I had done so. Everyone was astounded and wanted me to play again and I wanted only to escape.'

She took a breath. 'After we were back in the ballroom, Brandt asked where I had learned to play cards like that and I told him that Sir Preston had taught me and I could see he did not believe me. He said I was talented and I told him I did not want such a talent and he said that he doubted I would use it at the gaming tables.' She fixed her eyes on Belle's face. 'And tonight, I felt such a desire to win. Just as I did before. I never wanted to feel that way again. Or have everyone stare at me with such astonished expressions and then wager on whether I could win another game.'

'But it wasn't like before,' Belle said gently. 'Lucien was not there to coerce you into one more game and use you for his own means. You were not surrounded by drunken rakes, but by friends who only wished you well.'

'They would not wish me so well if they knew how I have deceived them. And how wicked I have been.'

'Chloe.' Belle took her hand. 'You were never wicked. You were very young, only thirteen, hardly more than a child. It was Lucien who was wicked—using you in such a way, taking advantage of your innocence.'

'But I felt what I was doing was wrong—I should have told Papa,' she whispered. Oh, how many times had she thought or said that? Lucien had been forbidden to come to the house, but he came none the less when Papa was away on one of his frequent journeys. Mama could not bear to turn him away and if Chloe whispered a word, Papa would be furious with Mama. So she had said nothing. Mama, often in bed with one of her headaches, had never guessed that Chloe was downstairs with Lucien and his friends.

'But Lucien convinced you he would make it much worse for you if you did. And for Maria. How could you fight against that?' Belle squeezed Chloe's hand and then looked up. 'Brandt is coming with your lemonade. You must put it aside—it is all in the past. Lucien is gone and he cannot hurt you or any of us now.'

'Yes.' Except she very much feared that, after tonight, she would not be able to put her past behind her as she had worked so hard to achieve.

Chapter Two

Brandt stood near the breakfast room window holding his newest cousin in his arms. 'Tree,' he said, pointing to an example on the other side of the glass. He had no idea what sort of conversation one made with a five-month old human, although the young Marquis of Wroth did not seem at all dismayed by his efforts. He made a gurgling sound and Brandt looked down to find the child's solemn unwavering gaze on his face. Was he about to cry? Brandt cleared his throat. 'I fear your mama has left you in very inexperienced hands. She should be back shortly. I hope.'

The small mouth suddenly moved. Brandt braced himself for a scream. To his astonishment, he realised his tiny cousin was actually smiling at him. He found his own mouth tentatively curving in response as he stared down at the babe. He gently touched the soft cheek and young Julian gurgled again. A small finger came up to grasp his. Unexpected warmth flowed through Brandt and he suddenly knew exactly why his cousin was so thoroughly in his son's thrall. Certainly he had seen Julian before at his christening when he had been the child's godfather, but he had resisted doing more than briefly hold the babe, fearing he would harm such a small and helpless life. Somehow

his cousin's happiness had made him feel left out, but now
he was beginning to regret he had stayed away so long.

He heard footsteps. He lifted his head. Expecting Belle,
he was startled to see Chloe instead. She looked equally
taken aback. Her gaze fell to Julian and her eyes widened
in astonishment.

'The Duchess decided I should play nursemaid while
she went to confer with Mrs Keith.'

'I see.' Her expression was controlled as it always was
around him. She wore a gown of creamy muslin tied with
a green sash. Her dark auburn hair was tamed into a knot
at the back of her head, but a few tendrils framed her face.
She looked fresh and pretty. And completely untouchable.
He had no idea why a girl whose smile could hold so much
warmth managed, at the same time, to neatly keep any
potential suitors at bay. That she disliked him he was well
aware of, and, to some extent, he could not blame her, but
that she would spurn the advances of other eligible young
men puzzled him.

As did her behaviour last night at the card table. Any
fool could see she was no novice. Then why go through
the pretence of having Kentworth instruct her? Even more
puzzling was how horrified she had looked right after she
had won, and even more so after he had taken her from
the card room. She had appeared much better after he returned with the lemonade, and Belle had said nothing more
than that Chloe had become overheated and that, after her
illness, she was still inclined to fatigue. Nothing had been
said about cards, so perhaps her reaction had been only in
his imagination after all.

Julian struggled in his arms. He looked down and saw
the babe was reaching towards Chloe. 'I think he wants
you.' He cast a doubtful look at her gown. 'If you
want him.'

'Of course.' She stepped closer to him, held out her arms and took the infant. The babe snuggled against her and then turned his head to look back at Brandt. He offered Brandt another tentative smile. Chloe glanced down at the child, her expression softening, and then back up at Brandt. 'He likes you.'

'I would hope so since we are related.'

'I doubt that is the only reason.'

'And what other reason might there be?'

'I...' She looked flustered. 'You are...are kind.'

'Ah. A compliment from your lips. I shall treasure it.'

Colour flooded her cheeks. 'There is no need to be so sardonic.' Her face closed again and she looked quickly down at the child.

He bit back a curse. He had no idea why he was so boorish around her. 'I beg your pardon.' He picked up the silver pot from the table. 'Will you take tea or coffee? Or chocolate.'

'I always take tea.' She looked flustered again. 'You do not need to pour me anything.'

'But you are occupied, so it is the least I can do.' He poured the tea into one of the china cups. 'Sit down. How much sugar?'

Still looking taken aback, she sat in the nearest chair. Julian promptly picked up a spoon. 'Two, if you please.' She watched Brandt spoon the sugar into the cup. Almost as soon as he set the tea in front of her Julian reached for it. Chloe pulled the child back just before he grasped his object. The spoon fell from his hand and he started to cry.

Brandt stared at him, completely at sea. 'Should I find Belle?'

'No. Pick up the spoon.' She stood and started to gently bounce the child, speaking to him in soft tones.

Brandt retrieved the spoon from under the chair. He held

it out to Julian, who had stopped crying. Instead of taking the spoon, he sniffed and held out his arms to Brandt.

'He wants you again,' Chloe said.

'I've no idea why. He would do much better to stay with you. What if he starts to cry again?'

Julian wriggled and reached towards Brandt. He made a little sound of protest. Chloe smiled at the child and then looked back at Brandt. 'He will probably start to cry if you do not take him. Here…' she held Julian out '…you were doing very well when I came in.'

Once again he found himself holding a chubby, pink-cheeked bundle who fixed him with a dazzling smile. It occurred to Brandt that he could not recall the last time someone had smiled at him with such pure, joyous pleasure at merely being in his presence. He smiled back at the babe with the oddest sensation he would never be the same again.

'See, there was nothing to be afraid of.'

He looked up at Chloe and found her watching him. Even more amazing, she actually smiled at him. For the second time in the space of a minute, he nearly reeled. 'No. He is…is charming.' That seemed completely inadequate.

'He is.' She was still smiling, the warm smile he'd only seen once or twice, the smile that lit up her face and rendered her incredibly lovely.

He felt as if he'd been punched in the stomach. Her smile faded as she took in his expression. Julian started to wriggle and make happy, impatient noises. When Brandt tore his gaze from Chloe he saw why. Justin and Belle had just entered the room.

The Duke of Westmore stopped. 'You look amazingly domestic. I feared I might find you cowering in the corner when Belle told me she had left Julian with you.'

'Fortunately Chloe came shortly after Belle departed and rescued me.'

'He really did not need to be rescued,' Chloe said.

He glanced at her, surprised at her defence of him, but her expression had reverted back to the same guarded one she always wore.

Julian squealed again and held his arms out towards his father. Justin's dark face broke into a smile as he took his son. He planted a brief kiss on the child's head and then looked at his wife. She met his eyes, a little smile on her face. For a moment, the three of them existed in a timeless bond that excluded the rest of the world.

Longing shot through Brandt, swift and hard. He forced his eyes away only to meet Chloe's. Their gazes locked and for an instant he saw the same yearning reflected in her face and he knew she read his mind as clearly as he read hers. She quickly looked away.

He pulled his gaze away as well, disconcerted by the connection between them. He wanted to escape. 'Now that you no longer need my services as nursemaid, I will take my leave. Carlton has the final papers ready for me to sign.'

'Then it is not yet too late for you to change your mind,' Justin said.

'I've no intention of doing so at this point.' He grinned at Belle. 'I fear you will find me underfoot more often than you might want.'

She smiled back at him. 'I doubt that. I am only a little angry you have not been to visit more often. I feared Julian would consider you a stranger.'

He glanced down at the child who had so suddenly stolen his heart. 'You no longer need to fear that,' he said softly.

He took his leave, only nodding to Chloe. For once he

felt no desire to tease her. In fact, avoiding her as much as possible seemed the best tactic.

He was nearly at the solicitor's office before he recalled that while he had been procuring a lemonade for Chloe last night, he had been approached by Miss Sutton. She had invited him to attend an afternoon of dancing lessons at her house. She hoped he might consider it even if Chloe had expressed the opinion that he would find it dull, which had been enough to secure his immediate acceptance. Particularly when he had heard Chloe would attend. He had looked forward to proving that he was not nearly the jaded sophisticate she seemed to see him as. Now, the prospect had lost some of its appeal.

This morning had merely been an aberration. Undoubtedly, she would be back to regarding him with the same disapproval as always and he would treat her in the same teasing fashion as if nothing had happened.

In the future, he would avoid any situations in which he found himself alone with her with only a baby as a chaperon.

Chloe sat back down at the breakfast table, her thoughts in turmoil. Whatever had happened? For a moment, when her gaze locked with Brandt's, she had known exactly what he was thinking, but more than that, exactly what he was feeling; she had glimpsed a vulnerable side to him that rendered him completely human. But she had already been thrown off when he had reluctantly taken Julian, the arrogant, cool peer suddenly stripped away by the mere thought of holding a baby. When his face had softened as he looked down at the child and then looked up at her and pronounced him charming, her antagonism had melted away.

'Chloe?'

She realised she had been staring at her toast. 'I…I fear I was wool-gathering.'

'I can see that. Are you still worried about last night? Or did Brandt say something to distress you?'

'He said nothing. He was worried about holding Julian.'

Belle smiled. 'Men do that. I have never seen Brandt look quite so dismayed as when I told him to hold Julian while I spoke to Mrs Keith. He tried to protest, but I told him it was time he became better acquainted with his godson. I imagine he was overjoyed when you arrived, although I was quite surprised to find him still holding Julian. I would have thought he would wish to hand him over to you straight away.'

'He did, but Julian made it very clear he wanted Brandt again. I told him if he did not take him, Julian would cry.'

Belle laughed. 'Very good.' She poured herself another cup of coffee and eyed Chloe. 'It does not sound as if you were at daggers drawn then.'

'For once we were not.'

'Good. I rather hope you might become friends of a sort.'

'I doubt that. We do not rub along well together.'

'Are you certain? I rather think it is mostly on your side. I still have no idea why you hold him in such dislike.'

'He is too arrogant, I suppose. He is just the sort of man I do not like very well.' Chloe looked down at her teacup.

'That is unfortunate, for I rather think he likes you,' Belle said gently.

Chloe's head jerked up. 'I doubt that. He teases me mercilessly and seems to delight in annoying me as much as possible.'

'I rather expect he does so to get your attention. Otherwise you tend to snub him.'

Heat stained Chloe's cheeks. She could not deny the accusation as much as she wanted to. It was not in her nature to deliberately hurt someone, but she had excused her rudeness to Brandt because she doubted he had any feelings to hurt. 'I suppose I still cannot forgive him for how he treated you in the beginning. To think that you could possibly be involved in Lucien's plot to destroy Justin.' She would never forget how cold he was to Belle, the first time Chloe had met him at a musicale. She had detested him on the spot for that alone.

'But that's in the past. And certainly you disliked Justin equally, but you do not seem to bear any ill will towards him now. If anything, he set out to hurt me whereas Brandt was merely attempting to protect his cousin. Just as you were attempting to protect me.'

'I know.' Certainly her feelings were irrational. When Justin had returned to England a year ago he had every reason to believe that Belle had been an accomplice in Lucien's plot to destroy Justin's father by killing Justin in a duel. Instead Lucien had been wounded and Justin had been exiled to the continent. Intent on revenge, he had set out to make Belle his mistress. So, if anything, Chloe should detest Justin, but how could she when he so obviously loved Belle and now Julian? And when he made her so welcome when he could very well detest her as Lucien's half-sister?

'There is another reason I hope you might come to like Brandt.' Belle paused. 'He is soon to become our neighbour.'

With a sinking heart, Chloe knew Mr Rushton had been right. 'He's bought Waverly.'

'How did you know that?'

'Mr Rushton said something about it last night.' She bit her lip. 'Why did you not tell me?'

'He asked us not to say anything as there was some dispute over the title that needed to be resolved and he did not want more rumours to complicate the matter. He will complete the purchase of Waverly today.'

'But I cannot imagine why he would want it! It is old and neglected and has no modern conveniences. Why can he not live at Salcombe House?'

'He does not like Salcombe House,' Belle said gently.

'But how can he possibly have the funds to do so?' she blurted out and was instantly ashamed when she saw Belle's quietly reproving expression. 'Oh, Belle, I am so sorry. I should not have said such a rude thing. It is none of my affair at all.'

'No, it is not, but I've no doubt others will ask the same thing. He sold most of his unentailed properties in order to pay off his father's debts and make the necessary improvements to his estate. He invested whatever was left and I assume it is from those monies he is purchasing Waverly.'

'He must want it very much. I suppose I do not understand why.'

Belle looked steadily at Chloe. 'I imagine it is because he fell in love with the house the first time he saw it. Just as you did.'

Brandt paused for a moment outside the gate to the Suttons' pleasant brick house. What the devil was he doing? He had no desire to participate in the sort of entertainment he envisioned; a gaggle of young ladies and their admirers going through the steps of the newest dances. Just the sort of rustic entertainment he would expect from an unsophisticated village such as Weyham. The sort of entertainment he had never had the opportunity to enjoy. His mother's constant illnesses and his father's rigid morality and cold disregard for most of his neighbours had not encouraged mixing with the local gentry. After his mother's death, when Brandt finally went out into society, he fell in with the most wild, rakish crowd possible. Not until his father was found dead in one of London's most notorious brothels did he come to his senses. By then, he was too disillusioned to enjoy such simple pleasures as an afternoon of practising dances.

Which was why he had no idea why he was standing here now.

'Planning to go in, Salcombe?'

Gilbert Rushton's voice startled him. He turned. 'I am still debating.'

'A bit too late for that. Miss Sutton is leaning out of the window. Bad *ton* if you were to walk away now.' He grinned at Brandt. 'Don't worry, only a couple of hours at the most.'

Miss Sutton was indeed waving at them from a first-floor window. He followed Rushton up the path. 'So, Miss Sutton talked you into this as well?'

'Precisely. However, when I discovered Lady Chloe would be here, I didn't need much persuading.'

'Lady Chloe?'

'She's a deuced pretty gal, clever, and an heiress to boot. Some men might resent a gal who could best them at the table, but not me. Always like a bit of spirit and brains. Besides, one never knows when a way with the cards might prove profitable.'

Brandt was unaccountably annoyed. 'I doubt Lady Chloe wishes to exploit her talent for profit.'

By now they had reached the front door. Rushton glanced at him. 'Not intruding on your territory, am I?'

'Not at all. I've no interest in Lady Chloe. That is, beyond that of a relation.'

'Then no objections if I pursue an acquaintance with her?'

Oh, he objected all right. He hardly wanted her to fall under the charm of a loose screw like Gilbert Rushton. 'No, unless you trifle with her.'

'Intentions are strictly honourable.'

That hardly reassured him. But the pink-cheeked housekeeper had opened the door and after taking their coats and hats and Rushton's cane, ushered them into the sunny, crowded drawing room. The furniture had been pushed aside to clear a space for the dancing. Half a dozen young people were already clustered around the piano. Chloe, however, sat on a small sofa with Sir Preston. She glanced up, her expression astonished, and then looked quickly away. Brandt quelled his desire to march over and say something to fluster her.

Mrs Sutton greeted them with a pleasant smile. 'Good day, Gilbert. How delightful to see you, Lord Salcombe. We cannot tell you how splendid it is to have you among us. We so feared Waverly would be pulled down and—' She stopped at his expression. 'Oh, dear! I fear I have said something when I should not…'

He had not quite been able to keep the surprise from his face. 'Not at all. I have just signed the final papers today so I no longer wish the matter kept private.'

The anxiety left her face. 'How delightful!'

'So the rumours were true! Congratulations!' Rushton said.

Everyone else gathered around to offer their congratulations and pleasure at the restorations taking place. Everyone except for Chloe, who hung back, her expression closed. Brandt was annoyed. She might not be delighted, but she could at least offer a token word.

Lydia finally turned to Chloe. 'See! I knew Lord Salcombe would come today. He assured me he would not find this at all dull as you said he would.'

'I see,' Chloe said faintly. She did not look at him.

Lydia was all smiles. 'Shall we begin? Harriet will play. We will first perform a country dance so Sir Preston might see how it is properly done. Then he can try it.'

Sir Preston tugged at his cravat. 'Er, certainly.'

'Do not worry. We can take it very slowly,' Chloe told him. She gave him a reassuring smile.

'But do you not think it will be too confusing if we are all dancing at once?' Emily said. She stood near the pianoforte, observing the company with her usual disdainful gaze. Her eye fell on Brandt. 'I think it would be best if Lady Chloe and Lord Salcombe demonstrate the steps first since they have been in London the most recently. I dare say they are the most expert.'

Chloe looked taken aback. 'I do not know if that makes me very expert at all.'

'And I rarely dance,' Brandt said. He crossed his arms, his mood surly. He had no intention of forcing himself on Chloe.

'But I was,' Rushton said. 'I should be happy to partner Lady Chloe.' He sent her a smile that set Brandt's teeth on edge.

'Then Lydia may partner Lord Salcombe,' Emily said.

Lydia, who had looked increasingly annoyed at Emily's interruption, suddenly brightened. 'That is a splendid idea. Two couples will make it much more easy to observe.'

'Here, here. Now that we've settled that, let's get on with it,' Tom Coltrane said. He stood near the pianoforte with Henry Ashton, attempting to affect a look of bored amusement.

They took their places in the middle of the room and Harriet launched into an uneven country dance. Brandt, who had danced at numerous balls with the most haughty members of the *ton* in attendance, suddenly found himself attacked by an unexpected bout of self-consciousness because he was on display in front of a mere handful of people. Harriet's choppy rhythm and the fact she tended to repeat passages whenever she hit a wrong note made keeping time nearly impossible. Rushton's low-voiced flirtation with Chloe threw Brandt off further. And when he handed off Lydia and found himself reaching for Rushton's hand, he had no idea whether to laugh or curse.

'Sorry,' Rushton said. 'Lydia, where are you? Salcombe, here, you take Lady Chloe.'

The others were beginning to titter. She stared at him and he saw her mouth begin to quiver. 'Chloe?' he asked. 'Are you all right?'

'Y…yes.' She bit her lip and then a laugh escaped her. She stopped and Lydia careened into her. 'Oh, dear… P…please do not say anything more.' She clapped her hand over her mouth and he saw she was laughing.

He grinned. The rest of the company was now laughing except for Lydia. 'Oh, do stop!' she cried. 'It was not that dreadful!'

'But it was!' Tom held his sides. 'Is that what they do in London? Had some idea those *ton* balls were a bit stodgy! Seems I was wrong!'

Even Sir Preston was grinning. 'Could have shown you that myself.'

Lydia marched over to the pianoforte. 'Harriet! Could you not have tried?'

Harriet jumped up. 'I told you I hate to play for dances!' She looked as if she were about to burst into tears.

'Never mind, Harriet,' Emily said briskly. 'Dances are always difficult. You can stand up with Tom, and I will play this time.' She gave her brother, who was still wiping his eyes, a meaningful look.

'Er, yes.' Tom held his arm out to Harriet. She beamed at him as they took their places along with the others.

This time everything went smoothly. When it was over, Emily stood. 'I know you play most delightfully, Lady Chloe. Perhaps you can play this time and I will show Sir Preston the proper steps.'

Brandt glanced at Chloe in time to see a peculiar look cross her face. She glanced at Sir Preston and finally said, 'I fear I am like Harriet and cannot play for dances.'

'Oh, I doubt that,' Emily said. The smile she bestowed upon Chloe was hardly sincere.

'Do play, Chloe!' Lydia said.

Chloe walked to the instrument and sat down, but it was obvious she was not pleased. Emily took Sir Preston's hand and then went through the steps in her no-nonsense fashion. When the dance began, it was apparent Emily's instructions had been adequate; Sir Preston only mis-stepped once.

After that, Mrs Sutton bustled in, followed by the house-keeper who carried a tray of refreshment. Despite the cheerful chatter of everyone else, Chloe seemed subdued and distracted. Brandt, intending to keep his distance, in-stead found he wanted to inquire what was wrong. Before he could extricate himself from Lydia, Gilbert Rushton took the place next to Chloe on the sofa. He said some-thing to her, and she gave him a slight smile that set Brandt's back up.

'Do you plan to make your home at Waverly, Lord Sal-combe?' Lydia was asking him.

'Yes, I am, Miss Sutton.'

'But you will keep a house in town, will you not? I

imagine you must find Weyham very dull after the delights of town.'

'Not at all. We rarely have entertainments such as this in London.'

'But you will be going to London often.'

'Do you wish to see me gone from the neighbourhood so soon, Miss Sutton?'

She coloured. 'Oh, no! I merely thought that you would wish to go there often.'

'Actually, I don't intend to spend much time at all in London except when necessary. Waverly will keep me occupied.'

She looked disappointed for some reason. Miss Coltrane, who seemed to have appointed herself in charge of the entertainment, stood. 'We can practice the waltz. However, this time Lord Salcombe and Lady Chloe must first demonstrate.'

Brandt looked over at Chloe and waited for the inevitable reason why she could not stand up with him. She met his sardonic gaze and lifted her chin. 'I would be glad to do so if Lord Salcombe does not object.'

'I do not object, as long as you don't, Lady Chloe.'

'I thought that was what I just said.' She came to his side.

'So, what has made you decide you would care to stand up with me after all?' he murmured.

'If you must know, I still owe you a dance. I merely wished to repay my debt.'

He'd nearly forgotten about that. 'Ah, although performing the waltz in someone's drawing room was hardly what I had in mind.'

Miss Coltrane played a few notes and then peered around the music at them. 'I believe the gentleman is to take the lady's hand and then put his hand at her waist.'

'If you don't know the waltz, Salcombe, I can take your place,' Rushton said.

Brandt started. 'Should we proceed, Lady Chloe?' He held up his hand.

She placed her hand in his. While he put his other hand on the small of her back. Miss Coltrane began the music. After a moment of hesitation, Chloe followed his lead easily. He forgot he was in a small drawing room with an assortment of onlookers—he was only aware of the pleasurable feel of her slender back, the delicate touch of her hand in his, the face so sweetly upturned towards him, her mouth soft and inviting. A vision of crushing those lips beneath his made him catch his breath.

He heard her own intake of breath and her eyes widened as if she guessed his desire. The music came to an abrupt halt and he jerked his gaze away. What the hell was he doing, practically making love to her in the middle of the afternoon in a country drawing room? He dropped his hands and gave a slight bow. 'Thank you for the dance, Lady Chloe.'

She curtsied. 'Thank you, Lord Salcombe.' She did not quite look at him.

There was silence and then Rushton applauded. 'Splendid! A worthy performance that quite makes up for the less than spectacular beginning.'

Chloe turned to Sir Preston. 'Do you wish to try, Sir Preston? I should be quite happy to show you the steps. Miss Coltrane did such a splendid job of playing I am certain she would be glad to play again.'

'Oh, most certainly,' Miss Coltrane said with a cool smile.

This time she played the waltz as if it were a requiem. However, Brandt was distracted from speculating why by Chloe's efforts to teach Sir Preston the finer points of waltzing. The sight of her guiding Sir Preston's hand in the appropriate position and the warm colour in her cheeks made him wish he were in need of instruction. The only gratification was that Sir Preston didn't appear to be nearly as affected by Chloe's efforts as Brandt was by watching them. The baronet's sole concentration centred on executing the steps correctly.

When Sir Preston finally danced without a misstep, she smiled at him in such a way that Brandt was pierced with jealousy.

Mrs Sutton insisted on playing so that everyone might dance. After another country dance and a cotillion, Miss Coltrane announced it was time for her to leave.

The others followed suit and the party broke up. Brandt took his leave of Mrs Sutton and she smiled up at him. 'How delighted we were to have you today! I hope you will not find our little corner of England too dull. We have the assemblies and sometimes there is a dinner party, but I dare say they are nothing compared to the splendid entertainments of London. Except for Lady Haversham's summer ball. I imagine you will be here for that?'

At that moment he heard Rushton say, 'Perhaps I could escort you home, Lady Chloe.'

Brandt realised Mrs Sutton was waiting for his reply so he pulled his attention back away from Chloe, irritated that he could be so easily distracted. 'Yes, I will be here.'

Mrs Sutton beamed. 'Splendid. It is always the most elaborate affair…'

He finally managed to escape, but once outside he saw no sign of Chloe. Rushton was conversing with Tom Coltrane, so at least Chloe had possessed the sense to refuse his offer. Of course, what she did was none of his concern. He'd best remind himself of that.

* * *

Chloe walked slowly up the lane, feeling curiously disgruntled. She had no idea whether today could be counted as a success or not. Certainly she had spent some time sitting with Sir Preston before the others arrived. But once Emily and Tom came, the conversation turned to racing, a topic Chloe knew little about. Brandt's unexpected arrival had only thrown the afternoon off even more, particularly when Lydia made the remark about him not finding the entertainment dull. Chloe had wanted to sink.

As the afternoon progressed, she realised that, for some reason, Emily was determined to keep her away from Sir Preston. At least Chloe had managed to thwart Emily in the end when she showed Sir Preston the waltz. For some reason, however, it had felt rather flat after waltzing with Brandt. Of course, Brandt was very experienced and had undoubtedly danced dozens of waltzes so naturally it would be more interesting. But that did not explain why, when Brandt took her hand and then rested the other on her back, a peculiar tingle raced through her. And why, when Sir Preston did the same thing, she felt nothing at all. Or why the look in Brandt's eyes when they finished made her heart skip a beat.

The only reason she had agreed to waltz with him was because of her promise last night. And because he had looked at her in that knowing way as if he was just waiting for her to cry off. She had wanted to prove him wrong.

Which was idiotic. As was thinking about him when she should be thinking of Sir Preston instead. He was the sort of safe, trustworthy man she wished to marry. A man she would be comfortable with. A man who did not overpower her, treat her as if she were incapable of thinking for herself. Not the way her father had. Or the way Lucien had. Or the way Arthur still did.

A cool, confident, overbearing man such as Brandt would be no different.

She heard her name. She turned to see Emily hurrying after her. She bit back a groan. Emily was the last person she wanted to see at this moment.

She caught up to Chloe. 'You certainly waltzed very well with Lord Salcombe. How kind of you to take the time to show Sir Preston the steps, although I doubt your expert instruction will have quite the same results for him as his expert instruction in cards has had for you. Particularly after last night.'

'I was merely lucky last night. As you pointed out.'

'I don't suggest it was luck for you. In fact, I think you are quite talented. But such talents run in your family, do they not?'

She was no doubt referring to Lucien. Chloe felt as if she had been struck, but she managed to keep her voice calm. 'Such talents seem to run in most people's families.'

'Perhaps. Lord Salcombe did not seem at all dismayed that he was bested by a mere female.'

'The game was not between Lord Salcombe and me. Sir Preston and Mr Rushton also played.'

'Poor Sir Preston. Anyone could see that you carried the game. I would imagine that must have been very humiliating.'

'I hardly think of Sir Preston as "poor"! He played very well and sometimes it is merely a matter of which cards are drawn. I should be happy to have him for a partner any time.'

Emily gave a little laugh. 'How quickly you come to his defence. One would almost think you have a *tendre* for him.'

Her manner indicated no woman in her right mind would ever consider such a thing. 'I can imagine any number of women developing a *tendre* for Sir Preston,' Chloe said.

'So you do! I would think you would prefer a man such as Lord Salcombe to someone as dull as Sir Preston.'

'I never said I had a *tendre* for Sir Preston.' Chloe's cheeks heated. 'I do not consider him dull, at any rate. I have no idea why you think I would prefer Lord Salcombe.'

'He is more sophisticated and has more address and I cannot imagine him thinking only of his land. Or his horses and dogs, and shooting. One must have something in common with the object of one's affection after all. I do not suppose you are interested in farming and dogs and sheep?'

'Of course I am.' She was beginning to resent this line of questioning very much. 'Not that it is any of your concern.'

Emily gave her a superior smile. 'Poor Sir Preston. Does he suspect? No, of course not. He is too thick.'

Chloe wanted to hit her. 'I do not have a *tendre* for anyone. If you must know, I have no intention of falling in love. I like Sir Preston because he is kind.' Thank goodness, they had reached the path Chloe needed to take to reach Falconcliff. 'I must go this way. I pray you will not repeat such speculations to anyone. They are quite untrue.'

'Oh, I shan't say a thing,' Emily said breezily. 'But I think you would do better to set your sights on Lord Salcombe. Good day, Lady Chloe.' She walked away, her head high.

Chloe stared after her. Oh, heavens! What if Emily said something? She would die of humiliation if anyone else thought she was setting her cap at Sir Preston.

Particularly Brandt. She could only imagine his amusement. No, she did not want anyone to know until she and Sir Preston were betrothed.

If, indeed, that happened.

Chloe's disgruntled feeling only increased when she entered her bedchamber and found a letter on her dressing table from Arthur. She tore off her gloves and picked up the missive. He never wrote unless he wished to admonish her for spending all of her pin-money. In her present mood, she looked forward to his certain lecture even less than usual.

Her first impulse was to put the letter off until later. On the other hand, she might as well open it and put it out of her mind. She broke the seal and spread open the paper. 'Oh, no,' she whispered. Surely, she had misread what he wrote.

But another read of his neat, precise handwriting left no doubt. *The Marquis of Denbigh and his sister, Lady Barbara, have most graciously invited us to a house party at Denbigh Hall. I will arrive at Falconcliff ten days after Lady Haversham's ball, but rather than going to Dutton Cottage we will leave directly for Denbigh Hall the following day.*

Not Lord Denbigh, who reminded her of a large frog with his great bulk, bulging eyes and clammy hands! She had met him this past Season and had hardly thought of him at all when he was first presented to her, except that he was the sort of man she disliked for he reminded her of Lucien's acquaintances. She had been puzzled as to why his widowed sister, the sophisticated Lady Barbara Grant, took an interest in her, inviting Chloe to the theatre, seeking her out at assemblies, taking her for drives in her stylish barouche. Chloe began to notice that Lord Denbigh was almost always present as well. She tried to avoid him; the expression in his eyes when he looked at her made her uneasy. But one evening, when she and Mama were invited to Lady Barbara's home for dinner, Lady Barbara left Chloe and Denbigh alone in the small garden behind the Denbigh town house. He suddenly declared that she was the sweetest creature alive and had pulled her into his arms and kissed her with his wet, thick mouth. His breath and odour had nearly made her gag and only when she had started to retch did he draw back. He had called for Lady Barbara.

Lady Barbara accepted his explanation that Chloe had suddenly taken ill while strolling in the garden. Maria had fussed over her, insisting she must stay in bed the next day. Horrified and ashamed, Chloe could not tell her mother about the kiss. Just as she had not told her mother about an earlier, even more brutal kiss. Chloe ended up ill anyway, for the day after that, she developed a fever and her body ached everywhere. After several weeks, she had still remained weak. The physician finally suggested that the air of London might be responsible and that the fresh air of the seaside would undoubtedly prove beneficial. By then she was eager to escape London and the fact that Belle had invited her to Falconcliff for an indeterminate amount of time pleased her even more. Thus her Season had ended, and, with it, she had thought, the attentions of Lord Denbigh, too.

What was she to do? The thought of facing Lord Denbigh again filled her with panic. If only Sir Preston would make her an offer! She turned from the window, still clutching the letter. If they were betrothed, then surely she would not be expected to go to house parties at Denbigh Hall or anywhere else. She could stay at Falconcliff until the marriage and then after that she would be here in Devon for ever.

She sat down on the bed. Certainly Sir Preston had been all that was kind and attentive, but he was not particularly polished in matters concerning females. He rather reminded her of Serena's betrothed, Charles Hampton. Serena, who was her dearest friend, had written that she had been forced to bring her Charles up to the mark.

How had she done it? Chloe rose and rummaged through the small wooden box where she stored her letters until she found Serena's letter.

I will own I was forced to take matters into my own hands, for I fear Charles would never come up to scratch if I did not. You would probably be shocked at my boldness, for I know how proper you like to be! During last night's assembly I asked him to escort me to the garden under the pretext that the room was far too warm. There was a nicely secluded bench and we sat. Then I told him I was rather cold and moved very close to him. I then smiled at him, but instead of looking away I held his gaze. In a most bold fashion! And then he kissed me, very nicely I must add, and after that he felt most obliged to make me an offer, which I modestly accepted.

The kissing aspect made her feel slightly ill, but if she married Sir Preston there would need to be kisses—as well as other more intimate contacts she shied away from thinking of. Perhaps one grew used to such things after a while.

Certainly Belle had, if the dreamy look in Belle's eyes when Justin regarded her in a particular way was any indication. But then she was in love with Justin and he was in love with her, so that undoubtedly made the difference. At such times, Chloe was uncomfortable, almost as if she had intruded on their privacy, but at least she had not felt repulsed by their mutual desire. Unlike the revulsion she experienced when Denbigh looked at her. Or when Lucien's acquaintances had stared at her so long ago.

Which was another reason, she felt safe with Sir Preston. He never looked at her in such a repugnant way. At least, she cared very much for Sir Preston, so perhaps she would not mind his kisses. And she wanted children, soft, rounded babies who would grow into lovable children, which meant she must learn not to mind such intimacies.

Could she possibly force Sir Preston's hand? She cringed at the thought, but she could see no other way to approach him before she was forced to leave with Arthur.

Arthur would arrive in less than a fortnight. She must think of something before then.

Chapter Three

Brandt looked down at the child who sat on his knee and wondered how he had managed to end up again with another human under the age of one. This time he held Lady Emma Peyton, the youngest daughter of Lord and Lady Haversham. Her wide blue eyes were fixed on him and when he tentatively smiled at her, her little rosebud mouth curved in an irresistible smile. No doubt she'd charm every man in sight in a few years. She had already charmed him.

'So we will have the picnic at Waverly two days after the ball,' Marguerite said. She sat across from him on one of the sofas in her drawing room.

He pulled his gaze away from Lady Emma. 'As long as it does not rain. The drawing room is still covered with plaster dust.'

'In that case we will just move the picnic here.'

Emma wriggled a little and he obligingly bounced her. She giggled.

'I think it is time you set up your own nursery,' Marguerite said.

'Why, when I can play uncle to your children and Belle's?'

'That is not quite the same as having children of your

own. What do you think, Giles? I think he would make a splendid papa.'

'Undoubtedly.' Giles grinned at Brandt from his position near the mantelpiece. 'You'd best be careful when she gets an idea into her head. You'll end up with a passel of urchins in no time.'

'But he'll need a wife first,' Marguerite said. She eyed Brandt. 'Is there not some woman who interests you? Someone respectable, that is.'

'I fear all the respectable, interesting women are either married or…' he glanced at Emma '…far too young.'

Marguerite rolled her eyes. 'Really, Brandt, can you not be serious for a moment? You cannot tell me there is no one who has caught your attention.'

He had visions of methodically looking at each eligible woman and tallying up her good and bad points. The thought was not appealing. 'So how does one go about, er…searching for the right wife?'

'Much like choosing a horse,' Giles said. 'The right breeding, fine lines, the right amount of spirit, and preferably an easy keeper.'

'You are not helping the matter. Brandt needs a wife, not a horse.' She rose and held her arms out to Emma, who had started to fuss. She pressed the baby close to her and planted a kiss on the soft cheek before looking up. 'Waverly needs to be filled with children, which means you must find someone who suits you. Someone you like.'

'At this point, I can hardly afford a new horse, much less a wife.'

'Certainly they cost as much to keep,' Giles added. 'You will need to find an heiress.'

Marguerite stared at her husband as if he'd said something brilliant. 'Of course. Chloe. She would be perfect!

She adores children and she adores Waverly! You could not find someone who would suit you more!'

Had Marguerite gone mad? 'I think you'd better suggest someone else. She would rather see one of us pole-axed before she'd accompany me to the altar.'

He realised Giles was watching them, a grin tugging at his lips. 'Well?' Brandt asked. 'What is it?'

'I am trying to imagine a marriage between you and Chloe. Rather like a Shakespeare comedy, I would think. Perhaps *The Taming of the Shrew* or *Much Ado about Nothing*.'

For some reason, Brandt was irritated. 'Since it is not likely to happen, I would save your imaginings.'

Giles only looked more amused. 'Why not? I doubt you'd be bored.'

'No. Only worried I'd wake up with a dagger at my throat.'

'You are both impossible!' Marguerite said with a look of disgust. 'Perhaps if you would cease to tease her in such an appalling fashion she would cease to be so cross with you,' she told Brandt and rose. 'I must return Emma to Nurse and then see to it the guest chambers have been properly readied. Our first guests will arrive today. As much as I look forward to the ball I am always relieved when it is over. Thank goodness it's the day after next.' She marched to the door and turned. 'If you do not consider Chloe, then I will be forced to find someone for you at the ball,' she challenged him as she left the room.

Giles laughed. 'Chloe is not that dangerous. In fact, she is quite kind and generous. Today she has taken Caroline and Will for a picnic. I do not know many young ladies who would be willing to spend so much time with two children who are not her relations. They adore her. You could do worse.'

'She is an heiress, that's true, although I've no intention of marrying anyone who brings more than a few thousand pounds to the marriage.'

'No?'

'No. In fact, I am not in the market for a wife.'

'You are now.' He laughed at Brandt's expression. 'If Marguerite has anything to say about it.'

Brandt rode along the path that ran across the top of the cliff towards Waverly. Below him lay the sparkling water of the sea. He paid scant heed to the scenery. Instead he was thinking of children. His children. At Waverly.

He must be mad. Surely he had not been so bewitched by first Julian and then Emma that he wanted to set up a nursery as soon as possible. If he had ever considered children, they had always appeared vague and faceless.

They were not faceless now. They had round cheeks and chubby little hands. And smiles that tugged at his heart. Despite the sense of rightness he felt at Waverly, it seemed lacking somehow, as if there was something else he wanted. Now he knew. The same things Justin and Giles had: warm, loving families.

Unlike his own family, with the mother who never smiled and the cold, stern father who angered at the least provocation. He could hardly remember a time when his mother was not an invalid and, although she never raised her voice, never openly wept, he had no doubt of her deep unhappiness. And his father had hardly been a father at all. If not for Justin's family, he would not have experienced any sort of warmth at all.

He had stayed with them often. The Duchess bestowed upon him the same love and warmth she bestowed upon her own son. She always listened when he talked, and had not been above getting down on her knees and playing games with them. The Duke, although more reserved, had been no less kind. Despite their welcome, Brandt could not forget they were not his own family or that, eventually, he would be summoned home.

Brandt had envied Justin. He still did.

Even if he wanted a wife, he could not afford one. Certainly he had started to recover some of the fortune his father had squandered, but he'd spent much of it on the repairs and improvements his father had neglected on the land and tenant cottages that belonged to Salcombe House. Some he had gambled on a venture that at the moment seemed fruitless. And now he had Waverly, the house he had wanted from the moment he had first laid eyes upon it.

He refused to marry for money. Or for mere convenience. Or to produce the heir his great-aunt, Lady Farrows, mentioned in every letter. He would not bring children into the world unless he married a woman who would adore them as much as Marguerite adored her children or Belle adored Julian.

A woman such as Chloe.

He wanted to curse Marguerite for even putting that notion into his head. Chloe was not for him. She was too untouched; too naïve; too good.

And he shared his father's blood. He'd set out to prove his difference when he'd run wild in London. Prove that he was not cold and passionless, prove he could sample all the pleasures of the flesh the capital had to offer. Pleasures his father had condemned.

But the irony was he had turned out to be like his father after all.

Brandt reached the ramshackle stables and then dismounted and handed his horse over to a groom. Instead of making for the house he veered off towards the path that took him to the edge of the cliff. Movement caught his eye on the beach below him. He had no difficulty identifying the children on the rocks as Lord Will Haversham and his sister, Lady Caroline. Or the woman whose head was bare and whose hair glinted red and gold in the sun.

He muttered a curse. By his calculations the tide would be coming in shortly. He hoped she had the sense to clamber from the rocks before that happened. He headed for the uneven stone steps that would take him to the beach.

'Look, Chloe!' William called. Chloe lifted her skirts and carefully stepped across the rocks to where William peered into a pool. She crouched down to look. 'What do you see?'

'A starfish! Is he not splendid?'

'He is.' She smiled at his enthusiasm. He was six and full of energy and spirits.

'I wish I could bring him home.'

'He would not survive very long away from the sea. He will be much happier here with his friends.'

William eyed her. 'What friends? I don't see any other starfish.'

'I'm sure he has friends close by.' She had no idea if starfish were particularly social. They didn't seem as if they would be.

She looked over at Will, and her heart swelled. She adored him as well as his more serious older sister, Caroline, and now, of course, little Emma. Lydia could not understand why she wanted to do dull things such as taking them on picnics or exploring tide pools or riding ponies to the fishing stream near the village. But then Lydia had grown up with an older brother and a younger sister and despite their little quarrels, no one could doubt the true affection between them. Lydia had had a neighbourhood of playmates as well. Chloe had never had playmates and Lucien had been worse than no brother at all. With Will and Caroline she could participate in all the things she had missed as a child.

'Chloe!' Caroline appeared at her side. 'I think we should go back. The tide is starting to come in.'

'You are right. Come, Will, we need to leave.'

'I want to stay. A little bit longer.' He wriggled further on his stomach.

'No, William,' Caroline said. 'We must make our way to the beach. We don't want to be caught on the rocks.'

'We won't be. Look, now there's a crab!'

'William!'

'If the tide does come in, we can escape by going through the sea cave. Then we'll end up at Waverly in the garden.'

Caroline shuddered. 'Ugh. It is too dark and slimy and smells like fish.'

'And I hate dark, cold places,' Chloe added. Will had dragged them over to the dark opening behind the rocks. The water swirling inside echoed in a sombre way that gave her the chills. Despite Will's assurance that the passage led away from the water and up the cliff she had horrible visions of being trapped while the water rose. And even if she did like climbing about in caves, she had no desire to end up in Waverly's garden. Not any more, at least. 'We can have the apricot tarts now.'

The mention of apricot tarts had the desired effect. Will stood up and scrambled over the rocks with amazing alacrity. He paused on the last rock. 'First one to the hamper gets three tarts!' He jumped down and dashed across the sand.

Caroline made a face. 'I would like to see him race in skirts.'

'I know. It doesn't seem fair, does it? Even for activities such as this women must wear skirts and shifts.' Of course, most ladies would never think of clambering around on rocks in bare feet as she was doing now.

Caroline hopped off the last rock and Chloe followed. Then the young girl turned to Chloe. 'The next person to the hamper gets two tarts!' She started to run and Chloe dashed after her.

Running on sand was no easy feat and they were giggling before they had gone no more than a few yards. They stopped, breathless and laughing. Chloe glanced towards William and the laughter faded. She wanted to groan instead. Why ever was Brandt here?

But he was. He stood with Will, watching them. 'Lord Salcombe is here!' Caroline's voice expressed delight. She began to walk towards him at a much more dignified pace.

Chloe trailed behind her, suddenly self-conscious of her faded gown with its wet, dirty skirts, the hair that had come out of its pins, and her bare, dirty feet. She probably looked like an overgrown street urchin. She pulled up her bonnet, which dangled down her back by its ribbons, and set it on her head.

William dashed towards her. 'Look, Chloe! Uncle Brandt is here! I told him we were having apricot tarts and he could have one!' He caught her hand, dragging her towards Brandt.

Brandt's eyes were on her and for a moment he did not reply. Then he seemed to start. 'Only if Lady Chloe agrees, and if there are enough.'

'I am certain there are,' she said, feeling even more awkward.

William had thrown himself down beside the hamper. 'Come and sit down,' he said, grinning up at them.

'Only after the ladies sit,' Brandt said.

'Oh!' William promptly rose. 'You need to sit down,' he told Chloe and Caroline.

They took their places and Will sat back down. Brandt settled his own long frame next to Will while Chloe opened the hamper and distributed the first round of tarts. She made certain her hand did not contact Brandt's strong, lean one when he took the pastry from her.

She sat back on the cloth, grateful Brandt lounged next to Will and the hamper provided a barrier between them. At least she did not need to think of conversation. Will chattered between mouthfuls of tart, excited to tell Brandt about starfish, tide pools and sea creatures. Chloe's name seemed to come into the conversation far too often for her liking. More than once she found Brandt's gaze on her, which only increased her discomfort.

'And Chloe doesn't mind getting her skirts wet! She even goes without shoes! Show him, Chloe!'

Chloe started. 'Show him what?'

'Your feet! They are bare!'

'I would rather not do that.'

'But why not?'

Brandt glanced down at him and his mouth twitched. 'Because it is not considered proper for ladies to show gentlemen their bare feet.'

'Oh.' Will digested that for a moment. 'Are you a gentleman?'

'Of course he is!' Caroline said. She gave her younger brother a reproving stare. 'He is a peer.'

Brandt looked over at Chloe and grinned with a boyishness she had never seen. 'I am not certain Chloe considers those terms necessarily synonymous.'

'I...I have never thought about it.' She found herself smiling back at him. His grin slowly faded and he stared at her with an awareness that brought heat to her cheeks and made her heart pound. She looked away. 'Does anyone want another tart?' Her voice sounded odd.

'I do!' William exclaimed.

Caroline did as well. Chloe was grateful for the excuse to bring out more of the delicious tarts and direct the conversation in another direction. After eating two more tarts, William grabbed Brandt's hand and urged him to wade with him.

He stood in a lazy, graceful movement. 'Actually, I had come to warn you about the tide. But I see I did not need to.'

'We come here all the time. Chloe knows all about the tides,' Will said.

'I am glad to hear that. I would not want any deaths on my property.'

'This is your property?' Chloe asked.

'Yes. I negotiated it as part of the estate. Do not worry, you are quite welcome to come here any time you want.'

'I see.' So he now was master of her favourite cove as well. She turned away, again with that little twinge of resentment and started to pack the linens back in the hamper.

'Come, Uncle Brandt! I want to show you where we found the starfish.'

'Do we have time?' Brandt asked her.

'A little time.' At least if he was occupied she could put her stockings and half-boots on without Brandt around. Not that he would watch, but she would rather not have an audience.

'Then I had best remove my boots,' he said. To her dismay, he sat down on a nearby rock. Cheeks pink, she looked away and busied herself putting the picnic dishes back in the hamper. He finally rose and left with William and Chloe found her stockings and boots and hastily put them on. She tried to pin her hair back up and finally Caroline offered to help.

As Chloe finished tidying up, William and Brandt remained standing in the waves. William was holding Brandt's hand. He turned and saw her and then said something to William. They then started back towards Caroline and Chloe.

Chloe wiped the sand from William's feet and then helped him put on his stockings and shoes. She tried to ignore that Brandt sat on the rock next to them and was engaged in the same task.

Brandt rose. 'Do you need me to carry the hamper back?'

Chloe shook her head. 'No. Marguerite said she would send a servant for it after we returned.'

'I will be glad to offer my escort back to the Hall, in any case.'

'That is not necessary,' she said sharply, then tried to sound more agreeable. 'But if you want to that would be very kind.' Now she merely sounded idiotic.

Which he must have thought as well from his quizzical expression. He said nothing, however.

They made their way up the stone steps that led from the beach to the top of the cliff. William continued to chatter about their excursion and even Caroline, who was normally reserved when in the company of more than one or two people, participated as well. Chloe followed along, feeling rather resentful, which was ridiculous. After all, William and Caroline had every right to like whomever they pleased. It was just…she felt rather left out. She had enjoyed being their special friend and now it seemed Brandt was just as special.

She had no idea why feeling special was so important, except that since Belle married she had felt a little lost. She knew Belle loved her no less, but now her husband and her baby were of first concern to her. She belonged to them and they belonged to her.

Chloe felt as if she did not belong to anyone.

By the time they reached the steps of Haversham Hall, she was still feeling sorry for herself. She followed them into the entrance hall, and Caroline turned to her. 'Will you stay for a while with us, Chloe?'

At least she hadn't asked Brandt if he would stay. Then chided herself for being so childish. 'No. I am too dirty to even enter the drawing room. But thank you.' She gave Caroline a swift hug, careful not to soil Caroline's gown and then shook William's hand.

'I will take you back to Falconcliff,' Brandt said.

'I walked. I would not want to inconvenience you if you rode.'

'I walked as well.'

'So you found them, Brandt,' Marguerite said as she came down the stairs. 'Now you can escort Chloe to Falconcliff.'

'Which is what I told her.'

Marguerite reached the bottom and came forward to take Chloe's hand. 'Thank you so much, dear Chloe.' She looked over to Brandt. 'The children adore her.'

'I've no doubt of that,' he said.

'She needs several of her own, do you not think?'

Chloe's face grew warm.

'If that is what she wants,' he said politely.

'Of course she will need a suitable husband first,' Marguerite persisted. She cast Chloe a mischievous look. 'That will be my next project.'

'I…' Why must Marguerite tease her about this now, when she was terrified she would end up with a most unsuitable husband? And in front of Brandt, of all people? 'I…I do not want a husband.' That was not what she meant to say either. 'I should return to Falconcliff.'

Marguerite made a wry face. 'I did not mean to put you to the blush. Sometimes my tongue runs away with me. I won't do anything you don't wish, but I would love to see you settled with your own children.' She glanced at Brandt. 'Just as I hope to see Brandt wed with a family of his own.'

To Chloe's surprise, a hint of colour tinged his cheek. 'Chloe is right. We had best go before you decide to post the banns.'

'I would not be that presumptuous!' For some reason Marguerite looked quite pleased with herself.

For the first time, Chloe was actually relieved to leave Marguerite. She could scarcely look at Brandt as they started down the path that cut through the Haversham estate to the back garden of Falconcliff. He did not seem inclined to talk either, which proved to be more unnerving than his teasing.

She finally stole a look at his face. He appeared to be concentrating very hard on the path. A lock of dark hair fell over his forehead and he looked rather boyish despite the set expression he wore. He cast a quick look at her. 'Don't let Marguerite's words trouble you. She habitually concerns herself in other people's affairs, particularly when it comes to marriage.'

'It is just rather awkward to have such things brought up in front of someone else.'

A slight smile touched his mouth. 'I agree. Particularly when it is quite apparent she intended to start her matchmaking in the middle of her hallway.'

A frown wrinkled Chloe's brow. 'Did she? With whom?' She had been so confused she had hardly known what Marguerite was talking about.

'With you and me.'

Chloe stared at him blankly. 'I beg your pardon.'

They had reached the stone gate that marked the beginning of Falconcliff's garden. He allowed her to pass him and then fell into step next to her on the walk that led to the house. 'She has already informed me she thinks that you and I would make a suitable match.'

Chloe's mouth fell open. 'Oh, dear,' was all she could say.

'Don't worry. You're in no danger. I am quite aware you would rather spend your life in Newgate than wed me.' This time he looked rather amused.

'That is not true!' Hearing him put the matter so bluntly made her cringe.

'Wouldn't you?'

'No, of course not!' What if he thought she was angling for an offer? 'I…I do not really want to marry anyone.'

He didn't blink at that. 'And why not? You seem fond of children. I would imagine you'd want your own some day.'

'I am very happy being an aunt,' she said stiffly. 'One must be married in order to have children of one's own. Or at least one should be.'

'That is preferable.' His mouth twitched. 'So what has caused you to hold marriage in such aversion? Most young ladies seem eager to acquire that status as quickly as possible.'

Well, she was not most young ladies and she found his amusement irritating. 'If you must know, I do not like the idea of a husband.'

'Why not?'

'I think in general they are too much trouble.'

To her satisfaction, he actually looked taken aback. 'Why do you say that?'

'They always wish you to do as they ask, frequently without consulting anyone's tastes; they wish everyone to be quiet when they want to be quiet and to make conversation when they wish to, and in general consider a wife there for only their convenience.'

'That is hardly a romantic view of marriage.'

'I am not very romantic. If I had to be married, I would prefer a comfortable marriage. In fact, I think being in love would be a great inconvenience and certainly clouds one's judgement. And I most certainly do not think it guarantees happiness!'

'But we have, under our noses, two couples who defy that theory.'

'But Belle and Justin made each other most unhappy until they resolved their differences. I would never want to go through that! And although Giles and Marguerite are very happy now, I dare say it is because they are so comfortable with each other. Marguerite told me that when she first met Giles, he seemed to dislike her and when she realised she had fallen in love with him, she despaired for months until he offered for her. The most odd thing was he confessed he had thought she did not like him. I cannot think of anything that would be more inconvenient. I would prefer to be comfortable right away and forgo all the stupid misunderstandings.'

'I will own that, on the whole, I tend to agree with you.'

She should have been pleased that he did; instead, she felt irrationally disappointed he did not try to argue with her. 'Why are you not married? You seem very fond of children yourself.'

He kept his eyes on the path. 'Even if I were so inclined, I am hardly in a position to take a wife.'

'But why not?' Then could have clapped her hands over her mouth as she recalled her earlier conversation with Belle.

This time he turned to look at her. He read her expression perfectly. 'Precisely.'

'I cannot think it would matter if someone cared for you!'

'And you are not a romantic?'

'Not at all! I merely meant that if someone cared for you it would not matter that you are not...that is...' she stumbled, but he said nothing and just watched her with that impenetrable look. 'Wealthy.'

'Most women expect a certain amount of comfort when they marry. I doubt if living in an old house on the Devon coast far from London appeals to many women.'

It appealed to Chloe, but she could hardly tell him that. 'Surely some women would not mind. Waverly will be perfectly lovely when it is finished.'

'By the time I am done with the repairs necessary to make it tolerably livable, I will have little money left to keep a wife in any sort of style. I no longer have a house in London so there would be no frequent visits to town.'

'Not every woman wishes to visit London. But you do have your other estate, do you not?'

A cool smile touched his mouth. 'Yes, unfortunately. If it were not entailed I would sell it in an instant.'

'Why?'

He glanced at her. 'Are you always this curious? If you must know, it is because I detest Salcombe House and all it represents.'

'I...I did not know. I am sorry,' she said. She had no idea what he was talking about.

'Don't be.' He kept his eye on the road. 'I do not intend to marry for money either. No heiresses.'

Was he trying to hint her away? As if she would ever fall in love with him! Irked, she said, 'What if you fell in love with an heiress?'

'I do not intend to do so.'

'What if you cannot help yourself? And she returns your affections?'

'That is unlikely to happen.'

'What is unlikely to happen? That an heiress will fall in love with you or you cannot help falling in love with her?'

'Both.' He stopped and looked down with her, the glint in his eye dangerous. 'If you persist in this line of questioning, I might start to think you are in love with me yourself.'

'I beg your pardon?' She backed away, heat flooding her cheeks.

His smile was sardonic. 'That is what I thought. Perhaps we could discuss something more pleasurable. Such as the weather.'

They continued on in an uncomfortable silence until they reached the terrace. He halted. 'I will see you tomorrow.'

'Tomorrow? But are you not dining with us?'

'Actually, no. I am to dine with Gilbert Rushton and Sir Preston Kentworth at the Inn.'

'With Sir Preston?' The name slipped from her lips before she could stop it.

'Do you have an objection to my dining with Sir Preston?'

'Oh, no, he is most kind.'

He was looking at her rather strangely. She should escape before she made things worse. 'I had best change.

Thank you.' She dashed through the French doors before he could say anything. Or before she said anything else stupid.

Sir Preston Kentworth rose from the table. 'Must be off.' He nodded to Brandt. 'Glad to have you in the neighbourhood, Salcombe. Night, Rushton.' He ambled away. Brandt liked him; he had a blunt, pleasant manner that was refreshing after the languid boredom affected by many of his London acquaintances.

Rushton leaned back. 'Wonder if he yet realises he is the object of affection of not only one, but two members of the fairer sex.'

'Kentworth?' Brandt asked, startled.

Rushton grinned. 'Hard to believe, but then who knows what inspires passion in a lady's heart? Causing quite a bit of speculation over which of the damsels will land their catch. Considered booking a wager on it, but didn't want the wrath of certain persons to fall on my head.'

'It is probably best in these cases.'

'Don't suppose you are interested in knowing the identity of the two rivals?'

'Not particularly.' Local gossip held no more interest for him than London gossip had.

'Ah, but in this case you might be intrigued to know.' Rushton leaned forward a gleam in his eye.

'Then you'd best tell me.' Even as he said the words, he was hit with a disquieting premonition.

'Emily Coltrane is one.' Rushton paused for effect. 'And Lady Chloe is the other.'

Brandt kept his expression bland. 'How do you know that?'

'Tom Coltrane. Says his sister's nose has been quite out of joint since Lady Chloe's arrival. Emily noticed straight away that Lady Chloe meant to set her cap at poor Kentworth. She's claimed all along that the card lessons were a ploy on Lady Chloe's part to gain Kentworth's attention. Seems Emily was right.'

He should have guessed. The signs were there; the look on her face at the dancing lessons, the way she blushed when he mentioned he would see Kentworth. 'Does Kentworth return her sentiments?'

Rushton shrugged. 'Hard to tell. Kentworth's a bit of a slow top in these matters. His mama's all for it, however. Been spreading subtle hints around the neighbourhood that she may soon have an intimate connection with Westmore's family.'

Hell. That harpy who had dragged Chloe into the card game? 'Does my cousin have wind of this?'

'Don't think so. Lady Kentworth is clever enough to keep it from the Duke until she has Lady Chloe in her net. Thought I should warn you so you might drop a word with the Duchess. Don't want to underestimate Lady Kentworth when she sets her mind on something. I wouldn't want to see Lady Chloe hurt. Or Kentworth, for that matter. From what I've heard of her guardian, don't think he'd welcome a country baronet into the family.'

Rushton was right. For all he appeared to be a loose screw, he was much more perceptive than Brandt had ever given him credit for, and he had no doubt Rushton was quite familiar with the local gossip. Although Justin and his family were warmly welcomed into the small tight-knit village, the local gentry still maintained a certain respectful distance and he doubted all the gossip reached Justin's ears.

Brandt finished his brandy. 'No, Ralston would not.' He eyed Rushton. 'You were wise to not book any wagers. You'd have not only Westmore to deal with; you would have me as well.'

'I rather thought so.' Rushton held up his hands. 'No need to look so grim. I promise Lady Chloe's reputation is safe in my hands. Just wanted to warn you.' He grinned. 'Besides, with Kentworth out of the running, thought I might have a chance in that direction myself.'

'I wouldn't wager on that either.' Brandt rose. 'I must take my leave as well.'

'I'll walk out with you.' The other man stood.

Rushton was silent until they reached Brandt's curricle. 'Don't want you to think I meant to spread gossip.' His countenance was sober. 'But Lady Kentworth has a reputation for interfering. Managed to compromise her own daughter into marriage a few years back—very nasty business—just wouldn't want the same thing happening to Lady Chloe.'

'No.' Neither would he. He would do everything in his power to prevent it, including keeping Chloe in his sights if Kentworth or Lady Kentworth were anywhere in her vicinity. But why had she been so adamant about her aversion to marriage if she had a *tendre* for Sir Preston? Or did she consider marriage to Sir Preston comfortable?

He did not intend to give her a chance to find out.

Brandt spoke to Belle the next morning after breakfast. He found her in the garden, Julian on her lap. She looked up and smiled, and then her expression sobered. 'I suspect you have something rather serious to say.'

'Yes. Rushton informed me that there are rumours circulating that Chloe is setting her cap at Sir Preston.'

'Oh, dear. I had hoped that no one would really notice or at least say anything. It is dreadful enough when one has a *tendre* for someone; then to have rumours spread about it is very humiliating. Particularly when one hopes to keep it secret.'

He started. 'You know Chloe has a *tendre* for Sir Preston?' For some reason having Belle confirm it only made him more angry. 'Then why the devil haven't you put a stop to it?'

'I cannot dictate how Chloe feels. As far as developing a *tendre* for someone, I would much prefer it be a decent, kind man such as Sir Preston than a charming fortune-hunter.'

'Are you saying you would welcome a match between them? Does Justin know of this?'

For some reason she looked as if she wanted to laugh. 'Yes, Justin does know, and his reaction was the same as yours. Once I convinced him that forbidding Chloe to have anything to do with Sir Preston would only make him even more romantic in her eyes, besides bewildering Sir Preston, he agreed we would say nothing. Of course, they are quite unsuited to each other. Poor Chloe, she knows nothing of farming and has been desperately reading all of Justin's *Gentleman's Magazines* in hopes of being able to converse with Sir Preston on topics he's interested in.'

Brandt wanted to grind his teeth. And curse. Belle's words were reasonable, but the thought of Chloe finding Sir Preston romantic only served to make his mood even surlier. 'Then perhaps you are not aware that Lady Kentworth has been hinting around that she expects a more intimate connection with your family. And that she forced her own daughter into a compromising marriage.'

'No, I did not know that.' She frowned a little. 'Do you know this for a fact?'

'Only what Gilbert Rushton told me.'

'Certainly Lady Kentworth has made it quite obvious she favours Chloe and fawns over her in a most deliberate manner. Oh, dear, I will speak to Justin, of course, but since Chloe will only be here for another week, I hate to create a stir. We will make certain she is well chaperoned and busy with other things so she will not have much time to think of Sir Preston.' She gave him a reassuring smile. 'I have no doubt everything will be fine. It is kind of you to worry about her.'

He felt rather idiotic since Belle seemed to have matters well in hand. 'I consider her a relation so, of course, I am concerned.' Now he sounded stiff.

'Of course.' Her eyes twinkled. 'I do hope you won't say anything to Chloe about this. I fear it will only antagonise her and then you will be at daggers drawn again. I should hate to see that.'

'I won't say anything.' Which did not mean he wouldn't keep an eye on her. At least he and Belle were in agreement on one point; she and Kentworth were not suited. He was a relation of sorts, so he had a certain responsibility for Chloe, and that responsibility entailed keeping her safe from her damnable romantic notions.

Chloe smiled down at Julian. 'I suppose we must take you back to Nurse.' She had just spent an agreeable hour with him in the garden. They had picked flowers, squealed at butterflies and watched the water spray from the fountain in the small pond. She rose and he wriggled until she turned him so he could more easily see where they were going. 'You are getting heavier,' she told him. 'Soon I won't be able to carry you so effortlessly.' He grinned at her and her heart melted. He smelled so sweet and felt so soft. Before Julian, she had never paid much attention to babies, but she had fallen instantly and irrevocably in love with him.

She wandered up the steps and entered the drawing room through the terrace door. Busy watching Julian, she did not notice the man standing there, until he spoke.

'Good day, Chloe. I see your clothing is in disarray as usual.'

She froze. 'Arthur? What are you doing here?'

Her guardian, Arthur, the Earl of Ralston, fixed her with his usual disapproving gaze. He was of medium height with light brown hair, and a bony face which always looked as if he were about to give someone a scold, most particularly when he focused his gaze on her. 'I see your manners have not improved either.' He clasped his hands behind his back. 'I decided there was no reason to delay the journey to Denbigh Hall as Lord Denbigh and Lady Barbara are most anxious to see you.'

'You cannot do that! I am to be here for another week, and there is Lady Haversham's ball tomorrow!'

'I did not intend to leave today. We will leave two days after the ball.' He cast a dismissive glance at Julian, who had become uncharacteristically silent. 'As soon as you return that child to its nurse, I would like to speak to you.'

That child? How dare he speak of Julian in such a way? 'I am certain you meant to say as soon as I return Lord Wroth to his nurse, you would like to speak to me.' She stalked past him and with no little satisfaction saw his brow snap down even further. In the hall, however, she felt less pleased with her little victory. She could never hold her tongue around him and put on the meek face he liked in young ladies. Instead, she always managed to make things worse.

She had started across the hall when Belle appeared, her expression one of dismay. 'Chloe, I fear Arthur has arrived. He wishes to speak to you straight away. He is putting up at the inn and arrived late last night, so we had no idea he was coming, or I would have suggested you stay away longer.'

Chloe handed Julian to his mother and made a face. 'I

have seen him. I came through the terrace doors and he has already chided me on my unimproved manners and disarrayed clothing.'

'Oh, dear.' Belle gave her a sympathetic look. 'Well, I suppose you must have your interview with him. At least you will have it over with.'

Chloe returned to the drawing room. Arthur stood near the window, hands clasped behind his back. He turned and moved towards her. 'Sit down, if you please.'

She took the chair he indicated and folded her hands in her lap. She vowed to hold back any unruly words that sprang to her lips.

He stood in front of her, a position that always made her feel like a chastised school girl. 'I hope that when you are married, your husband will be able to curb your tongue. As well as see that you dress properly.'

'Well, I do not have a husband yet,' she said brightly.

A wintry smile crossed his face. 'I trust you will before the summer is over.'

'Really? I cannot imagine why you would think that.' Had he somehow heard about Sir Preston?

'I intend to accept Lord Denbigh's offer.'

Her stomach lurched, and all thoughts of meekness fled. She jumped up. 'No! He…he is too old!'

'Nonsense. In fact, a man of his age will be able to guide you properly, which you most certainly need.'

'I will not accept him.'

'You will. Why else do you think we are going to Denbigh Hall?'

'So, I do not have any choice in the matter?'

He stared at her. 'You have had choices the last two Seasons, but you refused all of them. I've no doubt there are men who would be willing to overlook your advanced age, but I would prefer to see you betrothed before you are one and twenty.'

'I do not like him,' she said quietly.

His thin mouth tightened. 'What does that have to do with anything? You are young, and foolish if you think such emotions play a role in choosing a suitable mate. His bloodlines are impeccable. He is from one of England's oldest families. He is wealthy enough that no one could think he is marrying you for your dowry.'

'Love has nothing to do with it! I find him repulsive. He reminds me of a...a frog! In fact, I would rather marry a frog!'

Arthur stared at her and then his mouth tightened. 'You are disrespectful and childish. There is no reason why you should not accept him. I trust that after you reflect on the advantages of such a match you will come to your senses.'

'I won't. You cannot make me marry him.'

'No, but if you do not, I fear I will be forced to cut off your allowance. And your mother's as well.'

'You are despicable!'

His face contorted with such fury that she feared he would strike her. Without thinking, she turned and dashed into the hallway. She started for the staircase and then changed her mind.

If she went upstairs now, Arthur would undoubtedly find her. She whirled around. The next thing she knew she had crashed into a hard masculine chest. Strong arms steadied her and she was pressed into a coat smelling of outdoors and horses. Then she was released. She glanced swiftly up and found herself looking into Brandt's startled face.

Drat! Of all the people she must dash into! 'I beg your pardon,' she said stiffly. From the condition of his clothing, she knew he had been at Waverly. His coat was wrinkled and dusty; his breeches in no better condition. He looked rather like a ruffian. A very dangerous and very attractive ruffian. The unexpected thought flustered her completely.

His mouth curved. 'I will own you're the last woman I expected to throw herself into my arms.'

'I was hardly throwing myself into your arms.' She pulled away from him, still flustered. 'If you will excuse me, I...I must go.'

'Where are you going in such a hurry? It is nearly time to dress for dinner.'

'Nowhere. Outside, if you must know. I pray you will move.'

He stared at her; his expression changed to one of concern. 'What has happened?'

'Nothing. Nothing at all.'

'Then why do you look so agitated?'

'I...I don't.'

'Your face is far too expressive. You look as if the devil is on your heels.'

'Chloe!' Arthur's voice cut through the air. 'I have not finished with you.'

'I see. Not quite the devil, but close,' Brandt murmured.

'I must go,' she said desperately.

'Good day, Salcombe.' Arthur eyed Brandt with a look of distaste. Most likely disgusted by Brandt's dusty clothing. Arthur probably could not conceive how any gentlemen would ever be seen in such a condition.

'Good day, Ralston.' Brandt merely looked amused. 'Are you staying in Devon? Or did you merely stop by to have a word with Chloe?'

'Quite the contrary. I am to escort Lady Chloe,' he said with heavy emphasis on 'lady', 'to a house party.'

'Not today, I trust.'

'Naturally not. We will leave two days after Lord and

Lady Haversham's ball. However, I am certain you will wish to dress for dinner so we must not detain you. Chloe, come with me.'

'No.'

'I have not finished with you.'

Brandt shifted towards her. 'Apparently she has finished with you. And, as you pointed out, it is time to dress for dinner.'

His defence steadied her enough for her to say, 'And did you not point out my clothing is in disarray?'

'Yes, but…'

'Then I will see you at dinner, Cousin Arthur.' She gave Brandt a brief smile. 'Thank you.' She turned and started up the stairs before Arthur could detain her.

Once in her chamber, she shut the door and leaned against it for a moment. Her stomach began to churn again. Lord Denbigh. Even his name made her shudder. She had no choice; unless she brought Sir Preston up to scratch tomorrow, she would either be forced to marry Lord Denbigh or Mama would scarcely have a farthing to her name. Her latest letter from Mama had been full of news of purchases of lace and ribbons and two gowns; one a lilac crepe; the other a pale yellow cambric she could not do without. There had been a very small loss at whist as well. She so hated to ask Arthur for funds, for he would scold her terribly and threaten to cut off all her allowance entirely, so if Chloe had a very small sum…

And now if Chloe refused Denbigh, there would be nothing for her mother at all, which was why she *must* marry Sir Preston. Once she was married, Arthur would no longer control her fortune. True, it would then be in Sir Preston's hands, but she somehow doubted he would begrudge her the amounts she sent to Mama.

Chloe moved from the door. She really had no choice.

Just as her friend Serena had done with her man, Chloe must encourage Sir Preston to make her an offer.

Her only chance would be tomorrow night. At the Havershams' ball.

Chapter Four

'Chloe? Are you ready?' Chloe jumped when she heard Belle's voice. She nearly knocked her fan off the dressing table and caught it just in time. She snatched up the French shawl from her bed and draped it around her shoulders. She certainly did not want Belle to see her bodice; not until they were at the ball at any rate.

She turned and plastered a shaky smile to her face. 'Yes. I did not realise it was time to leave.'

'The carriages are below.' Belle stepped into the room, lovely and elegant in rose silk, diamonds at her throat and ears. Her smile was warm when she saw Chloe. 'Oh, Chloe! How beautiful you look and so grown up! I sometimes forget you are no longer a child until times such as this and I realise you are a young woman.'

'And nearly on the shelf according to Arthur.'

Belle made a face. 'He is ridiculous. You must put him from your mind. Do not worry, I will not allow him to ride roughshod over you. Come, let us go downstairs.' She paused and looked at Chloe's face. 'Are you all right?'

'Perhaps I am a trifle nervous.'

'Surely not after facing the patronesses of Almack's! Anyone who can win praise from Lady Jersey for her ''pleasing manners'' should not feel the least apprehensive about a country ball.'

She tried to return Belle's smile and followed her from the room. She could hardly tell Belle she had made up her mind to kiss Sir Preston. Or more to the point, to encourage him to kiss her. If a kiss had worked for Serena, then perhaps it would work with Sir Preston as well. If not, she might be desperate enough to propose to him.

Justin, Brandt, and Arthur waited for them in the drawing room. They stood near the mantelpiece in well-fitting dark coats and satin knee breeches. Although not as tall as the other two, even Arthur was not unattractive in his evening clothes.

Her gaze fell on Brandt. Tonight he was the elegant London lord, just as he had been this past Season. For some odd reason, she could not help but notice how well his corbeau coat fitted his broad shoulders or how his knee breeches and silk stockings emphasized his strong, muscular legs. Or that despite his civilized appearance he suddenly looked as male and dangerous as he had when she had crashed into him in the hall yesterday.

He looked up and his gaze met hers. Awareness shot through her and from the expression that leapt to his eyes, she knew he had felt the same jolt. She tore her gaze away, completely confused.

She felt no less confused when she found him at her side as they stepped out of the front door into the pleasant evening. 'You are to ride in my carriage,' he said.

'I am?' She looked up at him and wished she were a few inches taller. Or he was shorter. Although he was not the tallest man of her acquaintance, he was tall enough that she had to look up to him.

'Belle will ride with us as well so you will be adequately

chaperoned.' His eyes were laughing at her again, no trace of the earlier moment in his face. 'I thought you would prefer my company to Lord Ralston's, but perhaps I was mistaken.'

Usually she would prefer anyone's company to that of Arthur, but tonight she was not so sure as she glanced up at his face. Again she felt that disconcerting awareness of him.

She realised he was waiting for an answer. 'Of course.'

'Of course what? You would prefer my company?'

'Yes, I suppose so.'

'You only suppose? I look forward to the day when you have a definite preference for my company. Over Ralston's, that is.'

He was teasing her again. However, she was too distracted to even think of a response. He helped her and then Belle into the carriage. But as it rattled down the drive, worries about Sir Preston overtook any reaction she might have to Brandt. She would need to lure Sir Preston to somewhere private. What did one do next? She had no idea how to go about encouraging a man to kiss her. She would move closer to him as Serena had done, but what if that did not accomplish what she wanted? Should she—?

'Chloe, Brandt has just asked whether you are looking forward to the ball.' Belle's voice cut into her thoughts.

Chloe blinked. 'The ball?'

'The ball we are about to attend. Or perhaps it has slipped your mind,' Brandt said.

'I...no.'

He still watched her with that disconcerting intensity. 'Then do you look forward to it?'

'I...yes.' Thank goodness, they were already entering the arches of the drive in front of Haversham Hall. Brandt alighted and then helped them down. Justin took Belle's arm and Chloe found herself on Brandt's. Arthur trailed behind them up the marble steps to the entrance. The footman admitted them and another stepped forward to take her shawl. She reluctantly turned, and Brandt's gaze fell to her bodice. Her cheeks flamed at his blatant astonishment. She pulled her gaze away, telling herself that he had no business staring at her bosom in such a bold way. Even if it had expanded.

Thank goodness, Belle did not seem to notice anything amiss or Justin. Or Arthur, for which she was profoundly grateful.

Once they entered the ballroom, now lavishly decorated with fresh greenery, pots of plants and bouquets of flowers, her attention turned to finding Sir Preston. She spotted Emily straight away, looking like an overblown white rose in lace and flounces, and then she saw Sir Preston.

He looked quite splendid in his dark blue evening coat and black silk breeches. Yes, she could quite see herself on his arm in the future. Perhaps he was not the tallest man in the room or the most handsome, but he had a certain distinction that she found—

'Chloe, Brandt has just asked you to stand up with him for the first set.' Belle's gently amused voice broke into her thoughts.

'I...that would be very nice.' She found his gaze on her, but with a certain watchfulness she had noted in his eyes the past few days, particularly when they were in company. For some reason, it made her uneasy.

'Good.' He held out his arm. 'Shall we proceed then?'

'But the ball has not yet begun.'

'No, but I thought we could take a turn around the room.' His voice was still polite, but there was a certain note that told her he would not allow her to refuse.

She certainly did not want a scene. Rather resentful at his insistence, she rested her gloved hand on his arm. She would much rather seek out Sir Preston, but perhaps she should not make her move too soon. The ball would last for hours so there would be plenty of time.

Chloe was not so certain two hours later. She had not been able to even get near Sir Preston. He seemed to either be with a group of gentlemen or gone from the ballroom. Once she saw him talking to Emily and his mother. Then Emily had left and Chloe had started across the room. She was nearly there when Brandt appeared at her side. He had insisted she needed a lemonade and by the time she convinced him she did not, Sir Preston had vanished. She could barely conceal her impatience with Brandt. He had been in her way so much this evening, she would have accused him of following her if it weren't for the fact he would probably laugh at her. She could think of no reason why he would want to do so anyway.

She stood in one corner and looked around the room and then her heart skipped a beat. Sir Preston stood near the wall by a potted plant. For once, he was alone. She started forward, only to have Lydia grab her arm. At the same time, Brandt suddenly appeared.

'Chloe,' Lydia began and then her eyes widened when she saw Brandt. 'Good evening, Lord Salcombe.'

Chloe bit back a groan.

'Good evening, Miss Sutton.' He glanced at Chloe. 'And Chloe, of course.' His expression was rather mocking.

'I do not want to be rude, but I am feeling rather warm. So if you will excuse me I believe I will go to the garden.'

He held her gaze, a slight smile at his mouth. 'Did you not promise me this dance?'

'I do not remember doing so.' She was too frustrated to be polite. 'Besides, I do not care to dance now.' She glanced at Lydia who was staring at her, undoubtedly taken aback by Chloe's rudeness. 'However, I am quite certain Miss Sutton would like to stand up with you.'

'Oh! No...I...I...' Lydia stammered, turning pink. She managed to recover. 'I...I would be most honoured to stand up with Lord Salcombe.'

For a dreadful moment she thought he would refuse. He did not. 'I would be honoured as well, if you will favour me with the next dance, Miss Sutton.'

'That will work out quite well, then.' Chloe gave him a cold smile and marched off. Sir Preston was much where she had last seen him. His face creased in a smile as he watched her approach. 'Lady Chloe, haven't yet spoken to you. Seems you are always occupied. Hope you are enjoying the ball.'

'Oh, yes.' Her hands suddenly felt clammy and her stomach had started to churn. 'I...I am. And you? Are you not dancing at all? Even after the lesson?'

He grimaced. 'Fear it will take more than one or two lessons. Decided I didn't want to risk any lady's feet tonight.' He glanced out at the floor. 'Looks to be a waltz. You should be dancing.'

A waltz? She had hardly noticed. She spotted Brandt and Lydia straight away. Brandt had just placed his hand at Lydia's back and Lydia looked as if she had just swallowed a cream pot. Thank goodness, she had managed to evade waltzing with him, Chloe thought. She dragged her attention back to Sir Preston. 'Actually, I feel rather overheated. Do you think it is hot in here?' It was not exactly a falsehood, for she was becoming quite hot.

'Rather.' He looked concerned. 'Should I fetch the Duchess? You do look a trifle peaked.'

'Oh, no! I was rather thinking of a change of air. Perhaps I could walk to the gard—' Then she remembered she had just told Brandt that was where she wanted to go. 'Conservatory. I do not suppose you would care to accompany me?'

He hesitated. 'Most certainly. Wouldn't do for you to go alone.' He held out his arm and Chloe laid her hand on the sleeve of his coat.

She could not complain he was overly forward or flirtatious, which was fine with her. She led him from the ballroom and down the picture gallery, which connected the ballroom to the conservatory on the other side of the house. At least it should be private, which was what she needed for her plan.

No one else was there, thank goodness. A lamp was lit near the entrance, but the rest of the glass room was in shadows. The sweet scent of jasmine mingled with gardenias drifted up. Her partner shifted uncomfortably and sneezed. 'Beg pardon. Flowers make me sneeze.'

Hardly a promising start. 'We can sit on a bench,' Chloe said. She walked towards a wrought-iron seat on the other side of the room. He followed her. She sat down and patted the place next to her. 'You can sit here.'

He took the other side of the bench. Chloe frowned. Sitting this far apart would not do. She rubbed her arms. 'I fear I am getting rather cold.'

Sir Preston's gaze went to her low neckline for a second before he averted his eyes. 'Best return to the ballroom then.'

'Oh, no! I wanted to enjoy the flowers for a few minutes longer. Perhaps if I sit closer to you.' She shifted so her thigh just touched his.

He jumped. 'Er…' He looked at her face and she gave him her most demure smile. He swallowed. 'I…I do not suppose you would care to kiss me,' she blurted out and then wished she could vanish when she saw his startled expression.

As if mesmerised, he swayed towards her. His kiss was brief, and hardly enough to tell her whether she liked it or not. He drew away as if the kiss had startled him. 'Beg pardon. Not at all the thing to do.'

'I did not mind. I…I wondered if you could do it again. Longer, perhaps.'

He swallowed even harder. 'Anything to oblige.' He leaned towards her and his mouth came down on hers. This time he prolonged the contact, his lips moving over hers. It was not all unpleasant, particularly when compared to Denbigh's kiss. She would undoubtedly get used to it in time.

She tentatively kissed him back. A low sound issued from his throat and suddenly his tongue slipped into her mouth. She jumped. He pulled away, his expression stunned and then apologetic. 'Sorry. Suddenly carried away. If we go on…be obligated to offer you marriage. Not that I would mind. Have been thinking it's time to do the pretty. My mother would like it. Would be honoured if you—'

'I hardly think you've compromised Lady Chloe with one kiss.'

They both jumped at the sardonic voice that seemed to come out of nowhere. Chloe prayed she would disappear. Sir Preston half-rose. 'The devil take you, Salcombe! What do you mean by stealing up on a man like that! Having a private conversation!'

Brandt stepped out of the shadows. He folded his arms and regarded them with a stony expression. 'Lady Chloe is obligated to me for the next dance. I came to collect her.'

She had no idea whether she wanted to kill him or die of humiliation. Or do both.

'Er, had no idea.' Kentworth glanced at her. He looked confused. 'Lady Chloe was warm and wanted to cool down. So we walked here.'

'I see.' Brandt's hard gaze fell on Chloe and it took all of her will power to not look away. 'I am loath to tell you, my dear, but a kiss is hardly the way to cool down.'

She lifted her chin. 'Really.'

Kentworth took a step towards Brandt. 'Now see here. Won't have you insulting Lady Chloe. Will do my duty by her.'

'Why? I don't intend to tell anyone of this incident, and I trust you are gentleman enough not to do so.' There was a hint of steel in Brandt's voice that could almost be a threat.

Kentworth's hands curled. 'Calling my honour into question, Salcombe?' He sounded equally menacing.

They couldn't possibly be planning to fight, could they? That was not what she wanted. Brandt was deadly at fencing—she had watched him once with Justin. She suspected he was equally adept at handling a pistol. Sir Preston wouldn't stand a chance against him. She could not have him wounded or worse on her account! Not after she was the one who lured him to the conservatory. She jumped up. 'Stop this! No one is questioning anyone's honour!' She glared at Brandt. 'And none of this is your affair anyway!'

His eyes glinted. 'It most certainly is. You are now part of my cousin's family which makes you part of mine. Therefore, you are under my protection as well as my cousin's.'

'I most certainly am not!'

'Must say he is right, Lady Chloe,' Kentworth said, sud-

denly joining the enemy's side. 'Feel the same way about
my relations and their, er…relations. Has every right to
object to my, er…embracing you. Should never have done
so. Still willing to offer you my hand.'

The thought apparently gave him no pleasure. Whatever
was she thinking of? Trapping poor Sir Preston into a marriage he obviously didn't want only to save herself? With
sickening clarity, she saw how selfish, childish and, yes,
even wicked her plan had been. She could not have Sir
Preston taking the blame for her actions. 'That won't be
necessary, particularly since I threw myself at you. There
is no reason for you to sacrifice yourself on my account.
So, if you will pardon me, I believe I will return to the
ballroom.' She turned on her heel and walked as quickly
as possible from the conservatory.

But the humiliation hardly ended there. Emily stood outside the conservatory. She stared at Chloe, her expression
contemptuous. 'How dare you attempt to trap him into
marriage, you wicked creature! I swear if you have hurt
him I will make you very, very sorry!' Her mouth trembled
as if she were about to cry.

The truth hit Chloe with blinding force. 'You are in love
with Sir Preston,' she said, stricken. 'I am so sorry. I did
not mean to hurt him, or you.' She dashed away, unable
to bear any more, and ran into the nearest room off the
passageway.

The room was some sort of study lit only by the moonlight shining through the tall windows. There was a desk
and two wing chairs and shelves on one side lined with
books. She threw herself into one of the chairs and curled
her legs under her.

How could she have been so utterly stupid? And forward? She had behaved like the worst trollop, wearing a
low *décolletage*, padding her bodice, luring him to the con-

servatory, begging him to kiss her. She had never dreamed anyone would follow them there. Instead, two persons had witnessed that humiliating scene.

How long had they been there? Had they heard everything? That hardly mattered now, since she had already proclaimed that she had thrown herself at Kentworth. Brandt had looked at her with such icy contempt, she had no doubt she had made herself despicable in his eyes. And poor Emily! No wonder she had been so cold to Chloe. Why ever had she been so stupid as to not suspect Emily was in love with Sir Preston? If she hadn't been so selfish she would have seen that Emily was exactly the sort of wife Sir Preston needed. Not some silly creature who could scarcely tell one end of a sheep from the other.

She stifled a groan, and then froze when she heard footsteps and voices outside the study door. To her relief, they passed the room. She heard nothing for several minutes more. She supposed she should return to the ballroom before she was missed, but the thought of meeting Sir Preston or Brandt or Emily made her shudder. She was about to uncurl her legs from beneath her, when she heard more footsteps. She froze again, hardly daring to breathe. Surely no one would come into this dark study!

She was wrong. Her heart pounded when the person moved into the room. She folded herself more tightly into the chair. The footsteps stopped.

'Chloe,' Brandt said softly from somewhere behind her.

She fought down her panic. Perhaps if she did not answer he would go away. He came around the side of the chair and looked down at her.

'Please leave.' To her chagrin, her voice wobbled.

'Are you in love with him?'

'I beg your pardon?'

'Sir Preston. Are you in love with him?'

'I...' She should tell him it was none of his affair, but instead she said, 'I...I wanted to be. And he is the nicest man I know. I am very fond of him.'

'Is that why you wanted him to kiss you? Because you are fond of him?' His voice was harsh.

Her cheeks heated. 'I do not know,' she whispered.

'You do not know why you wanted him to kiss you? Do you know now?'

She jumped up, her humiliation turned to anger. 'Yes, I do know! I cannot see that it is any of your affair. I know you must think I am foolish and an utter wanton and undoubtedly hold me in contempt. But please do not make it worse by questioning me in such an odious fashion!'

'I don't hold you in contempt.'

'Don't you? I pray you will let me pass.'

'No.' He caught her arm and pulled her around to face him. Her eyes had adjusted to the dim light and she could see his grim expression. 'Did you like his kiss?'

She stared at him, completely taken aback. The cool, amused lord she knew had vanished. 'It...it was quite nice.'

'Quite nice?' He gave a short laugh. 'Is that all? Then allow me to give you something to compare it to.'

Before she could even think, he had pulled her hard against him. He tilted her chin with one hand and then his mouth found hers.

His kiss was nothing like Sir Preston's. Or Lord Denbigh's wet, repulsive kiss. Or the brutal, violation of her mouth so long ago. Her body seemed to meld with his; his warm, firm mouth moving over hers made her legs tremble so she was forced to cling to him. Her lips parted under his seductive pressure.

He released her so abruptly she stumbled.

'Hell,' he said.

She backed away from him. 'Oh, dear.'

'Yes.' He ran a hand through his hair. 'Damn it, Chloe, I did not mean to do that.' He wore the same pole-axed expression as Sir Preston had earlier.

'Didn't you? I…I pray you will not feel obligated to offer me marriage. After all, a kiss hardly obligates one,' she said brightly.

His expression darkened. 'No.'

She backed away. 'I…I should return to the ballroom.' The thought of facing Sir Preston and Emily was not as daunting as standing in this darkened room, the air heavy with a peculiar tension.

'Chloe, wait.' He lifted his hand towards her. 'Allow me to escort you.'

'No. You have done enough.' She turned and dashed from the room before she could humiliate herself further.

Brandt stood in the study, feeling as if he'd been punched in the stomach. What the devil had happened? No, he knew exactly what had happened. He'd allowed his baser instincts to crash through all his carefully constructed control and he had kissed Chloe. Not just any kiss. He'd kissed her with all the fierceness of a passionate lover, nearly ravishing her mouth until some semblance of rational thought had broken through. No wonder she'd fled from him.

All because of the searing, angry jealousy that had possessed him when he found her asking Kentworth to kiss her. He'd wanted to make her forget Kentworth's kiss, erase any *tendre* she had for the man.

Instead, he'd frightened her, which was undoubtedly for the best. Perhaps next time she asked for a kiss she would realise that not all men were as honourable as Sir Preston.

This hardly banished his remorse. He had only confirmed her worst opinion of his character. It shouldn't matter to him. She was far above his touch in every respect. Years ago, before he discovered what he really was, he might have allowed himself to fall in love with an innocent such as Chloe, but it was far too late for him now.

Chapter Five

Chloe rose, too nervous to sit, and went to look out of the drawing room window at the tidy garden behind the Coltranes' house. Like the rest of the house, the garden was carefully tended with a profusion of flowers and shrubs. Even on this overcast day, it looked green and inviting.

She twisted her hands together and hoped Emily would see her. After a restless sleep, she had decided she could at least try to make things right for Sir Preston and Emily. She had mustered all of her courage to come; Emily had witnessed her humiliation and, after Emily's words to her last night, she held no doubts that Emily detested her. At least she could explain and try to make amends.

Her stomach knotted even more when she heard footsteps. She turned, half-expecting to see the housekeeper, but instead Emily appeared. She wore a faded dress of yellow muslin but, despite its age, the style suited her. Her hair was pulled back in a simple chignon. Even with the smudge of mud on her cheek, she looked much more attractive than she usually did. Almost pretty, in fact.

She looked warily at Chloe. 'Mrs Potter said you wished to see me.'

'Yes.' Chloe took a deep breath. 'I wished to apologise to you.'

Surprise flashed in Emily's eyes. 'Why? I would think you would wish an apology from me for calling you a wicked creature.'

Chloe flinched, but did not look away. 'No, because you were right. It was very wicked of me to try and…force Sir Preston into marriage with me. I did not realise it until last night.'

'Are you in love with him?'

The same question Brandt has asked her, but Emily had a right to know. 'No. I thought I might be, but it was only because I wished to be. He is kind and decent and I can quite see how any woman would wish to marry him, but you are much more suited to him.'

Emily flushed. 'He does not notice me, so it hardly matters.' She twisted her hands together, a nervous gesture Chloe had never thought to see from her. 'I thought about many things as well last night. I only want him to be happy. If you would make him happy, then he must have you.'

'I do not think I would make him happy. At any rate, he does not care for me in that regard. I learned that last night as well.'

'But you were sitting alone with him. Quite close, in fact. Until Lord Salcombe showed up, that is. Then they argued and I was certain they were about to fight a duel over you.'

Thank goodness Emily had not seen the kiss. Chloe gave a little laugh. 'It was the most ridiculous thing. Lord Salcombe was angry because we were alone together. He blamed Sir Preston. When Lord Salcombe started to take me to task, Sir Preston accused him of insulting me and then I stepped in and told Lord Salcombe it was entirely my fault. Then they were both angry with me.'

'I see.' Emily did not look quite convinced, but at least she did not seem inclined to argue.

'So will you let me help you?'

'Help me do what?'

'Make Sir Preston notice you.'

Emily made a little gesture. 'Oh, no. I...I do not think that is possible. Besides—' she lifted her chin '—I have no intention of making a fool of myself over a man who does not care for me.'

Chloe sighed. 'It cannot be any worse than what I did. Besides, he does notice you. He has said the most complimentary things about you. I know he greatly admires your seat and light hands and your knowledge of farming.'

Emily coloured. 'But those are accomplishments that even Tom has. He does not notice me as a...a female. I know I am not pretty or graceful. And I hate most of my gowns. I always feel so ridiculous in lace and flounces.'

'Lace and flounces are not suited to everyone. I think you would do much better in simpler styles. The gown you are wearing today is very becoming.'

'This?' She made a face. 'But it is so old.'

'But the style is very nice for you. As is the colour. And I like your hair dressed in that particular fashion as well.'

Emily flushed, looking strangely unlike her usual forward self. 'Do you?' She looked at Chloe. 'Oh, how I wish I was as pretty as you are! You do not know how jealous I have been of you!'

'But I have red hair and freckles. I have always wanted to have a complexion such as yours. And your height. I am so tired of being short and ineffective!'

'Ineffective? I would never say that!' Emily looked

more like her blunt self again. 'Do you really wish to
help me?'

'Yes. I do not have much time. I am to leave with Lord
Ralston in two days, but we can at least find some gowns
that would be becoming and dress your hair. I thought if
you have some time today we could begin. Then you will
be ready for next week's assembly.'

'I still cannot imagine why you would want to help me.
I have not been nice to you at all.'

'I have not been nice to you either. Or Sir Preston.'
Chloe smiled a little. 'At the very least I can try to help
both of you find some happiness.'

Chloe cut through the shrubbery near Falconcliff and
then found the path along the cliff above the sea. She had
spent several hours with Emily going through her gowns,
finally choosing one in peach moiré that suited Emily's
creamy complexion. Mrs Coltrane had helped, and they
both agreed all the trim except two rows of flat ribbon
should be removed. After that, despite Emily's caustic
comments, they arranged her hair in several ways and finally decided on a style that softened her rather broad face.
Emily had stared at herself in the looking glass. 'I look
almost…pretty,' she finally said.

Mrs Coltrane hugged her. 'Oh, my dear child, you look
lovely. If only you had listened to me before, but you are
so stubborn! I hope you will from now on!'

Emily rolled her eyes. 'Mama!'

At least that had been gratifying. Chloe bit back a sigh.
She was dawdling because she dreaded returning to Falconcliff and the knowledge she was to leave soon. She
should be spending as much time as possible with Julian,
but it would only emphasise the reality of her leaving. She
had decided last night that she would marry Lord Denbigh.

What choice did she have? If she rebelled this time, there would only be another man. She could ask Belle and Justin for assistance, but they had already done so much for both her and Mama. If Arthur did as he threatened, then Belle and Justin would be forced to help not only her but her mother as well. They would be burdens until Chloe found someone else to marry.

Engrossed in her thoughts, she did not hear the horse until it seemed to be upon her. She whirled around. Her heart leapt to her throat when she saw the bay horse and its rider. Her first impulse was to run but she could not do that. She had done enough running last night. She waited, trying to quell the nerves in her stomach as Brandt drew to a halt. His expression was hard to read as he looked down at her. 'I want to speak to you for a moment.'

'Oh.' She tried not to think of how he had kissed her, but it proved impossible with him looking at her like that.

He dismounted in a graceful easy movement and caught the reins. 'I will walk back to the house with you.'

She nodded and started to walk. He fell into step beside her. 'I wish to apologise for my behaviour last night. I did not behave as a gentleman. First I insulted you and then forced my attentions upon you.' He did not look at her.

'I...I did not behave as a lady. I suppose you meant to teach me a lesson.'

He swung around to stare at her, two spots of colour in his cheeks. 'I was wrong,' he said flatly. 'I should not have presumed to do any such thing. My actions were all that were despicable.'

'I cannot blame you for thinking I was no better than a...a callous flirt. I should thank you for saving Sir Preston from a miserable fate.'

'You wish to thank me?' He gave a short laugh. 'I am

attempting to beg your forgiveness for my damnable actions. Not accuse you.'

She looked at him steadily. 'You are not guilty. I know how wicked I was.'

'Wicked? You?' He halted and faced her. 'You are the least wicked person I know. If you thought that was what I meant last night, then I must doubly beg your pardon.'

There was nothing of the flirt about him now. He was deadly serious, the intensity of his expression made her catch her breath. She looked away. 'Then I will accept your apology.'

'Thank you.'

They walked the rest of the way to the drive in an uncomfortable silence. She almost wished he would tease her; anything would be better than this sense that unspoken words hung between them. She was relieved when they neared the side of the drive where he would need to turn to go to the stables. 'Thank you for walking me home.' Her voice sounded much too high and breathless and she forced herself to look at him.

'Yes.' He hesitated a little. 'I hope we can be friends.'

'Friends? Oh, yes. That would be nice.' What a completely inane thing to say. She rushed on. 'I hope you will enjoy living in Devon. I will own I was quite jealous when Belle told me you had bought Waverly. I always thought of it as my house. So ridiculous.' Whatever had possessed her to say such a stupid thing?

An odd expression crossed his face. 'It is not at all ridiculous.' He hesitated. 'You are welcome to visit, you know.'

'Perhaps.' She felt rather sad. It was unlikely she ever would. She had no idea what her life would be when she was married to Lord Denbigh. She gave him a bright smile and held out her hand. 'Goodbye, Lord…Brandt.'

He took it. 'This isn't quite goodbye, is it? We will see each other before you leave. There is the picnic tomorrow. Marguerite has persuaded me to have it near the old chapel at Waverly. I would be more than pleased to show you the house as well then.'

The almost boyishly eager expression on his face made her want to weep. Perhaps if they had met under different circumstances, they could be friends. There would not be a moment like this again when for once, they were in perfect accord. Tonight, they would meet at dinner and she would have her defences firmly in place. He would revert back to the impenetrable, cool lord. She smiled anyway. 'I would like that.'

'Chloe.' He hesitated as if he were about to say something else and then dropped her hand.

She turned and had started up the wide shallow steps when the door opened. Lady Kentworth marched out, head high, her lips set in a thin, angry line. Her furious gaze fell on Chloe. She came down the first step, forcing Chloe back. 'You! You may think that because you are an Earl's daughter you are too high and mighty for the likes of us! I shall make you very, very sorry for the brazen way you trifled with my son!' She sailed past Chloe, who stood stricken against the pillar.

She finally moved and stepped into the cool entrance hall and saw Arthur standing in the door of Justin's study. As if drawn by a magnet, his gaze fell on her.

'I would like to see you now,' he said coldly.

'I must change.'

'Now.'

The look on his face did not bode well. Without a doubt she knew last night's débâcle had come to his ears. To complete her humiliation, Justin now emerged from the study. At the same moment, Belle came down the stairs.

'Chloe, there you are, thank goodness. We have been worried.' She glanced at Arthur and then back at Chloe. 'But first you must go upstairs and change. And rest.'

Arthur came up to Chloe's side. 'I intend to speak to her now.'

Belle lifted her chin. 'She needs to rest.'

Arthur's lip tightened. 'I intend to find out exactly why that creature seems to think Sir Preston has compromised Chloe, before she starts to spread her lies about the neighbourhood.'

'Arthur! Not now. You are distressing Chloe,' Belle said.

'Indeed. She will be even more distressed when her reputation is ruined.' He turned a cold gaze on Chloe. 'So, my dear Chloe, perhaps you will tell me whether Sir Preston compromised you last night or not.'

Chloe wanted to sink. 'He did not…that is, I…'

'Chloe was not compromised.' Brandt's voice broke into her disjointed speech. He suddenly appeared at her side.

Chloe jumped and Arthur swung his gaze to Brandt. 'What do you know of this?' he demanded.

Brandt met his eyes. 'I was there.'

'Precisely where is ''there''?'

'Precisely where did Sir Preston say he had compromised Lady Chloe?'

Arthur swung around to face him. 'See here, Salcombe, Lady Kentworth claims—'

Justin, who had been watching in silence, finally spoke. 'I suggest we should discuss this matter in my study. Belle, I would like you there as well.' He looked at Chloe. 'Belle is right, you must change and rest for a short while.'

'But I think I should…' Chloe began, but the look on his face stopped her. His expression was not unkind, but she knew he had no intention of relenting. 'Very well, your

Grace.' She quickly turned before she humiliated herself further by bursting into stupid tears.

Brandt watched her go, then followed the others into Justin's dark-lined study. Belle sat down on the wing chair near the desk, but the others remained standing. Brandt leaned against the desk. 'What has happened?'

Arthur folded his arms over his chest and glared at him. 'I had barely arrived, hoping to speak to my ward—who, by the way, was nowhere to be found, when that Woman, a term I have grave misgivings about applying in this case, appeared, wishing to speak not only with me, but with the Duke as well. If I do not consent to a match between her son and Chloe, she will spread it about that they were caught in a compromising situation.'

'Oh, dear,' Belle said.

Brandt bit back a curse. 'She's ridiculous.'

Justin spoke. 'Nonetheless, she claims several witnesses noticed Chloe and Kentworth leaving the ballroom together and that they did not return for nearly a half an hour.'

'They were not alone,' Brandt said. 'I followed them.'

Arthur's face turned red. 'What are you saying? Are you telling me Chloe actually left the room with her son? You let her out of your sight?' His voice rose and he turned a furious look on Belle.

Justin fixed him with a cool gaze. 'Might I remind you that you were also at the ball?'

'At any rate, my ward was not properly chaperoned.'

Brandt looked at him. 'They were chaperoned. I was with them.'

'Then why did you not insist they return to the assembly room?' Arthur asked.

'I did.' He decided it was not prudent to talk about the kiss.

'Obviously not soon enough.' Arthur gave him a cold look. 'I've no desire to have that tale put about either. I doubt there's a person in England who would consider you an adequate chaperon. Your reputation is not the most sterling.'

'Arthur!' Belle said.

Justin frowned at Brandt. 'Would you be willing to vouch you were with them if necessary?'

'Of course.'

Justin looked back at Arthur. 'Despite Lady Kentworth's bluster, she will find it difficult to convince anyone that Chloe was compromised, particularly if Brandt vows he was with them the entire time. I will not hesitate to apply more pressure if necessary. A very select dinner party, perhaps. With invitations to those who do not stoop to such vulgar speculation.'

'I will hope that will put that creature's threats to rest,' Arthur said, although he looked far from pleased. 'However, I intend to do one more thing to ensure she will pose no threat to Chloe and to prevent such schemes in the future.' He paced away from them and clasped his hands behind his back. 'Lord Denbigh has offered for Chloe. We intended to wait until we had spent a few days at Denbigh Hall to make the announcement, but in light of this, I feel it is prudent to announce the betrothal now.'

'Lord Denbigh?' Belle's usually calm voice rose. She jumped up, her face ashen. 'No! You cannot have her marry him! He is a…a lecherous old man who would make her miserable!'

'I have already told her where her duty lies. It is quite natural for a young girl to be a little timid around her future husband. As for your other objection, I hardly consider three and forty ancient. She needs a husband and I do not intend to wait any longer. I intend to see her betrothed as quickly as possible.'

'Is tonight soon enough?' Brandt asked.

They all turned to look at him and Arthur shot him a stony glance. 'I trust you are joking, Salcombe. I would never accept Kentworth. Not only is he most unsuitable, I would never risk letting that harpy get a shilling of her dowry.'

'Not Kentworth.' Brandt straightened. 'Myself.'

Arthur's mouth fell open. Belle made a little gasping sound. Only Justin remained impassive.

Arthur spoke first. 'You are offering for Chloe?' His voice was rather strangled.

'Yes. I am making a formal offer.'

'One that I will not accept. I will not see her fortune fall into the hands of a penniless viscount.'

'I would be willing to wager Denbigh has more need of her fortune than I do,' Brandt said coldly. 'You may write a codicil into the settlement that stipulates any money and property she brings to the marriage is hers to do with as she pleases.'

'That is hardly satisfactory. She is an Earl's daughter and can look much higher than a viscount. I cannot possibly consider your offer.'

Brandt folded his arms. 'I suggest you accept my offer. In fact, I insist, unless you want Lady Chloe moving in some of the most unsavoury circles in England. Of course, I will call you out before I would allow that to happen.'

Ralston's mouth tightened. 'Are you threatening me, Salcombe?'

'Yes.'

'I am her guardian.'

Belle stared at Arthur, her face set. 'Chloe will not leave

this house if you persist in this. She will not be forced into marriage with such a man, no matter how high his consequence. I will not allow it.'

'Nor will I,' Justin said. His own expression was cold. 'You will accept my cousin's offer. Chloe will not leave Falconcliff with you unless you decide to abduct her although I doubt you will like the consequences if you decide on that course of action. There are few who would sympathise with your efforts to marry your innocent ward off to a debauched man against her will. I would, of course, be forced to make it known my doors are no longer open to you.'

Arthur cleared his throat. 'I assure you there is no need for such measures. I would not want Chloe to marry someone with such a reputation, of course. Lord Denbigh, however, will not be pleased.' He glanced around at the others as if hoping for sympathy for his plight, but apparently finding none, he relented. 'Very well, Salcombe, I will accept your offer. I will inform Chloe that she is to marry you instead.'

'Let me speak to her first.' The last thing Brandt wanted was to have Ralston coerce her into this. Besides, there were a few points he needed to make clear to her.

'Very well. Although I prefer to inform her first so she will see where her duty lies.'

'I think in this case it would be best if Brandt talks to her before you do,' Justin said. He glanced at Brandt, his expression hard to read. 'In fact, I think you should do so now. I will send for her. You can talk to her here.' He walked to the door. 'Ralston.'

Ralston followed him, his stance showing displeasure. Belle waited until they were gone and then turned to Brandt.

'Why do you want to marry Chloe?'

He shrugged. 'I thought I might be preferable to Denbigh. Or the next unsuitable man Ralston sets his sights on.' His voice sounded too indifferent, but he felt as if he were in some sort of dream.

'Is that the only reason?'

'No. I need a wife.' It did not sound an adequate enough reason at all.

Her eyes searched his face. 'I see,' she said softly. 'I trust you will make her happy, then.'

'I will endeavour to do so.'

She gave him a little smile and then left the room. He watched her go and then moved to the window, too restless to sit. What the hell had possessed him to offer for Chloe?

He must have suffered a moment of temporary insanity. Perhaps he could blame it on Marguerite for her matchmaking. Or on Marguerite and Giles as well as Justin and Belle for being so damnably happy in their marriages. Or the feel of tiny hands against his skin. Or Chloe, herself.

His defences were already shot by the time he'd entered the study, so when Ralston had declared she was to marry Denbigh, he'd lost control of his reason. The thought of Chloe in Denbigh's arms had been so repugnant that he knew he'd do anything to stop such a match.

Including marry her himself.

Chloe stopped in front of the study and took a deep breath. She had no idea why Brandt would want to see her, and the peculiar look on Belle's face had confused her. She had not told Chloe what had happened during the interview and only said that she should see Brandt first.

She knocked and at Brandt's deep 'Come in' stepped into the room. Late afternoon sunlight streamed through the window. He moved and came to stand in front of the desk. Brandt stared at her for a moment before speaking. 'Please sit down.'

She perched on the edge of a hard-back chair and clasped her hands in her lap. 'Belle said you wished to see me about something.'

'Yes.' He leaned back against the desk and almost instantly moved away. He seemed nervous, which was odd because she did not imagine he was often nervous about anything.

He turned to look at her. 'Did she tell you why I wanted to see you?'

'No. She did not say much of anything.' She hardly ever felt annoyed with Belle, but she almost did today. But perhaps it was only because she feared she might cry instead. She raised her chin. 'In fact, I know nothing about what has been said. I suppose Arthur was very angry and demanded to know if it were true that I went off with Sir Preston. Of course, even if I was compromised Arthur would not like that because he wishes me to marry L...someone else instead.' She probably made no sense at all.

'Denbigh?'

Stunned, she stared at him. 'I suppose Arthur told you that. Yes, I am to marry Lord Denbigh. Unless I can think of another way to stop Arthur,' she added bitterly.

Comprehension dawned in his face. 'Is that what you were about with Kentworth? You hoped to compromise him in order to escape marriage with Denbigh?'

Her face flamed. How callous and selfish it sounded, as if she had no thought at all for Sir Preston. She at least owed it to him to try and explain that it was not completely that way. 'Yes, but that was only part of it. I...I thought Sir Preston was exactly the sort of husband I wanted. He is so kind and decent and I wanted to be in love with him.

I suppose I convinced myself that he returned my affections. When Arthur told me I was to marry Lord Denbigh, I decided I would force Sir Preston's hand. I…I realised as soon as he offered me marriage how wicked it was to try and trap him.' She took a deep breath and forced herself to look at him. 'I…I am grateful you followed us. I imagine you told Arthur, and Belle, and Justin that.'

'Only that I was with you in the conservatory. None of the rest.'

'Thank you.' She looked away for a moment. 'Does Arthur wish me to announce my betrothal to Lord Denbigh straight away?'

'No.' He hesitated. 'You are to become engaged to me instead.'

'Engaged to you?' Her head spun for a moment and her voice suddenly seemed far away. 'But why?'

'It was either me or Lord Denbigh. I've no intention of letting you fall into Denbigh's hands, so it was me.'

'You…you offered for me so I would not be forced to marry Lord Denbigh?'

'Yes.' His expression was watchful and she had no idea what he was thinking.

'I still do not understand why. You cannot possibly want to marry me! Is it because of last night? I told you that did not matter.'

'No, it is not because of last night,' he said quietly.

'But why? I still do not understand why. You cannot possibly want to marry me. I don't even think you like me! And I am an heiress! You do not want an heiress!'

A slight smile touched his mouth. 'I have no intention of touching a penny of your money. And you are quite wrong about the other,' he said softly.

A feeling of pure panic washed over her. She had no idea why, but the thought of having him want to marry her scared her. He was not at all the sort of man she wanted. Nor did she want him to…to like her. Not like that.

'No. I cannot!'

'Why not? A few days ago you informed me that Newgate was not a preferable option over wedding me.'

'We…we are not suited. I…I have no idea why you would think so.'

'We agreed earlier that we are both fond of children. You pointed out that you needed a husband to have a family of your own.'

'Yes, but not now!' She hardly knew what she was saying. 'I said I did not want a husband.'

'You are contradicting yourself. You wanted to marry Sir Preston.'

'But that was different!'

'How?'

'He…he would make a comfortable husband.'

'Ah. So you are afraid I will ride roughshod over you and consider you are a mere convenience?'

'Yes, if you must know!'

A little smile touched his mouth. 'I doubt I would ever consider you a mere convenience. Would it help if I promise not to be an overbearing husband? And you would have my house, you know.'

'Your house?'

'Waverly. I believe you told me earlier that you considered it your house and were jealous that I had bought it. It would now be yours as well.'

'It was a most stupid thing to say.' She tore her gaze away and looked down at her lap. 'I…I am much obliged by your offer, but I cannot marry you since—'

In two strides he was in front of her, his eyes blazing with anger. His hands clamped down on either side of her, imprisoning her in the chair. She stared at him and swallowed.

'What you don't understand, my dear Lady Chloe, is that you have no choice. You either accept my offer or you will find yourself betrothed to Denbigh. Or the subject of Lady Kentworth's vicious rumours. Since I will not allow either of those to happen, we will announce your betrothal to me instead. Furthermore, I'm not making you an offer, I am telling you what you are going to do. Do you understand?'

His face was inches from hers. She could see the colour of his eyes, a fascinating mixture of green and brown, and the shadow of beard around his mouth. Her heart was pounding and she felt breathless, and she had no idea if she was afraid or if it was something else altogether. Her gaze went to his mouth and she felt almost dizzy.

'Chloe?'

She blinked to clear her head. 'What?'

'Did you understand what I just said to you?' He pulled away, his voice impatient.

'Yes. I am going to become betrothed to you.' At least that was what she thought he said.

Now he was scowling. 'There is no need to sound so subdued. I am not planning to beat you.'

'I hardly thought that!' She stood and glared back at him. 'But there is no need for you to sacrifice yourself for me. If I hadn't acted so stupidly then there would be no need for you to do this. I think it would be best if I married Lord Denbigh.'

'I'll abduct you before that happens,' he said softly. He took a step towards her and this time she backed up. She could see he was truly angry and it scared her.

He stopped in front of her, but made no move to touch her. 'And you are wrong. I am not sacrificing myself.'

She suddenly felt alone and a little afraid. Everything had spun out of control.

He looked into her face and for a moment she believed he could read her thoughts. The sensation was not welcome. He suddenly stepped back. 'There is no need to look so stricken, I will not force you to the altar. I meant what I said before—I cannot afford a wife and I've no intention of marrying for money. Particularly not you. We will announce our betrothal, but make it clear there will be no wedding in the immediate future. After a suitable time, when all danger of gossip or Lord Denbigh is past, you may cry off. However, I suggest you wait at least two months.'

So, he really did not want her after all. She should feel relieved, but instead she felt as if she wanted to cry. Which made no sense because she did not want to marry him. 'Very well. I agree to your terms.'

'Good.' His voice was neutral. 'Then we should return to the drawing room and tell the others.'

'Yes.' She followed him to the door. He held it open for her and waited for her to pass. In a daze, she went with him to the drawing room. They were all there. She nearly turned tail and ran, but Brandt took her hand and he drew her forward. 'You may congratulate us. Chloe has agreed to accept my hand in marriage.'

None of them looked the least bit surprised, so, she realised, they had known what he planned to do. Justin came forward first. He took Chloe's other hand. 'I am more than pleased with my cousin's choice. Welcome to the family. Again.'

She managed a smile, although she felt as if she were in some sort of strange dream. 'Thank you.'

Belle was next. She planted a soft kiss on Brandt's cheek and enveloped Chloe in a warm embrace. She finally stepped back and Chloe saw she had tears in her eyes. 'Belle?'

'It is just…' Belle stopped. 'Please forgive me.'

Arthur was next. He shook Brandt's hand and then took Chloe's. 'Congratulations. I hope you will be most happy,' he said stiffly. He dropped her hand and looked at Brandt. 'I trust you will announce the betrothal immediately.'

'I will send the notice to the London papers tomorrow.'

'And the marriage? I assume it will take place as soon as the banns are posted.'

'We…' Chloe began.

Brandt glanced at her. 'The marriage will take place after I have finished the major renovations to Waverly. Chloe should at least have a drawing room and a bed-chamber that does not leak.'

'You do have another house,' Arthur said.

'Yes, but Chloe wishes to live at Waverly. It is near her family.'

Arthur looked unconvinced. 'Very well.' He eyed Chloe. 'We will need to inform Maria. I dare say she will be quite disappointed when she learns there will be no visit to Denbigh House, after all, since the purpose was to announce Chloe's betrothal to Lord Denbigh.'

'I am quite certain she will recover from her disappointment when she discovers Chloe is to marry my cousin and live near Belle,' Justin said. 'Of course, Chloe will remain with us until the wedding.'

Arthur cleared his throat. 'Her home is still at Braddon Hall until she marries. I've no doubt Lady Ralston would like her daughter with her.'

'Maria may come here and stay with us,' Belle said. 'I intend to write to her today. Also, of course, she will want to be present for the small party we will hold in honour of the betrothal. You will be invited as well.'

'A party? I would think it more appropriate if such an affair was held at Braddon Hall.'

Everything was going much too fast. 'I would rather there was no party at all.' They all turned to look at her. 'If you will pardon me, I would like to go to my bed-chamber.'

Belle instantly looked contrite. 'Oh, Chloe, of course you must. I have no doubt you must be feeling quite confused. Shall I go with you?'

'No. I shall be fine.' She wanted to be by herself.

'I will escort you.' Brandt moved away from the window.

'It is not necessary.'

'But I wish to.'

Out in the hall, she stopped and looked up at him. 'I do not need an escort.'

'Not even your fiancé?'

'You are not really my fiancé.' She started to move away.

He caught her arm. 'But I am.'

'We are only pretending.'

'Not until you officially cast me aside,' he said lightly, but there was something in his eye that made her think he did not find it amusing at all.

Her heart started beating in that odd way again and she felt that peculiar flicker of panic. He dropped her arm. 'I will take you to your room. It would not do if we are seen disagreeing so quickly.'

They did not speak until they reached the door of her bedchamber when she forced herself to meet his eyes. 'Thank you, Lord Salcombe.'

'What happened to my given name? Now that we are betrothed, do you no longer plan to use it?'

'Of course. I...I am just rather confused.'

He looked at her for a moment. 'Quite understandable. In the space of twenty-four hours you have expected to wed three men.'

She felt as if he had struck her. It sounded so callous. She turned away before he could see her expression.

'Damn it, Chloe, that is not what I meant to say.'

'It is quite true.' Her voice wobbled and to her dismay tears suddenly pricked her lids.

'Are you crying?'

'No.' She opened her door. 'G…good day.'

He stepped around so that he was facing her. With gentle fingers he lifted her chin. 'You are crying. I beg your pardon. I did not mean to say something so damnably stupid.' His expression was rueful. 'I only meant to say you have good reason to be confused. I am confused.'

'If you wish to stop this now, I will not mind.'

'No.' He dropped his hand away. 'I do not wish to stop this now. How would that look? Besides, you'd end up with Denbigh again.' He stepped away from her. 'I will see you at dinner.'

'Very well.' She forced herself to meet his eyes. She should not be arguing with someone so determined to save her from a horrible marriage. 'Thank you. You are very kind.'

'I am not kind at all,' he said abruptly. His gaze fell to her mouth and then he jerked it away. 'Good afternoon, Chloe.' He turned on his heel and left.

She watched him, a strange sense of loss creeping over her. Nothing seemed right any longer. She should be grateful to him, but instead she felt horrible that he had felt it necessary to come to her rescue in such a way. All of the things she had thought he was were completely untrue.

Now she had ruined his life as well.

* * *

What the devil had come over her? Brandt had returned to stare at her closed door. He'd fully expected her to take him to task and instead she had looked as if she thought he was about to beat her. The way she said his name.... He'd rather have her call him by his title if she intended to address him in that damnably contrite voice.

Hell. He raised his hand to knock and then dropped it. He could hardly stand here demanding she tell him what was wrong. She would probably retreat even further.

Which was perhaps for the best. He ran a hand through his hair and turned from her door. As much as he might want to tease her, he had no doubt the betrothal would end when the two months had passed. In all truth, despite the attraction he felt for her, she was not precisely the sort of calm, sensible wife he wanted.

Just as he was not the sort of comfortable husband she wanted. He shoved the unwelcome thought aside.

It was perhaps better if they did not appear to be too fond of one another.

Chapter Six

The soft knock startled Chloe from the daze she'd been in ever since Brandt had left her an hour ago. A book lay open on her lap, but reading had proved impossible. She had finally given up and curled up in the chair, staring out of the window at the clouds gathering in the distance over the water.

Belle entered the room and moved to Chloe's side. 'Why did you not tell us that Arthur had plans to marry you to Lord Denbigh? If I had known, if we had known, we would have stopped him.'

'He threatened to cut off my allowance and I did not want that. I have been helping Mama a little, you know she never has any idea of economy and I did not want her to go without. Lord Denbigh showed an interest in London, but then I became ill and I heard no more about him until Arthur wrote that we had been invited to Denbigh Hall. I knew nothing about Lord Denbigh's offer until Arthur arrived.' She avoided Belle's eyes. 'Then I thought that perhaps I might find another husband.'

'Sir Preston?' Belle asked gently.

Chloe drew in a breath. 'It was most ridiculous of me. He was only being kind. Oh, Belle, I was so wicked. I enticed him away to the conservatory and then asked him to kiss me. Then when he offered to marry me I knew it was only because he felt obligated.'

'I see.' Belle was silent for a moment. 'He is very kind and very decent and I've no doubt he considers you a friend. I do not suppose you have had many men that have been your friend. Under the circumstances, I can understand why you thought of him in that way, but I do not think you would have suited.'

'I know that now. Oh, Belle, I have made such a fool of myself.'

'I do not think Sir Preston will say anything. Or Brandt.'

'I cannot marry Brandt, you know.'

'Why not?'

'We are not at all suited either and, besides, I do not think he really wants to marry me. He felt obliged to offer for me so I would not have to marry Lord Denbigh.'

Belle looked at her. 'Then why did you accept his offer?'

'He gave me no choice. He said if I did not he would abduct me.' She was beginning to feel a little annoyed.

Instead of expressing outrage, Belle's lips twitched as if she wanted to laugh. 'Oh, dear. I will own that doesn't sound like a man who feels too obligated. If you really believe you are not suited, then you can change your mind. Justin and I will always help you or Maria if you are in need. But it would be best if you waited before deciding you wish to call off the betrothal. It will look most odd if you cry off right away. And there is Lady Kentworth to consider as well. She has threatened to spread it about you were seen leaving the assembly with Sir Preston. I know you would never want such a malicious thing spread about. At least if that should happen we can put it about that it was Brandt you left with. And that was when he made his offer.' She smiled a little. 'And if you wait, you might find Brandt suits you very well after all.'

'I doubt it.' Chloe plucked at the cover. It all seemed very logical but somehow Belle's assumption was quite irking. 'I doubt he thinks I suit him either. He said I should wait for at least two months before breaking off the betrothal.'

'Did he?' Belle started and then laughed. 'I must say it doesn't sound the most promising way to begin a betrothal with both parties intending to cry off. Oh, dear, what a muddle! At least we will have you with us for another two months and who knows what might happen during that time?' She stood. 'I came to help you dress for dinner.' She looked at Chloe's face. 'Please do not look so disgruntled. It is not a death sentence, you know. Brandt is not so very dreadful. There are any number of women who would envy you.'

Chloe rose. 'Well, I am not one of them. He is not the sort of man I want to marry.'

'But I thought you and Brandt have agreed you won't marry.'

'We did.'

Somehow she did not think Belle was taking her at all seriously, particularly when she cheerfully said, 'Then there is nothing to fret over. And one more thing, which should make you happy. Arthur is to leave Devon tomorrow so you can enjoy the picnic without his disapproving countenance. He is still rather disgruntled that we are not holding the betrothal party at Braddon Hall. However, he has consented to return with Maria in time for your party here.'

Chloe's frowned at the closed door after Belle left. Well, she intended to approach this betrothal in a practical, rational fashion. She certainly did not intend to make sheep's

eyes at Brandt or bring his name into every conversation
the way some of the young ladies did who had become
engaged in the past Seasons. Even Serena had seemed to
interject Charles's name a little too often into conversations and now into her letters. No, she would behave with
the utmost dignity. She had no intention of making a fool
of herself again.

To Chloe's dismay, the next day was perfect for a picnic. Already dressed in her riding habit, she stood at the
window, hoping to spot some indication that rain was im-
minent, but the clouds were fluffy and startlingly white
against the cerulean blue sky.

After the events of the past two days she felt little desire
to go on a picnic, particularly one that included Sir Preston, Emily and Lady Kentworth. And Brandt.

She closed her eyes for a moment. How had this ever
happened? She was betrothed to the arrogant, high-handed
Lord Salcombe; a man she had detested the first time she
had met him for his cold disdain towards Belle. Even after
Belle had told her that in the end he had been responsible
for bringing her and Justin together, she could not persuade
herself to like him.

Except her dislike was proving more and more difficult
to maintain. He and Belle treated each other with the easy
familiarity of old friends and Chloe had no doubt he would
do everything in his power to protect Belle and Julian if
anything should happen to Justin. And how could she detest a man who treated Julian with such gentle care or
showed such interest in Will and Caroline? Yesterday,
when he apologised, his arrogance gone, she had glimpsed
the eager, vulnerable youth he might once have been, and
she had known he was someone she could like very,
very much.

And for whatever reason, he had offered to marry her in order to save her from Denbigh.

She turned away from the window and wished she did not feel so confused. She would much rather think of him as an enemy, continue to keep him at arm's length. It would be much safer.

Also she did not want to see Waverly, the house he said would be hers if they married. She had no idea why that made her feel so uncomfortable.

Perhaps she could plead a headache. She did have a very slight one that sometimes resulted when she slept poorly, but they generally did not get much worse as long as she was not in the sun for very long. Certainly that would be an understandable excuse to not go to the picnic.

She would write a note now.

A few minutes after sending the note, she heard a knock on her door. She opened it and nearly jumped when she saw Brandt. 'Belle said you had the headache,' he said without preamble. His expression was cool.

'Well, yes. It is just a little one.' Taken aback, she had no time to formulate a more believable response.

'Are you certain? Or do you merely wish to avoid certain persons today?'

She had no doubt the heat flooding her cheeks gave her away. 'That, also.'

'You will need to see Kentworth and the others some time. Preferably today.'

'I would rather not. It is true that I do not feel at all the thing,' she said defensively.

'Then you might consider this.' He rested his forearm against the door jamb. 'Justin has decided it would be wise to informally announce the betrothal before the meal today. It would be best if you were there as well. Unless you would prefer the neighbourhood to speculate that the thought of marriage to me has sent you into a decline. Sir Preston might feel obliged to offer you marriage again in order to save you from my clutches.' There was a slight smile at his mouth that did not quite reach his eyes.

'Do you believe he might do that?' She could not think of anything more horrible at this point.

'Do you wish him to?' His smile suddenly looked rather dangerous.

'No, of…of course not. It would be the most terrible muddle. It would overset Em…everyone.' She took a deep breath. 'If you think it best, then I will go.'

He straightened. 'Are you certain you are well enough to ride today?' he asked abruptly.

'I have the very slightest of headaches, but I will be fine as long as I am not in the sun for very long periods.'

'Then you will ride with Belle and Julian in the barouche. Stay out of the sun and wear your hat. And let me know straight away if you begin to feel unwell. I will see you at the Haversham estate.'

She was too astonished to reply and could only gape as he strode away. Whatever had come over him? First, he had not seemed to believe her at all and then he was suddenly concerned about her health. And then he dictated she was to ride in the carriage.

He was completely incomprehensible. Just because they were betrothed did not mean he could order her about in such a way. Well, she had no intention of riding in the carriage as much as she might like to be with Julian and Belle. She would ride Maisy behind the carriage instead.

But as Chloe approached the edge of Waverly's property, she began to wish she had travelled in the carriage with Belle after all. When she had ridden up to the carriage with Maisy, Justin had told her that with her horse's dawdling pace, they would be fortunate if they arrived at Waverly in time to depart. She had best take the shortcut through the field with Brandt.

She realised Brandt had not informed them that he wanted her to ride in the carriage. She could quite imagine his sardonic expression if she showed up at the stables looking for him now. Instead of going to find Brandt, she dallied around until she was certain he would be gone.

By the time she reached the field at Haversham Hall where they were to meet the others, everyone had gone. Maisy had ambled along on her short legs, and if Chloe attempted to push her at all, she pinned her ears back and wheezed. She finally decided that they must cut through the sunny field rather than follow the path through the shady woods. The bright sun only increased her headache and now that she had finally reached Waverly's property she felt almost dizzy.

She urged Maisy forward, but once in the clearing near the old abbey, she halted again when she saw most of the guests had arrived. More dismaying, she could see no sign of the party from Falconcliff. Whatever would she tell Brandt when he came upon her?

Brandt was nowhere in sight, but she spotted Sir Preston standing with Tom Coltrane and Mr Rushton. Her heart pounded and she berated herself again for coming alone. At least, if she had arrived with Belle and Justin, she would not have drawn nearly as much attention to herself as she would if she rode up by herself.

'Chloe! Chloe!'

Will stood on a section of the old stone wall, waving at her. What if he fell? She urged Maisy into a trot, but before she reached the wall, Will had jumped down. Her heart leapt to her throat when he stumbled, but he recovered and dashed towards her. 'I was waiting for you! Why did you ride poor old Maisy? She can never keep up.' He gave the mare an affectionate pat on the neck.

'Because she wanted an outing. Will, you should not be standing on the wall. It is crumbling and you could be hurt.'

'I won't be! Papa says I climb like a monkey. Look! I lost a tooth last night!' He grinned up at her, the missing tooth making him look even more endearing. 'Come and sit with us! The groom brought Lion and he is sitting with Caroline. And we have a ball so I can help you practise your throws. You are getting much better,' he added encouragingly.

'That would be very kind.' Throwing a ball with Will and sitting with Caroline and their nearly grown puppy appealed to her much more than mingling with the rest of the guests. She must face the others at some point, but perhaps if she put it off a little she would feel better prepared. She slid from Maisy and Jennings, one of the grooms, took the mare's reins.

Will grabbed her hand and led her across the grass and around the east wall of the abbey towards the shade of some tall trees. 'Caroline and Lion are over there.'

As they passed the gate leading to the abbey garden, they nearly collided with Lady Kentworth and her cousin, an elderly lady who acted as her companion. Lady Kentworth stopped and stared at Chloe. 'I wonder that you dare show your face, but then I dare say because you are an Earl's daughter and great friends with a Duchess you think you can be as brazen and bold as you wish!'

The malice in her face made Chloe ill. Before she could say a word, Will marched forward and stared up at her, his face stern. 'You are not to speak to Lady Chloe in such a way! You must apologise immediately.'

Lady Kentworth's mouth fell open. Her cheeks turned

a dull, splotchy red. 'You are impertinent and ill mannered. If you were my son you would be beaten soundly for such manners.'

Chloe found her voice. 'It was wrong of him to speak to you in such a way, but it is just as wrong of you to say such a thing to him.' She looked down at Will. 'You must apologise to Lady Kentworth for speaking to her so rudely.'

'But…' He looked bewildered.

'I know.' She stooped in front of him and looked into his face. 'Please do it.' She feared that, if he did not, Lady Kentworth would take some sort of revenge on him. 'Please, Will.' He stared at her, his mouth stubborn, and then finally looked back up at Lady Kentworth. 'I am sorry that I was impertinent and ill mannered.' His voice was contrite, almost too contrite. Chloe prayed Lady Kentworth would not notice.

The woman stared at him for a moment. 'I trust that in the future you will remember to speak to your elders in a more suitable fashion.' She turned to her companion, who had stood with her eyes down cast the entire time. 'I would like to join the others.' She brushed past Chloe without speaking.

Will stared after her. 'I did not want to apologise,' he said in a low voice. 'She was the one who was impertinent and ill mannered and if she ever says such things to you again I will call her out!'

'You cannot call out a lady,' Chloe said gently. 'I know you did not want to apologise but sometimes it is better to do so even if you feel you are right. I did not want Lady Kentworth to become angry with you because of me.' She looked down at his bowed head. 'It was very gallant of you to stand up for me. I will always remember that.'

He looked up finally. 'I always stand up for my friends.'

'I know.' She smiled at him. 'Shall we find Lion and Caroline, and play a game of catch?' She hoped that would distract him.

He brightened a little. 'All right.'

Caroline sat on a blanket with Lion, a large gangly pup of indeterminate parentage. He bounded up, pulling Caroline with him, and nearly fell himself in his enthusiasm to greet Chloe. Caroline tugged on his lead with all her might in an effort to keep him from leaping on Chloe. 'Sit!' she said.

He sat for an instant and then leapt back up, his eyes intent on Chloe's face. 'Sit, Lion,' she told him in a stern voice. He reluctantly obeyed and she patted his head.

Caroline sighed. 'He never listens to me. I know I should tie him, but he hates it so.'

'Chloe! Here is the ball!' Will called. 'Stand back and I will throw it to you.'

'All right.' Although she really would prefer to sit for a while. She felt tired and the encounter with Lady Kentworth had only increased her headache.

She moved towards the wall and Will tossed the ball. She caught it.

'Very nice.'

She whirled around, the ball falling from her hand. Brandt stood behind her. She stared at him, suddenly breathless. 'What are you doing here?'

'This is my property.'

'I only meant what are you doing behind me. I did not see you.'

He stooped and picked up the ball and then straightened. 'I came over with some intention of greeting you as a proper host should. As well as to inquire why you did not inform me you intended to ride rather than drive. I believe we agreed you were to drive with Belle.'

'No, you told me I was to ride in the carriage and then walked away. I did not have a chance to agree or disagree with you. You merely assumed I agreed with you.'

'I was mistaken. I beg your pardon. Next time I will be certain you agree with me before I walk away.'

'But I might disagree with you.'

'Perhaps, but I will do my utmost to persuade you.' He had a little smile on his mouth.

She had no idea what he was talking about; it was turning into one of those conversations that made her feel out of her depth. She was relieved when Will ran up. 'Uncle Brandt! Have you come to play ball with us? I have been helping Chloe learn to throw and catch. Do you want her to throw the ball to you?'

'Once. Since I am the host, I should not be away too long from my guests.' He glanced at Chloe. 'And Chloe should not overtax herself. She should be sitting, not chasing balls around.'

'I rarely chase balls since I can now catch them quite nicely.'

'Another one of your surprising talents?' He looked amused.

'Yes. So if you will move back I will throw the ball to you.'

He stepped back a few inches. 'Is this too far?'

'No. You may move back.'

He took a few steps back.

'More, if you please.' For some reason, the grin on his face was most annoying. Obviously, he thought she could barely toss a ball. Although her habit was fitted rather tight across the bodice and she could not pull her arm very far back, he did not need to stand so close to her that she could hand the ball to him.

'Is this far enough?'

He'd moved way back now. Too far back. However, she had no intention of standing here all day, directing him to the perfect spot. She drew her arm back and then threw the ball with all her might. As she did so she heard an ominous rip. Brandt ducked as the ball narrowly missed his head and then it fell to the ground and rolled towards the assembled company. Suddenly Lion burst across the grass, his lead trailing behind him. There was a shriek as the ball rolled past Lady Kentworth's feet and Lion scrambled after it. Then Lady Kentworth fell.

Chloe froze, her mouth open in dismayed horror as Lion bounded over to Lady Kentworth and licked her face. The lady shrieked again, this time a much more bloodcurdling scream. Giles grabbed Lion's collar and pulled him away.

Will was jumping up and down. 'That was splendid!'

'But Lion knocked Lady Kentworth down,' Caroline said. She looked as sick as Chloe felt.

'That's why it was splendid!'

'No, it wasn't,' Chloe said. As much as she wanted to run in the opposite direction, Chloe had no choice. She started forward.

'I'd best go fetch Lion. Come with me, Will.' Brandt strode towards the group and Chloe followed.

By this time Lady Kentworth was sitting up and she waved away the vinaigrette Marguerite held under her nose. Giles thrust the lead at Brandt and then turned to Will. 'You will first apologise to Lady Kentworth and then you will come with me.'

Will turned pale. 'I…'

Lady Kentworth stared first at Chloe and then at Will, her eyes narrowed, her face a frightening purplish-red. 'You…!'

'William,' Giles said.

'It was my fault.' Chloe stepped forward and forced

herself to meet Lady Kentworth's eyes. 'I threw the ball. I...I am so very sorry. I did not think it would go so far. Will did nothing wrong.' She was quite aware that everyone looked at her and she felt mortified and foolish beyond belief.

Caroline came up beside Chloe. She bit her lip, but managed to look at Lady Kentworth. 'I was holding Lion. He pulled away from me. I should have tied him but I...I did not. I am very sorry.'

Lady Kentworth stared at them, her mouth thinning. 'Well!'

Brandt moved next to Chloe. 'And I am to blame as well. I stood too far from Lady Chloe so she was obliged to execute a rather forceful throw which undoubtedly accounted for the great distance the ball travelled. In addition, I did not assist in securing Lion and should have known he would most naturally go after a ball. So I must apologise as well.'

Lady Kentworth looked from one to the other, her mouth tight as if she suspected some sort of conspiracy. 'I quite see.'

Giles looked at them, his expression impassive, and then turned to Will. 'I see I erred in judging you without hearing the entire story. However, in the future I expect you to exert more control over your dog otherwise he will be banished from such excursions.'

Will hung his head. 'Yes, sir.'

'And, Caroline, if you cannot control Lion, then you will give him to someone who can.'

'Yes, Papa.' Caroline still looked mortified.

'Perhaps we should secure Lion now,' Brandt said. 'Come with me.'

The two children went with him, undoubtedly happy to get away. Sir Preston helped his mother to her feet while

Chloe made herself move forward. 'There are some chairs. Shall I have—?'

'You have done enough!' Lady Kentworth snapped. 'Do not come near me!'

There was a shocked silence. Chloe dared not meet Sir Preston's eyes, or anyone else's. Her head seemed to spin for a moment. 'If you will pardon me, I will go and see if I am needed…' She started to walk away before she humiliated herself further by bursting into tears.

Chloe found herself in the overgrown garden of the old chapel where she sat on a broken stone bench and prayed she would not weep. She had managed to humiliate herself again in front of most of the neighbourhood.

She had always considered herself practical and never prone to impulsiveness, but since she'd been at Falconcliff she had been nothing but foolish. Everything she did resulted in more disaster. And today appeared to be growing worse. If she had not set out to prove to Brandt that he could not dictate to her, then she would not be on his property with a stupid headache. She probably would not have met Lady Kentworth when she was with Will, so that Will was forced to defend her, thus incurring Lady Kentworth's wrath as well. If she hadn't been so stupidly determined to show Brandt she could throw a ball, Lady Kentworth would not have gone sprawling on the ground. And if she had not been so idiotic to begin with, then she would not be betrothed to Brandt after…

Someone stood in front of her. She slowly looked up into Brandt's face and, to her chagrin, tears pricked her lids.

His face changed. 'You aren't going to cry, are you? Chloe, it wasn't that bad,' he said roughly.

She gulped. 'Y…yes, it was. I knocked Lady Kentworth

down and nearly got Will into trouble again. And made a complete fool of myself.'

He sat down next to her. 'I have no doubt everyone knew it was an accident.'

'I nearly hit you.'

His eyes danced. 'I'm not certain that was an accident.'

'It was. I would never want to hit anyone, not even you.'

This time he laughed. 'I am gratified to hear that. Next time I will show you how to throw a ball properly.'

'I do not think there will be a next time.' She looked away.

'No? Why not?'

'Because it is a completely unladylike thing to do.'

'So?'

'So, I will not do it. I am too old for such things.'

'You will disappoint Will.'

'At least I will not create more trouble for him. He has already incurred Lady Kentworth's wrath twice today because of me.'

'He told me.' His eyes lost their amusement. 'At least come back to the picnic, Chloe.'

She bit her lip. 'I've torn my sleeve as well.'

'It does not matter. Nothing improper shows. And if it worries you I can have my housekeeper repair it for you.'

'Perhaps I should return to Falconcliff.'

'You cannot always run away.'

He undoubtedly referred to the night of the ball. 'Sometimes it is preferable.'

'Sometimes, but most of the time it only puts off what one has to face eventually. You cannot hide away from the neighbourhood. And as much as you might wish to…' his gaze held hers '…you cannot avoid me. We are betrothed.'

The denial she was about to make died on her lips. 'I am sorry,' she whispered.

'You don't need to apologise. I cannot make you like me, but if we hope to convince Lady Kentworth as well as your cousin that we are truly betrothed, it would be best if you could at least hold your dislike in check. And occasionally attempt to appear as if you take some pleasure in my company.'

'Brandt…' she began. 'I am sorry.'

'Don't be.' He rose. 'I think we should return to the others before we cause even more speculation. Belle has probably arrived and will worry if she does not find you.' He held out his hand.

She placed hers in his and stood. His hand, around hers, was warm and strong. She glanced at his face, finding no anger or censure there, something she might have expected after such a conversation. Her actions only seemed more childish.

Marguerite met them as they left the garden. 'There you are! Oh, Chloe, I meant to speak to you immediately but when I turned around you had disappeared. Emily thought you might be here and said she thought Brandt had followed you. Then Lady Kentworth began to fuss about the chair and the lemonade so I was quite occupied trying to mollify her before she ruined everything for everyone else.' She peered at Chloe's face. 'Oh, sweet child, there is no need to look so distraught. You must pay no heed to Lady Kentworth. She is the most unpleasant person and is always exceedingly rude when people displease her and the only reason we put up with her is because everyone is so fond of Sir Preston. I dare say more than one person present wanted to cheer when Lion knocked her down.'

Chloe was mortified all over again. 'I did not mean to do such a thing.'

'No one thinks that at all,' Marguerite said. 'Belle is here and wants to see you. Will gave her a rather confused and quite dramatic version of the event and Belle is now worried. So you must come with me and reassure her.' Her gaze fell to where Brandt still held Chloe's hand. 'Although I can see that perhaps she does not need to worry very much at all.'

Chloe pulled her hand away, self-conscious at the speculative look in Marguerite's eye. Brandt seemed not to notice. 'Then I will send Chloe with you,' he said easily. 'I will see both of you shortly.'

He strode off towards the others while Marguerite turned to her with a little smile. 'Well! I never thought to see you and Brandt walking hand in hand. You must be careful or everyone will start to speculate when the announcement will be made.'

Chloe's cheeks heated. She should say something, but Marguerite was already speaking again. 'I am only teasing you! I know very well Brandt provokes you terribly and is possibly the last man you would ever consider for a husband. However, I hope you will own he is not quite the ogre you thought him to be.'

'I really do not think he is an ogre at all.' She could only imagine the look on Marguerite's face when the betrothal was announced. 'In fact—'

'Chloe! The Duchess is here!' Will dashed up to them. 'Julian has just spat up all over the Duke! Just like Emma does to Papa. And to me,' he added with disgust.

'Oh, dear,' Marguerite said. She met Chloe's eyes over his head, her mouth twitching. 'I fear all babies do that. At least when they are your age, they stop.'

Will made a disbelieving sound. 'I've never spat up on anyone.'

'It is only that you do not remember,' Marguerite said

with maternal fondness. 'Perhaps you can escort Chloe to the Duchess while I see to the food. I am worried some of the hampers have not arrived.'

'Yes, Mama.' He took Chloe's hand. 'Don't worry, I will make sure nothing happens before we reach the Duchess.'

'Thank you.' Chloe hardly knew whether she wanted to laugh or cry at this touching show of male protectiveness. She smiled down at him, a little misty-eyed. 'I will need all the protection you can give me today.'

'Really, Brandt, I do not think you've attended to a word I've said for the last five minutes. If it weren't so impossible, I could almost believe you have developed a *tendre* for Chloe. Particularly after I saw you holding her hand earlier.'

Brandt forced his attention away from where Chloe sat on the quilt with Belle, Julian and Lydia Sutton. He was out of earshot, but it had not prevented him from noticing that her face had grown increasingly paler and her smiles had a strained quality to them. 'What did you say?' he asked Marguerite, who stood next to him.

Her brow arched. 'I said if it were not so impossible, I could think you have developed a *tendre* for Chloe.'

'What makes you say that?'

'You have been watching her for the past quarter of an hour. Although you have been frowning. Did you cross swords again?'

'I meant why would you find my having a *tendre* for her impossible?'

She stared at him. 'Are you saying you do? I cannot think of anyone I would rather have you marry, but I very much doubt Chloe would...that is, I am certain you could persuade her.'

'I merely asked why it seemed impossible.'

'Because…well, it is just that you usually do not like any woman under the age of five and twenty who is not either widowed or married, and you either tease her in a way that sets her back up dreadfully or else seem to be dictating to her in your overbearing fashion.'

His temper was not improved. 'I had no idea you had such a poor opinion of me.'

She laid a hand on his arm. 'Of course I do not. If I weren't so happily married to Giles and far too old for you, I might consider you for myself. You are kind and decent, something you could never quite hide even when you were attempting to be one of London's most notorious rakes. I never thought your heart was quite in it.' She smiled up at him. 'If it is Chloe you want, then I will do everything in my power to help you. However, you had best waste no time for she is to leave tomorrow.'

'Marguerite.' He hesitated. 'There is something you should know.'

Then he bit back a curse when Justin rose from the quilt where he sat with Chloe, Belle and the baby. He held out his hand to Belle and helped her rise. As if sensing something of importance was about to happen, everyone quieted.

Justin still held Belle's hand. 'I am certain all of you were delighted to discover that Waverly, which has stood empty for so long, once again has a master. I've no doubt you will be equally delighted to learn that Waverly will soon have a new mistress as well.'

'Brandt?' Marguerite gasped.

Everyone seemed to be staring at him. He crossed his arms, not daring to look at Chloe.

'Well, Duke, planning to tell us her name or must we guess?' Squire Heyburn boomed.

'That will not be necessary. Lady Chloe Daventry has done Lord Salcombe the honour of accepting his hand in marriage.'

'Chloe?' Lydia Sutton exclaimed.

Marguerite gaped at him. 'When I suggested you waste no time I had not expected...my goodness! Brandt, did you not tell Chloe? She looks as if she is about to swoon.'

Chloe's face was drained of colour. Brandt strode forward and reached her side just in time to catch her before she fainted.

Mrs Cromby, Waverly's kindly housekeeper, chatted away as she arranged cushions under Chloe's head and covered her with a quilt. 'Poor dear, we will have you feeling better in no time. The sun always affects my Molly in exactly the same way. 'Tis fortunate you were so close to the house so that Lord Salcombe could bring you in directly. I fear this sofa is not the most comfortable, but the others are much worse. I doubt old Nate Carington bought a stick of new furniture during his lifetime, the old miser that he was. Of course, in the end he let everything fall to ruin when his health failed him, which was no wonder with all the smuggled rum and whisky and all that climbing about in damp caverns and such. And the draughts in the house caused by all the passages—even one in his bedchamber! I trust his lordship will close that one up straight away!' She finished tucking the quilt around Chloe's shoulders and straightened. 'Now, you are to rest for a while. His lordship gave strict orders you are not to be disturbed.' She glanced at Belle who stood near the sofa. 'I do not think he referred to you, your Grace.'

'You need not worry, I promise I will not disturb Lady Chloe either.' Belle waited until Mrs Cromby had bustled out before turning to Chloe with a rueful smile. 'I dare say your poor head is spinning even more. I know mine is. Mrs Cromby is quite kind and very efficient, but she does tend to talk. I will own I could not follow half of what she said. Except for the secret passages. I must ask Brandt if there really is one in his bedchamber.' She touched Chloe's hand. 'Here I am, talking as much as Mrs Cromby, when you must want to do nothing more than close your eyes.'

'I really feel much better. I am certain I have recovered enough to join the others.'

'And risk Brandt's wrath? I have no doubt he would carry you back in here immediately.' Her eyes held gentle laughter. 'You would do much better to stay here for a little while. Besides, it is your chance to see something of Waverly. Haven't you always wanted to see the house?'

'Not like this.' She hadn't envisioned herself being carried in by the master of the house after nearly fainting in front of a crowd of people. And having the master scowl down at her and demand why hadn't she told him she was ill and why the devil had she insisted on riding instead of driving and then take her to task for running around in the sun after balls.

Never had she thought the master of the house would be her fiancé.

'Perhaps not,' Belle said. 'But Brandt is right, you need to rest. Today has been rather difficult.' She bent down and brushed a light kiss across Chloe's cheek. 'I will be back shortly.'

'Yes.' As Belle left the room in her quiet, graceful way, Chloe nearly called her back, but that was ridiculous. She was twenty, a grown woman, and she should not feel like a small child whose mother had just departed.

Her head still hurt and it was easier to close her eyes. The old library was quiet and in spite of herself, she drifted off.

'Chloe?' Emily Coltrane's soft voice aroused Chloe.

She struggled to sit, still a little dizzy. 'Emily, what are you doing here?'

'I came to see how you were.' Emily moved to the side of the sofa. 'Are you feeling any better?'

'A little.' Her head no longer hurt so much, nor did she feel so sick. 'I usually do not manage to humiliate myself this much in one day.'

'It certainly made the day exciting. Particularly when you fainted just after the Duke announced your betrothal. More than one person wondered whether you were just as surprised as everyone else.'

'It was only because of the sun. If I am in it too long, I sometimes develop the headache. I did not eat much breakfast, which made me feel rather ill as well.'

'I am glad it was not learning you were to marry Lord Salcombe.' She fixed her direct gaze on Chloe's face. 'Are you going to marry him because of what happened at the ball?'

Chloe stared at her. 'Why would you think that?'

'I suppose it is because you have always seemed to hold Lord Salcombe in such dislike. I worried that perhaps Lady…someone tried to cause mischief and you were forced to marry Lord Salcombe because of that.'

Emily was far too astute. 'No, it was not like that.' Chloe made herself look directly at Emily. 'It is true that I did not care for Lord Salcombe at first, but that…that is no longer true. I had no idea that he would even be interested in me and I…' she would undoubtedly sound fickle '…I suppose I was so determined to fall in love with Sir

Preston that I did not realise until I made such a sad mess
of everything that I...I cared for Lord Salcombe.'

'I see.' Emily studied her face. If she did not believe
Chloe, she gave no indication. 'I just wanted to make certain that neither you nor Lord Salcombe was forced because...'

She suddenly stopped. At the same time Chloe looked
up and saw Brandt standing in the doorway. Her heart
thudded and she wanted to dive under the quilt. What if
he had heard her tell Emily that she cared for him?

Emily rose. 'I wanted to make certain Lady Chloe was
better. We were all quite worried when she was so suddenly taken ill.'

He inclined his head. 'Of course.'

'I will not stay much longer.' She looked back at Chloe.
'Perhaps I can visit you.'

'I would like that. Besides, we must plan what you are
to wear for the next assembly.'

'But only if you are well enough.'

'I will be.'

Emily hesitated. 'I am glad you will be staying. And I
wish you well.'

'Thank you.'

'Then I will see you soon.' She left the room, only pausing to say goodbye to Brandt.

He crossed the room, coming to stand next to the sofa.
He looked down at her, his expression quizzical. 'So Miss
Coltrane wished to assure herself that we were not forced
into an engagement?' he asked.

'Yes.' Chloe plucked at the edge of the quilt. 'I suppose
you heard everything.'

'Much of it, including the part where you assured Miss
Coltrane you realised you cared for me after all.'

'Oh.' She could not meet his eyes.

'Chloe.' All of a sudden he was sitting next to her on the sofa. He tilted her chin towards him, his fingers gentle. 'Was that a complete falsehood? Or might I hope you do not hold me in complete dislike?'

She found herself staring into his changeable green-brown eyes. 'No. I…I really do not dislike you.'

'I am glad to hear that,' he said softly. 'Particularly since we are betrothed.'

She swallowed. 'But only temporarily.'

'Permanently for the next two months, perhaps longer.'

Her head was starting to spin again, but this time it was not from the sun. His eyes seemed to mesmerise her. Was she starting to sway towards him or was he starting to sway towards her? But it hardly mattered when his lips brushed hers in a kiss as light and gentle as the touch of butterfly wings. He lifted his head for a moment, his hand brushing a strand of hair from her cheek and then he cupped the back of her head, drawing her to him, his mouth returning to hers in gentle possession.

She should pull away, but the feel and taste of him was too intriguing. Her eyes fluttered shut as she gave herself up to his leisurely kiss. Except for the light touch at the back of her head, he made no move to hold her and so she found herself leaning closer to him. Her lips parted under his soft pressure and she hesitantly returned his kiss. The experiment was pleasurable enough that she repeated it with more confidence, this time lightly touching his lips with her tongue. He stilled, almost as if he'd stopped breathing.

'Oh! Oh, my!'

They jumped apart, Brandt uttering a curse. Mrs Cromby stood there, the shock on her face turning to mortification. 'I beg your pardon, my lord. I did not…' She started to back out.

Brandt stood. 'There is no need to leave. In fact, you may congratulate us instead. Lady Chloe has agreed to become my wife.'

Mrs Cromby stared at him and then a smile creased her plump face. 'Your wife? I…I had no idea! Of course, I wish you both much happiness! How delightful—Waverly will have a mistress as well!' She beamed at them and then started. 'Oh, my, I quite forgot. Four of the guests, including the young lady who was here earlier, have arrived and asked if they might see Lady Chloe for a moment if she is well enough to receive them.'

Brandt glanced at Chloe. 'Only if she wishes to.'

'Yes, that would be fine.' Anything to keep from being alone with him, or she might be tempted to ask him to kiss her again. Her cheeks were still heated from the encounter and she did not think she could look at him. It was bad enough she had submitted to his kisses without protest, but to kiss him back in such a brazen fashion…and then to want more.

In a few minutes, Mrs Cromby ushered in Lydia, Emily and Mr Rushton. Lydia stopped on the threshold and looked around the dark, bookshelf-lined room. 'Heavens! This room looks exactly like what one would expect to see in *Udolpho*!'

To Chloe's chagrin, Sir Preston followed. With everything else that had happened, she had nearly forgotten about Lion. Or the kiss in the conservatory.

There was nothing in his face to indicate disgust as he came to her side, however, followed by the others. Lydia swooped down upon her with a warm embrace. 'Oh, you sly thing! I never would have thought! I do hope you are much better. I was so worried when you suddenly fainted although—' she cast Brandt a coy glance '—it was rather romantic when Lord Salcombe carried you to the house!'

Mr Rushton shook her hand. 'You look much better. At least there's some colour in your cheeks. I should have guessed which way the wind was blowing when Salcombe warned me against trifling with your affections.'

'I should hope not,' Lydia said tartly.

Sir Preston also shook her hand. 'Must congratulate you as well. Wondered if something was up after the other night.'

'I am very sorry about knocking Lady Kentworth down, I hope she has recovered.'

'No need to be sorry. The dog knocked her down. Wished to apologise for her taking you to task. Afraid she doesn't hold her tongue when she's overset.'

'I quite understand.' She smiled at him, relieved he still considered her his friend after all that had happened.

'Lady Chloe has not yet recovered,' Brandt said so sharply Chloe looked up. Oh, dear, now what was wrong?

'Which was why I came,' Emily said. 'To make certain no one stayed very long. I did not know you would be here.'

Mr Rushton had strolled over to the mantelpiece. 'Isn't this the room with the entrance to the passage?'

'One of them,' Brandt said. He had his arms folded across his chest, his face impatient.

'There is a passage here?' Lydia skipped over to Mr Rushton's side. 'How exciting? Where?'

'Somewhere near the mantel,' Mr Rushton said. 'Heard a tale where a smuggler actually surprised old Nate when he was dozing in a chair in front of the fire.'

'Tale can't be right,' Sir Preston said.

Mr Rushton raised a brow. 'Why not?'

Sir Preston grinned. 'Entrance is in the fireplace.'

'Sir Preston is correct,' Brandt said.

'Really? Can we see it?' Lydia asked. She was already stooping so she could peer into the fireplace.

'Lydia, Lady Chloe needs to rest,' Emily said.

'I promise we can leave right after that.' Lydia moved closer. 'Nothing looks at all like an entrance! Are you certain it is here?'

'Best show it to her or we'll never drag her out of here,' Mr Rushton told Brandt. 'I'd do so but don't know how to get the thing open. Besides I don't want to cover myself in soot.'

'So you wish someone else to cover themselves instead. Quite understandable.' Brandt strode over to the mantel-piece. Chloe rose and trailed after him, curious about the secret passages she had heard so much about.

Brandt put his hand behind the old clock on the mantel and produced a key. He knelt, reached into the fireplace and inserted the key into the sooty iron grille in the back. With a creaky groan, the door opened to reveal a dark cavernous hole.

'Oh, my!' Lydia exclaimed as the men crowded forward. Even Miss Coltrane looked interested.

'Odd place,' Rushton commented. 'How did you know, Kentworth?'

Sir Preston's smile was sheepish. 'Actually been here years ago. Climbed through the passage with Dick Tenbury and found ourselves in the library. Nearly gave us a fright when the chambermaid came in.'

'Fortunate there was no fire.' Mr Rushton glanced at the company. 'Who wishes to go in first?'

Lydia squealed. 'You can't possibly think of doing that!'

'I will go in,' Emily said.

Sir Preston stepped forward. 'Not a good idea, Miss Coltrane. Dusty, spiders and all that.'

She gave him a cold glance. 'That does not bother me in the least.'

Puzzled by her tone, Chloe glanced at Sir Preston. He appeared taken aback, but said nothing.

'I've no idea what sort of condition the passage is in,' Brandt told them. 'I intend to do what my cousin has done with the passages at Falconcliff, close them.'

'Then I certainly must see it,' Emily said. She rolled her eyes at Lydia. 'Do not worry. I do not intend to do more than look.'

'But, Emily, you will dirty your gown!' Lydia said.

'I won't mind.'

Sir Preston backed out and allowed her to step past him. Chloe suppressed a shiver. She could think of nothing worse than finding one's self in a dark, cold tunnel where there were no exits except at the beginning and the end. She did not realise she was holding her breath until Emily reappeared. 'Well, it certainly is dusty.'

'No mice, spiders or ghosts?' Mr Rushton asked.

'None. The passage does branch off, however.'

'One to old Nate's bedchamber and the other to the cellar,' Sir Preston said.

'Salcombe is probably beginning to wonder if you've engaged in a bit of smuggling yourself,' Mr Rushton told him.

'No, just a bit of exploration.' Sir Preston looked rather guilty.

Brandt bent down and locked the door, then put the key back behind the clock. He rose and his eyes fell on Chloe. 'What are you doing up?'

'I wanted to see the entrance as well.'

He frowned. 'You should be resting.'

'I feel much better.' For some reason, her headache had completely disappeared while he had been...they had been kissing. Her gaze went to his mouth and she felt almost shaky again. She backed away. 'Perhaps I will sit down.'

The others instantly apologised for staying too long and took their leave. Almost as soon as they were through the library door, Belle and Justin entered and announced they had come to take Chloe home in the carriage.

'But Maisy?' She had forgotten all about her little mare.

'She will stay here,' Brandt said. 'The groom noticed she had strained a hock.'

'I did not know that.' Now she had even more reason to regret the day.

'We did not want to distress you further,' Belle said gently. 'At any rate, Brandt will see to it that she is well cared for.'

Chloe looked over at Brandt. 'Thank you.'

'Of course.' He was now polite again as if their encounter earlier had not happened. He was equally polite when he bade her farewell.

But then, she thought later, kisses did not always mean much to men. Lucien and his friends had been prime examples of that. She had been embarrassed to find him locked in an embrace with her governess and then, a few days later, embracing a chambermaid with equal fervour. Both times he had laughed it off and pinched her cheek and told her not to tell. The governess had never treated Chloe quite the same again and had left her position a short time later.

The friends Lucien invited to the house to spend endless hours gambling had been no better; after a while they had forgotten her presence and would speak of women as carelessly as they might their horses. She had not understood half of it, only enough to realise lust and regard did not necessarily go together.

Which was why she could not allow any more kisses, no matter how pleasurable she might find them. Her mother had warned her they could lead to other, more serious things. It did not matter that they were betrothed, for they would not marry, which meant she must do everything she could to keep their betrothal on a cool, distant basis.

Chapter Seven

Brandt followed the path that wound through Falcon-cliff's garden towards the narrow dirt lane that ran along the edge of the cliff. He had no idea why he had even bothered calling at the house—he should have known Chloe would not be there, but would be instead wandering around the property. Her illness yesterday had apparently not acted as a deterrent. Belle had been apologetic as she told him that attempting to keep Chloe inside was like trying to keep a fox in the house, but Belle had made Chloe promise she would sit in the shade.

At least the day was overcast and windy, the clouds a dark grey that hinted of rain. So she wouldn't become overheated again, forcing him to carry her back to Falcon-cliff with her soft curves pressing against his chest. Then he would not be tempted to steal a few more of the innocent provocative kisses that made him want to do much more with her.

The wind had whipped up noticeably by the time he left the stand of trees and started down the path that wound along the cliff. He finally spotted her near a stone bench. She stood facing the sea, her face lifted to the wind. Her bonnet dangled by its ribbons down her back and her hair had fallen from its pins and blew around her face. As he watched, she closed her eyes, held out her arms and twirled in a circle, her skirts flying around her legs. She looked like some sort of pagan worshipping the elements.

He strode forward. 'Your bonnet is off,' he said when he reached her.

She gasped and whirled around, her eyes wide with shock, her hands clasped to her chest. 'Oh! You frightened me!'

'Only because you were preoccupied with your ritual.'

'Ritual?'

'You were worshipping the wind and sea, were you not? Does the vicar know about this?'

The predictable colour rose in her cheeks. 'I loved to dance in the wind when I was a child. I would always feel as if I was part of the earth and the wind. The sea is so wonderful and wild when it is stormy like this—I just wanted to feel part of it.' She looked at him, rather shame-faced. 'I am not behaving as a lady should again. Proper young ladies do not dance in storms. I suppose you wish to scold me.'

No, what he wished to do was pull her into his arms, tangle his hands in her glorious red hair, and kiss her thoroughly while the wind whipped around them.

She watched him with her large eyes, waiting for his answer. 'No, I do not wish to scold you. Although you should wear your bonnet unless you want your skin to become burned from the wind.'

'But you are not wearing a hat. In fact, you do not wear hats very much at all.'

'I prefer to go bare-headed.'

'So do I. I think hats interfere too much with the weather. One cannot properly feel the breeze or... Oh!' A large raindrop had hit her on the nose. Before she could react further, the sky opened.

'In this case, hats would be useful.' He caught her hand and pulled her along the path. By the time they reached the shelter of the trees, they were both breathless, and thoroughly soaked.

He dropped her hand. 'You forgot to put your bonnet on.' It still dangled down her back, now wet and soggy.

'That would have taken too much time. I suppose it is ruined but it might have been ruined even if it were on my head.' She fumbled with the ribbons and then pulled it off.

'You are remarkably matter of fact about it. Many women would be in hysterics over the loss of a bonnet.'

'It is a very old bonnet, which is why I wore it,' she said defensively. 'In fact, Arthur suggested that I should give it away because it is so unfashionable.'

He grinned at her expression. 'I meant to pay you a compliment. I should hate to find myself taking shelter from the rain with a female who was in hysterics over the ruin of a bonnet.'

'Has that ever happened to you before?'

'Not over a bonnet. Over a ruined pair of gloves, however. I once escorted a woman to Vauxhall…' What the devil was he doing? He'd nearly told her about the time he and his then current mistress had been stranded by the rain. 'I should not be telling you these things.'

A little smile touched her mouth. 'I doubt I would be too shocked. Lucien was my half-brother, you know.'

He could not miss the sadness in her voice and she suddenly seemed far older than her twenty years. He'd not given any thought to what it might have been like for her with Lucien. Because Lucien was so much older he had assumed she had been sheltered from him by her parents.

'He spoke of such things around you?' He should not be shocked by anything Milbourne had done, but he was.

'Sometimes.' She avoided looking at him. She moved away and rubbed her arms and shivered. 'I hope the rain will let up soon. Perhaps we should hurry back to the house. I do not think we could get any wetter than we are.'

He followed her. 'Are you cold?'

'A little.'

'Then have my coat. The rain did not soak completely through it.' He shrugged out of it and held it out to her.

She stared at it. 'I cannot do that, then you will be cold.'

'I'm not wearing a thin muslin gown.' He stepped forward and draped it around her shoulders. His fingers brushed the nape of her neck and he had a sudden vision of exploring the soft creamy skin with his lips.

He backed away. Hell. Perhaps he'd best go stand out in the rain for a while and cool down his lust. Or pray the rain would let up and they could get out of here.

She cast a puzzled glance at him and then looked away. She seemed fragile, very young and rather lost in his coat. An uncomfortable silence fell between them as if she had sensed his unspoken thoughts. If anything, the rain seemed to be falling even harder, beating heavily on the canopy of the trees that sheltered them.

He cleared his throat and started to speak. At the same time she said, 'How…?'

He stopped. 'Please go on.'

'I was wondering how Maisy is.'

'She is fine, although my groom told me that she tried to nip Domino today.'

'Oh, dear. I am afraid Maisy does not like strange male horses.'

'Although Domino is not exactly male any more.' He

could have bitten his tongue. Why couldn't he remember she was a proper young lady?

She merely smiled. 'It does not really matter to her. Although she seems to be growing more irritable as she ages.'

'Why did you ride her yesterday? Surely Justin has given you use of a more suitable mount.'

'Because she is still my friend and she looked rather forlorn when I entered the stables. One doesn't desert friends just because they are old and not as useful as they once were. Arthur wanted to put her down because he said she was slow and ill tempered and we had no room, but I would not let him. I wrote to Belle and asked if they would have her and they sent for her straight away.' She gave him a defiant glance. 'I suppose you find that sentimental and ridiculous.'

'No, I find it commendable. You are not afraid to stand up for those you care for. I still recall how you declared you would make Justin very sorry if he hurt Belle, and that if I was not careful I would suffer the same fate.'

'I did mean it. I would not have let either of you hurt her.'

'I know,' he said quietly. 'In fact, that was when I started to change my mind about Belle.' He had come upon Chloe as she backed Justin into a corner at a ball, a young debutante in cream muslin, threatening Justin if he dared to hurt her beloved sister-in-law. When Brandt had made some idiotic remark about how Justin should watch his back, she had glared at him, told him it was rude to listen to private conversations and if she had to, she would spend the rest of her life making anyone who hurt Belle, including him, very sorry. He'd thought her a mouse before then, but her spirited defence had proved otherwise. He'd found himself watching her after that and noticing

things about her; the way her face lit up when she smiled,
her lack of pretence, her honest gaze. Most of all her belief
in Belle's goodness had made him question whether Belle
had been an accomplice in Lucien's plan to destroy Justin
after all.

'I am glad you did,' she said softly.

'As I am. She has made my cousin very happy.'

Her gaze locked with his. His eyes dropped to her mouth
and she swallowed. Almost without thinking he stepped
forward and then caught her by the shoulders, drawing her
to him. His mouth came down on hers. Her body seemed
to meld against his for a moment and then she stiffened
and pulled away.

He let her go. 'Chloe,' he began.

She took a step back, pulling his coat more tightly about
her as if to protect herself. 'I pray you will not kiss me
any more, my lord.' Now she was beginning to look like
the old Chloe, the one who made it obvious she held him
in complete dislike. The one who roused the devil in him.

He'd been about to apologise but her cool tone set his
back up and made him feel as if he'd been slapped. 'Why
not? You seemed to enjoy them well enough yesterday.'

She had the grace to colour. 'I do not want a betrothal
that includes kisses. I think it would be best if we had
a…a practical arrangement.'

'And what precisely is a practical arrangement?'

'An arrangement where both parties enter into a betrothal for purely rational reasons rather like a…a business
agreement. They are civil to one another, but there are no
other complications beyond that.'

'What sort of complications?'

'Well, kisses for one thing.'

'How would kisses complicate matters?'

She was beginning to look rather angry. 'I would imagine that is rather obvious!'

'Is it? Then why did you ask Sir Preston to kiss you?'

He knew he had gone too far when she took a step back, her cheeks suddenly pale. 'That was unkind,' she whispered.

'It was. I beg your pardon.'

'I…I suppose I deserved it.'

'No.' He now stepped away from her. 'You are right. We had best keep this arrangement on a practical basis. Kisses do make things damnably complicated. We can endeavour to be civil to one another.'

'Yes.' For some reason, she looked less than pleased by his capitulation. Another silence fell between them, this one even more profound. She finally looked away. 'The rain has stopped.'

No wonder it seemed so quiet. 'Then we should return to the house.'

'Very well.' She started to remove his coat. 'I must give this back to you.'

'Keep it on until we reach the house.' He was in no mood to argue the point.

She looked taken aback at his harsh tone, but said nothing. They walked back to the house in silence, both careful to maintain a distance between them. Once inside, she slipped out of his coat. 'Thank you,' she said.

'Of course.'

She searched his face as if trying to read his thoughts, her own expression unhappy. She finally looked away. 'I will see you at dinner.'

'Yes.' He watched her climb the stairs, a strange disappointment enveloping him. What had he hoped? That she might actually come to like him? That someone as decent as Chloe would accept someone as jaded as himself?

He turned away, impatient. Chloe ought to marry the sort of honourable sensible man she had her heart set on. As for himself, he would avoid thoughts of marriage. Particularly marriages that might involve complicated emotions.

He had no idea why the idea suddenly seemed so flat.

Chloe shut her bedchamber door. She leaned against it and wondered why she felt so miserable. She should be pleased with the conversation. She had made it quite clear they were to stay on a practical, impersonal basis with no ridiculous compliments or heady kisses to complicate matters. It was precisely the sort of betrothal she had always imagined.

Telling herself that did nothing to erase the fact that she had wanted nothing more than to melt into his embrace and see if his kisses were as pleasurable as they had been yesterday. It had taken every particle of will she possessed to break away. She had said the words she had so carefully rehearsed in her mind but somehow they did not feel so right when she actually said them to him, as they had when she was alone in her room. For an instant he almost appeared hurt, and then the cool, arrogant mask had slid over his face which had only goaded her more. The camaraderie they had experienced while dashing through the rain had vanished.

Perhaps it was for the best, because if she allowed herself to like him too much, she might make the dangerous mistake of actually falling in love with him, and he would have the power to hurt her much more than Lucien had ever done.

* * *

Chloe stood in the entrance of the assembly hall, her hands clammy. She should not be so nervous, but it was the first time she had been out in public since the picnic four days ago. Nor had she seen much of Brandt since their encounter in the rain. He had risen early to oversee the work at Waverly and returned late, often after dinner. Their exchanges were brief and all that was polite, and strangely unsatisfying.

In fact, although she was loath to admit it, she looked forward to seeing him tonight. He had told Belle he would drive over from Waverly. But she had not yet spotted him.

'I do not think Brandt is here yet,' Belle remarked, reading Chloe's mind. 'I am glad we were able to persuade him to come. He needs a diversion from spending so much time at Waverly. Although Marguerite tells me the rooms on the first floor are nearly finished. She has been trying to persuade him to hold your betrothal party there.'

'Why would she wish to do that?' She could not imagine Brandt allowing such a thing. In fact, she could not imagine he would want a betrothal party at all. She certainly did not. Even the mention of the affair was enough to send a tumult of emotions rushing through her, although desperation seemed to be the presiding one. Marguerite had been over twice to discuss the details with Belle and Chloe, which only increased her anxiety. Perhaps if she said something to Brandt he could talk them out of it. If she ever saw him long enough to do so.

'She seems to think it would be a good way to officially open up Waverly again as well as celebrate your forthcoming marriage, particularly since you are delaying it for so long.' Belle looked at her face and said with a sympathetic smile, 'I know you are not particularly pleased about it, but it is expected. You are the future mistress of Waverly in everyone's eyes.'

'It is just that it seems so deceitful.'

'Perhaps.' Belle turned away to speak to Mrs Sutton who had greeted her.

Mrs Sutton congratulated Chloe warmly on her betrothal. 'We are so pleased! You have become quite one of us and we were loath to have you leave! Now you will—' She broke off. 'Good heavens! Is that Emily Coltrane? Why, she looks quite pretty!'

Chloe spotted Mrs Coltrane and Emily standing near the door with Tom. Emily's dark hair was pulled back in a loose chignon that softened the lines of her square face. The pale peach silk she wore, now devoid of most of its trimming, fell in simple lines becoming to her figure and the vee of its bodice made her shoulders appear less broad. The colour, instead of making her face pale, brought out her creamy complexion. Mrs Coltrane beamed, but Emily's expression was apprehensive as if she had no idea how her startling transformation would be received.

'She looks beautiful,' Belle said.

They were not the only people who stared at Emily, who looked as if she were about to run. Chloe excused herself from Belle and Mrs Sutton and made her way through the crowd to Emily's side.

Emily fidgeted with her fan. 'What do you think?'

'You look lovely. In fact, Belle said you were beautiful.'

A slight flush coloured Emily's cheeks. 'Did she really?'

'That is what I told her,' Mrs Coltrane said with a fond smile, 'but now she refuses to step into the room.'

Tom made an impatient sound. 'Don't know why. For once she's in prime twig and now she doesn't want to go in. I would think you'd want to show off your dress like most girls.'

Emily sniffed. 'I'm not most girls.'

'No, that's for certain.' He grinned at his sister's stormy expression.

'Come with me,' Chloe said. 'We can take a turn around the room.'

'Do go on,' Mrs Coltrane urged when Emily hesitated. 'Now that everyone has seen you it would look quite odd for you to leave now.'

Emily still hesitated. 'Very well,' she finally said. She allowed Chloe to link her arm through hers.

Chloe smiled at her. 'Oh, Emily, I have no doubt someone will be quite smitten!'

Emily gave her a nervous smile. 'Do you think so?'

'I have no doubt. Shall we find Sir Preston now?'

'In a little bit. I do not want to appear overly eager to see him.'

'I quite understand.' Just as she did not want to appear overly eager to see Brandt, which of course, she wasn't.

Emily paused. 'Lord Salcombe is coming this way.'

'Oh.' Chloe flushed and forced herself not to turn around even when she sensed he stood directly behind her.

'Good evening, Miss Coltrane, Chloe.'

She turned slowly and managed a smile. 'Good evening, Lord Salcombe.'

His gaze sharpened for an instant before he turned his attention to Emily. 'May I tell you how charming you look tonight, Miss Coltrane? I almost did not recognise you.' His tone was polite, but there was no doubting the admiration in his eye. Chloe could have hugged him.

She was even more pleased when Emily, whose gaze had searched his face, smiled. 'You may, Lord Salcombe. And you may tell Chloe as well, for she is the one who wrought the change.'

He glanced at Chloe. 'I really did nothing but advise Emily on her gown,' she said.

'Your advice was sound.' His voice was still polite. 'Lady Chloe, perhaps you would stand up with me for the next set? I would also like to solicit your hand for the following dance, Miss Coltrane.'

'I...' Chloe suddenly saw Sir Preston standing near the wall. Perhaps if Brandt stood up with Emily first she could draw Sir Preston's attention to Emily while she danced with Brandt. 'Would you mind very much if I danced the following set instead? And you and Emily danced now?'

His face was a mask. He turned to Emily. 'Miss Coltrane?'

'I do not object.' She gave Chloe a curious look.

Chloe waited until they had joined one of the sets before heading towards Sir Preston. Halfway there she began to wonder what she was doing. He had congratulated them quite nicely at Waverly but that had been among the others. What if he refused to speak to her? She would not blame him, but to her great relief he did not walk away.

'Good evening, Lady Chloe.' He cleared his throat.

'Have you seen Miss Coltrane tonight?'

'Er, no. That is, haven't really looked.'

'She is dancing with Lord Salcombe at this very moment. She is quite transformed tonight. I scarcely recognised her. See, they are just now passing by.'

He looked. To her dismay, Brandt did as well. The dark expression on his face sent her heart through her throat. Emily did not seem to notice. Her eyes were on Brandt's face and she said something that made him turn from Chloe. Her only gratification was that Sir Preston was staring at the couple with a peculiarly stupefied air. 'Does she not look pretty?' Chloe asked him.

'Pretty? Er, yes. Doesn't look like Em...that is, Miss Coltrane. Never seen her dance quite like that, either.'

'I dare say she will be very much sought after tonight. Particularly since Lord Salcombe has stood up with her.'

'Undoubtedly,' he said absently.

'Perhaps you should ask her for the next dance.'

He tore his gaze away from the dancers. 'Couldn't do that. Can't dance like Salcombe.'

'Oh, that does not matter. I am certain she will be delighted to stand up with you.'

'Do you?' He stared at Emily for a moment longer, his expression bemused. 'Somehow don't think she'll like me stepping on her feet.'

'But you did very well when we were practising with the others.'

'There was just a few of us then.'

She could not persuade him. When the music finally ended, two of Tom's friends were already at Emily's side. Before she could make her way over with Sir Preston, Brandt appeared. He had a slight smile at his mouth, but the expression in his eyes was anything but amused. 'Good evening, Kentworth. I trust you do not mind if I steal my fiancée away for the next dance.'

'Of course.' He still looked rather preoccupied, which Chloe hoped was a good sign. 'Believe I will take myself off to the card room.'

Chloe stared after him and then slowly looked back at Brandt. He still appeared rather grim. 'Did you wish to dance?' she asked him brightly.

'Yes.' He took her arm, a trifle roughly and marched her into the set. He released her, but from his tensed jaw she suspected he was reining in his temper. He looked no less riled as the dance began.

Really! Whatever had put him up in arms? Her speaking with Sir Preston? Just because they were betrothed did not mean he should act so...so possessive.

They came together. 'You should at least make an attempt to appear pleased with my company,' he said.

'Only if you appear pleased with mine!'

'I am.'

'You look as if you are about to have a fit of apoplexy.'

He shot her a stormy look as they parted. At least she had the pleasure of seeing him on the edge of an explosion. Her pleasure was short-lived. The same sense of being trapped washed over her, just as it had with Lucien and her father and finally with Arthur. She was about to be scolded for doing nothing more than attempting to make things right. She had no doubt he intended to ring a peal over her.

Her trepidation increased as the dance drew to a close. And when he said, 'I wish to speak to you,' it was all she could do to keep from shrinking back. She went with him across the floor, her head high and he found a niche behind a large sickly-looking potted plant.

She touched one of its stunted leaves. 'I dare say this poor plant would be much happier if it was moved by a window.'

'I did not bring you here to discuss plants.'

She forced herself to look at him. 'I imagine you wish to give me a dressing-down for speaking to Sir Preston. I would prefer you did it somewhere other than a public assembly, but if you must do it now please begin so I might have it over with.' Her voice shook, but at least no tears threatened to fall as they once had when someone towered over her in a rage. She had learned to keep them at bay.

'Why are you looking at me like that?'

She started. 'Like what?'

'Like you think I am about to rage at you. Or strike you.'

'Aren't you? I mean, are you not about to rage at me?'

'No. Never that.' His mouth twisted as if something pained him and he looked away. Then back at her. 'You do not need to explain why you were with Sir Preston. Or why you did not wish to dance with me,' he said flatly.

She tightened her hands around her fan, not certain why his mood had so abruptly altered. 'I only wished to point out to Sir Preston how pretty Emily looked. I thought if he saw her dancing with you it might make him notice her a little and perhaps he would ask her to dance. But Tom's friends came and then you, and Sir Preston left for the card room. He probably has not even spoken to poor Emily.'

'I am not certain I quite follow this. You thought Sir Preston would ask her to dance after he saw me dancing with Miss Coltrane. Does Miss Coltrane want to dance with him?'

'She is in love with him.'

'Is Sir Preston in love with Miss Coltrane?'

'He could be. In fact, I am certain he will fall in love with her if only he can be persuaded to spend time in her company. I had so hoped he might ask her to dance but he said he did not dance as well as you and did not think she would like it.'

'That is why you were with Sir Preston? Because you wish to play matchmaker?'

'Yes, that is why. I…I was not flirting with him, if that is what you thought.'

'You don't need to tell me that,' he said shortly.

'I don't want you to think that I would be so callous as to do such a thing when I am engaged to you.'

'I know that.' He held her eyes.

She felt breathless and then he pulled his gaze away just as Marguerite appeared around the side of the pot. 'There you two are! Really, Brandt, from the way you dragged poor Chloe away I fully expected to find you quarrelling. Do you wish everyone to speculate that your betrothal is over before it is hardly begun?'

'I doubt that will happen.' Brandt glanced at Chloe. 'We were merely having a conversation.'

'I can see that.' Her fine brow arched. 'I suggest you have these sorts of conversations in private rather than at a public affair. It is not at all the thing to cast such intimate looks at each other in public.'

Chloe's cheeks heated. She didn't dare look at Brandt. 'We were not.'

Marguerite grinned. 'There is no need to look so flustered. I am only teasing you. I came to warn you that Gilbert Rushton and the Squire are demanding you two play cards against each other. They are already taking bets on the winner.'

Brandt looked over at Chloe, a little smile at his mouth. 'Well? Do you wish to play against me?'

She shook her head. 'No. I am certain it was nothing but luck last time.' She did not quite meet his eyes.

'Oh, Chloe! No one thinks it was completely luck!' Marguerite said. 'Just one hand, that is all. It will be fun. Besides, I have already wagered in your favour.' She smiled sheepishly.

Perhaps one game would not hurt, but she would not win. Not only had she scarcely beat Brandt last time, but this time she would play as poorly as she had when Sir Preston had taught her. That would surely discourage anyone else from asking her again. 'Very well. But only one hand.'

'Splendid!' Marguerite grinned at her. 'I am counting on you to increase my pin-money!'

Chloe assuaged her conscience but telling herself that it

was unlikely she would beat Brandt a second time anyway. Brandt said little as they made their way to the card room, but once or twice she felt his gaze on her face. She felt no less apprehensive as they sat down at one of the tables and a small crowd gathered around.

'Whist again? Or something else? Piquet?' He asked.

'Whist will do.' She could not imagine playing piquet with him.

She could almost feel the disappointment when she lost the first round. During the second round, his face held puzzlement and when he finally played the winning hand, there was no triumph in his face.

She hardly heard the good-natured teasing as she rose. She had proved to herself that she did not have to win— she was not Lucien. 'I...I am sorry.' She forced herself to meet Marguerite's eyes.

'Oh, Chloe, it hardly matters so I pray you will not look so stricken,' Marguerite said. 'I certainly will not miss a thing of my wager.'

'Certain you will do better next time,' Mr Rushton said. 'Undoubtedly offputting to play against one's betrothed.'

Other such remarks followed until everyone drifted off. Only Brandt remained silent. She finally excused herself and left the card room. Brandt followed.

Outside, he caught her hand and pulled her around to face him. 'Why did you play so poorly?' he asked quietly. 'And do not tell me it was only luck the last time.'

'It is unlikely I would have beaten you again, anyway.'

'That is hardly an answer.'

'Very well, if you must know, this evening is exactly why. I do not want anyone making a fuss over me or placing wagers on the outcome of games I play.'

'Then why did you agree?'

'I hoped if I played poorly then everyone would see last time was mere luck and not ask me again.'

'But why would you wish that? There is nothing to be ashamed of. In fact, most everyone finds it quite admirable.'

'But I don't! I hate it!' she burst out.

He stared at her. 'Chloe?'

'I pray you will say no more about it!' Ashamed at her show of emotion, she backed away from him, and promptly stepped on someone's foot.

'I beg your pardon.' She turned and found herself face to face with Lady Kentworth.

The woman's mouth curved in a patently false smile. 'Quarrelling again? Every time I have seen you together tonight you seemed to be out of sorts with one another. I would not consider that a promising beginning for a marriage but perhaps, Lady Chloe, that does not matter to you. How pleased you must feel to have captured such a grand prize as a viscount rather than a mere baronet. I am surprised, however, you did not hold out for a much grander title such as an earl or a marquis, but perhaps you had no choice after trying to compromise my son.' She looked at Brandt. 'I do have one piece of advice for you, Lord Salcombe. I would keep a very close eye on your little bride-to-be. She has the unfortunate habit of wandering off and not always alone.'

Brandt stepped towards the woman. 'And I have a piece of advice for you. If you even think of maligning Lady Chloe's character, you will be more than sorry.'

This time her smile faltered. 'Are you threatening me, Lord Salcombe?'

'Precisely.'

The look in her eye was that of pure hatred. 'You shall be quite sorry.' She moved off, a thin, cold figure.

Chloe was sickened by the encounter. Brandt looked down at her face. 'There is nothing she can do. Put her from your mind.'

'She is so very angry.'

He shrugged. 'Only because she wanted you for her son.'

'But I gave her reason to think it might be possible.'

'She would have been disappointed at any rate. I do not think your cousin would have approved the match.' Brandt's voice was impersonal as he took her arm and began to walk towards the assembly room.

'No.' She felt even more wretched. He was right, of course. But she had some sort of naïve idea that once Justin and Belle saw how happy she was they would have used their influence to persuade Arthur.

How ridiculous her plotting seemed in retrospect. It was a wonder Brandt did not completely despise her.

As they approached the corner where Belle stood with Marguerite, he dropped her arm. 'I am going to take my leave of you now. Tomorrow I depart for London. I have some business to attend to there, but I should return in a few days.'

'Oh.' A stab of disappointment pierced her. She managed a smile. 'I will wish you a good journey, then.' She held out her hand.

'Yes.' He took it and looked down at her face. 'Goodbye, Chloe.' He dropped her hand and after speaking a few words to Marguerite and Belle, left the room.

She watched him go and felt almost bereft as though he had taken something she wanted with him. And she had no idea what it was.

Chapter Eight

Brandt left the offices of Blakely, Blakely and Dedham with the solicitor's words still ringing in his ears, 'You are now an extremely wealthy man, my lord. Your investments have paid off nicely.' Edmund Blakely had looked up and said with his dry smile. 'Congratulations.'

He paused in the cool, misty air of a London morning. For the first time in years, he wished he had someone to share such news with immediately. Justin.

Or Chloe.

The desire to see her hit him with such force he was shaken. He wanted to tell her of his good fortune. That he could now do what he wanted.

He could rebuild Waverly from the ground up if he desired. Restore its overgrown gardens, buy back the lands around it.

He could afford a wife, if he so desired.

He could marry Chloe.

Brandt hardly noticed the passers-by as he walked down the street. He must be mad, thinking of Chloe and marriage, when he had hardly considered marriage at all. Although he could not now imagine living at Waverly without her. The house belonged to her as much as it had always belonged to him. He doubted the house would even accept any other mistress.

But would she accept him?

He would have to persuade her. Court her gently so she wouldn't run from him. Convince her that he would make the sensible, comfortable husband she desired. He wanted children, but he would not force her to his bed no matter how much his blood heated at the thought. He would prove to her that her fears were unfounded; not all husbands were overbearing or considered their wives a mere convenience.

He would prove to himself he was not his father's son after all.

Chloe smiled at Will. 'Shall we return to the house? Miss Withers probably thinks I have taken you prisoner.'

A hopeful look appeared on his face. 'Could you? And take me to the secret passage to Waverly? We could hide there for an age.'

She laughed. 'No, I think I should return you to your geography lesson. At any rate, the passage is blocked from the cliffs.'

'There is still an opening. Behind some bushes.' He gave her a sly look. 'I could show you, if you would like.'

'No, thank you. I doubt Lord Salcombe would like it if we invaded his house while he is not home.'

'He would not mind. Now that you are going to marry him.'

'Even then,' she said lightly. With Brandt gone, her betrothal seemed completely unreal. He was to be back late today or tomorrow.

They started up the path and Will took her hand in his. 'I'll help you,' he said. 'It is harder for girls to climb hills because of their skirts.'

'Thank you.' She hid her smile at this piece of male

observation. She supposed she should point out that skirts had never hindered her, but she did not want to crush his obvious desire to play the role of protector. He reminded her of Brandt. They were not related, but she could see the same desire to shield her from harm. So why did Will's efforts fill her with tender amusement while Brandt's made her shy away?

Perhaps it was because Will was so young, or that she knew it was really Will who needed her protection and she was merely indulging him. Or that the role of protector meant having all the power. She could never imagine Brandt in need of protection, or in need of anything, or anyone. Certainly he did not appear to need her.

They continued up the slope and to the top towards the house. Miss Withers, the pleasant-faced, middle-aged governess, waited for them near the garden gate. Chloe bent down and gave Will a hug. He smiled at her. 'When you live at Waverly we can do this every day.'

'Perhaps.'

Chloe watched Miss Withers lead him away and then started back towards Falconcliff, feeling heavy-hearted. Will's words only reinforced how much more of a mistake this betrothal really was. He would be terribly disappointed when she and Brandt parted, as would a good many others.

'Chloe!'

She looked up and saw Emily riding towards her on her grey mare. Chloe waited for Emily to halt beside her.

'I had hoped to see you today,' Emily said. 'Are you on your way back to Falconcliff?'

'Yes.'

'May I join you?' Without waiting for an answer, she slid gracefully from her mare and caught up the reins. 'I have not had the chance to thank you for the assembly. I had the most lovely time!'

'I am so glad, but I really did nothing. You were the one who danced and smiled and completely enthralled everyone.'

'I could not have done so if you had not helped me with my gown and hair and told me I must smile. And, of course, allowed Lord Salcombe to stand up with me for the first dance. I have no doubt that was what made the others take notice and decide I would be worth their while.'

'That sounds so callous! That is not the whole of it, at all.'

Emily merely smiled. 'Perhaps, but is that not how it works in Society? When someone of consequence notices one, others follow suit?'

'Sometimes, but not this time. I think it was because before you looked as if you did not want anyone to notice you. This time you looked much more friendly. As if you would not growl if someone dared to approach you.'

'Is that how I looked before? I suppose that is how I felt. But not any more.'

They walked towards Falconcliff, the mare trailing behind them. Chloe glanced at Emily. 'Did Sir Preston stand up with you?'

Emily gave a little laugh. 'No, but I decided that it did not matter. I am rather tired of waiting for him to notice me.' Nothing in her expression indicated this was not perfectly true.

'He did notice you. When you were dancing with Lord Salcombe, he said he thought you were very pretty and that he did not know you could dance like that. He worried that you would not want to stand up with him since he did not dance very well himself.'

She shrugged. 'If he really felt some sort of attraction to me, then he would have spoken to me. I have no intention of throwing myself his way any more.' She looked straight ahead and then turned to Chloe. 'I would rather hear about your betrothal to Lord Salcombe.'

They had just entered the part of the path on Falconcliff property. Chloe kept her voice light. 'It is not very exciting. An ordinary betrothal, I suppose.'

'Is it? Then why are you not very happy about it?'

'Of course I am. But it is merely a practical arrangement, not a love match.' Her voice came out as matter of fact as Emily's.

'On whose side?'

She glanced at Emily, surprised. 'On both sides, of course. We are both in agreement that marriage should be a practical union of two sensible persons who wish to be comfortable together.'

'That sounds exceedingly dull.'

'I think marriage should be dull.' One where the persons involved did not demand overly much from each other. Certainly no hot passions flaring between them that might lead to heartache and jealousy and who knew what other untidy emotions.

'Is that why you considered Sir Preston? You thought he was dull?' There was a sudden sharpness in Emily's voice.

'No, of course not. I thought him kind and very interesting. I thought we could be comfortable together. But now I see that was quite wrong of me. He needs someone with whom he can be less comfortable. Besides he was never interested in me in that way at all.'

'It is not wrong of you to consider Lord Salcombe because you can be comfortable with him?'

Perhaps it would be better to still be at odds with Emily if she meant to ask such probing questions. 'No, Br...Lord

Salcombe and I are in agreement that this is what we both want. A dull, practical marriage.'

'I cannot imagine Lord Salcombe wanting a dull marriage. His nature seems too passionate.'

Certainly, Emily was blunt. 'I assure you he is not,' Chloe said.

'Has he kissed you?'

Chloe's cheeks heated. 'Kissing is very dull as well.' This was nothing but a lie. She was relieved to see the drive of Falconcliff. 'Can you stay for a bit? The latest *elle Assemblée* has just arrived and we could look at the owns. I saw a morning gown that would be perfect for ou.'

'The *Belle Assemblée*?' Emily wrinkled her nose. 'It is he dullest...' She stopped. 'I am sorry. Of course I would ike to see pages and pages of gowns.'

Chloe laughed, relieved they were off the subject of Brandt. 'Please don't force yourself. We can do something else if you wish such as play billiards,' Chloe suggested. 'Sir...someone said you were a very good player.'

'Hardly, but I do enjoy playing.'

'I'm not very good at all.'

Belle was not at all surprised by their desire to play billiards. 'Please do so. I must own I rather enjoy it. At least now that I can hit the ball most of the time. Occasionally one goes in the right direction,' she said when hey asked her for permission to use the table. She was eated in a chair near the long windows of the library.

Justin looked up from the periodical he had been reading n the chair opposite hers. 'I would think that the number of hours I have spent instructing you would have more of an effect.'

'Except that you do not spend much time on instruct—' Belle broke off, her cheeks turning pink.

'Very true.' A look passed between them—one of those looks that filled Chloe with both embarrassment and envy. She looked away, shoving that last thought aside. She certainly did not want anyone looking at her in such a way.

Nor could she imagine what one could possibly do in a billiards room besides play billiards.

Emily was as delighted by the room as she was with the table since it possessed a magnificent view of the sea. Even on overcast days such as today it was possible to see fishing boats and an occasional sailing ship.

While Chloe found the cues, Emily set up the balls with a practised hand.

'Where did you learn to play?' Chloe asked her.

'My aunt and uncle have a table, so when we visit them, Tom asks me to play because he has no one else. When we visited Kentworth Hall...' She stopped and then continued in an off-handed fashion, 'We would play. Of course, I will not be doing that now.' She straightened up. 'Shall we begin?'

Compared to Emily's skill, Chloe's was dismal. Even after Emily's pointers she still hit few balls. Emily finally announced she must leave, but promised she would give Chloe another lesson soon. Belle insisted on sending a groom to accompany Emily home, despite Emily's assurances she always rode alone in the neighbourhood.

Chloe, feeling at a loose end, wandered back to the billiard room and picked up a cue. She had watched Justin and Brandt play and it had looked so effortless. She should be able to do the same. Chloe slammed the ball with her cue and then watched as it rolled off the table and towards the door.

'Drat!' She bent down to retrieve it. A pair of dusty masculine boots suddenly appeared in her vision.

'It might help if you hit the ball with less force.'

Her heart thudded to a halt. She looked up and met Brandt's amused gaze. 'What are you doing here?' she asked.

'That question could be answered in a number of ways.'

She straightened, ball in hand. 'I meant I did not expect to see you. Were you not to be back until tomorrow?'

'I finished my business early.'

'Oh.' She stared at him, unexpectedly glad to see him. He was travel-stained, a slight growth of beard about his mouth, and it occurred to her he had come straight to the billiard room from his journey.

Despite his certain fatigue, he had an air of suppressed excitement about him and a little smile played about his mouth as he looked at her. Again she experienced that odd breathless feeling. His eyes darkened and her heart began to beat most erratically. 'Did you come to play billiards?' she blurted out.

'Not quite.' His eyes were still on her face.

'Oh.'

'I came to see you.'

'Did you?' She resisted the urge to back away.

'Yes.' He took a step towards her. 'I missed you. Did you miss me?'

'Well, yes. A little.'

'Good. That is at least a beginning.'

'Is it?' Chloe had no idea what he was talking about. She bit her lip. 'I...I should put the ball back on the table.' Before she dropped it. Or begged him to kiss her.

Wherever had that thought come from? She scurried to the table and set the ball down. 'Emily, that is, Miss Coltrane, was here earlier. She attempted to instruct me in the finer points of billiards, but I fear it did not help one bit. I came back to practise but I still cannot hit anything.' She was chattering.

He had followed her. 'I would not say you couldn't hit anything. You had just hit the ball when I came in.'

'But it is not supposed to fall on the floor.' At least he had lost that intense look that made her feel so light-headed.

'No. I think you might profit from a few more lessons. We can begin tomorrow.'

'We?'

'Yes. I intend to take over your instruction.'

'I would not think you would have the time.'

He grinned. 'But for you, I do.'

Now she was certain he was teasing her. 'Do you not need to attend to your house?'

'Not every minute. I can find time for more pleasurable pursuits.' He leaned against the table. 'Such as instructing you.'

'I have no doubt you will be wasting your time. I suspect I will be a most disappointing pupil.' Now they were on familiar ground.

'I doubt it.' He still regarded her with that lazy, slightly amused look that had once annoyed her to no end. Now it merely felt familiar, unlike that intense look of earlier. She did not worry about this Brandt.

'We should probably return upstairs.'

'Probably.' He did not move.

'Do you not need to change your clothing?'

A slight smile touched his mouth. 'You are beginning to sound very wifely already.'

'I most certainly am not! If you must know, I do not care a whit about your appearance, I was merely suggesting that you might wish to change before dinner. Not that I care whether you do or not,' she added hastily.

'I am glad to hear that. When we are married, you will

not object if I occasionally come to dinner without changing.'

'We are not going to be married.'

'Aren't we? Then why are we betrothed?'

She gave him an exasperated look. 'Did a carriage accident befall you on your journey back to Devon? If you recall, this is a temporary state of affairs so I do not have to marry Lord Denbigh. You quite clearly told me you do not want to be married until you have amassed enough of a fortune to keep a wife. Not that I think that should matter in the least!'

'It does to me,' he said quietly. He looked at her. 'At any rate, that is no longer a concern.'

Something in his voice gave her pause. 'What is not a concern?'

'My fortune.' He smiled slightly. 'That was what I came to tell you.'

Her stomach lurched and she felt a sudden rush of fear for him. If he had lost everything after working so hard, she did not think she could bear it.

'My solicitor informed me that due to a number of investments I have made, I am now a very wealthy man. I need no longer worry about whether I have the means to do anything I wish.'

It took a moment for his news to sink in. 'Oh! That is absolutely wonderful!' Without thinking she launched herself at him, throwing her arms about his neck. He staggered back a little against the table and then caught her to him, his arms draped loosely about her.

For a moment her cheek pressed against the cloth of his coat and then she suddenly realised what she was doing. She stepped back, completely self-conscious. 'I beg your pardon. It was just I had such a dread that you meant to tell me you had lost everything. I did not mean to throw myself at you in such a way.'

An odd little smile played around his mouth. 'If I had known such news would bring you rushing into my arms, I would have tried harder to gain a fortune.'

'I did not do that because of your fortune.' He couldn't possibly think that it was only his wealth that caused such a reaction. She found herself desperately wanting to explain that. 'It was only because I was so pleased for you. You will have the funds to restore Waverly the way you want and do anything else you want without worry.'

'Yes.' His eyes were on her face. 'And take a wife.'

She forced a smile to her lips. 'That as well.' She looked away.

'I do not suppose you would consider the role.'

Her eyes went to his face. 'What role?'

'The role of my wife. Would you consider marrying me?'

'I…' She felt as if someone had knocked the breath from her. 'Why?'

He moved away from the table. 'Why not? I want a wife, and children. You need a husband. I strongly suspect you want children as well. Since we are already betrothed, it seems a logical conclusion. I've no doubt the arrangement would benefit both of us. There would be no need to go through the inconvenience of finding other suitable prospects.'

His words were rational, his voice calm as if he were proposing a mere business arrangement. Just the sort of arrangement she wanted for her marriage. Why, then, did she feel so panicked, and disappointed, as if it was not what she wanted at all?

'No, I cannot.' She barely whispered the words.

'Why? Did you not tell me you wanted a sensible, practical marriage? That is what I am offering you.'

'Yes.' *But not to you*, she wanted to say. She looked at
him, the strong planes of his face, the hair curling at the
nape of his neck, the strength of his well-formed physique,
but most of all his eyes. Emily was right. He was too
passionate. He would not be sensible or practical. The way
he looked at her, with that intense dark gaze told her that.
He would storm her senses.

And her heart.

'Do you recall I said I wanted a comfortable husband?
I do not think you would be very comfortable.'

He turned, his arms folded. 'Are you certain that is what
you want? A comfortable husband?'

'Yes.'

'Why do you not think I would be comfortable?'

'You are not dull enough.' The words came before she
could think.

His eyes glinted. 'No? I consider that a compliment. I
would not want you to think me dull.' He took a step
towards her.

'I prefer dull.'

'Do you? What are you afraid of that you need a dull
husband?' He took another step.

She backed away, this time finding herself against the
billiard table. 'Nothing. I thought we agreed that falling in
love was very inconvenient.'

His eyes still had that strange glint, as if he was barely
holding back some strong emotion. 'So you fear you will
fall in love with me?'

'That is the last thing I would ever do!'

'Is it?' He moved towards her, so she was completely
backed up against the table. His body was only inches

from her. 'What if I decided to make you fall in love with me?'

'I…I do not think you could do that,' she whispered.

'I consider that a challenge.' He closed the gap between them, his body pressing hers against the table, his hands imprisoning her on either side. Then his mouth found hers, in a hard demanding kiss that left her breathless, demanding her surrender. Her lips parted under his and his tongue slipped inside her mouth, creating sensations that made her head spin. Her legs were trapped between his and she was wholly and completely his prisoner. There was nothing else but him, his mouth moving over hers, his hands, the hardness of his body pressed against hers. Her body seemed to be on fire, a warmth growing in her abdomen making her want more than just kisses. Somehow she was half on the table, and he was leaning over her, her hands clinging to his shoulders, her skirts tangled about her legs. His hand was stroking her, her breasts, her belly and then his hand was beneath her skirts, moving up her leg. She panicked then, a little gasp of fear escaping her.

He released her suddenly as if a bucket of water had been thrown on them. Her eyes flew open in time to watch his expression change to one of pure shock. He backed away from her. 'Chloe,' he whispered.

She straightened, hardly knowing what had happened, as with trembling hands she pulled down her skirt.

His eyes were on her. 'Did I hurt you?' He looked almost sick.

'No.' She turned away. 'Not really.' Except the worn fabric of her gown had torn where the bodice joined the skirt. She was completely confused by her reaction at both wanting and fearing what he had been doing—what they had been doing.

'I did,' he said flatly. 'I beg your pardon. I did not

mean...' He paced away from her. 'I vow I will never touch you again. Not like that.'

She looked up in time to see the anguish on his face. 'You did not hurt me,' she said, not knowing what else to say.

'I could have,' he said in a low voice. 'You are right, we are not suited. I will release you from this betrothal as soon as I can do so without creating more gossip and speculation than necessary.'

He spoke in the same low, impassioned voice. She had never seen him like this, as if all his defences had fallen away. He looked as if he was in the worst agony and she had no idea why.

'What is wrong?' she asked.

'Wrong?' He gave a short laugh. 'Nothing, except that because I was angry I nearly seduced you. It was no better than an act of rape.'

'But you did not seduce me. You stopped.'

'It does not matter. I forced you.'

'You did not. It was not...' *like the other time.* The words stuck in her throat.

She took a step towards him, but he seemed to recoil, his expression now shuttered. 'You ought to return to your room and change,' he said.

'Brandt...'

'I suggest we avoid each other as much as possible.' He did not look at her.

There seemed to be nothing else she could say. 'Very well.' She started towards the door and then stopped and looked back at him. He was staring out of the window at the sea. 'Goodbye.'

She could not tell if he even heard her.

Chloe had wanted to escape to her room, but she met Justin on the stairs. If she had hoped to hide her dishevelled state from him, one look at his face told her it was impossible. His gaze went briefly to where her hand held her bodice together. 'What happened?'

'I...I had an accident.' She tried to meet his eyes. 'It is nothing.'

'Your gown is ripped.'

'Yes.' She started to move past him. 'I must change.'

He caught her arm, his touch light, but she had no doubt he did not mean to let her go until he had an explanation. 'Were you with Brandt?' he asked carefully. 'Belle sent him to find you in the billiard room.'

She bit her lip. 'Yes, but this has nothing to do with him.'

She was a miserable liar. Justin's face changed. 'What did he do?'

'He did nothing. Please, do not ask me any more.'

'He is my cousin, but I consider you my relation as well. You are a guest under my roof and therefore under my protection. I will not allow you to be distressed or abused in any fashion. Go to your chamber. I will send Belle to speak to you. I am going to seek out my cousin.'

'That is not necessary.' Brandt spoke from below.

Chloe's gaze flew to his face, but he was not looking at her. He had that same closed expression and nothing about him told her he knew she was even there.

'I wish to speak to you,' Justin said.

Brandt inclined his head slightly. 'Of course.'

They might have been strangers instead of cousins closer than brothers. She caught Justin's arm. 'Please. He did nothing more than...than kiss me.' She had no idea if Justin had heard. With a sick feeling, she turned, started up the steps, and prayed things would not get any worse.

* * *

Brandt followed his cousin into his panelled study. He felt curiously numb, as if he were observing himself from outside. When Justin turned and faced him, he waited for the verdict to fall.

'What happened? Chloe assures me nothing, that her ripped gown and dishevelled appearance was an accident, but I find that difficult to believe. She has all the appearance of a woman who has been ravished. Or nearly so.'

Brandt met his cousin's eyes. 'I did not ravish her but I might as well have.' He would never forget the little sound she made and the confused, frightened look on her face when he let her go. It was her bewilderment afterwards, as if she could not comprehend what had happened, which sickened him most.

'Why?'

'Because I forced myself on her. I asked her to marry me and when she turned me down and told me that she would never fall in love with me, I lost my head. I suppose I had some damnable notion of proving her wrong. I kissed her, but it was not a pleasant kiss. Not the sort of kiss you give a young and inexperienced girl.'

'How did her bodice come to be ripped?'

'I backed her against the billiards table,' he said bluntly. 'I suppose it came to be ripped then.' He gave a short laugh. 'I did not tear the cloth deliberately.'

'Did you set out to seduce her?'

'No, but I came damnably close.'

'Why did you stop?' Justin's expression was merely curious.

'Because it penetrated my damnable conscience that I could hurt her, that I was hurting her.'

'She said you did not hurt her. And you did stop.' Justin met his gaze squarely. 'You did not force her.'

'She did not ask for my kiss, I forced it on her because

I was angry and I came close to losing complete control and taking her on the table. I vowed I would never touch a woman in anger. And I did.'

'You are not your father,' Justin said quietly.

'No? I have his blood running in my veins. I have inherited his temper and his lack of control. And his appetites.'

'I have not noticed that. Nor has anyone else.'

'Only because I am careful to keep my passions under control.'

'So you are telling me that underneath your iron control you harbour the desire to seduce virgins for sport and engage in perversions that are best left unspoken of? You'd force yourself on unwilling women?'

'Of course not, dammit.'

'I did not think so. Not even when you were determined to sow as many wild oats as possible did you behave in a less than chivalrous manner.'

Brandt shrugged. 'It does not matter. Chloe has told me that we are not suited. She is right, of course. She wishes for a dull husband. She informed me I am not dull enough. I will, of course, release her from the betrothal as soon as possible.'

'I suggest you wait unless you want Ralston to hurry her off to Denbigh Hall, or Lady Kentworth to spread rumours.'

'I've no doubt you could put a stop to both of those.'

'Perhaps. Or perhaps not.'

'Damn you,' Brandt said softly. 'Do you not see the necessity of my staying away from her?'

'I doubt Chloe is in any danger from any more displays of passion. Quite the contrary, I suspect.' Justin was silent for a moment. 'Do you think I did not feel shame for what

I did to Belle? Forcing her to become my mistress was hardly the act of an honourable man.'

'You thought she had hurt you and your family in the worst possible way.'

'That did not justify my despicable behaviour,' he said. 'I am only grateful that Belle forgave me.'

'She loves you.'

'Yes.' A slight smile touched Justin's mouth. 'Little though I deserve it. I like to think that because of that, I am perhaps a more honourable man that I might have been.'

'You are fortunate.'

'Very.' He looked back at Brandt. 'Chloe could be your redemption as well.'

'She hates me.'

'I doubt it. She seemed more concerned about protecting you than accusing you.'

He shrugged, determined to quell the slight hope that sprang within him. 'She is an innocent. She has no idea what I am.'

Justin merely looked at him. 'I do not think you know either.'

Brandt moved away. 'I must return to Waverly. I trust Belle will understand if I decline her offer for dinner.'

'As you wish. You can dine with us tomorrow.'

'I think not.' He left before his cousin could say anything more.

Chloe stood in front of the window, too numb to move. She supposed she should summon the maid to help her undress, but could not seem to act. She only turned when she heard the door open.

Belle had quietly entered the room. She quickly took in Chloe's appearance. 'Are you all right?'

'Yes.'

Belle came across the room. 'What happened?' she asked quietly.

'Can you first make certain Justin does not call Brandt out?'

Belle stilled. 'Why would Justin wish to do that?'

'I imagine because he thinks Brandt hurt me.'

'Did he?'

'No.' She took a deep breath. 'He…he just kissed me. He did nothing more.'

'And your dress.'

'Somehow it became torn. Brandt did not do it.'

'I see.' Belle looked thoughtful.

'Can you make certain Brandt is safe?'

'I am certain he is.' Belle took her hand. 'Come and sit by me.'

She followed Belle to the bed and sat next to her. 'Do you wish to tell me about it?' Belle asked. 'Only if you wish.'

'He asked me to marry him. He said that we could have a sensible, practical marriage, just as I wished. That because we were already betrothed it would save us the inconvenience of finding other spouses.'

'That is perhaps true. What did you say?'

'I said "no" and told him that I did not find him dull enough to be the sort of husband I wanted. Then I told him I would never fall in love with him. And then he…he kissed me.'

'Then what happened?'

She flushed. 'He let me go and then asked if he had hurt me. I said no and he told me he would never touch me again like that. He said I was right, we were not suited and he would release me from this betrothal.' She turned her eyes on Belle. 'He said he…he nearly seduced me. He looked in such anguish—I have never seen anyone so!'

'I imagine he was angry with himself for kissing you in such a way,' Belle said carefully. 'You are young and have not much experience with men or their passions, which, of course, is what is expected of young, unmarried women. It is not acceptable for a man to do more than plant a chaste kiss on the cheek of his affianced bride. He probably feared he had frightened you and was horrified as well at his ungentlemanly behaviour. He has always wanted to protect you, whether you wanted him to or not.'

'Yes.' That was very true.

'There is one more thing.'

Chloe looked up at her, the tone of Belle's voice giving her pause. 'What is it?'

'I do not know what you know of Brandt's father, but he was far from a kind man. He was considered a pious man but he was cruel. Cruel to his wife, and to his son. At the least provocation, real or imagined, his father would strike him. Brandt's mother was a frail invalid and although Brandt loved her, she did not help him. Instead, he bore his father's wrath to stand up for her. He still thinks there was something he should have done or could have done. When Brandt left home after his mother died, he behaved in the worst way possible. Perhaps he wished to punish his father for her death. In the end, he discovered his father did things that were far worse than anything Brandt could ever do. Justin says that Brandt fears he has inherited his father's tendencies.'

'How can he think that?' Tears sprang to Chloe's eyes. Shock and pity mixed with anger towards a father who would abuse his son rushed through her. She could not imagine Giles ever raising a hand to Will in such a way.

Or to Caroline or to his wife. Or Justin striking Belle or little Julian no matter how angry he might be.

'Because despite the fear and the helplessness, one feels such terrible anger. You cannot show that anger and so it is buried along with any other emotion. When you feel again you fear that you will never stop the anger…that you are no better than the person you feared and loathed. You will do anything to prove you are not.'

'Is that how you felt with Lucien?'

Belle hesitated. 'Yes, that is how I felt. After Lucien's death, when Justin returned, determined to make me pay for the terrible wrong Lucien had done to him and to his family, I thought the only way I could atone for Lucien's wrongs and my own was to give him what he wanted. I never thought I would fall in love with Justin or that he would come to love me. So I tried to run from him and from myself. I feared that the happiness I felt with him was only an illusion and I would wake up and find it all gone, that I was not deserving after all. I suspect Brandt feels much the same. He feels he has no right to care for you.'

'But he doesn't. Not in that way.'

'He does.' Belle smiled a little. 'Why else do you think he kissed you with such passion and then instantly regretted it?'

'Do men not do that? Kiss women, whether there is any attachment or not?'

'Sometimes, but I do not think that was what happened today.' Belle hesitated. 'Sometimes when one is first kissed it might not be quite as enjoyable as it will be later. Sometimes it is rather frightening but when you hold someone in regard and they return your affection, it will soon become one of the most pleasurable activities of marriage.'

Chloe's cheeks burned. 'Perhaps. At any rate, I...I am not going to marry Brandt. He does not want me. In fact, he suggested we avoid each other as much as possible.'

'Then you must persuade him otherwise.'

'Why? We are not suited.' But Chloe's words did not quite ring true.

'Oh, but I think you are. As does everyone else.' Belle's face was filled with kindness and understanding. 'He needs you. Sometimes the strongest men are the ones who need the love of a woman the most.'

'I do not want to fall in love with him,' Chloe whispered. 'Or have him in love with me.'

Belle touched her hand. 'Sometimes we do not have a choice about these things.'

Chapter Nine

Chloe did not see Brandt the next day, or the day after. Meanwhile, Belle and Marguerite proceeded with the preparations for the betrothal party as if nothing was amiss. They solicited Chloe's advice at every turn and if they noticed Chloe's lack of enthusiasm, they made no comment. Marguerite cheerily informed her that progress on Waverly was proceeding at a furious pace and she had no doubt it would soon be ready for its new mistress. Chloe tried not to cringe.

Even the news that her mother was coming for the party failed to cheer her. On the third day after the kiss in the billiard room, she accompanied Belle to Haversham Hall. Marguerite shooed her from the drawing room. 'Will and Caroline had been plaguing me for an age to ask if you would take them to the shore. Since I know you love to do so, I think you should go.'

Glad to escape from the betrothal plans which were suddenly turning into a small ball, Chloe left.

Will and Caroline were just as delighted to escape from the house, as was Lion, but rather than stopping to view the sea as they almost always did, they seemed in a hurry to get to the cove. She scrambled down the path after them, almost losing her balance. They ran ahead of her and she followed. Her shoes, adequate for a walk on a tame path, were no match for the sandy beach.

She nearly gave into the urge to pull her stockings and slippers off when they finally rounded the slight promontory and came to the cove. Picking her way over the rocks she did not pay much attention until she heard Lion's excited barks. She looked up to see him dashing towards an all-too familiar male figure.

Her heart leapt to her throat and every instinct told her to flee, but he had already looked up and spotted her. She could almost feel his gaze from across the distance. Will had followed Lion across the sand and now flung himself at Brandt. Caroline stopped and waited for Chloe to catch up.

Her serious eyes searched Chloe's face. 'Mama thought it would be nice if we asked Uncle Brandt as well, but she wanted us to keep it a surprise. I hope you do not mind too much. I will own I do not like surprises very well.'

'It is all right. Sometimes I do not mind a surprise.' But not this one. 'Is this to be a surprise for Uncle Brandt as well?'

'Yes.'

Splendid. She could think of nothing more awkward. Well, she would try to maintain a calm, friendly distance towards him.

At least he seemed to be heading in their direction with Will and Lion. She waited, heart pounding, until he joined her and Caroline. 'Good day, Lady Chloe,' he said.

'Good day.' She was not about to call him Lord Salcombe, but she certainly did not want to use his given name if he intended to be so stupidly formal.

Will beamed. 'Are you not surprised?'

'Very much so,' Brandt said. His gaze was impersonal

as it swept over Chloe. 'Was this a surprise for Lady Chloe as well?'

'Yes, but why are you calling her Lady Chloe? You always call her Chloe.'

'That is the proper way to address her.'

'Only if you aren't her friend. Since you are her friend, then you should call her Chloe.'

Chloe looked at him. 'He is right, of course.' She patted Will's head and smiled at Caroline. 'What shall we do now?'

'Look at the tide pools,' Will said promptly.

'Is that what you wish to do, Caroline?' Chloe asked.

'Oh, yes!' Then, recalling she was trying to behave more as a proper young lady, added, 'But only until the picnic arrives.'

Chloe glanced at Brandt. 'Is that plan agreeable to you?'

'Of course.'

The neutral tone in his voice made her want to hit him. She gave him a determined smile. 'Well, then, shall we go?'

'Yes!' Will dashed ahead and then turned. 'Hurry, Uncle Brandt!'

Caroline and Chloe followed at a more sedate pace. Unfortunately the only access to the tide pools was over a pile of rocks. Caroline was wearing sensible boots, but her own slippers would undoubtedly be cut to shreds if she wore them. Well, she would just have to remove them. At least there was one advantage to always removing shoes whenever possible. She sat down on one of the rocks. 'Please go on with the others. I am going to remove my stockings and slippers.' So what if Brandt thought she was improper? He obviously did not want to marry her anyway. He could think what he liked.

Caroline hesitated. 'Are you certain?'

'Yes.' Chloe shot her a quick smile.

'Very well.' Caroline still looked uncertain. 'Is Uncle Brandt well?'

'Well?'

'It is just he looks rather grim. Like Papa when something is troubling him.'

'Perhaps something is.' She had no idea what to say to this astute child. 'But do not worry about it. I am certain it is nothing very important.'

'I see.'

Just then Will shouted something and Caroline turned and started to climb over the rocks. Chloe bent down to untie the laces of her slippers, her mood growing more foul by the moment. Really, it was one thing for him to look so out of sorts, but another thing altogether if it overset Caroline. If he wished to make it obvious he wanted nothing to do with her, then at least he could do it in private, rather than in front of anyone else.

Not that they would ever be private again. She scowled at the knot she had been attempting to undo and finally pulled the slipper from her foot. After that she rolled down her stockings and climbed up the first rocks. The others were already at the next pile of rocks by the tide pool. She gingerly made her way over the rocky ground. Will looked up from his position on the edge of a pool and waved.

Brandt had removed his coat and laid it across one of the rocks. He knelt next to Will, but she almost saw the muscles tense beneath his shirt at her approach. 'Hello,' she said brightly. 'What have you found?'

Will looked disappointed. 'Only a few anemones. No starfish like last time.'

'Anemones are very interesting,' Chloe said. She moved slightly closer to Brandt. 'So what are your favourite things to look for, Lord Salcombe?'

He started to glance up at her, but his attention was suddenly arrested. He looked slightly stunned before his gaze shifted to her face and narrowed. 'Where are your shoes?'

'That was not my question.'

Caroline looked from one to the other, her expression slightly anxious. 'Chloe often removes her shoes. She says it is much easier to keep her footing. Mama removes her shoes as well and Papa does not mind. At least, not very much.'

'Yes, so there is no need to discuss this now,' Chloe added. She refused to quarrel with him in front of Caroline and Will.

'Very well.' But the look he gave her told her he did not intend to leave the matter alone.

Will jumped up. 'The picnic is here!' He scrambled off the rock with great alacrity. 'Whoever gets there first gets all the tarts.'

'That's hardly fair!' Caroline scrambled after him, her attempts to be lady-like swallowed by the natural competition between siblings.

'Well, I certainly do not intend to go without tarts.' Suddenly shy in Brandt's presence, Chloe jumped off the rock to the one below. She picked up her skirts to better clamber after them, and stumbled on a rock.

Strong arms caught her. She gasped and found herself looking into a cool pair of green eyes. 'What the devil do you think you're doing?'

'Laying claim to my share of tarts,' she replied.

He released her. 'More likely trying to cut yourself or sprain an ankle.'

'I won't. I do this all the time.' She lifted her chin. 'At any rate, since you have made it clear we are no longer to be engaged, you have no business dictating to me.'

'It does not mean that I don't have a responsibility towards you.'

Hurt shot through her. 'No? Well, I don't need your protection!' Chloe stormed away from him and climbed down the last rock. Her slippers and stockings were where she had left them. She had no intention of putting them on with him glaring at her so she picked them up and started across the sand towards the sheltered overhang.

At least he didn't attempt to catch up with her. Will and Caroline were seated on the cloth spread on the ground next to the hampers. The footman had pulled out plates and utensils and she sat down by Caroline. Brandt joined them, carefully sitting as far away from Chloe as possible.

Will chattered most of the time they were eating. Chloe's normally healthy appetite had somehow vanished. She forced a tart down her throat as Will had relented and said everyone should have one since there were too many for him to eat alone.

Afterwards, Will pressed back against Brandt's arm, tart on his face while Caroline sat on his other side. Brandt was smiling at something Will said. Then he looked up and caught her gaze and the smile suddenly shuttered.

Anger shot through her. Did he dislike her so much that every time he saw her he would close up? She hadn't asked him to kiss her in that way! She rose. 'I believe I will walk along the shore.'

'Do you want me to come?' Caroline asked.

'Oh, no. I can take Lion for company.'

But even Lion refused to leave Brandt's side. She walked away, the sand cool between her toes, before anything else could be said. She fought back the tears of anger that threatened to squeeze from her eyelids. Despite Belle's words, she could see no evidence he needed her or even liked her, much less loved her. No more than she loved

him. In fact, she was quite certain she disliked him. The
romantic picture she had built in her mind of somehow
rescuing him from his unhappy life had fled. Not when he
made it clear he did not wish to be rescued.

He did not need her. She had always been a failure at
that anyway. Her mother had never listened to her advice
even when Chloe knew what she was about to do would
be a disaster. She had thought that last year she might save
Belle from Justin, but instead it had turned out Belle did
not need to be rescued, that Justin was her destiny.

Sir Preston hadn't needed her, or wanted her. Her attempts to make that right had failed, too. Emily did not
want Sir Preston after all.

Even Caroline and Will did not really need her. They
had their parents, and Brandt, whose company they probably preferred anyway.

Feeling sorry for herself, Chloe had hardly noticed she
had walked around the small promontory until she felt the
water swirling at her ankles. She looked down, vaguely
surprised and then realised the tide was coming in. She
looked back but could not see the others. The water was
starting to lap up over the smaller rocks.

She should undoubtedly return. Not that anyone would
miss her.

Which was completely idiotic. Of course they would. At
least Belle. And Julian. And Justin. And Marguerite, Giles,
her mother, and Will and Caroline, although perhaps not
as much as they would Brandt if he was the one walking
away to nowhere.

She started back and then halted. Her path was blocked
by the incoming tide. She had quite forgotten that the water first surrounded this particular point, turning it into a
tiny peninsula before creeping up to cover all but the tallest
rocks. She would have to climb over the rocks and make

her way to the daunting cliff behind them. She would need to hurry before the water covered the remaining smaller rocks.

Gaining a foothold on the first rock, which came only up to her knee, was not too difficult, but the next circle of rock was much more tricky. She slipped once, scraping her elbow. Her feet were beginning to feel raw and she had to fight the absurd desire to sit down and cry. She reached the end of the rocks and saw the ledge above. She could not imagine how she could climb it.

A shout startled her. She looked up and saw Brandt climbing towards her. She cringed. It was bad enough she was in this predicament—worse that he must come to her rescue again. She made her way over another pile of rocks before he reached the rock ledge directly above her and knelt down.

'Give me your hand.'

She looked up at him, half-expecting to see disdain or impatience, but there was nothing of that in his face, only calm reassurance.

'Chloe, you need to give me your hand so I can help you up. Do you see the rocks to your right? There is a small indent like a foothold.' His voice was firm as it would be if he were encouraging a child.

She found it and placed her foot in the recess. She was able to stand up enough so that he could reach her hand. He pulled her up and she collapsed on the ledge next to him.

He helped her to her feet and then released her hand. For a moment she could not think and then realised he was speaking. 'The water has come in so that we cannot go back to the beach now. We can either wait for the water to fall or climb through the passage in the cave.'

'The cave?' She looked up and saw the dark opening a few feet from them. 'It is Will's cave.'

His mouth curved faintly. 'Actually, it is my cave.'

'I cannot go in there.'

'Why not?'

'I do not like dark places.'

'We have no choice unless we wish to stay here on the rocks until the tide goes out again.'

'I…I would rather do that. You can go without me. Will and Caroline need you.'

'They have gone to Waverly with my groom. Chloe, I will be with you. The cave leads to the grotto in my garden. I've done this trek a number of times, the most recent a few weeks ago with Will. Come with me.' He held out his hand.

The dark opening loomed over her like some sort of cavernous mouth. She shook her head. When she did not take his hand, he took hers. Her gloves were gone so his warm, firm flesh was against hers. She realised it was the first time she had ever held his hand without a glove between them. 'Come, Chloe.' He started to climb and, in a sort of daze, she followed him.

She stepped on a loose rock and flinched. He glanced down. 'Your feet.' He grimaced. 'I would offer you my shoes, but I am not wearing them.' His gaze went back to her face. 'It's not very far. Can you make it?'

'Oh, yes. My feet are perfectly fine.' She would die before admitting they felt as if they'd been cut in a million places.

'I suppose you plan to tell me that you do this all the time?'

'Not exactly this part.'

'I didn't think so.' His hand closed more tightly around hers. 'We can go slowly.'

The cave was dark and damp and smelled of salt water and seaweed. She could barely stand and Brandt was forced to stoop. 'This way.'

She felt the first twinge of panic as they headed into a dark narrow passage. She took a deep breath in an attempt to steady her nerves, but as they advanced further into the tunnel, now completely dark, it was all she could do not to flee. Or scream. She made a little sound.

Brandt turned. 'What is wrong?'

'N...nothing.'

He moved closer to her. 'Are you afraid? Don't be. It's not very far and I am here with you.'

'I...I know,' she whispered.

'I will take your hand again and you can close your eyes and pretend I am leading you through a garden.' His voice was matter of fact and calm, as if he frequently led half-hysterical females through dark, narrow passages.

Somehow that steadied her. 'Yes.' She closed her eyes and gave him her hand.

He started to walk. 'Now we are near a rose bed. There is a particularly red rose just to your right. Further on is a clump of, er...gillyflowers.'

She almost smiled. He kept up a stream of nonsense as they slowly climbed through the narrow tunnel. Time seemed to stand still until a branch brushed against her cheek. Her eyes jerked open. Dazed, she saw they were completely surrounded by shrubbery and tangled over-grown vines, and a tumbling stone wall directly in front of them.

He dropped her hand. 'You are safe.'

She nodded. His clothing was damp and streaked with dirt; a lock of hair had fallen over his forehead giving him a rakish air and his feet were bare and dirty.

She undoubtedly looked worse. From the expression on

his face, she guessed she looked like the survivor of a
shipwreck. 'I need to get you back to the house.'

'I should return to Haversham Hall.' She should apologise to him as well for all of his trouble, but she felt too
miserable to say anything.

'Not like this.' Before she knew what he was about he
had stepped forward and swept her up in his arms.

She gasped. 'I...I can walk.'

'I doubt it.'

'Please put me down. I weigh too much.'

'Not at all.'

'But...'

'Be quiet.'

The deadly calm in his voice quelled her more effec-
tively than if he had shouted at her. She knew then that
he was very angry.

Which he had every right to be.

They were met in the hall by Mrs Cromby. 'Oh, my!
Whatever has happened? I could not make heads or tails
of what the children were saying except you were rescuing
Lady Chloe and taking her through the grotto. We have
already sent word to Haversham Hall. The children are in
the kitchen having gingerbread and milk. You must bring
her into the drawing room. I will have a fire set straight
away!'

She kept up a stream of chatter as she proceeded Brandt
into the drawing room. He set Chloe down on the sofa and
Mrs Cromby caught sight of her feet. Her eyes widened in
shock and sympathy. 'My poor love!' She turned to the
footman standing near the drawing room doors. 'We need
a basin of water, rags and bandages. And a blanket. I will
get that myself!' She bustled out.

Brandt sat down on the sofa next to her. 'I am going to
see to your feet.'

'No!'

He looked up, that same impersonal expression on his face. 'I need to see how badly you are hurt.'

He would not allow her to refuse so she nodded. His touch was gentle as he turned her foot although she could not help flinching when his fingers brushed a particularly sore place. She whimpered a little when he touched her ankle. His hand stilled. He looked up. 'Did you twist your foot?'

'Perhaps a little. I cannot remember.'

'It is bruised and a little swollen, but I do not think it is sprained. You are fortunate that your cuts are small, but you have bruised your feet. Walking will not be particularly comfortable for a few days.'

He sounded exactly like Dr Abbott, the physician who had seen her in London. Brandt stood when Mrs Cromby and the footman returned. The loss of the warmth of his hand made her feel suddenly cold.

He spoke to Mrs Cromby and then turned to Chloe. 'I am going up to change. I'll be back down shortly.'

'Yes.' She should thank him, but the words seemed to stick to her tongue. He had already left the room.

Mrs Cromby set to work washing her tender feet and then bandaging them. After that, she helped Chloe wipe her face and comb her hair and then wrapped her in a quilt. She stood. 'Are you ready for visitors? The young lord and lady are impatient to see you.'

'Of course.'

Will flew into the room with Caroline following close behind. 'Will! Please do not jump on Chloe! You might hurt her,' she called.

Will stopped by the sofa. 'Are you very badly hurt?' he asked.

'No, not much.'

'Oh.' He stared at her. 'Why did you keeping walking? We shouted and shouted at you and you did not stop. Were you running away from us?'

'Oh, no, Will, that was not it at all. I was lost in thought and I did not hear you. Of course, I would never run away from you.'

'I'm glad.'

'So am I,' Caroline said. 'We were so worried when we saw how the water had risen, but Uncle Brandt said he would see no harm came to you.'

'Did you like the cave? Did Uncle Brandt show you where the passage begins that leads to the house?' Will asked.

'No, I fear I had my eyes shut most of the way.' She gave him an apologetic smile. 'I am afraid of dark, tight places.'

'How did you see to get out?'

'Br…Lord Salcombe helped me. He knew the way.'

'So you did not see any of the slimy creatures that live in the cave?' He glanced at his sister, his eyes dancing.

Caroline shuddered. 'Will!'

'None at all,' Brandt said as he came into the room. He was in an immaculate shirt and pantaloons and coat and no one would ever guess that a mere hour earlier he had waded through sea water, crawled over rocks and then crept through a cave.

Although Mrs Cromby had helped wash most of the grime from her face and limbs, Chloe still felt horrid. She pulled the quilt more tightly about her.

Brandt looked down at the children. 'Your papa has sent his carriage for you. Your groom will see Lion safely home.'

'Is Chloe staying here?' Will asked.

He glanced at Chloe. 'Only until I take her home.'

'Can she not come home with us?' Caroline asked.

'Your papa has asked that I escort her back to Falconcliff.' Again that polite neutral tone as if they were strangers.

Chloe managed to smile and embrace Caroline and Will before they departed. Brandt escorted them to the waiting carriage and she was left in the silent drawing room. Her chagrin was mixed with anger. She would rather he came out and told her he did not like her than treat her with such icy politeness. It was a wonder he deigned to rescue her. Then why had he been so kind? If he wished to prove they were not suited, he was going about it in the wrong way.

At any rate, she was not staying here like some sort of helpless invalid. She threw off the quilt and stood. She would rather walk home than impose upon him any longer.

Or at least ask that Belle or Justin send a carriage for her. She grimaced. Her feet were sore and the bandages would make walking more than a very short distance difficult. And she had no shoes.

She hobbled to the door only to come face to face with Brandt. 'What are you doing?' he demanded.

'I am going to ask Mrs Cromby to send a message to Falconcliff. I would like a carriage sent.'

'I am going to escort you home in my carriage.'

'I would really prefer that you did not. I have no desire to impose on you any longer.'

'You are not imposing on me.'

'If you must know, I did not purposely go around the promontory so that you would have to rescue me.'

'I never thought you did.'

'There was no need to put yourself out to rescue me. I was perfectly capable of rescuing myself.'

'How?'

'I would have sat on the rock until the tide receded.'

'You are quite mad if you think I intended to let you do that.'

'Why not? You have made it quite obvious you wish to rid yourself of me. I have no idea why you did not finish your picnic and leave.'

'For one thing, Will would have tried to save you himself.'

'I quite understand. The only reason you did so was so that Will would not come to harm.'

'That is not what I said.'

She knew she made no sense, but at least his indifferent politeness had left. 'That is what you implied. So now that Will is gone you can allow me to make my own way home!'

'Did you hit your head?' he demanded.

'No. Did you?'

'You need to sit down.'

'No.'

'This is ridiculous.'

'No, it's not,' she snapped. To her chagrin, she felt tears prick her lids.

'Hell.' He took her arm. 'Come and sit down.'

'I do not wish to.'

'But you will.' He led her to the sofa. 'Sit.'

Chloe sniffed. 'I am not Lion.'

He looked confused. 'No.' He pulled her down on the sofa next to him. 'Don't cry.'

'I'm n…not.' She dashed a tear away. The next thing she knew he was pressing a handkerchief into her hand.

She swiped at her eyes. 'Now…now I have ruined your handkerchief and your clothes. It seems you must go on being kind even though you wish only to…to rid yourself of m…me.'

'I do not wish to rid myself...' Brandt stopped. 'We are not suited. You told me that yourself and I would think that after the other day you would realise I would make a damnable husband.'

'Why?'

'Because...' He turned and looked at her. 'There are things about me you do not know,' he said flatly. 'No gentleman would have kissed you the way I did. Nor would have frightened you as I did.'

'I know about your father. I know you are nothing like him.'

He stilled. 'How do you know that?'

'Belle told me.'

'Did she? Did she also tell you that I frequented some of the worst hells in London? That I had a string of mistresses? That once I fought a duel over another man's wife? Do you know why? Because I wished to prove to myself that I was nothing like my father. In the end, it turned out that my stern, moral parent did all of those things, and he had no compunction in forcing himself upon any woman he desired. Just as I forced myself upon you. Twice, in fact.'

'You merely kissed me. Never once did I think that you intended to hurt me. Or did you?'

'No. I would never hurt you.' He ran a hand through his hair. 'But that does not excuse my behaviour or that I frightened you.'

'It was only that I am not very used to such kisses.' Not his sort of kisses; ones that made her want more, much more.

'I would hope not. Not until you are married and even then I would hope your future husband would exercise more restraint when with a young, innocent wife.'

'What if I hope he doesn't?'

'You've no idea what you are talking about.'

'So men only lose their restraint when they are with their mistresses, but not with their wives?'

To her surprise, a dull patch of colour appeared on his cheek. 'I am beginning to think we have both gone mad. This conversation is exceedingly improper. Most certainly you should not be talking about mistresses.'

'I am not so naïve that I do not know what they are. I heard enough whispers about Lucien's affairs. I am not so stupid or blind that I did not know what Justin intended when Belle left London with him,' she said quietly. 'Nor am I as innocent as you think.'

'Another one of your rhetorical arguments? I suggest we stop this line of conversation before you argue that there is no reason why we would not suit.' His voice was light and mocking. Brandt rose. 'I must take you back to Falconcliff, before my cousin accuses me of abducting you. You have been with me far too long as it is.'

Now he was back to the bored gallant. With sudden insight, Chloe realised that he adopted the role most often when he wanted to hide his true feelings, as he carefully deflected the conversation like a skilled swordsman deflecting an opponent's thrust when the topics were too close to his hurt.

She watched him leave to send for the carriage. He was impossible; arrogant, stubborn, and controlled, but also kind beyond measure. She was beginning to think they were perfectly matched after all.

Brandt handed the butler the bouquet of flowers. 'I will not disturb Lady Chloe while she is receiving other visitors. Please see that she gets the flowers.'

'Of course, my lord.'

He turned away, trying to convince himself that he was

relieved he had a convenient excuse not to deliver the flowers in person. It was best that he not see her nor allow himself to be engaged in any more conversations such as yesterday's. Conversations that might lead him to hope for things he could not have. Such as Chloe.

'Brandt!'

Belle's voice stopped him. He turned. She was coming across the hall towards him, her usual smile of welcome on her face. The longing and envy for the happiness his cousin had found with her hit him with renewed vigour. He forced himself to smile. 'Good day, Belle.'

She seemed to notice nothing amiss. 'Are these for Chloe? How lovely! But you must deliver them to her in person. I know she wishes to see you. She said she never thanked you properly for your gallant rescue yesterday. I believe she would like to do so.'

'Indeed. Yesterday she indicated that there was no need for such a rescue. She told me she had planned to wait on the rocks until the tide receded.'

'I believe she felt extremely foolish to have gone so far in the first place. She has never liked to inconvenience anyone or to feel beholden to them.' She touched his hand. 'So come and see her. Her injuries are much better and she is insisting she should be able to walk about. Perhaps you can convince her to stay down.'

'I doubt it. Does she not have a visitor already?'

'She has had several. Miss Coltrane left a quarter of an hour ago. Miss Sutton arrived shortly after that. And, oh yes, Sir Preston is here.'

Kentworth? What the hell was he doing here? Did he somehow know that their betrothal was only temporary and hoped to stake his claim early? He'd best look elsewhere, for Chloe was still his until the betrothal formally ended.

After that, he still had no intention of allowing Kentworth to have her.

Even as he told himself his speculations were ridiculous, he found himself saying, 'Very well, I'll see her.'

He took the flowers back from the butler and followed Belle through the hall to the staircase. They met Miss Sutton and her mother at the bottom, which meant Kentworth was with Chloe, unchaperoned. To his irritation, the departing guests insisted on exchanging a number of pleasantries, which Belle seemed in no hurry to discourage. He shifted impatiently. At this rate, Kentworth would have time to seduce Chloe if he had a mind to.

He finally broke in. 'I trust you will understand if I take my leave of you and go to see Lady Chloe.'

'Of course,' Mrs Sutton said kindly. 'I have no doubt you are anxious to see how the poor girl is doing for yourself. You must go.'

He started up the stairs, only to hear Mrs Sutton say, 'How nice to see two such suitable young persons in love. Perhaps I am too modern, but I do think love matches are so much nicer than marriages made only for convenience.'

He did not hear Belle's reply. His mind was reeling. In love? Did everyone actually think he and Chloe were in love? He had no idea how they came to such a conclusion when everything in their behaviour should indicate otherwise.

Still unsettled, he stalked into the drawing room just in time to see Kentworth take Chloe's hand and bow over it. 'So I might hope? Never thought to tumble head over ears until…'

It was all he could do to restrain himself from grabbing Kentworth by the throat and backing him up against the wall. 'Is there a reason why you are holding my fiancée's hand?'

They both jumped when Brandt spoke. Kentworth dropping her hand as if burned. Brandt had no idea how to read the emotions that flashed across Chloe's face.

Kentworth straightened. He eyed Brandt with an amazing calm for a man on the verge of being challenged. 'About to take my leave. No need to look like a dog with a bone.' He picked up his gloves and then stopped to face Brandt. 'Hope you know what a right-goer you have, Salcombe.'

Brandt stared at him. 'I do,' he said shortly.

'Good.' Kentworth left.

He turned to Chloe on the sofa. She looked lovely and rather fragile with the quilt over her lap, and completely in need of protection. His protection.

'What the devil was Kentworth saying to you about tumbling head over ears?'

'What lovely flowers! Are they for me?'

He stalked towards her. 'Yes.' He held them out to her and she took them.

'How pretty! Daisies and gillyflowers are my favourites. And there is a rose! Is that from the old shrub that is growing near the south wall? I thought all the roses were spent.'

'I found one. You have not answered my question.'

'Haven't I?'

'Yes. No!' He folded his arms. 'You are still my fiancée, you know.'

The slight smile left her face and he saw she looked rather angry. 'Am I? If you must know, I found your question rather stupid.'

'You think it stupid to question why another man is holding your hand and speaking to you of love?'

'Yes.' She met his gaze.

'Is he in love with you?' Because if he was, he would be dead.

She took a deep breath. 'No, of course not. He is in love with Emily. He realised it as soon as she decided not to be in love with him any more. Except that I think she still cares for him, but does not want to admit it. Perhaps she wishes him to suffer the same pain of unrequited love she did.'

'So he is not in love with you.'

'That is what I said.' Now she sounded exasperated. 'He was referring to Emily. He wished to know if he had any hope.'

There was nothing in her clear gaze that belied her words. He was beginning to feel foolish. 'I see.' He paced away. 'None the less, I would ask you to refrain from holding Kentworth's hand in the future or encouraging such confidences.' He sounded unbelievably pompous even to his own ears.

'Why?'

'We are betrothed. It is not seemly for you to do such things with other men.'

'Would it be more seemly if I did such things with you?' There was a tinge of anger in her voice.

'Yes.'

'Except I can't imagine you would ever need to hold my hand or confide in me!' Now she sounded truly angry. 'At least Sir Preston makes me feel useful!'

'Does he?' He had no idea what she was talking about, but the jealousy he had tried to smother burst forth. 'Since you have nothing but praise for him, then perhaps you should consider him for your future husband after all.'

Something flashed in her eyes and then she lifted her chin. 'Perhaps I will, if Emily does not want him.'

'Hell will freeze over before I will allow that to happen!'

'It will be none of your business.'

'It is as long as you are betrothed to me.'

She smiled, a cool little smile that made him gnash his teeth. 'I won't be betrothed to you for ever.'

He stared at her, but before he could say anything, she continued, 'In fact, I think it best if we end this idiotic farce now.'

He took a step towards her, wanting to kiss her until she admitted she was his. Instead, he gritted his teeth. 'I am loath to inform you, that however you might hate it, we will continue this farce until the agreed-upon time. I've no intention of allowing your guardian a reason to cart you off to Denbigh Hall. And you might consider how Belle will feel if you decide to throw me over two days before the party.' He picked up his gloves with a deliberate move-ment. 'I will bid you farewell for now. I will see you the day after next at our betrothal celebration.' He gave the words sardonic emphasis.

He did not give her time to reply, instead he stalked from the room, his temper at breaking point. He ran into his cousin coming from his study. 'In the future I trust you will keep Chloe better chaperoned,' Brandt ground out.

'From you?'

'No, dammit, from Kentworth or any other man who comes to call.'

'I quite see.'

It wasn't until he had swung himself upon his horse that he recalled he had not even inquired after her health. In-stead, he had allowed his own temper and passions to take over.

But then, she did not want him. She had made that very clear today.

* * *

Chloe stared at the lovely bouquet of flowers. The gillyflowers had already started to wilt. She had been tempted to throw the bouquet at Brandt, but now it only looked sad and forlorn. Just the way she felt. Her temper had cooled almost as soon as he had gone, leaving her with nothing but an overwhelming desire to burst into tears.

Provoking him had given her a great deal of satisfaction at the time, but in the end nothing had been gained. What had she hoped to do? Force him into saying that she could not marry Sir Preston because he loved her? Or he had no intention of letting her go? Instead, he had become more angry by the moment until he had stalked out.

Why he cared whom she married was beyond her. He did not want to worry Belle, he had made that clear.

Chloe clutched the bouquet tighter. The daisy heads had begun to droop as well. She began to cry.

Chapter Ten

Chloe avoided glancing at herself in the looking glass. She did not want to see her undoubtedly pale face or the lovely gown that she had no desire to wear. She picked up her fan and then looked up when the door opened.

'Oh, my love! How beautiful you look!' Her mother entered the bedchamber, a misty smile on her face. 'I still cannot believe that my sweet girl will soon be a married woman!' She traipsed across the room and caught Chloe's hands, her eyes tearing up as they had frequently ever since her arrival yesterday with Arthur. 'You look like an angel. Lord Salcombe will be enchanted, although from all reports he is already quite under your spell.'

There seemed to be no answer other than a sickly smile. Lady Ralston's brow puckered. 'Are you quite well? You have been very quiet since yesterday. I can only imagine how much your feet must hurt! I will not scold you, but I pray you have learned your lesson and will not go about barefooted any longer! I trust your future husband has already persuaded you of that!'

Chloe did not want to discuss Brandt. In fact, she did not even want to think about him. 'Shall we go? I suppose I should not be late.'

'Most certainly not.'

The carriage ride with Arthur and her mother was far too short. For once, Arthur actually attempted to engage her in conversation, but she was too nervous to respond. Thank goodness her mother answered for her. Her stomach churned as they halted in the drive. The house was transformed; lights shone from the windows and the overgrown vines and shrubs had been cleared so the front door and ground-floor windows were visible. Arthur helped Lady Ralston and then Chloe from the carriage. She winced as her tender feet touched the ground.

Chloe entered the hall on Arthur's arm and after Justin and Belle. She had been too preoccupied last time she was here to notice the changes but now, under the gleaming candlelight, she could see the newly polished floor and the gloss of the banister. The footman took her shawl and she, her mother and Arthur were following Justin and Belle up the staircase and to the rooms on the next floor.

Her stomach fluttered as Brandt broke away from the elderly lady at his side to greet them. In his black coat and pantaloons, a diamond gleaming in the folds of his snowy cravat, he was completely elegant, completely male and very disturbing. His eyes met hers and she trembled at the answering surge of awareness she saw in them.

He was not indifferent after all.

He held her gaze as he took her hand. 'You have not met my great-aunt, Lady Farrows. She is anxious to meet you.'

He guided her to the elderly lady and Chloe found herself looking into a pair of intelligent grey eyes in a sharply wrinkled face. She took Chloe's hand. 'So you are the young lady who has finally persuaded my nephew to marry. Certainly you are pretty enough. I trust you have some semblance of intelligence as well.'

Lady Farrows released Chloe's hand. She turned to Brandt. 'Since I did not trust you to remember the necklace and ear-rings I have brought them down myself. She should put them on now. Her gown will do very well with them.' She handed him a jeweller's box.

'I do not think the ballroom is quite the place for Chloe to change her jewellery.'

Lady Farrows waved a hand. 'Then take her to another room. There are certainly enough in this monstrosity. I trust you will find one without plaster raining from the ceiling. While you do that, the Duchess, Lady Ralston and I will greet any guests.'

He glanced at Chloe. 'We have our orders, it seems.' His expression was rueful.

'Yes.' She found herself smiling at him. She had no idea what to think of Lady Farrows who seemed to speak her mind, but it was somehow so artless that she was not certain if she should be offended or not.

His own lips curved in a smile and for a moment they were in perfect accord. She suddenly looked away, remembering they had no business being in such harmony. He took her arm. 'We will return shortly.'

He led her to a small room off the ballroom. 'I have found it best not to argue with my aunt in these matters. She always has her way in the end, it seems.'

He opened the box. 'I had hoped to avoid giving you this set, but I fear I have no choice. It is a family tradition.'

'I promise I will not lose it and, of course, I will return it to you as soon as possible.'

'Actually, it would be a great favour to future wives if you would lose it. The setting is atrocious and will undoubtedly make you look as if you are wearing a harness collar.' He held the necklace up.

Diamonds and emeralds adorned an intricate gold circle,

which was not quite a collar but certainly heavy enough. 'It is not too awful,' Chloe said doubtfully. 'I am certain it must be very valuable.'

'Yes, and it is never to pass out of the family, otherwise I've no doubt it would have been sold long ago or broken up. Do you want me to help you put it on?' His voice was calm and impersonal.

'I might be able to manage.' She undid the clasp to the simple strand of pearls she wore, and set it on the table. Brandt handed her the necklace, but she found the unfamiliar clasp beyond her. She finally gave up. 'I must ask for your help.'

'Of course.' He stepped forward and his fingers brushed her nape as he caught the ends of the necklace. A spark shot through her. He fumbled with the clasp; his light touch was making her knees weak. 'I have it,' he said, but his hand stilled at the nape of her neck. 'Chloe,' he said. 'This is impossible.' His voice was husky.

'What is?'

'All of this. This betrothal. Touching you like this. Having you so close and wanting more than anything to kiss you.'

'Oh.' Her heart started to pound. 'I…I would not mind if you did.'

'Wouldn't you? You told me you did not want my kisses.'

'Perhaps I have changed my mind.'

His hands slid to her shoulders and he slowly turned her to face him. 'I shouldn't do this, you know.'

'Why not? We are betrothed.' She held his gaze.

'Last time I frightened you.'

'No, you did not. Not really.' She hardly thought she could breathe.

He slowly lowered his head. His mouth covered hers in

a kiss that was so gentle she thought she would melt. She found herself pressing closer to him wanting more. He finally lifted his head. 'I forbid you to think about Kentworth.'

'No.'

'Good.' He hesitated. 'Chloe...'

'I trust you intend to show yourselves to your guests at some point.' Justin's voice broke into their reverie.

Chloe jumped back, her cheeks heated. She could hardly meet Justin's gaze, particularly when he said to Brandt, 'You were wrong. It is you who needs to be chaperoned.'

Brandt laughed, but it held genuine amusement. 'I think you are right.' He looked at Chloe. 'I suppose you must put on the equally atrocious ear-rings so at least you have a matching set.'

She nodded, hardly able to speak. She removed her ear-rings with shaky fingers. What had just happened? There was the kiss, which had been the most breathtaking thing imaginable, but something else had changed as well. The look in his eye, the gentleness of his touch had promised things even more wonderful.

'The ear-rings, Chloe.' He held them out. 'Or should I help you with these as well?'

She coloured. 'No, it is not necessary.'

His smile held a hint of wickedness. 'I agree. It might be dangerous.'

He was flirting with her again, but instead of annoyance, she felt breathless and vulnerable and happy all at once. She managed to put the ear-rings on. They felt as cool and heavy as the necklace but somehow she did not mind. When he held out his arm, she took it, her fingers trembling very slightly, but it was in anticipation.

She hardly noticed the guests they greeted. She was too aware of the man next to her; the strength of his lean hand, the timbre of his voice, the way his chestnut hair curled at the nape of his neck. Not even Lady Kentworth's tight smile and angry eyes burst her happy anticipation.

Gilbert Rushton sauntered in. He took Chloe's hand. 'From the besotted expression on your faces, I am surprised you have not escaped the formalities and gone for a romantic moonlight stroll in the garden.'

Brandt glanced at Chloe who felt as if her cheeks were on fire. 'I've plans for that later,' he said.

'Splendid.' Mr Rushton released her hand and grinned before strolling off.

Chloe did not dare look at Brandt until the musicians struck up the notes of the first set. Belle turned to Chloe. 'Under ordinary circumstances you and Brandt would head the first set, but I do not know if you should dance. Not with your feet still so tender.'

'In fact, I must forbid her to do so.' Brandt smiled down at Chloe. 'Come and talk to me for a moment instead.'

'After that you may stand up with me,' Lady Farrows told him.

Arthur levelled a frown at Brandt. 'I trust you will refrain from doing anything that might cause gossip.'

'I will endeavour to do my best.' He held his hand out to Chloe. She placed hers in his and he led her near a small alcove. He looked down at her. 'I am serious, you know. I want you to meet me in the garden at midnight. By the grotto. Do you recall where it is?' He paused, his expression suddenly less certain. 'Only if you wish to. Perhaps I am being presumptuous.'

'No.' She held his gaze. 'I want to be there. I will be there.'

His eyes darkened in the way she had seen Justin's when he looked at Belle. Instead of wanting to flee, she wanted to go to him, and press her mouth to his.

Was this what it was like to be in love?

The realisation hit her with such force she nearly reeled. She stared at his familiar face, and wondered why she had not known this before. Perhaps she had but had not wanted to admit it, out of a fear that she would be badly beyond her depth.

'What is amiss?' His eyes were watchful.

'Nothing. Everything is quite all right.' She touched his sleeve. 'You must go dance with Lady Farrows.' Everything was suddenly moving too fast and she needed a few moments to sort her tumultuous feelings.

'I will see you at midnight?' It was a question.

'Yes.'

She watched him go and then nearly jumped when Lady Kentworth appeared beside her. 'Another assignation, Lady Chloe? At least this time it is with your fiancé.' She gave Chloe a malicious smile before walking off.

The glow of happiness faded as a feeling of unease stole over her. How much had Lady Kentworth heard? Enough, apparently, to know she planned to meet Brandt alone. Such behaviour was not quite proper even for an engaged couple, but certainly meeting him was nothing Lady Kentworth could turn against them.

Perhaps she should have insisted on meeting somewhere else, or at another time, but she sensed this was too important; that whatever Brandt wanted must not be put off because of propriety or doubts, or anything else. And certainly not because of Lady Kentworth.

If only she could have a few minutes alone to collect her thoughts. First Lydia approached her and after that Belle insisted she must sit so she might watch the dancers. She was never alone after that. Finally Sir Preston stopped to speak to her and she recalled she had promised to help him with Emily. She finally spotted Emily and Mr Rushton near the same alcove where she had stood with Brandt. She rose and asked Sir Preston to escort her to Emily. Emily pasted a strained smile on her face when she saw them. Chloe was too tired to dissemble. 'Sir Preston wishes to dance with you, Emily.'

Sir Preston tugged at his cravat. 'Only if you wish, that is. No obligation to at all, Em…Miss Coltrane.'

'I have promised Mr Rushton…' Emily began.

Chloe cast a meaningful look towards Gilbert. 'I am certain Mr Rushton will understand.'

Gilbert's face was bland. 'Most certainly. Care for a turn about the room, Lady Chloe?'

'I think I would prefer to sit. My feet are rather sore.'

'Of course. I will escort you back to your chair.' He smiled paternally at Sir Preston and Emily. 'Time to take yourselves off to the dance floor.'

Sir Preston held out his arm. 'Miss Coltrane?' Chloe was pleased to see he looked her directly in the eye.

'Yes. I suppose.' Emily placed her gloved hand on his.

Rushton watched him lead Emily to the floor before turning to Chloe. 'Almost as entertaining as watching you and Salcombe dance circles around each other. Glad to see you two have finally come to your senses. Well, let us find your chair and then a glass of lemonade.'

He saw her back to her chair and then left to procure the drink. She quickly spotted Brandt moving through the dance with effortless grace. Had she really fallen in love with him? Was that what this attraction was all about? This half-hope that she would see him, the disappointment when he was not there, the breathlessness when he looked at her? The desire to feel his arms around her, his lips on hers?

It was a much worse feeling than she had ever anticipated. When she had been with him, everything had seemed to fall into place but suddenly she felt less certain, less happy and much more frightened. If she met him as she had agreed, she would be giving herself to him; perhaps not in the most physical, intimate sense, but in every other way. If she did not go, she would be telling him that she did not want him.

If only she could draw Belle aside and ask her what to do. But this was not something she could discuss with Belle. She must make up her own mind.

She saw Mr Rushton returning with the lemonade. After that, her mother came to sit with her. She scarcely saw Brandt, but when she did she found his eyes on her in a sober, considering way. She was quite aware of passing time and, as half-past eleven approached, she felt as if she was on pins and needles.

It was after eleven thirty that she made up her mind. She was about to excuse herself from Emily and Lydia when a footman appeared next to her. 'I have a message for you. I am to tell you that it is imperative that you read it immediately and then wait for your reply.'

'Thank you.' She took the paper and opened it. It was brief. *Meet me in the west wing chamber. It is important. Salcombe.*

Why would he wish to meet her there? Except for the library, she had never been to the west wing and doubted she could even find her way there. But why else would he send her a message unless he had a reason for changing?

'Is something wrong?' Emily asked.

'Nothing at all.' The footman still waited for a reply. She took a breath. 'Yes, I will be there.'

'I am to escort you.'

At least that would be better than wandering around on her own. She followed the footman from the room and across the hall to the corridor that led to the older wing.

He carried a brace of candles, but they provided little light in the dim passage. He finally stopped in front of a heavy wooden door and waited for her to enter. She stepped inside, grateful to see a burning candle on the heavy table near the door. It took a moment for her eyes to adjust to the dim light. 'Brandt?' she said softly.

She heard footsteps and nearly screamed.

'Lady Chloe? What the devil are you doing here?'

To her astonishment, Sir Preston appeared. He looked as taken aback as she was.

'I was to meet someone here,' she said. 'What are you doing here?'

'I was to meet someone here as well.' He cleared his throat. 'Don't suppose you came to meet Emily, did you?'

'No.'

'Deuced odd. Got a note from Emily saying she needed to see me urgently but shouldn't tell anyone where I was going. Thought it strange but didn't want to not show in case it was important.'

'Yes, I know. My note was very similar.' It must be very close to midnight. Brandt would be waiting for her. 'I must go. There is something I must do.'

'Will accompany you back. Rather dark.'

'I think it would be best if you did not.' She nearly ran to the door, but when she turned the handle it would not budge. She tried again, but still the door would not move. 'Drat!' Growing desperate, she pushed then she turned and found Sir Preston behind her. 'The door will not open!'

'Let me try.' He waited until she stepped aside and then tried the handle, but his efforts were no more successful than hers. He shoved and finally said to her, his face mirroring her own frustration. 'Appears we are locked in.'

'We cannot be!' Brandt would think she had changed her mind. And if she was discovered locked in this ancient bedchamber with Sir Preston... 'There must be some way to force the door. Or another way out!'

'Door is thick oak. Don't think I can break it down.' He looked at her with a doubtful expression. 'Not planning to have hysterics are you?'

'I never have hysterics.' However, if she were going to, this would be the time. She went over to the heavy curtains and pushed them aside; the cloud of dust that rose from them making her sneeze. She tried the window sash, then realised she had forgotten to unlock it. She managed to work the lock only to find the sash would barely move.

'Don't think climbing out is a good idea,' Sir Preston remarked over her shoulder. 'The roof has a devilish pitch. Probably end up in the garden with a broken leg, or worse.'

She whirled around. 'But what should we do then? I cannot stay here. I promised Brandt that I would...would meet him and if I do not...I cannot imagine what he will think!'

'No doubt he'll understand once he sees the note. Kept mine.'

'I kept mine as well.' But it would not be the same. Tears pricked her eyelids. She would not cry because then she would never be able to think, but she was beginning to feel hopeless.

Sir Preston suddenly straightened. 'Thought of something.'

'What?'

'There's a panel in this room. Leads to a passage.'

'A panel? I thought that was in the library.'

'One here as well. Goes to the library.' He strode over to the wall near the cobweb-draped tester bed and she hurried after him. He shoved a small table aside and began to push on the panels then suddenly jumped when the wall opened and Emily stepped through.

Sir Preston goggled. 'Emily? What the devil!'

Dust covered her gown, but she appeared as composed as ever. 'I came to rescue you. Actually, I came to rescue Chloe.'

'How the devil did you know we were here?' Sir Preston demanded. He looked quite stern. 'And what do you mean by coming by yourself?'

'It will take too long to explain.' She looked at Chloe. 'You must hurry, Lord Salcombe is waiting for you. You must go through the passage and continue to your right and then you will come out in the library. Take my candle.'

'Yes.' Chloe took the candle and took a step towards the dark hole and then paused. 'You and Sir Preston are not coming?'

'Not for a while.' Emily's face wore a peculiar little smile. 'I will see you tomorrow and tell you all about it.'

Chloe stepped into the passage and took a deep breath. She would not panic, she would find the library.

And Brandt.

Brandt glanced at his pocket watch but it was not necessary. He knew it was past midnight, nearly twenty minutes past, and there was no Chloe.

She had changed her mind. He was not prepared for the bitter disappointment that washed over him. For a moment in the ballroom, when she had looked up at him, he had hoped that she perhaps wanted him after all, but she had not. For whatever reason, she did not trust him.

He could hear the faint laugher and music issuing from the house. Soon it would be time for Justin to make the formal announcement. His hopes of having her consent to marry him before the announcement were dashed. Instead, he would stand next to Chloe and know that the betrothal was truly a façade.

He must return to his guests, and find Chloe. He left the bench in the grotto and headed towards the terrace and the newly installed French windows that led inside. At the top of the terrace steps he was hailed by Tom. 'Lord Salcombe!'

Brandt turned. 'What is it?' He knew he sounded curt, but he was in no mood for idle talk.

'Have a note from Emily for you. She wanted me to find you and give it to you directly. She said it is imperative that you read it straight away. Had no idea you were in the garden or would have given it to you earlier.'

'At least I have it now. Thank you.' He started to fold it.

'She wanted you to read it as soon as possible,' Tom insisted. 'She looked worried. Can't find her now. Or Lady Chloe, and the Duchess has been asking for her.'

Brandt opened the note. *Lady K. locked Sir P. and Lady C. in west wing chamber. Have gone to rescue them through the passage. I will send Chloe to library through passage. Emily Coltrane.*

She had not changed her mind! His relief was short-lived. He had to find Chloe and then he would deal with Lady Kentworth.

'Something wrong?' Tom asked.

Brandt looked up. 'No. Your sister is fine. I am going to find Lady Chloe. You may tell the Duchess not to worry.'

The best way would be to go through the side entrance, which would allow him to proceed directly to the library. If Chloe had gone through the passage, then he would meet her. Unless she had become confused and taken the wrong turn. He cut around the corner of the terrace and then leapt lightly to the ground. The side entrance was nearly hidden by overgrown ivy, but the door was unlocked. He nearly ran to the library and then realised he had not brought a candle with him.

He prayed Chloe was already there.

The room was empty, but a candle burned in its holder on the mantel. Thank goodness for Miss Coltrane's never-failing efficiency. He took the candle and bent down. The heavy door was unlocked so he pulled it open and climbed through the grate into the dark passage. He would go first to the bedchamber, then, if she was not there, head for the sea. And hope Chloe had not gone very far at all.

Chloe leaned against the wall, hugging herself with her arms, trying to stem the rising tide of panic that threatened to overwhelm her. The passage was completely dark and she was completely lost. Her candle had blown out moments earlier. From the sudden cool breeze that touched her cheeks she knew she was near the sea, far from the passage to the library.

How could she have been so stupid? She should have had Emily repeat the directions, but she had been so determined to reach Brandt she had not waited. She had come to the fork in the passage but could not recall at all what Emily had said. The passage to the right had been narrow and full of cobwebs and the left had been wider. So she had chosen the latter and been completely wrong.

She had realised that when the path suddenly sloped downwards. She panicked then and had stood, immobilized, until she forced herself to turn around. But a few steps later, Chloe saw another fork in the tunnel she had not noticed before. Her mind had gone blank. She had suddenly had no idea where she was or how she had got there. She had forced herself to move and found herself in this gently sloping passage. Then, turning a corner, the candle had slipped from her hand.

Chloe closed her eyes and took a deep breath. She would not panic; she would *not* go mad. She would think of...of gardens. Roses and gillyflowers and daisies.

Then she shrieked as cold water touched her slippers, and her eyes flew open. She looked down and saw the water lapping at her feet. She stared for a moment, wondering how that could be, then her mind began to work again. She was in one of the sea caves. One of the caves that would be submerged with water.

She must move. Chloe forced herself away from the slippery wall and began the slight climb upwards. She must find where the walls and floor became dry. But it seemed to take an age before the surface was no longer slippery. Her feet hurt and her slippers felt as if they were worn to shreds. She slid down the wall and closed her eyes. She was exhausted, the effort to hold her fear at bay taking all her strength. Perhaps if she rested.

'Chloe!' At first she thought she was dreaming, but when she heard her name again she opened her eyes. She could see a faint light down the passage.

She stood. 'Here.' Her voice sounded feeble to her ears.

It must have been enough. 'Stay where you are. Do not move.'

Brandt was coming for her. She waited and then he came into view. He carried a candle. 'Thank God,' he said, and then he was at her side.

'I...I wanted to meet you,' she managed and then burst into tears.

With one arm, he pulled her against him. 'It is all right, Chloe. You are safe.'

She couldn't seem to stop the sobs, so he held her until they finally subsided and she leaned into him, spent. She wanted to stay in the comfort of his embrace for ever, but he finally shifted. 'We must return to the house.'

'Yes.' She stepped away from him and shivered a little.

'You can wear my coat. Can you hold the candle?'

She took it. 'I think so, but I dropped the other one.'

'My poor girl.' His voice was a caress. He shrugged out of his evening coat and draped it around her shoulders, then gently removed the candle from her hand. 'Come with me.'

'I tried to think of gardens.'

'Did it help?'

'A little.' Until the water came. She did not want to think about that. In fact, she did not want to think at all. She followed him up the passage in a daze, aware of nothing but his solid, warm presence. She had no idea how much time had passed when they halted.

'This leads to the library. You will need to bend down a little.' He stepped through and then held out his hand and helped her. In a moment, she was standing in the library with him. Brandt looked down at her. 'You need a change of clothing and a bed. I will send for Mrs Cromby and let Belle know you are safe. But first I need to get you to a more suitable room.'

She nodded. The ball, the guests seemed very far away. He took her hand and led her across the floor to the closed door. He tried it, but it would not open. He stared at it for a moment and then retried the handle again. 'Damn.'

'Is it locked?' Somehow it seemed almost natural for it to be so.

'It appears to be.' He turned and looked at her with the same frustrated expression Sir Preston had worn earlier.

'I suppose we could always go back through the passage to the bedchamber.'

'We cannot,' he said flatly. 'The door is locked from

the bedchamber. I asked Miss Coltrane to lock it. It is doubtful they are still there.'

He tried the door once more, this time pressing his shoulders against the wood, but it did not move.

Her lethargy dissipated. 'Could we call for help? Or climb through a window?'

'The window is impossible. It is a straight drop down to the garden. I can try to call.' He sounded doubtful.

Brandt began to pound on the door and shout. Chloe joined him. After a few tries, he finally turned to her. 'I suspect they cannot hear us. I fear we must manage the best we can until someone comes to look for us. I would hope that would be soon since they should notice that their host and the guest of honour are missing.'

She nodded, suddenly too sleepy to care much. She was cold, tired and exhausted. 'I believe I would like to sit down and wait.'

'Of course.' He ran a hand through his hair. 'There is the sofa, but it is devilishly uncomfortable, you know.'

'I do not mind.' Anything would do.

He took her arm and led her to the heavy, old sofa. She nearly collapsed on it. He stood looking down at her. 'Hell. Your clothing is wet and you must be cold. I would build a fire but there is no wood. Unless I use the furniture.'

'Oh, no, please do not do that. You would need an axe at any rate.' The last thing she wanted was to create more problems than she had already. 'I will be fine.'

'Your gown is soaked.'

'Only the hem.'

'At least I can remove your stockings and slippers.' Before she could protest, he had set the candle down on a side table and knelt down in front of her. He slanted a slight smile at her. 'I have done this before, you know.'

'Yes.' As before his hands were gentle and she closed

her eyes, mesmerized by his soothing touch. When he was done, he straightened. 'You had better lay down. You look as if you are about to fall asleep.' And then he sneezed.

For the first time she noticed how fatigued and cold he looked. The bottoms of his pantaloons were wet and his fine embroidered waistcoat was streaked with mud. Since she was still wearing his coat, he had not had even that extra protection.

'You must be cold as well. You must have your coat.' She started to remove it only to have his hand come down on her shoulder.

'Hardly. I don't need the coat. Lay down, Chloe.'

'I am always much colder when I lay down.'

'You won't be because I intend to lay down with you.' His brow lifted slightly at her expression. 'I am not planning a seduction. I merely intend to keep you warm. This room is damnably cold and the longer we stay here the colder you will feel. I've no intention of allowing you to catch a chill.' He sat down next to her. 'First I'd best remove my own wet stockings and shoes.' He bent and swiftly removed them. After he shrugged out of his damp waistcoat, he turned and held out his arms. 'Come here, Chloe.'

She shifted next to him and his arms came around her, drawing her back against him. He half-reclined against the back of the sofa, legs outstretched in front of him. He moved a little so that he could arrange his coat over her and then settled back against the sofa. His heart beat strong under her ear; his scent was comforting and pleasant, and the feel of his hand on her back made her feel protected and safe. His feet entwined with her colder ones and they, too, soon began to warm. Her eyes drifted shut as a drowsy warmth seeped through her.

She did not even notice when the candle burned its last for she had already drifted off to sleep.

'Brandt!'

His eyes jerked opened. At the same time he realised his cousin was standing over him.

And Chloe was nestled in his arms.

He bit back a curse just as Chloe stirred. She opened her eyes, her face filled with confusion. And then she blanched. 'Oh, no,' she whispered. She tried to push away from him.

He tightened his arm around her and rose to a sitting position with her still cradled against him. 'It is all right, sweetheart,' he said softly. He looked up at Justin. 'What took you so long to find us?'

'We were rather confused about your whereabouts. There seemed to be a number of missing persons including yourselves.' Justin's gaze fell on Chloe. 'Are you all right?' he asked quietly.

'Yes,' she whispered.

'She needs a change of clothing, a warm bath, and a decent bed.'

Justin's gaze raked over him. 'You look as if you need the same. Where were you?'

'In the tunnels. I would prefer to leave the explanations until later.' He rose and gently set her on her feet. 'I am going to carry you to my bedchamber. It is the only one that is truly habitable.'

'I can walk.'

'Your feet are bare.'

'So are yours.'

At least she was showing some spirit. 'Yes, but yours are cut up again. And this is my house.' He swept her into his arms before she could protest and strode with her towards the door.

Justin followed. 'I will at least inform Belle that she is safe. We spent the night here.'

'Please put me down,' Chloe said in a low voice.

'Hush.'

'I am not very light.'

'You are not very heavy.'

'But...'

'Don't argue with me.'

Surprise flashed briefly in her eyes, but she said no more as Brandt carried her into the hall. He nearly cursed when he entered the main part of the house and nearly slammed into his aunt, Lady Ralston and Belle. He did curse when he saw the Earl of Ralston behind them.

Lady Ralston let out a little shriek and dashed forward. 'My poor child! What have you done to her?'

'He has done nothing, Mama,' Chloe said.

'But your feet are bare and your gown is ruined!' She turned accusing eyes on Brandt. 'How could you?'

Belle took her arm. 'Maria, I think it best to wait and hear what has happened.'

'Which can wait until Chloe has been attended to.' Justin had come up behind them.

'So if you will pardon me.' Brandt pushed past the assembled group.

Ralston's face was black. 'I trust you have a rational explanation for this, Salcombe.'

'I've no idea.'

He thought he would be relieved to finally set her gently on his bed, but the sight of her lovely face against his pillows nearly sent him mad. The ache that had consumed him most of the night with the feel of her soft, light body snuggled into his suddenly burst into full, flaming desire.

If it weren't for the fact that Belle and Maria had trailed him upstairs he would have lain beside her and pulled her back into his arms.

He moved away. 'I will send Mrs Cromby to you.' His voice was more curt than he had intended.

Chloe sat up, her face worried. 'But do you not need a change of clothing? And something warm to drink? I fear you are about to catch a chill.'

'I assure you I am not.' Her concern was unnerving. 'I will see you later.' He stalked out and then realised his clothing was in the small room off of his bedchamber. He found Henry, the Crombys' son who had been serving as his valet, and sent him to retrieve a set of clothing and stockings and boots. He pulled them on in one of the empty bedchambers and was about to set off to find Justin when his cousin entered the room. He carried two glasses of brandy and shut the door with his foot. 'Thought it best to corner you here before Ralston tracks you down.' He handed Brandt one of the glasses. 'You look as if you need this.'

'A decanter would be better. Where did you find it?'

'Mrs Cromby. An exceedingly competent housekeeper. I trust you plan to keep her on.'

'With an increase in wages.' He took a sip of the brandy. He'd probably regret it on an empty stomach, but right now it was what he needed. 'How did you come to unlock the library?'

Justin eyed him. 'A short time before that I received a rather mysterious, anonymous note suggesting that we look for you and Lady Chloe in the old library. It also suggested the key might be found in a potted plant.'

Brandt set his glass down on the table nearby. 'There seems to have been an excess of mysterious, anonymous notes circulating last night. Both Chloe and Kentworth received such notes as well. Except it turned out Lady Kentworth was undoubtedly behind those. Chloe's was to arrange an assignation with me in the old master suite and Kentworth's was from Miss Coltrane for the same purpose.'

'So Chloe and Kentworth ended up together?'

'Not only that, but locked in together,' Brandt said.

'Very odd. For when that particular door was forced open at Lady Kentworth's insistence, Kentworth and Miss Coltrane were together. In another rather compromising situation. There will be a wedding shortly.'

'So that was what Miss Coltrane was up to.' Brandt's mouth curved in momentary amusement.

'You do not seem overly surprised. I suppose you know how Miss Coltrane came to be there instead of Chloe.'

'I did not have the time to gather all the facts from Miss Coltrane when I found her in the bedchamber with Sir Preston. She suspected Lady Kentworth might do something to interfere with last night's announcement so she kept an eye on Chloe. After Chloe was handed the note, Miss Coltrane feared something was wrong. She followed Chloe to the old wing where she saw Lady Kentworth close the door and then lock it. I can only surmise she must have stolen the key Mrs Cromby kept in the kitchen. Miss Coltrane asked for pen and paper and then wrote me a note informing me she planned to enter the room through the library passage, and that she would send Chloe to the library.'

'That did not happen?'

His mouth tightened. 'No. Unfortunately, I did not get Miss Coltrane's note until some time after she wrote it. Chloe is afraid of tight, dark places. I did not expect her to even want to enter the tunnels, but when I arrived at the bedchamber she was gone. I feared she had become disorientated and had gone the wrong way.' He looked at his cousin. 'She had. She was nearly at the sea caves. By the time I caught up with her she had started back, but she had lost her candle. She was shaking and terrified.' His blood still ran cold at the memory of her stricken, pale face. 'We managed to get back to the library, but when I tried the door, I found it was locked. The doors in this place should be used in a fortress. No one heard our shouts and we finally sat down to wait. Except it was damnably cold, her gown was wet and her shoes ruined. The only way I could keep her warm enough was to lay down with her.' He gave a short laugh. 'That was all that happened, I swear.'

'You do not need to defend yourself to me.' He looked steadily at Brandt. 'However, Ralston is another matter.'

'That doesn't surprise me.'

'He insists that you and Chloe marry by special licence as soon as possible.'

Brandt stilled. 'Does he? For once he and I are in accord. However, I suspect Chloe will prove less amenable.'

'To what will I prove less amenable?'

They both turned to see Chloe standing in the doorway. She was clothed in a plain, woollen dress that was far too big for her and no doubt belonged to Mrs Cromby. Her hair was caught in a ribbon and hung down her back. Her face was clean but still pale.

Brandt strode to the door. 'What are you doing out of bed?' he demanded roughly.

'I need to speak with you.'

'Where is Belle?'

'With Mama, who is having hysterics. Arthur has convinced her I am now completely ruined. And that we should marry as soon as possible. I told her I would not and she became overset.' She spoke with a sort of calm detachment, but from the way she knotted her hands together he knew she was far from calm.

'The devil take him,' he said softly. More than ever he would enjoy mowing Ralston down, this time for oversetting Chloe and Lady Ralston before anything was decided.

Her eyes were huge in her face. 'I thought you should know before he accuses you of…of ruining me. I tried to tell him that nothing had happened and he was ridiculous but he would not listen.' She took a deep breath. 'And I told him I would not marry you under such circumstances.'

'You've little choice,' he said flatly. '*We've* little choice. The circumstances in which we were discovered were damning to say the least.'

'But you did nothing, and it was not your fault or mine that the door was locked.'

Justin had come up beside them. 'Brandt is right, you have no alternative. Most of the countryside knows you were missing. We came up with some story about lingering effects from the excursion a few days ago and Brandt's desire to see to you, but I doubt few believed the story. Most certainly Lady Kentworth did not, since she knew perfectly well why you were gone. I've no doubt she will not let this ride.'

'But…'

'It is not only your reputation that will suffer—it is Brandt's as well. I do not think you would want him to be accused of seducing you and then abandoning you.'

'No, I would not, but…' She had a hopeless, trappe look on her face that tore at Brandt.

'He will be good to you.' Justin touched her cheek and then looked at Brandt. 'I will let you sort this matter out between yourselves, then I suggest you leave for London as soon as possible.' He quietly left the room.

Chloe's face was pale, the only colour the sprinkling of

reckles across her nose. Brandt wanted to take her in his arms and comfort her but he had no idea what she would do.

'Come in for a moment,' he said.

She hesitated and then stepped inside. He shut the door behind her, not wanting them to be interrupted. She jumped as his hand brushed her arm.

Brandt moved away from her. 'There is no need to look so terrified. It won't be so bad.'

'What won't be?'

'Marriage to me. I will not beat you or lock you up or keep you closeted at Waverly for the rest of your life. You can come and go as you please, you will be able to visit Belle as often as you want and your family. You will have your own money—I have no need of it. I will not interfere with you.'

He hoped his words would bring some sort of relief to her face but instead she looked even more wretched. 'You are very kind.'

'Hardly.' He folded his arms. 'There is one more thing. I will not touch you until you wish me to.'

Colour flooded her cheeks. 'I see.' She looked away for a moment, then back at him. 'This cannot be the sort of marriage you want.'

'Or the marriage you want.' Not when she looked as if she was about to be tortured. He shrugged, not about to let her know he cared. 'If I recall, neither one of us wanted a marriage of passion.'

She looked stricken. 'Yes. But I…' Her voice trailed away.

'I will inform your cousin that we will marry as soon as I procure the special licence.'

'Very well.' She did not quite look at him.

'I will leave today.'

This time she did look up. 'Should you? I have no doubt you are very tired. Perhaps it would be best to wait.'

'So that we might delay the wedding further? I think not,' he said coldly.

She turned away, but not before he saw the swift hurt in her face. 'I had better return to Belle and Mama.' She looked up briefly. 'I wish you a safe journey,' she said before she left the room.

He stared after her, suddenly weary.

Chapter Eleven

Chloe watched the rain pour down in front of the library window at Falconcliff. It had been like this for the past five days ever since Brandt had left for London. Most of the time she liked watching the rain; liked watching the wildness of the sea beating against the rocks while she sat safe and snug in the warm library. But she had felt none of that safeness this time.

Instead she felt restless and waiting. Waiting for Brandt to return.

How had everything become so complicated? Not that her relations with Brandt had ever been simple, but she had never expected their lives to become more and more inextricably intertwined, almost as if fate had decreed it so.

Soon they would be joined together in the most holy and inseparable of bonds until death made its claim.

She rose, too agitated to sit. He was to return today, but she had no idea if the weather would prevent him. She both longed for and dreaded his return. She had not seen him after that last distressing conversation in which they had suddenly become strangers again. Nothing she had said had turned out right. She had been so distressed at

Arthur's accusations that she had fled directly to Brandt.
She had meant to warn him, but it had been too late. When
he had said that neither one of them had wanted a marriage
of passion she had wanted to tell him he was wrong, that
she had changed her mind, but somehow, under his cold,
remote exterior, the words would not come.

She had no idea if the opportunity was now lost for ever.

She shivered, suddenly needing to find Belle and Julian
and escape her thoughts. She left the library and came into
the hall just as the butler opened the door. 'Lord Salcombe,' he said, his voice surprised.

She stopped and her heart began to pound as a tall,
cloaked figure stepped into the hall. He started to speak
and was suddenly overcome by a fit of coughing. He
straightened and then swayed. The butler grabbed his arm
to steady him. 'My lord! You are not well!'

Chloe ran to his side. 'Brandt, what is it?'

He looked down at her. Beneath the dripping brim of
his hat, his face was drawn and pale. 'I have the licence,'
he said and then promptly collapsed at their feet. Only the
fact that Eliot still held his arm as he went down kept him
from dashing his head against the floor.

Chloe fell to her knees, fear gripping her. He was
breathing, but when she touched his forehead her hand
nearly burned.

He groaned a little and she looked quickly up at Eliot.
'You must find Justin or Belle. He needs a bed and a
physician.'

'Yes.' He turned. 'Stephens! Find the Duke and tell him
Lord Salcombe has taken ill. And send Timmons to help
me carry him to bed.'

She hadn't noticed the footman who now scrambled
away. She laid her hand on Brandt's burning forehead.
'Can you hear me?'

He turned his head and opened his eyes. 'Chloe? Or are you an angel?'

'Certainly not.' Did he think he was dying? 'We are sending for Justin and a physician. And someone to help you to bed.'

'Not necessary. Apologies for fainting on you. Must get up.' He started to push himself up with his arms.

'No! Just wait for help.'

'Floor is hard.'

'Then put your head in my lap.' She moved so she was sitting in front of him. He obligingly shifted so his head rested in her lap.

A slight smile tilted his mouth. 'Nice. Must do this again.' Then he closed his eyes.

'I pray you will not.' Her voice was sharp with worry. What if he was dying? A sick dread gripped her. She could not bear it if he was gone. A future without him would be a hopeless swirling void. She bent over him and closed her own eyes and whispered a silent prayer.

'Chloe.'

Her eyes flew open. Justin was at her side. 'What happened?' he asked quickly.

'Eliot admitted him and then he fainted. His head is so very hot—he must have a fever.'

'Has he awakened at all?'

'A few moments ago. He spoke, but did not make much sense.'

'The fever, undoubtedly. I've sent for Dr Crowley, but for now we must get him upstairs.' He signalled to Eliot and the young, burly footman who hovered nearby.

Chloe stood aside as the three men lifted and then carried him up the stairs. She trailed them, feeling completely helpless. Belle met them at the top of the stairs. 'Mrs Keith is preparing the blue bedchamber. How is he?' Her face looked as sick as Chloe felt.

'He is alive. He has a fever,' Justin said as they moved past her.

Belle saw Chloe. 'Oh, my poor dear!' She hurried forward and caught Chloe in an embrace. They held each other for a moment and then Belle released her. 'You must go to him. I must tell Lady Farrows and then I will join you as soon as I can.'

They had just laid him on the bed when Chloe entered the room. His eyes were open but unfocused. She stood in the doorway, not certain what to do as Justin's valet set to work removing his muddy boots and stockings. Justin and one of the footmen had already helped him out of his outer coat and were now stripping him of his waistcoat and stock.

Justin looked up. 'You should leave. We need to remove his clothing and put him into a dry nightshirt.'

'I would like to help.'

His face was not unkind. 'For now you should go. He would not like to have you see him like this.'

She backed away, knowing he was right, but wanting something to do, anything to rid herself of this utterly helpless feeling. She felt even more helpless as the servants bustled in and out, and then Lady Farrows, after giving her a brief embrace, joined the others behind the closed door. Dr Crowley arrived just before her mother and Arthur returned from their excursion to the village.

Lady Ralston flew at her. 'I have just heard! My love! How worried you must be!'

Chloe was enveloped in a smothering embrace. 'Mama, please…' She would lose all patience if her mother suddenly had hysterics.

Her mother pulled away. 'My dear, you must come and lay down.'

'No, I must stay and hear what Dr Crowley says.'

'But you are so pale! I fear you are about to become ill as well.'

'I am fine.'

'Chloe... Arthur, you must reason with her.'

Arthur spoke. 'She will undoubtedly be more distressed if forced to rest before she knows the diagnosis.' He took Lady Ralston's arm. 'Come, Aunt. You should change before you catch a chill as well.'

This unexpected support apparently stunned Lady Ralston as much as it did Chloe. Her mouth fell open. She snapped it shut. 'I...I suppose you are right.'

'Good.' Arthur glanced at Chloe. 'I, of course, join you in hoping that Lord Salcombe will soon be fully recovered.'

'Thank you.' She was too taken aback to say any more before he led Lady Ralston away.

Then the door opened and Justin stepped out, followed by the physician.

Her heart slammed to her throat as Justin came over and touched her arm. 'He has the influenza, but his lungs are severely affected.' He paused. 'There is some indication he has developed pneumonia as well.'

'Oh, no,' she whispered. 'What can be done?'

'I have bled him and then administered a dose of laudanum to help him rest more easily. Cool compresses to help lower his fever. In these cases I have found a cool bath to be helpful.' Dr Crowley paused. 'And prayers.'

'Yes.' She caught Justin's arm as soon as the doctor had left. 'I want to see him.'

'It would be best if you waited.'

'No. I will not sit by and do nothing. I cannot bear to do nothing. I can help nurse him.'

'My dear…' Justin began.

'She needs to do this,' Belle said quietly from the doorway. 'She will go quite mad if she doesn't. I know I would.'

Justin looked down at her. 'There is the risk of becoming ill yourself. You are not long recovered from your own illness.'

'I am quite recovered. It does not matter at any rate for this is what I want to do. What I will do.' She walked past him and Belle into the room.

Brandt lay very still on the bed, his chest rising and falling beneath the quilt. The darkness of the stubble around his mouth only emphasised his terrible pallor. She knelt beside him and took his hand. 'Brandt, it is Chloe.' Her voice thickened with unshed tears and she could not say any more. She hardly noticed when Lady Farrows quietly departed and left her holding his hand in silence.

The small sound awakened Chloe from the light sleep into which she had fallen. She opened her eyes, disorientated at first, and then remembered; she was in the dimly lit bedchamber, sitting next to the bed in which Brandt had tossed and turned in feverish delirium for the past four days.

She left the chair and moved to the side of the bed. He slept, one bare arm flung over the quilt covering his chest. She watched him for a moment. His breathing seemed less laboured, nor did he seem quite as restless. She felt his forehead. It no longer felt so hot. Perhaps Lady Farrows had been right in declaring the medicine Dr Crowley had prescribed only contributed to his delirium. She had refused to allow Mrs Keith to give him the last two doses, despite the older woman's great objections. Hope flickered in her.

Where was Mrs Keith? Unable to sleep, Chloe had come to his bedchamber what seemed like hours ago. Mrs Keith, who sat with him, was clearly exhausted, so Chloe had sent her away, promising she would stay with Brandt. Mrs Keith had protested but then said if Chloe did not mind staying she needed to fetch fresh cloths. So Chloe had sat in the wing chair next to the bed, her eyes on Brandt's face, praying his fever would break. She had thought the housekeeper would be gone for only a short while, but the candle on the table by the bed had burnt almost completely. Not that she minded that. She would have sat with him every hour of his illness if they had allowed her. She would return to her chair and stay with him until morning.

Before she could move, his eyes opened. 'An angel,' he murmured.

He had said a number of nonsensical things in the past few days.

'I am Chloe.'

'Then I am in heaven after all.'

'You are at Falconcliff.'

'No.'

So he was still delirious. 'You must rest.'

His hand caught her arm and his grip was surprisingly strong. 'Water, please.'

'You must let go of my arm then.' The hope began to grow. He had not asked for water before. She moved to the bed table and poured him a glass and then returned to the bedside. 'I can help you.' She sat next to him and lifted the glass to his lips. He sipped slowly, but soon finished it. 'Do you want more?'

'Later.'

'I must tell Mrs Keith that you are awake.' She started to rise, only to find her arm again in his grip.

'Later,' he said. 'Stay with me.'

She sank slowly down on the bed next to him. 'Do you know who I am?'

'An angel, and I am in paradise.' His eyes were fixed on her face, but she had no idea if he was truly seeing her.

'No, you are at Falconcliff.'

'Allow me my delusions.' His other hand had come up and caught her other arm. He began to draw her slowly down on his chest. 'Will you kiss me, my angel?'

'You are not well.'

'Perhaps not.' His expression changed and she saw the desire, but even more the longing and vulnerability. 'I need you,' he said simply.

She bent down and kissed him. He lay still under her soft kiss, allowing her to explore his mouth. She touched his face, his hair, his eyelids wanting to feel him, wanting to reassure herself he was alive.

He drew her down to his chest and she found his mouth again. He did not move for a moment and then he groaned. His arms pinned her to him and somehow she was underneath him and he was kissing her with a hot passionate need that swept her away with its force. Her own hands tangled in his hair and she returned his kiss, the horrible worries and fears of the past few days driving her own passion. She wanted to be part of him, to press into him, to reassure herself he was alive, to become part of him. He opened her dressing gown and his hand cupped her breast through the thin linen of her nightrail.

She gasped when he circled the sensitive nipple with a gentle finger. Her stomach contracted and her body arched in an effort to press closer to him. The voluminous folds of the dressing gown suddenly seemed in her way and when he pushed it away she did not object.

There was nothing between them except the thin cotton of her nightrail. His hand stroked her bared leg, moving in sensuous circles upwards until he was stroking the silky soft skin between her thighs. She stiffened at the unfamiliar touch, but then his mouth was on hers and his fingers were inside her, stroking, caressing the most private part of her being.

Waves of tension radiated from where his fingers continued their seductive ministrations. Her legs closed around his hand and she pressed against him, begging for relief from the hot heavy wanting. And then his leg was between her thighs, gently parting them. He removed his hand and she felt the unfamiliar firm, fleshy tip at her opening. He hesitated. 'Chloe?'

'Yes. Please,' she whispered. Her legs seemed to part of their own accord in invitation.

He slowly entered her and then paused and touched her face with his hand. 'My sweet angel,' he murmured and then thrust deeper into her. She bit her lip, startled by the dull pain, and then he was moving in measured, rhythmic strokes inside her. She closed her eyes, and clung to him as his thrusts deepened and quickened. She was a part of him, her own body swept away by his passion as the tension built in her. With a final thrust, his seed spilled into her.

He hovered over her for a moment before withdrawing. He cupped her face, still lying half on her. 'If this is a dream, I pray I will never awaken. You have taken me to paradise.' He kissed her again. And then coughed.

Her eyes jerked opened. The candle had burnt completely, but in the faint moonlight she saw his eyes were glazed. His hair was damp and his forehead wet with perspiration. His hand felt hot against her face and his body heat burned through her nightrail. 'You are feverish,' she whispered. Oh, heavens! What had she done to him.

'Yes, my lovely angel,' he murmured. He closed his eyes, his arm draped over her. She tried to move and he stirred, his eyes opening. 'Don't leave me,' he whispered before his eyes shut again, and she saw he had fallen asleep.

She managed to remove his arm and sat up, her dream-like state rapidly disappearing. *I have been seduced.* No, that was not quite true. If anything she had seduced him, gone to him, wanting to assure herself he was alive, wanting to keep the fears away, and when he had said he needed her, his face vulnerable, she had given herself to him. Somehow, in that peculiar state she had been in, it had seemed only right to surrender to the final, natural conclusion.

She had no idea if he would even remember what had happened. He seemed to think she was an angel. Perhaps he would consider it a dream.

She had no idea whether that would be for the best or not. She rose from the bed on shaky legs and retrieved her dressing gown, which had become tangled under them. The dark stain in its folds seemed to jump out at her; clear evidence that it had not been a dream.

She clutched it to her chest for a moment and took a breath. She could not think about this—she must check on Brandt, for what if she had sent him into a relapse? He was breathing better, but when he coughed again, she jumped. She brushed her hand across his head. He was hot, but not quite as hot as he had been in days past. She straightened the covers around him and prayed she had not harmed him. She looked down at his face, the strong contours of his cheeks, the way his lashes closed over his eyes.

He looked both strong and vulnerable and she wanted nothing more than to lie with him again.

She spun around when the door opened. Mrs Keith bustled in, her face contrite under her ruffled nightcap. 'I am so sorry, Lady Chloe. I meant only to put my feet up for a bit and I fell asleep. I do not know what the Duchess will say as I was not to let you sit with him at night when you so much need your own sleep.'

'There is no need to tell the Duchess, or anyone else. I would not want to be scolded for leaving my bed.' Which had just been long enough for her to seduce Brandt in the midst of his fever.

Mrs Keith looked relieved. 'Then that is all right.' She moved to Brandt's side. 'How is our patient?' She touched his forehead. A little frown crossed her forehead, which only deepened when he coughed. 'His fever has gone up a trifle.'

Chloe felt guilty and sick all at once. 'Is it very bad?'

Mrs Keith glanced at Chloe's face. 'Oh, my dear, 'tis nothing to fret yourself over. Now, you must go to bed— it is nearly dawn. I have no doubt a spoon of Dr Crowley's potent will bring the fever down straight away.'

'Are you certain?' Chloe asked. 'I thought perhaps he seemed a little better without it.'

Mrs Keith moved to the bedside table and picked up the bottle. 'Now, I have no doubt Lady Farrows meant well, for after all he is her great-nephew, but his fever is up again and he is coughing so 'tis best to heed Dr Crowley.' She looked back at Chloe. 'You must go to bed. I promise you I will take the best care of him. He will not want to find you ill when he awakens.'

'No.' There seemed to be nothing else she could do. Her head was reeling and she felt again that she was in some sort of dream.

She was too tired and she must go to her room. Chloe backed away from Mrs Keith and towards the door, not wanting the older woman to see the faint stain on her nightrail. There was no one in the hall as she made her way to her bedchamber. The faint rays of dawn were already creeping across the sky as she climbed into bed.

An enormous fatigue overpowered her almost the moment she hit the pillow, but the last thing she thought of was being in Brandt's arms.

Chapter Twelve

His head hurt and his throat was parched but for the first time in an eternity, the heat that had consumed him was gone. As was the sense of floating in a dream where voices and faces drifted in and out of his consciousness. Except for last night. That dream had been so vivid, so real he had no idea if it had been a dream at all.

He shifted and slowly opened his eyes, half-hoping, half-dreading that she would be there but there was no soft, slender body nor any sign at all in the smooth covers that anyone else had shared the bed with him. He prayed he had only seduced Chloe in his dreams after all.

'Brandt?'

His aunt appeared by his bed. For a moment he had no idea why she would be there and then he recalled the ball. The tunnel. And the licence.

Relief flooded her lined face. 'Oh, my dear boy! Thank God! You are awake. Do you know me?'

'Aunt,' he managed to croak. 'Water, please.'

'Oh, yes.' She bustled over to the night stand and then returned with a glass that she held to his lips. He had a vague memory of Chloe doing the same thing, but perhaps that had only been a dream as well.

'You do not know how we have worried about you!' To his astonishment, he saw her eyes were filled with tears. 'There were times when we did not know if you would live!'

'But I did.' He wanted to close his eyes again, but he needed to know about Chloe. 'Lady Chloe? Is she here?'

'Yes, the poor lamb. She has been at your bedside every day, and sometimes at night, nearly ill with worry.'

Had she been with him last night? 'Must see her.'

'Of course. But first I must tell the Duchess you are finally awake.'

'No, Chloe.'

'I will send her to you as soon as possible. You must rest for now.'

He watched her leave and then tried to sit up, but he was as weak as a newborn. He finally fell back against the pillows. He needed to see Chloe as soon as possible, reassure himself that nothing had happened between them.

Or find out if it had.

He willed himself to stay awake, but dozed off anyway. He jerked awake when the door softly opened, but it was Belle who entered. She moved to his bed. 'How are you feeling?'

'Weak. Beg pardon for the inconvenience.'

A little smile touched her mouth. 'We are only grateful you managed to make it to Falconcliff in time to inconvenience us. I've sent for Justin. He should be here shortly.'

'Chloe. Need to see her.'

'I know.' She hesitated. 'She is resting now. She has not eaten or slept much in the past few days and Dr Crowley felt it best that she stay in bed. He gave her a draught, but I promise that she will see you as soon as she is able. Do not worry, she is not ill, only tired.'

He bit back a curse. 'Should have taken better care of her.'

'Yes, but she insisted she could not stand by and do nothing. She wanted to stay with you.'

He recalled his aunt's words. Day and night. 'Last night? Was she here?'

A puzzled expression crossed her face. 'I do not think so. Mrs Keith was with you and then your aunt.'

'I see.' So she hadn't been there but he still felt uneasy.

'You must rest. I will sit with you until Justin arrives.'

He nodded.

Chloe awoke, her head heavy. She forced her eyes open, disorientated to see the evening shadows on the wall. Why was she in bed at this time? Then she remembered the draught Dr Crowley had administered. She had awoken in the late morning. Dr Crowley had just seen Brandt and Belle had insisted he see her as well. He had proclaimed her fatigued, had prescribed a draught and told Belle she must stay in bed the rest of the day.

She should get up, but she felt too drugged to move. Her head hurt, but more than that was the unfamiliar soreness between her thighs.

A reminder that she had indeed given herself to Brandt. She had allowed a passion she did not know she possessed to overcome her judgement, her morals and her resolution. She was stunned at how swiftly it had happened—had she made a deliberate decision from the moment he had taken her arm and begged her to stay to let matters proceed so far? Or had she allowed herself to be carried away without regard to the costs?

That would be the worse thing of all. A deliberate decision would be one thing, but possessing so little control

that she would do something with such grave consequences was much more serious.

She felt as if she did not know herself at all and she
had no idea what she would say or do when she saw
Brandt.

Brandt shoved aside the thin gruel that his aunt and Mrs
Keith had deemed appropriate. It was hardly his choice for
his first meal in nearly a week but at least he could keep
it down. He had his wits about him enough to refuse the
vile potion that he was certain contained laudanum and
kept him in a perpetually drugged state.

'Only a few more spoonfuls, my lord,' Mrs Keith said,
picking up the spoon. She had taken on the role of nurse
with a vengeance and was determined to strong-arm him
whenever possible.

'Although it was delicious I do not want to overtax my
system.' He gave her his most charming smile. 'I would
like you to send for Lady Chloe.'

'Doctor Crowley was quite insistent that you not have
too many visitors.'

'Lady Chloe is hardly a visitor. She is my fiancée.'

'Yes, of course, but perhaps I should consult with the
Duchess first.'

'Either you inform Lady Chloe I would like to see her
or I will inform her myself even if I am forced to crawl
down the hall.' He started to throw back the covers.

Alarm crossed her face. 'Of course, my lord.'

'One more question.'

She paused. 'My lord?'

'Did Lady Chloe ever sit with me at night?'

She hesitated and then stiffened. 'The Duchess did not
deem it proper for Lady Chloe to sit with you at night.'

He fell back against the pillows after she left. The sun

had set nearly an hour ago. He knew Chloe was up because Mrs Keith had informed him she had come downstairs to dine which had not improved his mood. It would seem she was in no great hurry to see him despite the concern everyone declared she had shown when he was racked with fever.

His mood only darkened when the door opened and Belle entered. 'Where is Chloe?' he demanded.

'Behind me, if you would exercise a bit of patience.'

He saw the figure behind her then. Chloe followed Belle into the room, her hands folded in front of her as if she did not know quite what to do next.

She glanced at Belle, then moved towards the bed and looked down at him with no trembling, no revulsion, no shirking, nothing at all in her quiet countenance to indicate he had done something as vile as taking her virginity while he was half out of his mind. 'How are you feeling?' she asked softly.

'Better.' He saw there were shadows under her eyes and her face was pale. He scowled. 'You look as if you need Dr Crowley's attentions more than I do.'

'It is probably because I slept most of the day. Dr Crowley gave me a draught and I always feel horrid when I wake up.'

She spoke matter-of-factly and Brandt began to relax a little. Surely if he had seduced her there would be something in her manner, some sort of fear or accusation in her face, but he still needed to talk to her alone. He looked at Belle. 'I would like to talk to Chloe a few minutes in private, if you please.'

'I suspect it matters little whether I please or not, so I will not waste my breath. However, I trust you will not scold her for the past few days.'

'No, because I intend to scold you as well as my cousin for allowing her to become this fatigued.'

Belle smiled. 'I will warn Justin,' she said as she left the room.

He fixed his gaze on Chloe's face. 'Sit down. I do not like having you hover.'

She took the chair near the bed. Again, he had the odd sense of having woken up and found her in that exact position. 'Was it true that you insisted on sitting with me?'

'Yes, but we all did. You were so very ill that we did not want to leave you alone for an instant in case you…in case you needed something. Even Justin. He sat up with you one night. Belle is very nearly worn out because Julian is teething and has been fussing most terribly, which is why you should not scold her. I could not sit idly by while they made themselves ill.'

'I am beginning to think that they should ring a peal over my head for running the household ragged.'

'That is not what I meant at all. I only meant that we were so very worried about you that none of us wished to leave you for an instant.'

'Us? Does that mean you worried about me as well?'

'Yes.'

He kept his eyes on her face. 'Then perhaps you no longer hold me in such dislike.'

She flushed a little, but did not look away. 'I do not hold you in dislike.'

'I am glad to hear that.' Then it had been a dream, obviously a vivid one brought on by a combination of fever and drugs and desire, for surely if he had used her so badly she would hate him.

'I should let you rest.' She started to rise and he found his hand clamping around hers. She jumped, her eyes startled, and he had that bizarre sense he had done this before.

Except then he had pulled her down on top of him. He could almost feel the weight of her light, delicate body on top of his. Desire shot through him, hot and immediate.

He released her abruptly. 'I beg your pardon. I had something else to say to you.'

She had frozen at his touch. Now she looked apprehensive. 'What is it?'

He had no idea why she suddenly looked so fearful. 'I want us to marry as soon as possible. Tomorrow, in fact.'

'Tomorrow?' She looked completely uncomprehending as if she had no idea what he referred to.

'Surely you recall I had just returned from London with the special licence when I collapsed at your feet.'

'Oh. Yes.' She flushed. 'But surely you wish to wait until you are well.'

'No. And risk some other damnable thing happening before we are wed?'

'What else would happen?'

'I've no idea.' He only knew that he wanted her safely under the protection of his name and that he did not intend to let her go.

'I do not think...'

'Chloe.' He suddenly felt weary. 'Don't argue with me. I do not have the strength.'

Something changed in her expression. 'I will not argue with you,' she said quietly. 'I will wed you tomorrow if that is what you wish.'

'It is.' He wanted to tell her they would marry only if that was what she wished as well, but it was too late for that. They had no choice. He was not sure if fate had ever given them one.

Chloe sat in the chair by her window, feeling numb. He had not remembered after all. Perhaps last night had seemed part of the restless dreams that had plagued him. For a moment, when he had taken her arm, she had thought he was going to say something about the previous night, but instead he had spoken of the marriage. There had been nothing in his manner to indicate he recalled her even being there.

Perhaps it was for the best to go on as if nothing at all had happened.

But she had agreed to marry him tomorrow. She was hardly aware of what he said at first, and then when it dawned upon her that he wanted to marry tomorrow, she had panicked.

Until she had seen the vulnerability beneath his cool arrogance. The tiredness…the need. And she had responded to it, wanting to erase the weariness from his face.

She knew now why she had gone to him last night.

She loved him.

Chapter Thirteen

Belle sat down on the bed next to Chloe and took her hand. 'It is only natural to be a little afraid before one's wedding. My knees were shaking quite horribly and I scarcely remembered saying the vows.'

'When you married Lucien?'

'Yes, and when I married Justin as well. But particularly with Lucien, I did not know what to expect. I did not know how a wife was supposed to be, and I knew nothing of the intimacies between a man and a woman. Lucien had only kissed me once before we married.' She hesitated. 'Has Maria talked to you at all of this?'

Chloe felt her face grow warm. 'No.' She had no idea what to say.

'I do not want you to go into your marriage as unprepared as I was. The first time a woman is with her husband, she finds the intimacy a little bewildering and perhaps not so pleasurable. But when one is with a man who cares for one and whom one cares for in return, it will soon become one of the most wonderful pleasures of marriage.' Her hand tightened around Chloe's. 'Brandt cares for you. I know he will be patient and kind. He will not hurt you.'

'I…I know.' She wanted to sink through the floor, but

there was nothing she could say. Her unhappiness and self-reproach deepened as Belle gently described the marriage bed. She could only sit, frozen, until Belle finished and then enveloped her in a tight embrace.

Belle released her. 'You must dress. I will send Ellen to you but please, if you need anything, I am here.'

'Yes.' She wanted to cling to Belle, but she could not. 'I know.' She forced a smile to her lips. 'I think I would like to be alone for a little while.'

'Of course.' Belle left the room.

Chloe rose from the bed and went to the window, not really seeing the blue sky or the high fleecy clouds. She felt more and more as if she was about to enter into the worst sort of deception. She was presenting herself as a virginal bride, but she was not.

What would Brandt do when he discovered the truth? If and when he decided to exercise his rights as a husband. She must think of some way of telling him.

She had no idea how.

The short journey to the chapel passed in a sort of dream and then she was stepping down from the carriage into the cool, misty morning. Arthur took her arm and escorted her up the stone steps of the old chapel with her mother trailing behind her. Inside, Caroline and Will waited for her, their faces solemn. Will stepped forward and handed her a bouquet of flowers with a formality so unlike his usual self that she had no idea whether she wanted to smile or weep. Instead, she bent down and hugged him and was rewarded by a fierce hug in return. 'Now, you'll be here for ever with us,' he told her.

'Yes.' She embraced Caroline and then stepped from the vestibule and into the chapel. With some amazement, she saw there were a number of people present. She looked towards the front and her heart leapt to her throat when she saw that Brandt already stood there, elegant in a dark coat and pantaloons, his starched cravat tied in an intricate knot at his neck. His eyes met hers, his gaze dark and intense, and she caught her breath.

Justin came to her side. 'Chloe, are you ready?'

'Y…yes.' To her chagrin, her voice shook.

'Then come. Brandt is waiting for you.'

The ceremony passed in a haze. She hardly heard the vicar's words and barely recalled repeating her vows. She was aware only of Brandt, of his cool but increasingly husky replies, of his body next to hers. Then he was taking her hand and slipping a ring over her third finger and finally tilting her chin towards him. 'Chloe,' he whispered and then his lips brushed over hers in a kiss that made her legs weak. He released her and promptly began to cough.

'You must sit down,' Chloe said, alarmed. His face was white and she feared he would swoon. Justin caught his arm and guided him to a front pew. He sat abruptly, still coughing. Lady Farrows and Marguerite rushed to his side and then the vicar appeared with a glass of water.

Brandt took a few sips and then his coughing subsided. He looked over at Chloe, who had come to stand a little to the side. Chagrin crossed his face. 'I beg your pardon.'

She wanted to brush back the lock of hair that had fallen over his forehead, but she doubted he would welcome it. 'Please do not. One always has such dreadful coughs with influenza.'

'You are too kind,' he said softly.

Giles spoke. 'Perhaps we should congratulate the bride and groom and then see them to Falconcliff before the groom collapses.'

'I've no intention of doing that.' Brandt rose and held out his arm to Chloe. 'Shall we?'

She took it, hoping he would make it to the carriage without another bout of coughing. The others followed them, speaking in quiet voices. The carriage already waited in the small drive in front of the chapel.

'I had better ride with you,' Lady Farrows said. 'Shouldn't want you to collapse on Lady Salcombe.'

Lady Salcombe? Chloe started before she realised Lady Farrows referred to her. But Justin was helping Brandt into the carriage and then Chloe, and finally Lady Farrows who took the place next to Brandt.

Brandt began to cough as soon as the carriage was in motion. Lady Farrows handed him a handkerchief and when he finally stopped, told him to lean back and close his eyes. Chloe watched, feeling useless, for Lady Farrows seemed to have everything well in hand.

She could scarcely fathom she was married and watching Brandt resting against the pillows only increased her sense of unreality. She looked away, fighting the most absurd desire to burst into tears and when she glanced back at him and saw how vulnerable he looked with his eyes closed, she wanted nothing more than to gather him into her arms and comfort him. She could hardly do so with Lady Farrows in the carriage, and even if they were alone, she doubted she would have the courage to do so.

They finally reached Falconcliff. Brandt roused himself when the carriage halted and insisted on stepping down without help. He assisted his aunt down and then held out his hand to Chloe. To her dismay, she stumbled so he was forced to catch her against him. She pulled away. 'I beg your pardon.'

For the first time that day, the familiar smile touched his mouth. 'There is no need to. In fact, I look forward to many such moments in the future.'

'But I might have hurt you.'

'Never.' His arm tightened around her and she caught her breath. His expression changed. 'Chloe.'

For a heart-stopping moment, she thought he was about to kiss her. Lady Farrows voice broke in. 'My dear boy, I suggest you go inside before you catch another chill. I doubt Chloe wishes to nurse you through another illness.'

Brandt's hands fell from her arm. 'Of course.' He escorted Chloe into the hall where Belle, Justin and Marguerite waited. Belle took one look at Brandt's pale face and insisted he go upstairs immediately. 'We can have the wedding breakfast brought upstairs.'

'And crowd into your bedchamber,' Justin added. He grinned at his cousin. 'You may be served in bed if you like.'

'I think not.' Brandt looked at Chloe. 'Unless Chloe wishes to join me.'

She flushed. 'No, I...'

'Really, Brandt,' Marguerite said. 'You can put her to the blush later. After your guests have gone.'

Chloe looked away, her stomach lurching. In the presence of family and friends, she could easily think nothing had changed, but everything had. Her life was now irrevocably intertwined with his and he had every right to ask anything of her he wished.

She managed to force a few bites of the delicious breakfast down her throat and smile and join in the conversation, all the while aware of Brandt who sat in the wing chair near the fireplace. He ate very little, his pallor only increasing as time went on, his gaze frequently resting on her with a brooding expression she could not interpret.

And finally Belle and Marguerite announced it was time to leave, and that Brandt needed to rest. Marguerite took Chloe's arm. 'The bride needs to rest as well. She is nearly as pale as the groom.'

Brandt rose from his chair. 'I wish to speak to Chloe for a few minutes first.'

Marguerite gave him an arch look. 'Very well, but I hope you remember that you are far from well.'

'I am quite aware of it,' he said drily.

He leaned heavily against the bedpost while the others left. His breathing was more laboured and he was starting to cough again.

The room was quiet at last. Brandt still leaned against the bedpost. He opened his mouth to speak and then coughed.

Chloe poured a glass of water and gave it to him. 'You should be in bed.'

He took a sip. 'I need to talk to you.'

'You can do so in bed.' She took his arm. 'Please.'

He looked down at her, a peculiar light in his eye. 'Will you join me?'

She dropped his arm and froze. 'I...'

His expression changed. 'Chloe, I swear there is no need to look like that. I promised I would not touch you unless you were willing.' His voice was thick. 'Sit down, Marguerite is right, you need a bed as much as I do.'

'I am fine.' But he had already seated her gently on the bed.

He sat down a careful distance from her. 'I beg your pardon for my damnable tongue. I did not mean to frighten you. It was just...' He frowned. 'It will not happen again. This is what I wished to speak to you about. I told you before I would not expect you to share my bed, at least until we are better acquainted. Until you are ready, I will not force myself on you. We will keep our relationship on the businesslike basis we both want.'

She felt as if she were in a waking nightmare. 'Brandt...'